MW00908029

Waterfall Way

Natasha Murray

NATASHA MURRAY

WATERFALL WAY

First published in Great Britain in 2021
Copyright © Natasha Murray 2021
The right of Natasha Murray to be identified as the author of this work had
been asserted by her in accordance with the Copyright, Designs and
Patents Act 1988. All rights reserved.
No part of this publication may be reproduced, transmitted, or stored in a
retrieval system, in any form or by any means, without permission in
writing from the author, nor be otherwise circulated in any form of
binding or cover other than that in which it is published and without a
similar condition being imposed on the subsequent purchaser.
All characters in this publication are fictitious, and any
resemblance to real people, alive or dead, is purely coincidental.
A catalogue record for this book is available from
The British Library.
Published by Natasha Murray ISBN 978-1-9996351-9-0

NATASHA MURRAY

Chapter One

Seth and Charlene Hearn walked briskly towards Crow Farm. It was a dark, cold evening and a cruel breeze bit into them as they walked along the ice-covered lane. Seth's little niece Bryony and his two nephews, Michael and Rowan, ran on ahead. Charlene's youngest, Finn, was asleep in his pushchair and sucked his thumb as he slept. Seth couldn't help but notice how big Finn was compared to his little Darragh. *The same age and twice the size at least!* As they approached Crow Farm, Seth was beginning to feel nervous. The farmhouse looked dark and foreboding.

"Mam?" Bryony called. "We are going to run home to see Dad. Don't be long; we are starving."

"Stay together, and go straight back. It's too dark and cold to play outside. Don't run…"

"Ok, Mam," Michael shouted as the three of them tore off.

"They never listen; they are a lively bunch."

"Bryony has got tall while I have been away. I hardly recognise her. She's so grown up now. She is very good with Finn. She is like a little mother to him," Seth said, opening the gate for Charlene.

"She can be a bit of a handful and likes things done her way. She keeps singing Baby Shark to Finn. That song drives me crazy, but Finn doesn't seem to mind. The four of them keep me busy, and as for starving, I swear they all ate their body weight in cupcakes at yours. Jules is really good at baking. It was lovely to see you both together again. She's missed

1

you, you know. The first few months were the hardest. Jules really has been through a lot. She told me about nearly being kidnapped by that awful Tom Stone. That must have been a hard time for you both. You must promise me to take good care of her. I know she makes out that she is not bothered about it, but something like that will leave its mark. Do you hear me, Sebastian?"

"I do, Charlene. I'll look after her, I promise. That bastard drugged her with ketamine. She doesn't remember much about that day. She doesn't remember that he raped her. I found a used condom on the floor by our bed, and he said he had her. Jules doesn't know that. Please don't tell her."

"My God! Rape! I didn't realise. I won't tell her, but I think that you should. If it were me, I would want to know. He shouldn't be allowed to get away with rape. You need to talk to her about it and get that man charged!"

"I know, but she is so fragile at the moment. News like that might break her. When we are back home at Waterfall and settled, I will talk to her then. I really don't want to hurt her. All I want to do is make her happy."

"I know you do. She thinks the world of you. It's good to have you back, sweetie, even if it is just for one day. You look worried. Are you ok?"

Seth glanced at the front door of the farmhouse and sighed. "I'm not sure if this is a good idea. Only you and Maureen came to see me when I was inside. When I was in prison the first time, James, Sam, and Doreen used to visit me. I don't think my brothers and sisters have missed me that much. Do they blame me for Dad's disappearance?"

"Oh, sweetie, I am not going to lie to you. They did at first. Mam saw to that," Charlene said as she stopped a bag from falling out of the pushchair. "At first, they were after your blood. Mam said that you two had been fighting. Then on the night, you escaped, Mam got drunk and declared to everyone that Dad had left her for another woman. From that moment on, everyone started to get on with their lives again. Apart from Mam, that is. She was drunk most evenings and stopped cleaning and cooking. Those that were relying on her for cooked meals had to fend for themselves. Our family has become dysfunctional, and we are not close anymore. Those that live in this house eat in their rooms alone. I am so glad I am not living in the farmhouse anymore, and I have my own family to look after."

"Really? It's funny, as it is dinner time, I imagined walking into the kitchen and seeing everyone sitting around the table eating and laughing together. The house looks sad and empty. Void of laughter and without a soul."

"I promise you, everyone will be pleased to see you. You will have to knock on their bedroom doors to find them. I wouldn't bother with Patrick. He is staying in your old rooms now. He is too up himself these days and is best avoided. I know he is my brother, but I can't stand the man. He said that I was a traitor for turning Mam in. It had to be done. He gives my Joe such a hard time, and he is on his back all the time to work harder. You know my Joe. He is not lazy."

"So come to Waterfall West and work on the estate. Jules doesn't know this yet, but I plan to farm the land, and I will need a good manager. Joe is more than able to manage an arable farm. I can't think of anyone better. Farming is in my blood, and the estate has many fertile acres crying out to be farmed. If you come over to Ireland, it will mean that I will always have my favourite sister, brother-in-law, niece and nephews close by. Please come over."

"Oh, sweetie, you have the kindest heart. I might just take you up on your offer. It would mean the children would have to change schools, but I do miss Ireland. I will speak to Joe. Oh, Seth, everyone should know that you went to prison for Jake. Does your father-in-law know what you did? Does he realise that his daughter is married to a hero?"

"No, we don't really talk to each other. I wouldn't say that I am a hero. A bit soft in the head, perhaps. I am sure Jake would have done the same if the boot were on the other foot. I am definitely not a hero."

"You are. Jake has not been himself lately. He is feeling guilty that you did time for him. You two need to talk. He won't come to you, and he should really, but he finds it difficult to talk about what happened. I've tried, but he hides and drinks. There is no getting away from it; Jake is an alcoholic. Go and see him. He will be in the caravan with Mark. Do you have your key with you, or do you want me to let you in the house? I've got to get back and cook now and then get everything ready for school tomorrow."

"I've still got a key, but I can't go in. I don't know why. I will go through the field and climb through the post and rail fence into the back garden. Jake and Mark's caravan is still at the end of the garden, isn't it?"

"Yes, it's still in the same place. If they offer you any homebrew, then say no, Seth. It is not what it seems. I don't want to see any ambulances in the lane," she said, laughing.

"I promise I won't drink anything. I am going to miss you, Charlene. As soon as I get my farm going, I will call you and then please come over. The kids will love living at Waterfall West, and Darragh will have family to play with."

"I'll talk to Joe. Take care, sweetie, I will miss you. Don't forget to give me a ring when you get back home. I want to make sure you get back to Waterfall safely."

"I will. Miss you lots already," he said, continuing up the lane and then blew her a kiss and waved.

***

Seth climbed through the post and rail fence and into the back garden. The security light lit up, and he walked across the frozen grass towards Jake and Mark's mobile home. The garden was void of fairy lights and flowers. The summer parties and his family making merry in the garden and house were now just distant memories. *Crow Farm is a sad and lonely place! It is giving me the shivers just being here.*

"So, you think you can just walk into the garden like you own the place!"

Seth spun around. "Fuck! Patrick! Where the hell did you come from?"

Patrick sneered and came a little closer. "I saw you talking to Charlene in the lane. You were as thick as thieves. You do know that you are not welcome here anymore, cousin?"

"That's not what Charlene said. What do you mean, cousin? I am your brother, you eejit. We have the same father." Seth scowled at him.

"So, it's true then. Mam took you in like she took Jake in. I was ten when you appeared, and Mam told me that you were a gift from God. How wrong she was."

"What do you mean by that?"

"Like I said, you are not welcome at Crow Farm, and I want you to leave."

"Like I am going to take notice of you. You don't own the place. I can go where I like and see who I please. I am going to see Jake and Mark, so you can sod off."

"You take one more step, and you will be sorry,"

"Seriously? Are you threatening me? Look, I don't know what you are on. You need to take a long, hard look at yourself. You are not Dad or Mam. You have no authority here."

"I don't know if you noticed, but I am in charge here. What I say goes. I swear I will kill you if you had anything to do with Dad going missing."

"So, this is what it is about. You know as well as I do that Dad is one sick bastard, and he is probably in bed with someone's daughter fucking as we speak. He fucked Ivy, and he's probably fucked every woman in Findon. Look what happened to our sister Claire. Christ, Patrick, smell the roses. He had to go, or he would have been strung up by his own children." Seth could feel the heat rising in his cheeks but knew that he had got through to his brother, who was now looking shocked. "Please tell me that you knew that Claire's baby was Dad's."

"No, I didn't. Nobody tells me anything around here. Our Claire?"
Seth nodded.
"Shit!"

***

Seth walked back to Farm End, using the torch on his phone. Jake and Mark were not in the caravan, and he guessed that they had gone down to the pub. It would have been good to see them both before he left. *Should I go to the pub with Jules? It's probably best if we don't.* He was eager to get back to Jules and Darragh. He thought back to what Charlene had said about him taking care of her. Earlier, while Darragh slept, they had found each other again and had made love. After, he had held her in his arms and felt her body trembling as she cried. *Ten months apart has hurt her. She is a little broken. My poor, sweet dote. Tomorrow we will travel to Ireland and start our lives over. In time your broken heart will mend.*

As Seth made his way across the courtyard, being careful not to slip on the ice-covered cobbles, he looked up at the night sky, amazed at how many stars were up there shining down on him. It was so good to be a free man and see this. From his cell in prison, through a locked window, he had stared up at the sky, longing to be free and back in the arms of Jules. The past ten months had limped by, and being separated from her had been so unbelievably painful. When there were no stars, dark thoughts had entered his head, and some nights he had cried out in his sleep, feeling his father's hands around his throat as he tried to drown him in the silent pool. He breathed deeply, drawing in the frozen air and brought himself back to the here and now. The icy air filled his lungs and soothed his troubled soul. Tomorrow would be the start of a new chapter in their lives. He felt a wave of euphoria wash over him, and he smiled. *It's so good to be a free man and back with my family. I have missed them so much.*

Chapter Two

Darragh giggled as Seth lowered him gently into the bath. His big brown eyes stared up at him, questioning his actions. "That's right, it's me again. Do you remember me holding you when you were born?"

Jules smiled as she watched them together. Seth was being so gentle with Darragh, and he was treating him so delicately as if he might break.

"Does he need to lie back on my arm like this, or is he ok to sit up?" Seth asked, looking towards Jules for advice.

"Sit him up but just be ready to stop him keeling over. He loves the water and sometimes gets a bit excited and then slips over." As she spoke, Darragh hit the water with his hands and laughed.

"I see what you mean," Seth said, laughing. "He loves it, doesn't he?" Seth sat him up and then carefully let him go. "Look at you sitting up so strong. Is it good to have your Dad bathe you for a change? Do you want this dolphin to play with?" Seth asked, picking up a toy from the side of the bath and then looked at it. "No, it's not a dolphin. It's a killer whale. I didn't know they made such gruesome toys for children."

Jules laughed, "I think it's quite cute. Look at its big eyes and big white teeth. Give it to him and see what he does with it."

Seth swam the whale to him, and Darragh squealed with joy and reached out for his toy. He picked it up, looked at it for a moment and then rammed it into his mouth.

"You're hungry, are you? So, you like to eat whales, do you? You are going to be one strong little boy when you grow up."

"He's doing really well for a preterm. He's teething. That's why he is putting everything you give him into his mouth. I am so glad that you will be here to see his first tooth." Jules smiled at Seth. It was such a good feeling to have him back in their lives. While Seth had been in prison, it had been a hard ten months to get through. If anything, it had made their relationship stronger. Today, for the first time in ages, she felt euphoric and earlier, she had cried happy tears. "It's just so good to be together. I can't wait to go back home to Ireland. The only thing is, I won't have a job when we get back. May had to hire someone to clean the Manor House, and our savings have nearly gone. I will think of a way to earn some extra money again. I guess we could go busking. I won't feel right again until we have sung together. I think we should hire a studio and create an album. We can play a couple of our songs on YouTube and Facebook to get people interested and then use a distributor. We can be our own record label. S&J."

Seth laughed. "I knew you would come up with something. Oh, hold on. Our little man nearly went then." Seth sat Darragh up straight and held on to him. "We will be ok for money. I can work part-time in the riding school. Sinead said that Luke is doing really well teaching, and there is something I would like to do too. I had an idea the other day, and I was going to tell you about it. When I was in prison, I realised how much I missed being out in the fields and working the land. Waterfall West has acres and acres of unused pasture, and it is a crying shame that these fields are not used to grow food. I was going to ask May if we could cultivate some of the fields and start a small farm. I've been researching the trending crops, and it would be good to grow oats, root vegetables and soya beans, perhaps. We could also do 'pick your own' strawberries in the summer. What do you think?"

"I like the idea but won't the start-up costs be expensive?"

"I have some money in my old bank account, and there is an old tractor and equipment in one of the outbuildings. I would just need to buy seeds and petrol for the tractor and hire workers during harvest. I've looked at the profit margin and think that we would do really well."

Seth's eyes shone with enthusiasm. She couldn't throw cold water on his plans and wanted him to do what made him happy. "I've always wanted to be a farmer's wife," she teased. "If you think we can make a living from the land, then there is no harm in trying."

"That's grand. Now, where's the soap for our wee lad."

"It's in that bottle on the side. The one with the purple label. It's got lavender in it and will help him sleep. When we give him his bottle in a minute, you will be able to smell it, and you will find yourself drifting off too. It's my secret weapon. Darragh will sleep through until eleven, and then after some milk, he will sleep until seven. I don't know if I will sleep. We have been sleeping in the same room since he came home from the hospital. I know he will be fine, but it is going to be odd not seeing him next to me."

"We can stay in your room tonight, although I might have to sleep on the floor as I swear your bed is meant for a baby."

"No, it's ok. I know he needs to be in his own room now. He is strong enough for me not to worry. I also know that we will need to be private from time to time. It was so good to be in your arms again this morning. I am lost without you."

Seth could see that she was tearing up. "It's ok, don't cry. Everything will be ok. I'm here for you," he said as he poured too much bath lotion into his hand.

Jules smiled. "You only need a little. Darragh might slip through your fingers and then sleep for a week."

After Seth had washed Darragh, Jules lay a towel on the bathmat, and Seth lifted Darragh out and lay him on the towel. Jules wrapped him up and then picked Darragh up. "We'll go and dry and dress him in my room. Do you mind emptying the bath and cleaning the sides down?"

"No, of course not. Do you do this every day, then?"

"Yes, the same time every day unless he has a late nap, and then the routine goes haywire."

As Jules walked out onto the landing, she met her brother, Peter, coming up the stairs. He was looking smart, and he was wearing a newly pressed shirt. His aftershave, however, reminded her of sweet tropical flowers and was overpowering and sickly.

"My, you look like you are going on a date." Peter looked shocked and then went a little red.

"Is it that obvious?"

"All I ever see you in are torn farm clothes and boots. I don't think I have ever seen you wearing normal clothes. I'm pleased for you. Are you going to tell your sister who she is? It's a first date, isn't it?"

"Christ, you miss nothing!"

"Where did you two meet?"

"Ok, it's not like I do something like this all the time, but I went through Bumble, and I am dating a girl from Worthing. Her name is Josie, and she is at uni. She lives on a farm too."

"Does Dad know?"

"This is going to sound really weird, but to get him on side, I let him go through the profiles so he could see that there are some really decent women on the site. I said he should try and find someone too, but he said he was happy as he was. He chose Josie so he is ok about it."

"I'm pleased for you. Will you promise to bring her over to Waterfall in the summer? I want you to see where I live and see the beautiful Irish countryside. I won't see you in the morning. We are setting off before you get back from doing the milking. You've got my number. Will you message me and let me know how you are doing?"

"I will…"

Seth came out of the bathroom and smiled at Peter. "It's time you found yourself a good woman. It's been the making of me. Jules is right; you need to visit Waterfall. I am going to start farming there and would be grateful if you would check out my business plan and see if there are any holes. Bring Josie too; she will love it there."

"Wow! You've got us married off already. Let's hope this evening goes well."

***

Was that Darragh? Jules opened her eyes and stared into the darkness as she listened for his cry. She had lost count of how many times she had woken in the night worrying about him alone in her bedroom for the first time. Back in Ireland, she had made a nest for him on Seth's side of the bed so she could check on him through the night. *I hope he is ok. Come on now, he is ten months old and is big and strong, like his Dad. What time is it? She sat up in bed and picked up the phone to check. It's just after four. Too early to be getting up. Good, another hour of sleep left. I'm so tired.* She could hear the kettle boiling and realised that someone was in the kitchen. *It's probably Peter getting ready to milk the cows. I wonder how his date went?*

Although she was tired, Jules was wide awake, too excited to go back to sleep. *Today we are going home. I wish Seth could drive us home and not Dad. No, he offered to drive the horses and us over to Ireland. At least Seth will be able to help him get the horses in the trailer. Dad should have made more of an effort to speak to Seth. I wonder how they will get on today. I hope Connor and Barney don't kick up a fuss when they are loaded into the horsebox. It's ok. Seth is here, and he will get them in, no problem.*

12

By the light of the phone, she could see his handsome features and his strong shoulder. He was sound asleep next to her. She smiled. *You always look so peaceful when you are asleep. It is so good to see you next to me. It is how it should be.* Wanting to feel his warm body next to hers, she put the phone on the side table, lay down and then slid over to him. With her back against him, she whispered to him to hold her.

Somewhere in his dreams, Seth could hear Jules calling to him. He had to find her. He was in a strange land. He had been there before but couldn't quite remember when. *If only I could see where I am going, then I will be able to help her.* He held his arms out and tried his best to find her. Her voice was louder now, and she was growing impatient. Finally, his hand felt her bare skin, her soft curls, and he drew her to him and wrapped his arms around her. Her body felt cool against his, and he could smell her. A sweet smell of vanilla and baby powder. He sighed a contented sigh and then fell back to sleep again, lost in her being.

Chapter Three

Feeling a little anxious, Seth waited by the gate for Mr Bridgewater to back the horsebox up to it. Seth directed him back until the truck was just inches away from the opening. Seth was glad that he had brought a lantern with him as it would have been too dark to see properly. He opened the gate and waited for his father-in-law to get out of the cab. *Why is he taking so long?* Seth opened the gate and was pleased to see that the gaps on either side of the horsebox were too small to let a horse or pony through. Connor and Barney had wandered over to see him, unaware that soon they would be loaded into the horsebox and transported to Ireland to start a new life at Waterfall West.

Seth patted Connor's neck gently and realized that Barney had his nose by his coat pocket. "You don't miss a trick, do you? You can smell apples, can't you? If you two boys load nicely into the box, then I promise I will feed you treats all the way home. So big fellow, here's your head collar." Connor allowed Seth to slip it over his head and fasten it. Barney, however, looked wearily at the horsebox and then cantered off.

"Damn, I should have done you first," he called as he watched Jules' old pony disappear into the darkness. *I'll load Connor first and then sort Barney out.* Seth tied Connor to the fence and collected his rugs and boots, ready to prepare him for travel. It was a cold February morning, and he didn't want the horses getting chilled or hurt. Connor's ears pricked up as they heard the lorry's engine turn off and the handbrake go on. Seth took a deep breath and waited for his father-in-law to appear. Since he had arrived

14

at Farm End, they had exchanged pleasantries but had not actually had a conversation. *Let's play this by ear. No, I've got to get him talking. We can't spend the whole day travelling to Ireland in silence. Jules says he's changed.* His mind flashed back to the night that Mr Bridgewater had stormed over to Crow Farm and had dragged her away from Jake and Ivy's party, determined to keep her away from the Hearns, and him.

Michael Bridgewater appeared by the gate and scowled. "Where's the pony?"

"He's gone off, but he will be back in a minute. He's not going to let his buddy go off without him and get all the apples," Seth said confidently, but he knew deep down that he would have trouble catching him. Shetland ponies could be a handful. "We really appreciate you giving us a lift back to Ireland. It's really kind of you." *Should I try to joke with him? Maybe not; he still has a stony face.*

"Well, you don't have a license, do you? And Julia has only just passed her test." Michael sighed. "Look, I am doing this for her sake. I have no idea why she married a Hearn and had a kid before she was twenty, but she did. Her happiness is all that matters to me now, and for some reason, she thinks the world of you. At least you have given her a decent home in Ireland. She keeps telling me that you shouldn't have gone to prison. All I ask is that you treat her well and never cross her. If you do, then I will be after you. Let's hope you are not a jailbird and that you are not like your father."

"You've got my word, Mr Bridgewater. I love your daughter, and I promise that I will treat her well. I am not like my Dad."

"Mm... We'll see. Let's get these horses loaded. We don't want to be late for the ferry."

Feeling like he had been chastised, Seth opened the gate and waited for him to lower the ramp down so that he could load Connor into the horsebox. Seth threw the last blanket over the horse's back and then collected the long boots to protect his legs. The gentle horse waited patiently as Seth got him ready. He knew that he was going to have no trouble getting him into the horsebox, and he patted him, talking soothingly to him. Out of the corner of his eye, he could see Mr Bridgewater watching him. His arms were folded, and he knew that he was impatient to get going. *This trip is not going to be an easy one. I wonder if he remembers me giving him mouth to mouth after he tried to hang himself.*

Jules rushed around the kitchen, loading sandwiches, bottles of milk and several cold items out of the fridge into an icebox. Darragh was still asleep, and she had been so relieved to see that he had made it through the night. The heating was on full blast, and her room had been warm overnight. He had kicked off his duvet, and she had felt a little guilty that she hadn't covered him up sooner. *Perhaps he was too hot. I wonder how Seth and Dad are getting on. It's twenty to six. Just twenty more minutes, and then we are off. They should be back in a minute.* As she thought that, she saw the horsebox pull up in the courtyard. *Good, hopefully, all went well. I hope Dad is being kind to Seth.*

As Jules zipped up the cool box, she stopped for a minute to listen to the news on the radio. *I swear there is more news than music these days. Not more Coronavirus news! Surely China has the virus under control.* Jules turned the radio off and stared silently around the kitchen as if it were the last time she would see it. *No, silly, we can come back for holidays. Yes, we will come and visit again in the autumn.* Her attention turned to Darragh. She could hear him crying, and she smiled as she knew that as soon as he saw her, then he would stop, and his face would light up.

Seth and her dad entered the kitchen, and both looked solemn.

"Did everything go ok? You both look very serious."

Seth smiled weakly at her, but he said nothing.

"They are in, but Barney gave us a run for his money. Did you know that your old pony has an aversion to horseboxes?" her dad said, rubbing his hands together. "It took both of us to get him in there. Poor Seth got kicked."

"Oh no! Are you hurt, Seth?"

"I'll live. I can manage without a kneecap. Is that Darragh crying?"

"He's just woken up. Let's go and get him. I'm ready, Dad. I just need to dress Darragh and give him a bottle, and then we can go." She looked over at Seth and could see that something was bothering him. *Is his knee hurting, or is it something more?*

As Seth followed her up the stairs, she could see that he was limping. "Aww, poor you. Barney is usually so gentle. He must be thirty now and has become a grumpy old man. A bit like Dad."

"No, it was my fault. I shouldn't have been standing behind him when we had him on the ramp. Your Dad was pulling him rather than letting him walk freely. I was going to lead Barney, but your Dad was getting impatient and took the lead rope off me," he whispered.

"Oh, dear. How are you getting on with Dad?"

"Ok, I guess. Let's just say it is going to take a bit of work for him to warm to me. I think you should sit up front with him, and I'll sit in the seats behind with Darragh. I think he would prefer that."

"If that will make things easier, then that will be fine. You are going to have your work cut out, though. I am not sure if Darragh is going to like being in his carrier for so long. I'm hoping that he will sleep a lot."

"We will have to stop after four hours to walk the horses. Your Dad has agreed to that. He has picked a spot to stop. Let's hope we get to the ferry on time. Otherwise, he will be spitting feathers."

"Let me handle him. He will do anything for his little kitten."

"I promise I will do my best to charm him. What is he interested in? Does he have any hobbies?"

"You are not trying to date him," Jules said, chuckling.

"I know, but it will make things easier if I know, and then I can talk to him."

"Oh goodness! It's funny, you don't think of your parents as actually having a life with interests. Let me think. He likes reading thrillers. You like reading, don't you? He knows everything about steam trains, and oh yes, he is a black belt in karate. When he was in the army, he used to instruct others."

"Crikey, now you tell me," Seth said as he thought back to earlier when Mr Bridgewater said that he would come after him if he treated Jules badly. "Does he like music?"

"He loves music. Mostly music from the eighties, though. He listens to Heart Radio, so he likes some of the modern stuff too."

"That is good to know. I will have to think of a plan to win his heart," Seth said, laughing.

They walked into her bedroom, and immediately Darragh stopped crying. He was sitting up in his crib and was looking at the stars on the walls cast by his nightlight.

"Oh my, you're sitting up all by yourself. You are too big for your crib now. I love picking him up in the morning. He is always so warm and smells so sweet until you smell wee." She picked him up and felt his nappy. "No wonder you were crying; your nappy is so wet."

Seth smiled. Darragh looked so happy to be in his mother's arms. "I still can't get over being here with you both. This is what I've dreamed about for months now."

Jules carried Darragh over to her bed and lay him on a changing mat. She had everything she needed next to the mat and started to undress him. Darragh was wriggling quite a lot and wanted to play rather than be dressed. She had some plastic keys ready and handed them to him. He became calm and looked at the keyring and then bit on the green key. "I think his favourite colour is green. He always has that one in his mouth. Is that tooth coming through then? Does that feel good?" Jules changed his nappy and dressed him in cord dungarees and a check shirt. "I haven't had to buy any clothes. Charlene has given me all of Finn's old clothes. They've hardly been worn. When we get back, we are going to have to get Darragh a cot. He is too big for his crib. I am not going to bring that with us. It won't be long before he is crawling."

"No problem, we'll go and get one in Cork tomorrow. Can I give him his bottle?"

Jules smiled. "Of course, you can. You don't have to ask. I found a cot on Facebook Marketplace. If you think it is ok, then May will pick it up today for us from a woman in Carrigrohane. It's in really good condition, and she only wants twenty for it. It comes with bumpers and bedding."

Seth laughed. "You are so organised. Yes, I'll give May a ring when we are travelling. It will be good to have a chat with her."

"Oh Seth, I am so looking forward to going home and seeing May and Sinead again. You have no idea how much I have missed the cat. I rang Sinead yesterday, and she said that Barney is missing me. I hope he isn't put out that I have a pony named Barney too. Sinead said that May is going to throw us a little party when we arrive. Dad will like May, and if anyone can make him see how wonderful you are, then she can."

"I'm not wonderful, Jules, just your average husband trying to do his best. A party, you say? Now that sounds like a lot of fun. Although I might be on a crutch by the time I get there. My knee is throbbing and starting to swell up."

Chapter Four

Deep in thought, Jules stared out of the horsebox window at the cars ahead of them. *Where are they all going to? Are they going to Fishguard too, or are they all businessmen looking for their next sale?* They had been on the road for nearly four hours, and we're going to stop at a country park to give Connor and Barney a walk. Seth was doing really well looking after Darragh, and he was chatting to him about Waterfall West, May, Sinead, the riding school and how he was going to farm the land. He had made her laugh, and she had noticed her dad smiling too. She hoped that he was beginning to warm to him.

Darragh was due to sleep, and Jules could tell that he was getting tired and wanted a bottle of milk. An hour ago, Seth had given Darragh a jar of banana and yoghurt. *Seth is going to be a great Dad. I wonder how he will cope when he has to change a messy nappy.* Jules smiled. *Let's hope he has a strong stomach.* "How are you doing, Dad? You haven't driven this far for quite a while."

"I'm fine, kitten. It's good to go for a drive. Although I could do with a coffee and a sandwich. What sandwiches did you make?"

"I made you some ham ones, but there are plenty of cheese and pickle sandwiches if you would prefer those."

"Ham is good. I can't get used to you being a vegetarian. We are going to stop soon and exercise the horses. Let's hope we can get Barney back in the box."

"Let Seth take him in this time. He is used to handling horses. I can't wait for you to see Seth's horse, Moss. I would love to show you Cork too, although it would look better in the summer. Last February, Cork was knee-deep in snow. Did we check the weather forecast?"

"Just clouds and sun today. It's cold, though. It is cold enough to snow but not today. I don't think that we will be able to visit Cork. I'm only staying one night."

"I know. It's a shame you can't stay for longer."

"I will come and stay in the summer. I have to get back and help Peter with the farm. I'm really proud of him. He has turned the business around. So, Seth, do you have the directions for the country park?"

"I do, Mr Bridgewater. Hold on, I'll have a look on my phone. The signal here is a bit hit and miss."

"Dad, you can't let Seth call you Mr Bridgewater!"

"No? I suppose not. Seth, call me Michael."

"Dad!"

"He can't call me Dad! Mike then."

"Ok... Mike. We need to take the next turning and then find a place to stop when we enter the woodland. If that is ok."

"You only have half an hour to walk them. I don't want to miss the ferry. There isn't any room for error. I want to get on the ferry as soon as we get to the port."

Goodness! I feel like I am in the army! "I know, Mr Bridge... I mean Mike. We don't want to keep the horses in the horsebox longer than is necessary. Jules, does this little fellow need a sleep yet?" Darragh was looking straight at him and was rubbing his eyes. "It would be handy if he did. I really need you to lead Barney down the track."

"I thought that he would have slept after breakfast. You are obviously doing too good a job of entertaining him. When we stop, I'll change his nappy, give him a bottle and then he can go in his pouch carrier. The warmth of my body will soon send him off."

Mike stopped the horsebox in a layby. The road was quiet, and there was a track leading off into the woodland. Seth jumped down from the cab and groaned. His knee was really sore. He could barely bend his leg, and he wondered if he would have to cut his jeans off later. He took in a deep breath, determined not to let anyone see how much pain he was in. *Perhaps walking Connor will help. I need to keep moving and not let my knee seize up.*

Jules came over to him and looked at him suspiciously. "It's your knee, isn't it? You look white."

"I'm ok, really."

Mike joined them and shook his head. "You might have a fracture. That pony really got you good and proper. You are going to have to rest your leg and put an ice pack on it. Do you have any in the cool box?" he asked Jules.

"I'll be fine. Let's get the horses out, and then when we are on the ferry, I will be able to put my leg up and put an ice pack on it then."

Darragh started to cry. "He's just tired," Jules said, reassuring Seth, who was looking alarmed. "I will change him while you two get Connor and Barney out. Seth, be careful with your knee. I don't like to see you in pain."

"Don't you worry, my sweet girl, I'm tough as old boots."

Mike opened up the back of the horsebox and then looked at Seth with his mouth open. Barney was lying on the floor. His legs were tucked underneath him, and his head was being held up in the air at an odd angle by the rope. The old pony was abnormally still, and they could both see that there was something very wrong with him.

"He's dead, isn't he," Mike whispered, running his hand through his hair. Connor neighed as if in agreement. "Christ! What now?"

Fearing this too, Seth limped into the horsebox and then ran his hands over the lifeless pony, trying to find a pulse or any signs of life.

"No, he's gone. Jules is going to be really upset."

"What do we tell Julia?"

Seth looked sadly down at the pony and sensed that Mike was starting to panic. "I'll handle this." He untied the rope and lowered Barney's head down to the floor. "Jules will be fine about it. Trust me. Barney was thirty; that's the equivalent of a hundred in human years. He's had a good life with you all at Farm End."

Seth got Connor out and then walked him over to the front of the horsebox. Mike followed. They found Jules in the cab feeding Darragh a bottle of milk.

She didn't see them at first, and then when she looked up, she could see by their anxious faces that something was wrong. "You both look very serious. What happened?"

"It's Barney," Seth said. "You know how he is really old? I don't think he suffered. He's passed away. He looks like he is sleeping."

"I'm sorry," her dad added. "We are going to have to call someone to take him away. Is it ok to have a coffee?" he asked, opening up a flask of coffee he had found sticking out of a bag in the footwell.

"Yes, Dad, help yourself."

Seth watched her face, fully expecting her to burst into tears. Her blue eyes shone back at him, and she looked sad, but she didn't cry.

"Oh dear," she said eventually. "Can we take him with us to Waterfall?"

"I don't know. Perhaps it will be better to get him taken away at the port. We've got no signal to call anyone to come here," Seth said, looking at Mike, who had almost spat out his first mouthful of coffee.

"I know that bringing him with us sounds crazy, but I want Barney to be buried near the summer field. That way, he will be near Conner and would have made it to Ireland with him."

"If the authorities find out that we are transporting a dead pony, we might get done for animal cruelty," her dad replied. There was a stern note to his voice.

"Please, Dad. If he looks like he is sleeping, then nobody is going to ask questions. It is very unlikely anyone will look in the horsebox anyway. Please, Dad."

"I don't know. This is not a normal thing to do."

"I know, but it feels right. If we hang around for someone to come and collect him at the port, then everyone will be staring, and we will miss the ferry. Also, Connor will be in the box for too long, and we don't want to have another casualty."

"She's right, Mike. It makes sense to bring him. We can work out what to do with him when we get to Waterfall. I'd better get this horse exercised. Are you going to come with me, Jules?"

"Yes, I need to stretch my legs. Darragh has had his bottle, and I am sure a little fresh air will send him off to sleep. I won't be a minute."

It was cold in the country park, but winter sunshine streamed through the trees and made walking Connor through the woodland enjoyable.

Seth studied Jules' face. He was having trouble reading her. He couldn't work out why she was so relaxed about losing Barney. *I am going to have to help you feel again.*

"I don't think that your Dad was too happy about taking Barney on the ferry."

"Are you ok with it?"

"You know that I'd do anything for you. The only thing that I am worried about is digging a hole in frozen ground when we get home. Would you mind if we got him cremated and then just buried his ashes?"

"Sure," Jules said, stroking the top of Darragh's head. "Our boy is fast asleep now. I hope he doesn't wake up when we put him back in his car seat."

"Jules, I'm worried about you. I thought that you would be in floods of tears when I told you that Barney was dead. It's ok to cry."

Jules looked up at his concerned face. *Oh God, he thinks that I have a cold heart. Do I?* "Oh, Seth, he was so old and slow. I don't know why, but I half expected to find him dead. So, when I saw yours and Dad's face, I just knew that he was dead. I am sad, really. I am just done with crying. I don't need to cry ever again now I have you back in my life. It's just so good to be together again. I love you so much."

***

The ferry was quiet. Jules had gone off to warm a jar of food for Darragh, and Mike sat looking wistfully out of the window. Seth had taken his shoe off and laid his foot on the seat opposite. He held an ice pack on his knee and could feel it throbbing. There was no denying it; Barney, slow or not, had caused serious damage. He sighed and wondered if he had actually broken something. *This knee is going to stop me running for a while. Damn!* He looked over at Darragh and smiled. *He looks so peaceful when he sleeps. When he's gone, he's gone, and nothing will wake him, just like his Mam.*

"You know, I've never been to Ireland before. It's a country that I've never wanted to visit," Mike said, taking Seth by surprise as he hadn't expected him to chat.

"Ireland has some beautiful cities to visit, and Jules wants to see more of Ireland. It's a shame that you couldn't have stayed longer, and I could have shown you two round."

"Julia seems to love living in Ireland. I am going to miss her. It's not easy to let her go."

"She will keep in touch and Facetime you. I know she will."

"Facetime?"

"You know, video call you on your phone or computer."

"Oh yes, I'd like that. I'd also like to see how my grandson is doing too. I'd forgotten what it was like to have a baby in the house. He's quite a character, and he has grown on me."

Darragh's eyes opened, and he looked around, and not recognising where he was, he started to cry.

"Oh dear, Seth said, lifting his leg down so that he could go to him. "You don't look very happy. Do you want to come out of your chair? Are you hungry? Your Mam is just coming. Here, come out of your chair and sit on your Dad's knee. You are all right, little fellow."

Clenching his teeth together as he felt the pain in his knee, Seth unbuckled Darragh and then lifted him out of the chair. Darragh continued to cry but then stopped when he realised that he was in safe hands.

"You're a natural. I don't think I've held a baby before."

"Not even your own? Not even Jules?"

"No, I left that side of things to Sarah."

"Do you want to hold him?"

"No, it's ok. I don't want him to cry again."

"There, look, that's better. Don't cry. You are not smelling so good. I would change your nappy, but I haven't got a clue what to do. Your Mam is going to have to train me when we get home. She won't be long."

Darragh started to cry again, and Seth was relieved when Jules returned.

"It is not like him to cry so much. I wonder if he is in pain with his teeth."

"It might be his nappy. He smells a bit odd."

"Yes, that might be why. Come on then," she said as she put a jar of food on the table and then picked up a bag. "Let's go to the toilets and sort him out."

"You know I would," Seth said. "But I need to rest this leg. We may have to go to A&E later. It really hurts."

"Oh, I forgot. It's ok. We'll spare you this time."

Seth passed Darragh to Jules and felt just a little guilty that he wasn't being more helpful. When Jules had gone, Mike stood up.

"I think that you had a lucky escape. Do you want me to go and check on the horse?"

"That's ok, I think I should go. I can't work out if I should try and keep my leg moving or rest it."

"RICE—Rest, Ice, Compression, and Elevation. That's what you need to do. If the swelling in your knee hasn't gone down in three days, then go to A&E. Is there anything I should be doing to Connor?"

"He should be fine. He's a grand horse and is as calm as they come. Here, give him some apples," Seth said, pulling out a plastic bag full of chopped apples from his pocket. "Do you know how to feed a horse?"

"No, not really."

"Just lay some pieces of apple on your open palm with your fingers squeezed together, and he will gently pick them up with his lips and not eat your fingers. There's nothing to it, and he will be your friend for life."

***

It was nearly dark and late in the afternoon when they drove the horsebox off the ferry at Rosslare Harbour. Seth felt the tension in the air dissipate when they left the port. Having a dead pony in your horsebox did not sit well with Mike. Seth stretched his knee out, trying to get comfortable. He sat sideways with his back against the window, and he was thankful that his knee hadn't gotten any larger and that he had been able to walk back to the horsebox without needing to lean on anyone. They planned to stop off soon to walk Connor again at Killinick before it got too dark. The weather was icy cold, and it was good to be in the warm cab. *I hope Connor has enough blankets and is not too stiff and cold. No, he seemed happy enough when I last checked on him.*

Darragh was wide awake, and he was grouchy. His little cheeks were bright red, and he kept chewing on his keyring. A syringe of Calpol suddenly appeared from the front seat.

"Seth, could you give Darragh this, please. I really think that he is in pain. He is usually the happiest little soul. Isn't he, Dad?"

"I don't think that I have heard him cry much."

"Ok, no problem. Do I just squirt it in, or will he suck it down?"

"I've no idea. This is the first time he's had it. Just give him a little at the time, so he doesn't choke."

Seth took the syringe from Jules and looked at the syringe with concern. "I think that his teeth are bothering him; he looks tired too. Ok, here goes. I just need to prize the plastic key out of his mouth and hope he doesn't cry. Look what I've got for you."

Seth needed to distract him for a moment and dangled his own keys in front of him. Darragh immediately stopped chewing and dropping his own keys reached out for the shiny jingling ones. Gently Seth inserted the syringe into his mouth and pushed the plunger so that the sweet liquid entered his mouth. Darragh's eyes grew wide, and then he smiled. Seth put away his own keys and sighed. "Mission accomplished, he likes it. I think he might have a sweet tooth like you, Jules. Are you feeling better already, little fellow?"

"Oh, good, but it will take about fifteen minutes to work. If only we could get him to sleep for a bit before his dinner. Seth, will you sing to him? He likes listening to your voice, and it calms him down."

"I don't know," he said, hesitantly looking at the back of Mike's head.

"When I had trouble getting him to sleep at night, I used to play him our CD that Jane recorded for us. He likes hearing us sing, but your voice makes him sleepy."

"Do you think I am boring, Darragh?"

"No, silly. You have a settling tone to your voice. When I was pregnant, he must have heard us sing at The Elbow, and that's when I am happiest and relaxed. Dad, you heard our CD. What did you think of S&J then? You never said."

"I think you have something. I am not sure I like Irish music, though."

"I guess it's not for everybody. We do modern songs too. I know one both you and Darragh will like. Seth, sing Rockabye. Do you remember it?"

"You are not going to make the poor man sing a lullaby, are you?"

"No, it's not a lullaby. I remember singing it at The Elbow. I never forget the words to a song once I've sung it. Mike, it's a modern version by Clean Bandit. We do covers. You've probably heard it on the radio. Jules, you've got to help me out. You can rap if you like."

"Ok, but Dad, I don't want you to laugh." *I don't care what Dad thinks. I feel alive when we sing.*

29

"Ok, baby boy, let's give you a song. You are going to love this one," Seth said, and then he started to sing.

Jules watched her dad's face and could see that he was impressed. *I hope you never get depressed again. Life can be so cruel sometimes.*

Chapter Five

"Dad, the Manor House will be on your left, just after the next bend in the road."

"At last! These lanes are dark and twisty and are making my head ache."

"Thanks for driving. We really do appreciate it. I am so excited to be back home. Seth, do you think Resting Horses will be at the stables yet? How long ago did you call them? Was it an hour ago?"

"I hope not. I was hoping to get home before they came for Barney. I want to take Connor to the lower field first."

"Here, Dad, do you see the sign? Oh, look, May has put a banner up saying 'Welcome.' It must be for us. How sweet."

"Yes, I see it? At last! I am exhausted. What are you doing about dinner tonight?"

"May said that she has party food for us, and she is bound to do enough to feed an army."

"I don't think that I am up for a party. Are there any sandwiches left?"

"No, they've all gone. Just come down to say hello, have a little food and then say you need an early night. Nobody will be offended. We have been on the road for over twelve hours. Look, Seth, the house is all lit up with fairy lights. May has gone to town with the decorations. Are all those lights really to welcome us back? I can't wait to see her and Sinead. Is Darragh still awake? I want him to see the lights."

"He is wide awake, and he is looking at me and laughing," he replied. "Are you glad to be home too? What are we going to do with him this evening? He'll be ready to go to bed for the night soon."

"I was thinking that we could change him for bed, give him a bottle and then put him in the pram and wheel him down to the Manor House. He can sleep in that."

"Is this where I stop, in this car park?"

"If you drive up the hill, we can park in the riding school car park, the yard lights will come on, and we will be able to see what we are doing," Seth replied. "There's no sign of the Resting Horses' van, thank goodness. I will give Sinead a ring and ask her to give you both a lift down to the Old Barn with Darragh and the suitcases. There is no point in us all waiting for them to collect Barney."

Seth got out of the cab and slid to the floor, fully expecting to feel a little pain when he put weight on his bad leg. "Oh fuck!" he gasped quietly, not wanting anyone to hear him as the terrible pain shook him. *I thought my knee was getting better.* Holding his knee and trying not to faint, he lent over for a minute to recover. As the pain subsided, he stood and saw headlights approaching. "I can see a car coming up the hill, " he called. "I think it's Sinead." Jules and Mike joined him as he hobbled to the end of the horsebox to greet her.

"I can see May too," Jules said. "I won't get Darragh out for a minute. He has just drifted off to sleep."

As soon as May got out of the car, Jules ran up to her and gave her a big hug. She then hugged Sinead too. "Oh, it is so good to be home. I've missed you both so much."

Seth hugged them both, trying not to show that he was in pain. *I feel like such an eejit for standing behind a horse. Sinead is going to tell me off.* "Yes, it really is grand to be back. We had a good trip, although…"

32

"We've missed you too," May said, laughing.

"We've come up to see if you need any help," Sinead said, looking towards the horsebox and at Mike.

Seth looked over his shoulder and noticed that Mike was stood behind them in the shadows. "Mike, this is May and Sinead. Jules must have told you lots about them."

Mike came over and shook each of their hands. "Nice to meet you both, and thanks for coming up to help us. We've had a bit of trouble on the way over."

"Sinead, I will need your help getting Connor out of the horsebox. I am practically a cripple. The pony kicked me this morning, and he's done a bit of damage to my knee. It was my fault I was behind him, trying to get him in the box."

"Seth! You loon!"

"I thought that you would say that. I was standing too close. He's had his last laugh, though. I don't know how to tell you this, but the pony passed away on the ferry," he lied.

"Barney was too old to travel. I feel bad for bringing him." Jules was starting to feel tearful. *As soon as they opened the back of the horsebox up, I will see him. I can't. I want to remember him as he was when I last saw him - eating grass at Farm End.*

"No! Oh, Jules, you must be devastated. I'm really sorry," both May and Sinead said in unison and then looked at each other as they realised that they had said the same thing.

"The Resting Horses people should be here any minute," Mike added.

"I am sad, but he was so old. Poor Connor is going to be lonely without Barney." Jules could feel tears welling up. *I mustn't cry.*

"He won't be lonely. He will have all the other cobs to play with," May said gently, looking at Jules with concern.

33

"Tonight, we'll get Pringle from the field to keep him company in the barn. He's a Shetland pony like Barney, and he is friendly enough," Seth said, hugging her. *You need to cry.*

Sinead started to undo the back of the horsebox. "Seth, you wait here with Barney, and I will sort Connor out, no problem. May, please would you take Jules and Mike down to the Old Barn in the Mini."

"Yes, of course. Please, will you all come down to the Manor House at eight? We've got two surprises for you," May said, grinning. "Where's Darragh? I'm longing to see your darling little baby again."

"He's in the cab, sleeping. I'll get him out. You won't believe how big he's got. I can barely lift his car seat these days."

"I'll get him out for you," her dad said, heading towards the front of the lorry.

"Thanks, Dad," and then she noticed that Sinead and May were holding hands and beaming at both her and Seth. *That's a bit weird. Oh my, are they a couple?*

"We've got something to tell you. This is surprise number one," Sinead announced. "May and I got engaged today!"

Seth gasped with surprise, not sure if he had heard her correctly. *May and Sinead are getting married*! *I didn't see that one coming*! "Holy cow! Congratulations! When did this happen?" he asked, hugging them both.

Sinead laughed. "We've been living together for a while, and I asked May to marry me today!"

"I am so happy for you both," Jules said. "I love surprises. So, when is the big day then?"

"We want to get married soon. Jules, please will you help me arrange everything? May is not to do a thing," Sinead asked.

"Yes, I'd love to,"

"We are going to get married in the orangery if we can find a day that is free."

"Are you still getting wedding bookings then? Didn't our wedding put people off?" Seth asked.

"I thought that it would, but after all the media attention we've had, for some reason, a beautiful murder scene is attractive to some couples," May said, going over to inspect Darragh. "Oh, he is so big now and has so much hair. He is like a mini-Seth. When he wakes up, I will have to have a cuddle."

"We still get journalists on our door wanting to interview us," Sinead said. "You wouldn't believe how popular it is to have a wedding at Waterfall West Orangery. We are booked up for this year and the next!"

"Who would have thought it?" Seth was speechless.

**

Jules opened the front door of the Old Barn and sighed with relief. Her home looked just the same, if not better than she remembered it to be. The barn still had a smell of new paint, and the wood burner had been lit. Flames danced merrily from within and had warmed the living area up so much that Jules had to take off her coat instantly before she melted. After bringing in all the bags, her dad put Darragh on the kitchen table, and he continued to sleep soundly.

"Goodness! I didn't expect this," her dad said, taking off his coat. "You and Seth have done an amazing job here." He continued his inspection and walked around the lounge area, studying the pictures on the wall.

"I'm so glad you like it. Seth took all those pictures. They're great, aren't they?" Jules opened the fridge and was relieved to see that May and Sinead had stocked up the fridge for them.

"Julia, I am going to say it now. I might have been wrong about Seth."

Jules smiled. *That's all I need to hear.* "He's the best, and he is my soulmate. I am lost without him."

"I can see that now. Although he is a complete bell end!"

"Why?"

"For taking you away from me."

"I know. I will ring you every week, and we will visit, I promise... Dad, there's eggs and cheese in the fridge. Do you want me to make you an omelette with fried potatoes?"

"Do you have time?"

"There's plenty of time, and Darragh is asleep."

"Ok then, I could eat a horse. Sorry, bad choice of words. This will be the last decent meal I will have for a long time. Peter is a dreadful cook."

Jules laughed. "You will have to learn to cook. I learnt using YouTube videos."

"I burn everything. I just start listening to the radio and forget that I am cooking. I could find me a woman to look after me."

"Dad! You sound like you are from the fifties."

"I was only joking. After I've eaten, is it ok if I stay here with Darragh? I get tired easily these days and need to rest. I don't think that I am up for socialising tonight."

Jules looked at her dad's tired face and then at Darragh and realised that it would be better for him if she put him to bed. "Ok, that's fine, Dad. We won't stay out too late. I will be back to give Darragh his last bottle. You can ring me if he wakes up. I wonder what May and Sinead's next surprise is. I can't believe they are getting married. Now that I think about it, Sinead did spend a lot of time with May, but I never suspected that there was anything going on."

Seth sat in the cab of the horsebox and rubbed his hands together, trying to keep warm. He was longing to see the Old Barn again and see his horse, Moss. *Please come and collect Barney soon. I wonder how they are going to get him out of the horsebox. Drag him? I am glad Jules is not here to see this.* His thoughts were interrupted by the sound of a lorry. *Oh, thank God!* He carefully climbed down from the cab, trying not to put any weight on his sore leg and hoped that his ears had not deceived him. He sighed with relief as the lorry drew up next to him. *At last! Poor old Barney, I forgive you for the pain you have caused me. Forgive me for swearing at you earlier.*

Chapter Six

Holding hands, Jules walked, and Seth limped up the path towards Waterfall West Manor House. The fairy lights twinkled in the darkness, guiding them towards the front door.

"It feels like Christmas," Seth whispered. "I hope they haven't gone too mad and invited everyone in the village. I was hoping that we could slip back here and just carry on from where we left off without any fuss. I wonder what May and Sinead's second surprise is going to be? I still can't get my head around them being a couple."

"I know. I was so shocked too when they told us. There's about a thirty-year age difference, but I guess age is irrelevant if you love someone," Jules whispered and then squealed with joy. "Oh, Seth. Barney, my lovely cat, is sitting on the doorstep. What is he doing down here?"

"I guess he lives with May and Sinead in the Manor House. I am sure when he sees you, he will be overjoyed. Come on, Barney, show us some love."

As they reached the door, Barney meowed to be let in.

"Oh my, he just wants us to open the door." Jules could feel a lump in her throat. *Please don't give me the cold shoulder. I have only been away for six months.* "I don't think that he likes me anymore. I can't bear this."

"He's probably just hungry. I am sure he still loves you."

"I've lost him..." she sobbed. The tears began to fall, and she couldn't stop them. "Damn, I'm crying again!"

Seth drew her to him and hugged her. "It's ok to cry. He does love you. He just needs his dinner. We will come and collect him tomorrow. Come on, don't cry, we have a party to go to. Do you hear music?"

Jules dried her eyes on the back of her hand and nodded. "I'm just tired. Why am I crying? I will win him back with tuna and Dreamies. Seth, I can hear Sonar Cell playing, actually playing live. Listen, May has invited them to our welcome party. That's the second surprise. I know it is."

The door opened, and Barney shot inside. May stood in the lit hall and was smiling at them. "Come in," she said, laughing. "I thought that you would never get here. I invited some of your friends over, and they insisted on playing."

"Well, I never, this is such a surprise. I don't know what to say," Seth replied. "Thank you for throwing us a party. We really don't deserve this."

"Of course, you do. I have been so looking forward to you both coming back to Waterfall, and so has everyone else. Come on in and say hello."

As they walked into the lounge, they were amazed to see a room full of people smiling and cheering. Shawn and his band were playing at one end of the room, and all the stable hands and their partners were there to greet them.

"It's so good of you all to come. Jules and I are blown away!" *I wonder if they know that I spent the last ten months in prison? Would they be so happy to see me if they knew?*

"Oh, it's so lovely to see you all. We are so happy to be back in Waterfall," Jules announced, smiling broadly.

Shawn's girlfriend, Jane, beckoned them over to a table and gave them each glass of champagne.

"Welcome back. Shawn and I have missed you so much. The Elbow has not been the same without you."

"Thank you, I really didn't expect such a welcome. It's great to be back. How have you all been?" Jules asked.

"We've been just grand. The band has been doing really well, and they have had two number ones. We've been travelling around Europe. Next month we are on tour in America."

"We were lucky to catch you. Do you still play at The Elbow, then?" Seth asked.

"We haven't for ages, but this weekend we will be there. Are you planning to perform soon? I hope so."

"Seth has written so many songs while we've been away. I can't wait for everyone to hear them."

"You really should have signed up with our manager. He's not so bad when you get to know him. Shawn doesn't take any nonsense from him, though."

"We thought about it, but we've decided to produce and distribute our songs ourselves. That's the plan anyway."

"You do realise that you are going to have to sing for us tonight."

"Oh, I don't know. I think everyone is enjoying Solar Cell playing," Seth said, smiling. "I don't mind. It's been a while. Maybe later then."

"Well, you are going to have to sing Waterfall Way. That's for sure. Shawn has been going on about that song all year."

"Ok, we'll see. Jane, I need to sit down. I injured my knee, and this champagne has gone straight to my head."

"Oh dear, poor you. There's a space on the sofa. I'll get you some food," Jules suggested.

"That would be grand. I am starving."

"You look pale. Do you want me to have a look at your knee?" Jane asked. "I am a nurse. Did you fall?

"No, a horse kicked me," I will be fine. "I just need to rest it. Jules' dad said RICE it. I had an ice pack on it earlier, and my knee felt a lot better. I've been standing up too long, and it's starting to hurt again."

"I don't think that you have fractured it, but you might have a crack in the bone. I'll get you some ice. I'll ask May for some. I would go and have an x-ray in the morning. You do need to put your leg up. Sit down while you can. I won't be a minute. I just saw May going into the kitchen."

Seth sat down on the sofa next to Sinead and groaned as another wave of pain hit him. "How's my favourite girl doing then?"

"I'm fine, but you sound like you are in agony."

"I'll live. Jane has gone to get me some ice. How does it feel to be engaged? When I rang you from prison, you never said that you were in a relationship. I have to say, you took me by surprise. I knew you liked girls, but I had no idea you liked May."

"I don't think May knew herself until recently. I was planning to go up North and visit a relative and said I would be away for a week. We had a big row about me going, and it was then that she realized that she didn't want to be apart and that she loved me."

"Do you feel the same?"

"Well, obviously! We got engaged, didn't we?"

"I just wanted to make sure that you were happy. You know I care about you."

"I know. I've missed my bossy younger brother. Oh, fuck! She's staring at you again."

"Who's staring? What are you talking about?" he asked, looking around the room.

"It's Gemma. I think she has a bit of a crush on you."

"Gemma? Gemma, stable hand Gemma? She's just a kid. She's about twelve, isn't she?"

"No, she's sixteen. Don't look her way and encourage her. She is standing by the fireplace. I am only telling you this because while you were away, she kept asking me a lot of questions about you. I didn't think anything of it, but yesterday she was wearing your riding jacket."

"I left it in the office. It was probably a cold February day, and she was desperate. I don't think she owns a coat from what I remember."

"Perhaps."

"She knows I am a married man, right?"

"All I am saying is that you should be careful when you talk to her. She's been through a rough time recently. Her dad died at Christmas. She isn't a child anymore. Most of the boys at the yard have fucked her."

"Ok, Christ, poor Gemma. I will be mindful." *Jesus!* Seth saw Jules approaching with two plates of food, and he was relieved to see her. It was quite unnerving knowing that he was being stared at. He tried his best to focus on Jules, and then his eyes strayed towards the fireplace, and he caught sight of Gemma - she didn't look away and then scowled when Jules blocked her view. *Sinead is right; she is staring at me!*

"Here, Jules, you sit in my seat. I've got to go and get some more wine out of the fridge," Sinead said. "Oh, yes, Seth, I was going to say Luke is going on holiday tomorrow. Is it ok if you start teaching straight away? This is the first fully booked Saturday we've had since last year. Are you going to manage with a bruised knee?"

"I can teach, no problem. I am sure my knee will feel a whole lot better after I've had a night's sleep."

"Great, I'll see you just after eight," Sinead said as she headed towards the kitchen.

Jules sat down and handed Seth a plate of food. From under her arm, she produced a bag of frozen peas wrapped in a tea cloth. "Jane gave me these. May has run out of ice. You really need to put your foot up."

"Thanks for the peas. I'll look a bit odd. It's bad enough having to hold peas on my knee. I am trying to keep it quiet that I am injured. I don't like everyone knowing that I have been an eejit."

"People don't think that."

Shawn appeared, holding a footstool. "Jane says you need to put your leg up. I wouldn't argue with Nurse Jane, or she will read you the riot act." Shawn placed the stool in front of Seth. Reluctantly, Seth lifted his foot onto it, trying not to show that he was in pain and lowered his heel onto the stool. Silently he screamed inside.

"Thanks, mate. How are you? We've been listening to your songs on the radio. You've made quite a name for yourselves."

"I'm grand, and so is Jane. She's taken to life on the road like a duck to water. I am sorry to hear about all that trouble with your Mam at the wedding. Still, it's all over with now. Did Jane tell you that we are going on tour in America soon? If you fancy a trip over, then you are more than welcome to stay with us. We are hiring a huge house with a pool and everything."

"That's really kind," Jules said. "We have a baby now, so it would be difficult to travel all that way with him. We had enough trouble getting him over to Ireland."

"A baby, you say. That was quick work."

"He was born on our wedding day. I delivered him. Darragh will be one in April," Seth said, smiling.

"Crikey, that really was quick work," Shawn said, laughing. "So, where is the wee lad?"

"He's with my Dad. I hope he's ok." Trying not to be rude, Jules quickly looked at the phone to see if she had missed any calls. "Hopefully, he is asleep."

"Don't tell Jane, she'll be wanting one too."

"Have you married the woman yet?"

43

"No, I will, though. One of these fine days when the band is rich and famous. You two should really be going down the same road. It would be a crying shame not to. Me and the lads were talking. We think that we should record your song Waterfall Way together. I tell you, it would make it to number one! That song will launch your music career, and you will never look back. What do you say?"

"That sounds good in theory," Seth replied, "but wouldn't your manager have something to say about that? We were going to see him, but he wouldn't see us other than on our wedding day, so we couldn't make the appointment. We weren't that keen on him."

"I've got Roger eating out of my hand. The more successful we are, the more money he makes. It's a win-win situation. Have a think about it anyway. Will you both come over and sing for us all, for goodness' sake? Jane wants to hear you again. She's been chewing my ear off about it all night."

"We would love to, wouldn't we, Jules?"

"Of course, but we might have to carry you across the room. I think you should have someone look at your knee in the morning."

"No, you must rest your leg. We'll come to you. I'll go and get the lads. Eat first. I won't be long."

Seth grinned at Jules. "It's been a while since we sang together. Are you up for singing with your old man, my gorgeous girl?"

"I can't wait," she said as she picked up a cheese and onion roll. *Seth is so excited. He has a sparkle in his lovely dark brown eyes. How I have missed those eyes.*

Jules gasped as she felt a soft furry head rubbing up against her hand. Barney had jumped up on the sofa next to her and was purring as he waited to be loved. She ran her hand over his head and back. "Seth, he remembers me. He has come back to me." She was laughing and crying at the same time. *Just happy tears!*

"There, I told you. You daft thing. Don't cry."

***

Sonar Cell sat opposite them, and everyone, realising that there was going to be a joint performance, gathered around them to listen.

"This song, Waterfall Way, was written by S&J last summer, and we think that it is a winner," Seth declared. "We've updated the words a little to make it even better. Enjoy."

The band started to play their introduction to the song. Seth smiled as he remembered them being on stage at The Elbow like it was only yesterday. *How quickly time flies.* He gave Jules a reassuring squeeze. Barney had curled up on her lap and was unfazed by the loud music. *Perhaps he's deaf. She looks so happy tonight.*

> *Nearly lost our lives when the sun went down*
> *To a crazy man and his plans and a withered clown*
> *We fled golden fields for county Cork*
> *Too poor to eat, so we found work*
> *We declared our love with a Claddagh ring*
> *now all we do is laugh and dance and sing*
> *You laughed and stole a kiss, and I stole one back*
> *looked up at the sky and the stars, and I made my wish*
>
> *If we are going to Waterfall Way*
> *oh, then can we stay?*
> *I need you today*
> *Say you'll take this ring and be my wife*

Oh, how long, I've waited all my life
And if you're planning on leaving, then listen, dear
I'll do whatever it takes to convince you that you should be here

Don't dance with that badass guy; he'll make you cry
Oh, be with me instead, he's in another girl's bed
You cringe, you hang your head because you know it's true
When all I want is to save this dance for you.

If we are going to Waterfall Way
oh, then can we stay?
I need you today
Say you'll take this ring and be my wife
Oh, how long, I've waited all my life
And if you're planning on leaving, then listen, dear
I'll do whatever it takes to convince you that you should be here

Together we can climb our tree
Seal our love
Just you and me
We don't need to think
Just let our bodies sink
And I'm crazy; you're in my head
You're in my bed
In my head

The song went down well. They were applauded, and Luke called out that he wanted them to sing another song. Requests continued to come, and an hour passed quickly.

Jules looked around at everyone's smiling faces. *It is good to be home*. Barney meowed a little. She looked down at his warm body and realised that her phone was ringing. *Did my phone disturb you?* She stopped singing and looked at her phone, knowing that it was her dad that was calling her. She took the call. "Hold on, Dad." She lifted Barney down and then stood up and made her way to the hall. "Dad, is everything ok?"

"Well, yes, but Darragh is crying. I let him cry for half an hour, but he hasn't stopped. I think he wants his nappy changing or an early feed. I am not that keen on picking him up."

"That's ok, Dad. Half an hour to cry is a long time. I will be about five minutes. I will let Seth know."

"Won't he be walking you back?

"No. He is resting his knee. I could get Sinead to run us home, but… I've got a torch. I'll be fine. I'll feed him, and then if he settles, I will come back to the party."

"Ok, kitten. See you in a minute."

Jules stood in the doorway of the lounge and decided to wait until the next song finished. Seth was singing These Days with Shawn, and she felt a little sad that she wasn't singing with him. She sighed. *Life has changed so much since Darragh came along.* She didn't want Seth to stop singing as he was enjoying himself so much. It was then that she noticed Gemma sat on the stairs behind her. "Gemma, are you ok? Are you not joining in?"

"I was, but I got a bit hot. So, I am having a cool off. I didn't realise that Seth could sing. I love that song, Giants, he sang earlier. He sounds a bit like Dermot Kennedy. Seth is looking good, isn't he?"

"Um… I guess so. He's in a lot of pain. He's hurt his knee. Although you wouldn't know it the way, he is singing. Gemma? You wouldn't do me a favour, would you? I've got to go and give Darragh a bottle. I don't want to interrupt the singing. I should be back in half an hour. Would you tell him that?"

"What? Actually speak to him?"

"Yes, when the next song finishes."

"Ok, I'll look after him while you are gone."

"Thanks, Gemma, you are a brick,"

"A brick?"

"Yes, a brick. A sweetheart."

Chapter Seven

Darragh was howling, his cheeks were bright red, and there was nothing Jules could do to soothe her fevered baby. She had fed him, changed his nappy and was walking him up and down the lounge, rocking him gently, hoping that he would stop crying.

"It's not like him to cry so much. He must be in pain," her dad declared, appearing in the doorway of his bedroom. He was dressed in his striped pyjamas, and he looked tired and sleepy.

"Did he wake you? I think it must be his teeth cutting through the gum. If I touch his bottom gum, he bites my finger and cries more. If only he could speak and tell me what's wrong. What time is it, Dad?"

"It's nearly one in the morning. Can't Seth rock him for a bit? You look exhausted."

"Seth's staying over at the Manor House."

"That doesn't seem right. Leaving you to hold the baby."

"It's all right. Seth's knee is causing him grief, and everyone thought that he should stay where he is. Apparently, he nearly passed out when he went to the toilet. May gave him some painkillers, and he is asleep on the sofa. I think that he should go to A&E in the morning."

"A likely story!"

"Dad!"

"It just doesn't seem right. I'm just saying."

Jules didn't have the strength to argue. She was near to tears. It would have been good to have Seth back home for moral support. Her dad was making things twice as bad. "You go back to bed and try to sleep.

49

You've got a long trip in the morning. I am going to give him some Calpol and his keys to chew on. I've put them in the fridge. He feels hot. I wish I had a thermometer."

"Let me feel his head," her dad said, walking over to them. He placed his hand on Darragh's forehead and looked concerned. Darragh stopped crying for a moment and looked at him suspiciously. "He does feel hot. My hands are always cold, and he definitely has a temperature."

"You've got the magic touch. He's quiet now. I just need a moment to think. This is the first time he has been sick. It is freaking me out."

"Strip him off down to his nappy and try and cool him down a bit."

"Ok. Do you think his temperature is over forty?"

"Pretty close."

"Do you think he is really ill?"

"Don't panic. Kids get temperatures and all sorts when they are small. Your Mum and I were always at the hospital with you both. Peter especially. I bet you anything, after some medicine, by the morning, Darragh will be back to his old self. Babies have a way of bouncing back when you fear the worst. See if you can cool him down, then that will help. If he doesn't settle in the next hour, then maybe we should take him to A&E. Just to get him checked out and put your mind at rest."

"In the horsebox?"

"Oh dear, yes, I forgot that we came in that beast. It will be fine. I am sure that there will be plenty of parking spaces free. It is the middle of the night."

"Ok, you try to sleep. I'll ring Seth in a bit and let him know what's going on."

"I wouldn't bother. He's probably wasted."

"Dad! He's not like that."

***

I can smell roses. A sweet, sickly smell. Where is it coming from? Why can I smell roses? I need to wake up. There's somewhere I need to be. Seth tried to wake himself from his dream. It seemed like only moments ago he had been singing with everyone. *Why aren't I singing now?* He shifted his body a little to try and get more comfortable. He could feel pain. *Fuck! Something hurts so bad. Why is my bed so small? Am I still in prison? No, not anymore.* He smiled as that pleasant thought filled his head. He could see Jules waiting outside the prison for him. He wanted to hug her so much. Suddenly she was there. He felt her hand on his chest, and he could feel his heart beating against it. Her hand ran down his body. Down to his groin, and she tugged at the buttons on his fly. He was shocked. *She wouldn't do such a thing outside the prison, would she?*

Seth opened his eyes wide, aware that there was somebody sitting next to him, with her hands at his waist, tugging at the top button of his jeans. He could smell roses again. *It's not Jules. Hell no! Somebody is undoing my trousers.* He sat up and pushed whoever it was away. A girl screamed. Seth yelled too, the pain in his knee was too much to bear. He found his phone, and the room lit up enough to see who it was. "Christ, Gemma! It's you. What the fuck are you doing?"

Gemma got up from the floor. She was still wearing her party dress and looked a little embarrassed. She pulled the strap up over her shoulder and stood up.

"You scared me. I didn't mean to hurt you. What were you doing?" he asked.

"I was making you more comfortable. It's not very nice to wear your clothes all night. You looked agitated, so I thought it would help if I undid your trousers. I'm sorry."

I don't think she is telling the truth. Her eyes are telling a different story. "How long have you been here?"

"All night."

"Why? What am I going to tell Jules?"

"That you'd rather be with me than her. I bet she doesn't look after you like I do."

"Gemma, I've been back a day, not even that. I am a happily married man, and I really am not interested in you."

Gemma started to cry. "Jules asked me to look after you."

Seth was still shocked and a little confused. "Look, don't cry. I am sure you are really nice, and everything, but you shouldn't have done what you did. What if May or Sinead came in here. What would they think? It was very kind of you to stay with me, but there really was no need. I won't say anything. You should go home. It's nearly two o'clock. Won't your Mam be worried about you?"

"I live here in the attic. Don't tell May. I've got nowhere else to go."

"Christ, Gemma! You can't live here uninvited. Why are you homeless?"

"I fell out with Mam. She's not been the same since Dad died," she said, snivelling.

"I'm sorry to hear about your Dad. You're earning a wage now, cleaning this house. Surely you can find a room somewhere in Waterfall?"

"I can't afford rent on my wage. Anyway, I like living here."

"You need to speak to May. I won't say anything. I have to go. I should be in my own bed with my wife," Seth said, getting up from the sofa. The pain in his knee was a little better, but it was still painful to move. His phone started to ring, and he saw that it was Jules calling him. *Why is she calling me at this time of night?* He took the call. "Is everything ok?"

"Oh, thank goodness you picked up. Darragh has a raging temperature, and Dad and I are going to take him up to A&E to get him checked over. He has been crying for hours."

"No! Poor thing. I'll meet you at the end of the drive."

"I am so relieved. Can you walk?"

"I'll manage."

"You might as well get your knee looked at while we are there. We are just getting into the horsebox. I'll see you in a minute."

I can hear Darragh crying. "See you soon." He put his phone in his pocket and looked up. Gemma had gone. He sighed. *That girl is trouble.* Cautiously, he stepped forward, testing his leg. He could put weight on it, but his knee hurt like anything.

It was good to be outside the house, and he did his best to push his brief encounter with Gemma to the back of his mind. *What a stupid girl. Should I tell Jules about what happened? I should, but not tonight.*

The lorry pulled up beside Seth, and he saw Jules' worried face at the window. She pointed at the front seat, indicating that he should get in there, next to Mike. Seth took a deep breath and opened the door, ready to haul himself in. He was feeling nervous about sitting next to him. He had a feeling that he was in his bad books again. As he sat down, he looked over at his father-in-law and knew that he was not pleased with him. "Jules, I'm sorry I didn't make it back to the barn. May gave me some crazy pills that didn't work well with champagne, and I just passed out on the sofa. How's Darragh doing?"

"You are here with us now. That's what matters. I think he is exhausted from crying, and the drive down here has calmed him. Seth, he has a rash on his body. I'm really starting to worry, in case he has something awful."

"The hospital is only minutes away," her dad said. "He has probably just got heat rash."

"Mike, do you want me to guide you to the hospital. I can get a route up on my phone," Seth asked, trying to sound friendly.

"I know the way. Julia has told me how to get there."

Darragh started to cry again, and Seth could tell that he was in pain. He felt like crying too. For his son, and for not being a good husband or father.

Darragh continued to cry as Jules and Seth waited in the kids A&E. There was one other family waiting with a toddler. The little girl had blonde hair tied up on top of her head in a small bunch. Jules wondered what was wrong with her as she showed no signs of being ill.

"She fell down the stairs and was sick," the child's mother announced. She was a thin woman with long black hair and was wearing her dressing gown. "She bumped her head. I feel terrible about it."

"Oh dear, she looks so happy," Jules replied. "She is the cutest little thing."

"What's wrong with your baby?"

"I don't know. He has a temperature and is in pain somewhere. I hope that we don't have to wait too long. Seth, you need to register yourself to get your knee seen. Did you see how busy the main waiting room was?"

"It's Friday night, and there's lots of drunk eejits in there."

"I heard someone say there is a three-hour wait to get seen," the woman declared.

For a second, Seth had a flashback of his drunken mother, lying in a pool of sick on the streets of Cork and imagined himself sitting next to someone like that in the waiting room. He silently sighed and then realised how tired he was. "I don't think I will bother. I want to see the doctor about Darragh. My knee can wait. I wish they would hurry up. I don't like to see him so distressed."

Jules was hugging and rocking Darragh, who had the hiccups and occasionally cried out in pain. "It's our turn next…"

"Darragh Hearn?" a paediatrician called out. Seth picked up the empty carrier, and limping, he followed Jules and the doctor into a consultation room.

"So, how can I help?" the doctor asked. "He's not very happy, is he?"

"He's got a temperature, a rash, and he won't stop crying. He wouldn't take his last bottle."

"I think that he is in pain," Seth added. Jules shot him an anxious look.

"Undress him down to his nappy and lay him on the bed. Let's have a look at the wee fellow. He's quite small for ten months. Was he a preterm?"

"Yes, he was six weeks early."

"Were there any birth complications?"

"No, he could breathe by himself straight away."

Jules lay Darragh on the bed and undressed him. The rash on his body looked angry. The doctor took his temperature and checked Darragh over as he tried to work out what was wrong with him. "You don't think he's got meningitis, do you?"

"No, when you press his skin, the rash fades. I think there is something wrong with his ears. He probably has an infection, and that is why he has a rash. He has very small ear canals, and they can get infected easily. Sit him on your lap, and I'll have a look in his ears."

Jules picked Darragh up and sat down with him. He had stopped crying and was looking around at the brightly lit room curiously.

The doctor looked in both ears and nodded. "He has an ear infection in his right ear, and his eardrum has burst."

"Oh my! No wonder he has been crying. Will his eardrum mend? This is the first time he has had an ear infection," Jules said, running her fingers through Darragh's soft hair.

"It has probably just burst, and that will relieve a lot of pressure. He won't be in pain now. It will heal, and we will give him some antibiotics to get rid of the infection. I am surprised he hasn't had an ear infection before."

Jules was so relieved that Darragh didn't have anything more serious, and she could feel a weight lift off her shoulders.

"Thank you for helping him."

"Get him dressed and go and get him his prescription. The sooner he starts on the antibiotics, the better. If his temperature doesn't go down by tomorrow lunchtime or gets higher, then bring him back."

***

Seth breathed a sigh of relief as he opened their front door and stepped into the lounge. There was something very satisfying about being back in his own home. *It is just as I remember it. Thank God!* The walls were still covered in pictures, and the side lamps cast their light on their modern furnishings, making their home feel warm and welcoming. "It's so good to be back. I don't think that I will ever get over having a place like this to live in," he said, smiling.

"Yes, it's good to be home. I am going to put Darragh in his cot. He is asleep at last," Jules said, walking through to the bedroom."

"You get some sleep too, kitten, it's practically morning," her dad said.

Jules stopped and turned around. "Dad, stay another day. You will be too tired to drive home tomorrow."

"Yes, please, Mike. I will ring the hire company and see if we can keep the horsebox for another day. I don't think that they will mind," Seth said, eager to try and win him over. "I think the weather is going to be rough tomorrow too. We really would like it if you did."

Mike sighed and then nodded. "I am feeling pretty tired, and it would be good to see Waterfall West in daylight. Ok then, I will."

After putting Darragh to bed, Jules returned to the lounge and sat down heavily at the kitchen table. Seth could see that she was exhausted. He was tired, but he wasn't feeling too bad, having had a few hours of sleep earlier. "Do you two want a cup of tea?"

"No, thanks. I am beat. I need to sleep," she said, yawning. "What about you, Dad?"

"I'm knackered. I will see you both in the morning."

"Night, Dad."

"Night, kitten."

When Mike had gone, Jules stood up and walked over to Seth and hugged him. She lay her head on his chest and breathed him in. "Come to bed, Seth, I need a hug."

"I will in a minute. I just need to shower and then strap my knee up."

"It's a shame you didn't get it seen to."

"I would still be sitting in A&E now if I had waited. I know it's not broken, so all they would have done is give me a knee brace. I can create one myself." He hugged her tighter, enjoying feeling her body against his. "I would be quite happy if we stayed like this forever."

"Me too. It is so good to be in your arms again. It's been a long day, hasn't it?"

"Such a long day! Thank goodness Darragh is going to be ok. He doesn't feel as hot as he did. I think the antibiotics are starting to work."

"Seth, tomorrow we need to get him a thermometer. It's crazy that we haven't got one."

"After work, we will get the bus into Cork and get one. Sinead has put me to work tomorrow. Is that ok? We could do with the money."

"Sure. It will be just like old times. I am so enjoying this hug, I am falling asleep in your arms, and you may well have to carry me to bed. You smell so sweet tonight. Just like roses."

Chapter Eight

Seth woke up with Jules in his arms. It was so good to be in his own bed again, holding his beautiful wife. This was the happiest he had been in the whole of his life. Jules was fast asleep, and he knew that he shouldn't wake her. He drew her a little closer and shut his eyes again, wishing that he could lie in with her. He knew that he would have to get up soon and get ready for work. Although he had only had a few hours' sleep, he was feeling refreshed. He smiled. A whole new chapter was starting and today felt like the first day of the rest of his life. *I wonder what the time is. Did I set my alarm? No, I didn't. What time did I say I would meet Sinead at the yard? Eight-thirty, I think.*

Reluctantly, Seth let Jules go and gently slid out of bed to look at the time. It was quarter past seven. He sighed with relief. *I've got plenty of time to get ready.* He shivered and quickly put his hoodie on. *I'll go and put another log in the burner. I can't have the house getting cold. Mike wouldn't be impressed. What are we going to do with him today? Jules wants to take him with us to Cork.* He looked up at the roof window and saw angry grey clouds. *It's a bit of a wild day for sightseeing.*

Seth limped over to Darragh's cot and looked at his sleeping son. He had rosy cheeks and had kicked off his covers. *You sleep deeply, just like your Mam.* Seth couldn't help stroking his thick brown hair, and then he pulled the covers over his shoulder, not wanting him to get cold. Darragh opened his eyes and then looked at him. Seth stayed very still, hoping that he would go back to sleep. His baby smiled at him and then kicked the duvet off himself, rolled onto his tummy and started to crawl towards him. Seth was not sure what to do. *I should take him into the other room so poor Jules can sleep for a bit longer.* "You clever boy. Come on then," he whispered. "Let's go and get you a bottle and let your Mam sleep." He picked him up and collected a cardigan for him he saw lying on one of the suitcases.

Seth sat on the sofa and put the cardigan on Darragh, and then turned him around so he could talk to him. "There. Is that better? Are you warmer now?" He felt his cheeks and forehead to see if he still had a fever. *Just bed warm. Good.* "You gave us both a scare yesterday." Darragh laughed. "So, you are laughing now. Do you want your milk? I saw some bottles in the fridge. I guess I have to stand the bottle in hot water to warm it up for you. The question is, where do I put you?" Seth stood up and looked around for the car seat and then saw May walking up the garden path. She was holding an umbrella over her to protect her from the rain. *Oh, God! It's pouring now.* He carried Darragh over to the front door and opened it to let her in. The weather was wild outside, and May was almost blown into the barn.

"Oh heavens! It's not very nice out there. Thank goodness we don't have any weddings booked for today. I had to come up and see you. Gemma just told me what happened last night," she added as she put her umbrella on the doormat. "I'll have to get you an umbrella stand."

Seth's heart stopped for a moment as he had a flashback of Gemma wrestling with his trousers. "What did she tell you exactly?"

"She said that you had to take this little one to the hospital. I just had to come up and see if he was ok. What was wrong with him? He is smiling, so I guess it wasn't anything too serious."

"He's got an ear infection, and his eardrum burst. He was in terrible pain. He's on antibiotics. He seems much better today."

"Oh, you poor baby," she said, stroking Darragh's cheek. "Can I hold him? I wonder if he remembers me. I used to give him lots of cuddles when you were away."

"Yes, sure. I need to warm some milk up for him." Seth passed Darragh to her and then saw Jules emerge from the bedroom. She stood in the doorway looking very sexy in her short nightshirt. She smiled at him and then gasped when she realised that they had company. She ran back into the bedroom to put on some clothes. Moments later, she reappeared in a dressing gown he had not seen before and had her hair tied back.

Jules walked over to Seth and gave him a morning hug. He hugged her back and kissed her gently on the lips. "Morning, beautiful. May has come up to see how Darragh is."

May was showing Darragh all the pictures on the wall and telling him where they were taken. Jules smiled at them both. *She is so good with Darragh, and it is obvious that they have a bond.* "May, I was going to call you later to tell you what happened. I guess Seth has told you about our hospital visit?"

"I am so glad that he is not in pain now. He is such a cute little darling," May said, sitting down on the sofa. "He must have doubled in size since I last saw him. I've knitted him some clothes for the winter. I hope they are going to fit him."

"That's really kind of you. He has nearly outgrown all of the clothes Charlene gave me. I was going to say thank you for getting him the cot. It is perfect, and it was such a relief to see it all ready for him yesterday."

"It was no bother, the woman that sold it to us actually delivered it to the door in one piece. All Sinead and I had to do was bring it in. It was spotless, but Sinead insisted on wiping it down with antibac wipes. You will probably have to get Darragh a high chair and perhaps a baby walker too. Do they still make those things?"

"I think that they do. I'll have a look on eBay later."

"Do you want a cup of tea?" Seth asked, flicking the kettle on.

"Yes, please. Do you have coffee? I haven't had my morning cupper yet, and my brain doesn't function properly until I do."

"No problem, I'll make you one. Jules, how do you heat Darragh's milk up?"

"I usually stand it in a jug of hot water for ten minutes. Don't worry, I'll do it. You make us our drinks and some toast. Thanks to May, the fridge is full."

"That was Sinead's doing. Seth, you are going to have your hands full this morning. She is going to have one terrible hangover. I don't envy you two having to teach outside today. It's raining cats and dogs out there!"

"I can handle Sinead, I'm used to being verbally abused, and then I laugh, and she laughs too. How is Moss, by the way? I am itching to see him again."

"Luke has been looking after him. Moss won a few best of breed classes last year. We put all the cobs in the barn last night. The forecast is rain with gale-force winds today. They might cancel the ferries. Jules, your dad should delay going home until tomorrow. I don't think that it is a good day to travel at all."

"He's agreed to stay another day. He drove us to the hospital in the horsebox last night and needs to rest. I wanted to take him around Cork today and show him the Manor House and the estate. It's a shame that the weather is so terrible. I hope that he is not going to be bored."

"Come down to the Manor House, and I will give him a guided tour. The house has a lot of history, and just lately, I have been giving tours when people come to stay in the B&B. It will be fun. You had quite a day yesterday. You should have called me, and I would have driven to the hospital. It can't have been easy parking the horsebox."

"I didn't like to call. It was really late, and Dad volunteered. We managed to park it ok. Oh, I was going to tell you. I passed my driving test first time thanks to all your help."

"That's great news. You really need to be able to drive when you live out here. You can use my car if you like. Sinead hates it. Well, hates me driving it anyway. We use her Mini all the time."

"I couldn't! I am sure we can get one soon."

"Well, use it until you can save up for your own. It would make me feel less guilty."

"Why do you feel guilty?" asked Seth.

"I had to give Jules' job to Gemma. Not that she's any good, mind you. Seth, you don't earn much as an instructor, and things are going to be tight money wise for you."

"We will get by. We were going to ask you if we could farm some of the land. I thought I could grow vegetables and sell the produce locally. Perhaps open a farm shop in one of the outbuildings. It will just be a small farming venture to start with. I would buy the horse manure from you."

May laughed. "That sounds wonderful. The estate will be like it was hundreds of years ago. How delightful. You really don't have to buy dung. It is a headache for me to get rid of."

Jules smiled as she handed May the bottle of milk to give to Darragh. She had always loved doing this. "You are the best!"

***

Seth and a very grumpy Sinead had stood out in the rain and taught riding to a handful of resilient riders. The students' love for the sport knew no bounds, and they were happy to pay for lessons and brave the elements, regardless.

Seth had a break at lunchtime and was sodden. He had limped down the track to join Jules and Mike for lunch. She had helped him peel off his waterproofs and had found him some dry clothes as his coat had failed miserably. She wondered where his waterproof jacket was. Seth did his best to chat to her dad, but there was tension in the air, and she noticed that Seth was doing most of the talking. She felt a little sad that his opinion of Seth had altered. *Why doesn't he like him? Seth is a good person.*

Jules fastened the popper of her mac under her chin, determined to keep her hood up and protect her hair from the rain. The wind was fierce. Her dad had the hood of his waterproof coat tied tightly around his face. Jules thought that he looked ridiculous and laughed when she saw him. He laughed too and said that he wasn't going to take any chances and was determined to stay dry. They were late to visit May as they had waited a while for a break in the weather so that they could walk down to the Manor House without being drenched or blown to pieces. If anything, the wind had become even more ferocious. As Darragh had fallen asleep, they laid him in his pushchair with the rain cover over it and set off along the track towards the stable yard.

That morning, Darragh had been the model baby and had taken his medicine without complaint. From the moment he had been awake, he had laughed and played as if nothing had happened. Still a little shell shocked from their ordeal at the hospital, Jules had kept a close eye on him, fearing that he may get sick. Her fears were unfounded. Darragh was his old self again.

As they approached the stable yard, Jules could see that her dad was looking nervous.

"It's ok, Dad, May and Sinead are really nice. May can talk the back legs off a donkey. We are going to have a lovely afternoon. The Manor House has a really interesting history."

"I am sure that we will. I find it hard to face people when they know that you have been in a mental hospital."

"There's nothing to be ashamed of. It is quite obvious that you are recovering and everyone will be so pleased for you. Even Winston Churchill battled with depression."

"How did you know that?"

"I did do A-level history! Seth should have finished his lessons for the day. I thought we could pick him up on the way."

"Do we have to?"

"Dad! I really don't understand why you don't like him," she was starting to get angry.

"I was only joking. I just find it difficult to accept that you have married a Hearn. You know his parents have made our farm unsellable. Nobody is going to want to buy it knowing that multiple bodies were found on it."

"You can't blame Seth for that. Anyway, you are not selling the farm now. Dad, you really make me mad sometimes."

***

With no stable hands in sight, Seth and Sinead led Soldier into his stable and started to remove his saddle and bridle. The stable was surprisingly warm, and Soldier seemed happy to be out of the rain.

"Well, that was one hell of a day. I bet you are really glad to be back. I feel like shit!" Sinead said, hooking up a hay net.

"It's not so bad. I feel alive when I am outside. I actually like the rain. As long as you have good waterproofs, then you are ok. My jacket wasn't in the office. I could have done with it as this old thing I am wearing is useless. You said that Gemma had it. Will it be ok if I order some new waterproofs?"

"Yes, of course. If you want me to see Gemma and get it off her, then I'd only be too happy. She's been driving May and me mad lately. I know she's lost her dad, but there's no excuse for being late to work every day and moaning all the time. She says she has to get the first bus in, and it's always late."

Seth was starting to feel uncomfortable knowing that Gemma was telling lies. *Should I say that she is sleeping in the attic? No, better not.* "Gemma can have my coat, I don't think she has one, and it was a bit small for me. She is only young and probably needs you to mother her a bit."

Sinead looked at Seth and smirked. "Fuck off!"

Seth laughed. "If it is ok with you, I am going to have to go home and change before I come down to the Manor House."

"You don't have to ask. We are partners, remember?"

"I know, but I feel like I don't contribute enough to running this riding school."

"Don't be so hard on yourself. You did a great job today. There's not many that would stand for hours in a gale and teach after a night you've had. How is your knee, by the way?"

"I think that it is improving. Now and again, I catch it, and I could scream. You should see the bruise. I took a photo of it before I strapped it up," he said, getting his phone out of his pocket. "Christ, my phone is soaked too." He managed to find the photo and smiled. "Here, have a look. That old pony got me good and proper."

"Shit! That looks horrible. You should have got it looked at last night."

As Seth and Sinead walked into the yard, they saw Jules making their way up the track towards them. Mike was pushing Darragh, and he was having difficulty as the path was full of potholes. "I will have to make that track pushchair friendly."

"The rest of the way is going to be tough going too," Sinead said, pushing a strand of wet hair behind her ear. "May said she is going to lend you her old car. You will be able to drive home later."

Jules smiled when she saw Seth and Sinead waiting for her. *Seth looks like a drowned rat.* His dark wavy hair was flattened, and his clothes were wringing wet again and were hanging on him. Despite his dishevelled look, his big brown eyes were sparkling. *The rain doesn't bother him. He looks happy.* When she reached him, Seth hugged her.

"Are you wet, my sweet girl?"

"Not as wet as you are." The wind hit them hard, and he clung on to her, frightened that she might be blown away. "Are you ok, Mike? You are doing a grand job with little Darragh and that old pushchair."

"It has been hard work and a bit bumpy. I don't think that Darragh has noticed. He's dead to the world. This cover is protecting him from the worst of it."

"You will be able to drive home tonight. May has got her old car out of the garage and has sorted out the insurance," Sinead declared. "Jules, you are going to be driving around in style now."

"Seriously? That is so kind of her. I've never seen her car."

"I have," Seth said. "Do you think you are going to be ok driving a vintage Jaguar?"

"Oh, my," Jules said, laughing. "That does sound grand. I'll give it a go. I am just so grateful. We had better go and see May. We are running a bit late. You are both so wet. Seth, are you going to change?"

"Yes, but first, I am going to see Moss. I won't be long. I'll check on Connor, too, while I'm there. I will be with you in half an hour."

***

Seth battled against the wind as he made his way towards the hay barn. The building was huge. At the far end of the barn, bales of hay were piled high, and the other end was fenced off, forming a substantial paddock large enough to house all the horses when the weather was particularly bad. They were free to roam into the adjoining field if they wished. *This would make a great indoor riding school. I don't know why we aren't using it on days like this.*

Seth had butterflies in his stomach. He knew that Moss would recognise him, but he also had a niggling fear that his horse might prefer Luke to him. Seth stood in the doorway and looked at all of May's coloured cobs, and scanned the barn for a shiny black stallion. Nearly all the mares had large foals with them. The majority of them were black. *Well, that's a surprise! I think Moss is a father too.* Connor and Pringle stood side by side, and both looked at him curiously. "It's ok, boys. I've not come to get you." He smiled when he saw Moss. His horse was standing in the far corner, dozing. He still had his winter coat and was covered in mud. Not wanting to frighten him, Seth limped over to him and shook his head when he realised just how muddy and thin he was looking. "So, my old mate, are you going to come and say hello."

Moss woke with a start, and his ears pricked up as he realised that Seth was talking to him. "Yes, it's me. I am back for good now." Moss snorted and then calmly walked over to him. Seth put his arms around his neck and hugged him. *He smells of hay and something foul. What have you been rolling in? Fox shite!* "You look tired, old friend. Did you miss me? I missed you. It's ok. I'm here now." Seth patted his neck and sighed. "You don't look well."

"He's been pining for you."

Seth's heart nearly leapt out of his chest. Gemma was sitting on the haystack watching them. "Christ, Gemma! You gave me a fright." He noticed that she was wearing his rain jacket. Her curly blonde hair was tied back, and her black mascara ran in streaks down her cheeks. She looked away when she realised that he was staring at her. "Are you ok? Have you been crying?"

She nodded.

"What's wrong?"

"It's all your fault. Seth Hearn, you won't want to hear this, but you are breaking my heart."

Chapter Nine

Seth stepped out of the hot shower and started to dry himself off with his towel. *It's so good to be home and be able to use my own bathroom again.* Lost in thought, he looked at himself in the mirror and sighed. He was feeling guilty. Gemma's announcement that he was breaking her heart had taken him by surprise. He had told her that she didn't know him and needed to grow up. *Perhaps that wasn't the best thing to say. What the fuck am I going to tell Jules?*

Dressed in his jeans and his favourite t-shirt and hoodie, Seth loaded the washing machine with all the wet clothes he'd worn that morning. He threw in his coat as well, which was so heavy with water that he could barely lift it. *So, what coat am I going to wear down to the Manor House?* Seth looked out of the windows at the rain beating down hard on the ground. *I'll have to run down as I am. Damn, I can't run with this knee. How about I wear a dustbin sack? Not the most glamorous of looks, but it will do.* As he pulled out the roll of dustbin bags, he saw May's old green Jaguar draw up, and his mouth opened in amazement. Jules was at the steering wheel with a big smile across her face. *My clever, gorgeous girl. So tiny in such a big car. Perfect timing.*

Jules beckoned to him, and picking up his keys and phone, he limped outside to join her. The wind and rain hit him, almost knocking him off his feet. *This wind is getting stronger. Strong enough to blow down a tree.* He was so glad to get in the car and to be alone with her. *I should tell her about Gemma. We promised that we will always be honest with each other. Will she be upset?* "You are so good to me," he said, kissing her. Her lips were warm. "Saving your poor husband from getting drenched again. How does it feel to be behind the wheel of something so grand?"

"I was a bit nervous to start with but compared to Dad's old jeep, this is a dream to drive. The only thing is; this car is going to cost us a fortune to run. I swear I have used nearly half a tank of fuel to get here. I don't think that it is environmentally friendly, either."

"We will save up for a little run around for us. I'd like to get an electric car if we could."

Jules started to reverse out of their drive and onto the track. "This road is treacherous. I don't remember it being so bad."

"The winter weather does terrible things to the roads here. I will order some scalpings to fill the holes."

"Scalpings? What are they?"

"Just gravel that you can compact down into the holes. Dad used to use them to repair the tracks around Crow Farm."

"Is that an Irish word?"

"No. I don't think so. You're handling this car well. I miss driving."

"When do you think you will get your license back?"

"As soon as I get a moment, I am going to apply for it. I should get it back before the end of March." Seth huffed. He couldn't get the image of Gemma running away from him after he had told her to grow up out of his mind.

"What's the matter? Are you tired?"

"No, I'm not tired. I've got a bit of a problem."

"What's that then?" Jules said, looking quickly at Seth's worried face. *Oh, dear!*

"You see… I have been having a bit of trouble with Gemma."

"Have you? She didn't turn up for work this morning at the Manor House. What happened?"

"Well, here's the thing... I think she has the hots for me. When I went to see the horses, she was in the barn, wearing my rain jacket, and she was crying. She told me that I was breaking her heart. I told her that I wasn't interested, and she ran off crying. There, I said it." *Crap, Jules has gone quiet!*

Jules looked at the road ahead, trying her best to avoid the potholes. Seth's words were slowly starting to filter through, and she needed a moment to process what he was telling her. *Am I shocked? No, not really.*

"Jules?"

"Oh, dear. I am sad for her."

"Really? You don't mind that women are coming on to me?"

"Of course, I mind, but let's face it, Seth, you are hot property. When we are famous, I am going to have to get used to women swooning when they see you. When we sang at The Elbow, there were plenty of female fans who only had eyes for you."

"I didn't notice. So, you're not mad then?"

"No, but I don't think you handled things with Gemma very well."

"You're right. I didn't. What do you suggest I do?"

"I'll talk to her."

"I don't know if that is a good idea. What are you going to say?"

"That I'll share you with her."

"Surely not!"

"No, I'm only joking," Jules said, laughing. "Your face! I'll be kind to her. Don't you remember what it was like to fall in love with a pop star and feel the pain of unrequited love? Each day is torture because you know that you will never be with them."

"No, not really. So, who has caused my beautiful girl so much pain?"

"I might have been just a little upset when Ed Sheeran married Cherry Seaborn."

"I never knew that you liked him that much. It's a good job I snapped you up when I did then! I think that the closest I've come to feeling that pain is being apart from you for ten months. You do realise that I will never leave your side, and you are stuck with me forever."

"Ahhh, you sweet thing. It's ok, we're together now. So, this thing with Gemma…"

"I don't like you to call it a thing."

"I think that Gemma is star struck. She has put you on a pedestal without knowing you and is obsessively in love with you."

"Christ, you are making her sound like a bunny boiler! I don't know if I can handle this."

"Did you like that film, Fatal Attraction?"

"It was ok. I don't remember the plot very well, but I remember seeing a rabbit in a cooking pot. We should watch it again when our boy is in bed."

"I'd like that. I've missed watching films with you. It's a good job you don't have a rabbit."

Jules parked the car in the lower car park by the Manor House, and they both ran up the path, through the wind and the rain, doing their best to stay dry.

The house smelt of jam and cakes and welcomed them in with open arms. "May's been baking," Seth said, wiping his feet on the mat. "I hope that there is some cake left."

"There will be. May usually cooks too much." She could hear the sound of laughter coming from the lounge. *I can hear Dad laughing.* "I think they are all in the lounge. I haven't heard Dad laugh so much in a long time."

"I'll have to ask May for some tips. Your dad is a hard nut to crack."

"You are trying too hard. Just give him time."

As they walked into the lounge, Jules saw her dad holding Darragh high in the air, and he was pretending that he was an airplane. Darragh was laughing, and Jules could see how happy her dad was looking. *My, that's a first. He's actually holding Darragh.* Seeing them arrive, her dad returned his grandson to a standing position on his knees, and he was looking embarrassed about his tender outburst.

I can't believe that he is holding him. He looks so guilty. Seth grinned at everyone. "It's good to be here in the warm with you all."

"Oh, Jules and my lovely Seth, I am so glad you got here in one piece. How are you finding my old car?" May asked.

"It's just grand. We are really thankful to you, and it has saved us from getting blown away. What a wild day. How has my wee boy been then?" he asked, walking over to Mike to see him. "Is it ok if I take him off you for a hug?"

"Please do. I think that he is growing tired of me."

"No, I think you are wrong. I've never seen him so happy. He loves his granddad." Seth picked up Darragh and hugged him. His body was soft and warm, and he smelt of baby powder. Darragh's big brown eyes looked up at him, and then he saw tears. "Oh no, you are not going to cry, are you? Do you want to go back to your granddad?" Darragh started to cry.

"I better take him," Jules said. "He probably needs a bottle and a nap. Come here, my little kitten."

Feeling a little sad, Seth handed Darragh to Jules, and instantly he stopped crying.

"In the bag next to Sinead's chair is his bottle of milk in a cool bag. Will you heat it up for him, and then will you feed him?"

Seth smiled. "Ok, I'd love to give him his bottle. I'll make some tea while I am in the kitchen. Does anyone else want a cup?" he asked, looking at their empty mugs. It was then that he noticed the side table laden with hundreds of cakes. "May, you have done yourself proud! Please tell me that these cakes are for us?"

"Thank you. Of course, they are. I know that you love a slice of cake. I will have tea, please, Seth. Sinead, do you want one, my lovely? You are so quiet this afternoon."

"I think that I need a brandy. I swear the rain has bored down into my bones, and now I am a block of shivering ice."

"Let me get you one, " May said, walking over to the drinks table. "Do you want a brandy, Mike?" May asked.

"No, thanks. I will have a coffee, Seth. Black with two sugars, please, and is that coffee cake I see?"

***

Feeling emotional, Seth gazed down at his son. Darragh had finished his milk, and his eyes were closing. Gently he removed the teat from his mouth and looked over at Jules, who was sitting next to Sinead. Sinead had a blanket around her shoulders, and her cheeks were pink and warm. She was sipping a large brandy and was looking so much better. He listened in to their conversation and realised that they were talking about wedding dresses. He smiled; he had never seen Sinead in a dress and wondered what she would wear when she walked down the aisle. He waited for them to finish talking. "Jules," he whispered. She looked across at him. "Would you take Darragh, please? He's asleep, and I haven't had my cake yet."

"Oh, good. He has gone to sleep at the perfect time. May, can we take Dad on a grand tour of the house while he naps? I'll go and get his pushchair from the hallway. I won't be a moment."

"How long have you lived here?" Mike asked May.

May laughed. "All my life! My mother was the housekeeper here, and my father the chauffeur. They came from England and served the O'Sullivan family, and we lived in the servant quarters at the top of the house. I must show you them, the rooms look like a 1950's film set."

"I never knew that," Seth said as he got to his feet, trying his best not to wake Darragh. He lowered him into the pram. *I wonder if Gemma is appreciating the 50's vibe. Christ, I hope she isn't up there when we go on our tour.* "So, how did you end up owning Waterfall West?"

"I married Edward O'Sullivan."

"Oh! I didn't think that you ever married," Sinead said with a look of horror on her face.

May sighed. "We were married for a week. I should never have married him. Edward was a widower, and he had two children. One of his sons died in World War II. His other son took his own life when he came back from the war. He had PTSD, although they didn't call it that back then. He went to a rehabilitation unit. Nobody liked to talk about mental illness in those days."

"I'm sorry to hear that," Mike said and then shook his head and looked distressed. "War can break a man."

"I know, dear. I am sorry that you have not been well. We are all so proud of you for battling with your demons."

"I am getting there."

"Where was I? Oh yes. When I was eighteen, I lost both my parents in a plane accident, and I took on the housekeeping duties here. I also had to look after my younger brother Tom."

Jules shuddered when she heard his name, and she saw May cast her an awkward glance at her. *Take a deep breath. All that is in the past.*

"It was a difficult time for us, and Mr O'Sullivan, Edward was very kind to me. We were both lonely, and although there was a huge age

76

difference, I agreed to marry him. We were companions and nothing more. It was a marriage of convenience. We kept each other company, listened to music and read books together. I have to say, I never for one moment thought that he would leave Waterfall West to me.

"One Christmas morning, I took him in his breakfast and newspaper. The room was dark, and so I pulled back the curtains and saw him sitting up in bed. His face was a deadly white, and he was so... so still. I knew immediately that he was dead. They said that it was a heart attack. All his arteries were blocked. Questions were asked, and some people in the village said that I had murdered him for his money. You know how people like to gossip in Waterfall? I think that they called me the black widow for a while."

"That's crazy," Jules said. "People can be so cruel."

"I shouldn't have married him. I didn't love him, and for years, I hated this house. I swore to myself that one day I would give this house and estate to someone who would truly appreciate it. That's why I chose you two, Sinead and Seth. You have the biggest hearts and work hard. You are like a son and daughter to me. I can think of no one better to inherit this estate."

Jules looked at Seth and could see that he was embarrassed. Her dad was looking surprised too. *I didn't tell him about Seth inheriting half of the estate. I wonder if he will like Seth any better now.*

"So, are you ready for a grand tour of the house? There's quite a few ghosts here!" May asked Mike. "I really want to show you the honeymoon suite. When you go through that door, you will be transported back in time. The four-poster bed is as old as the hills; possibly medieval. You like that room too, don't you, Sinead?"

"I did, but isn't that the old master bedroom? Is that where you found him?"

May laughed. "You are not afraid of ghosts, are you, darling?"

"No, of course not. But I am not going in that room again. Just in case."

May was giving a splendid narrated tour of the house, and Jules was impressed by her knowledge and the stories she was telling about the people that had lived in there. *This house has quite a lot of dark secrets and more than its fair share of ghosts.* As they approached the servants' quarters via a narrow staircase, which led to May's old home, Jules could see that Seth was becoming uneasy. "Are you ok?" she whispered.

"No, not really. Did you know that Gemma has been living up here? May and Sinead have no idea," he whispered back. "Let's hope that she is not in this afternoon."

As they reached the top of the winding staircase and approached the door to the servants' quarters, they all became aware of a peculiar screaming sound.

"What is that?" Sinead asked, her eyes wide with fear.

"I have no idea," May replied. "It sounds like cats fighting. I hope that Barney hasn't brought another cat up here," she said as she tried to open the door. "That's strange. The door is locked. It's never locked? Not to worry, I have the master key here. May held up a huge bunch of keys and methodically went through them, looking at the labels until she found the right one. After struggling to open the door as there was a key inserted on the other side of the lock, she let them all into a cosy lounge. The room was furnished with 1950's furniture, and there was a large TV in a wooden case in front of two worn-out green sofas. The room was littered with empty takeaway cartons and used dishes and plates. "What on earth is going on here?" May asked, sounding shocked. "Somebody is living up here!"

The screaming noise was coming from a bedroom at the end of the corridor. With her eyes blazing, May stormed down the corridor, flung the door open and then gasped. Everyone followed, eager to see what was causing such a terrible noise and to find out if it were indeed cats having a spat.

The group, shocked into silence, watched in dismay as they witnessed a naked man with a blond ponytail having wild sex with Gemma. She was lying on the bed, her legs and arms tied to each corner. Both unaware of their spectators, they were both screaming out in pain on the brink of orgasm.

"What the hell are you doing?" May yelled. The man froze and then, with a look of horror, flipped himself around and glared at May. Gemma screamed out and then turned her head away, embarrassed and humiliated. "Tom? WHAT THE HELL ARE YOU DOING HERE?"

Silently, Jules screamed inside as she realised that May's brother was back in Waterfall. It sickened her to see him, and shivers ran up and down her spine. She could feel the pulse in her neck beating hard and she was sweating with fear. *I need air. Is this what he did to me? Please, no!*

"For heaven's sake. What is going on?" May demanded. "And in our parents' bed too!"

Jules looked towards Seth for reassurance and then realised that a red mist was descending over him. His dark eyes were flashing dangerously. *Fuck! He is going to kill him.* Jules grabbed his hand hard and yelled at him. "Seth, don't! He's not worth it. I don't want you to go back to prison. Let May deal with this."

Seth shook his head. "No, he needs to be taught a lesson. The sick bastard!"

"Don't, Seth. Please!" She looked desperately at her dad to back her up and then felt Seth's hand slip out of hers. She saw him rush towards Tom. "Dad, you have to stop Seth. Tom hurt me last year and tried to kill Seth's horse. He…" Jules didn't have to say anymore. Her dad flew into the bedroom and pulled Seth off of Tom, and dragged him away, putting his arm behind his back. Seth struggled to get free and yelled out in frustration that he couldn't get at his foe. Tom, who was now lying on the floor, whimpered pathetically.

"Get a grip, Seth! He is not worth it," Mike yelled.

"He's a maniac!" Tom yelled, getting up from the floor. "He should be locked up." He was rubbing his elbow and seemed totally unaware that he was standing in front of everyone naked and erect.

"You're a sick bastard," Seth spat. "You raped Jules and tried to kill my horse. I should have punched your lights out when I had the chance. Fuck! I shouldn't have said that!" He looked over at Jules. Her mouth was open and her eyes wide.

"I did no such thing! Like the rest of them, she was gagging for it. Look at this one here. She was crying out with pleasure until you all turned up. What the fuck are you all doing here? Can't a man have a bit of privacy in his own home?"

Gemma was crying. "Can someone please help me?"

In defiance, May put her fists on her hips. "This is not your home. I own this house. You need to leave this minute and never come back. You are not welcome here," she said sternly.

Tom went quiet for a moment, and his eyes narrowed. "I have nowhere else to go. I am your brother. There is something wrong with me. Please help me. I have an addiction to sex."

"He's talking bullshit," Sinead spat. "We should call the police."

"No, please don't do that. I love him," Gemma announced.

"There! See? I have done nothing wrong, but I am ashamed of myself. I came back here to say sorry to Julia."

Seth looked at Tom with disgust. *He is bluffing. He thinks that we are all eejits.* "You need locking up," he yelled at Tom. He felt the grip on his arm tighten. "It's ok, Mike, you can let me go. I need to go back to Jules. I am calm now." Mike released him, and then Seth looked over at the empty space where Jules had been standing. "Oh no! She's run off. I've got to find her." He glared at Tom and then, unable to stop himself, punched him hard on his chin, sending him flying. It was quite satisfying knowing that he had hurt him. Seth didn't look back, and he ran off to find Jules. *I hope that sick bastard's jaw is broken for good!*

Chapter Ten

Jules stood by the lounge window and watched the wind and rain battering the front garden. The bare rose bushes lining the path were fighting for their lives. She feared that any moment they would be ripped from the ground and, with earthy roots flaying, be hurled across the lawn. She took in a deep breath to steady her breathing and to try and calm herself down. She was furious. *How could Seth just blurt out to everyone that I was raped? What possessed him? How does he know that's what happened? He wasn't there. Was he? What is Dad going to think? Jesus!*

She looked across the room and was relieved to see that Darragh was still asleep. She saw the door open and then saw Seth enter into the room. He was looking worried. "I can't deal with this now." She looked away and knew that she was going to cry. The ugly truth was beginning to sink in.

Seth walked over to her and put his arms around her. He felt terrible and was grateful that she hadn't pushed him away. "Please don't hate me. It was the shock of seeing that prick again." *Oh God, she's crying!* "I love you so much. Please don't cry."

"Why didn't you tell me?"

"Believe me, I wanted to, but you couldn't remember anything, and I didn't want that bastard to destroy your life. If you remember, you told me not to tell you if anything bad had happened."

"How can you bear to be with me?" she sobbed. "I feel so dirty now."

"What are you talking about? You are my world." He turned her around and drew her to him and kissed her, and wiped away her tears with his thumb. "You are perfect. You must never think anything less of yourself. Deep down, you must have known."

She nodded and lay her head on his chest. "Everyone knows now." She looked up into his eyes, trying to read what he was thinking. He looked away for a moment, and she knew there and then the truth. "Everyone knew before me, didn't they?"

Seth looked back down at her. "Sinead knows, she was there when he told us about what he did to you. She has probably told May. Look, I am really sorry about upstairs. You know what I am like when I am angry. I just lose it."

"What on earth am I going to say to Dad?"

"You are going to tell him why you didn't call the police and get that bastard locked away."

"Dad!" she exclaimed, startled by his appearance.

"She didn't know," Seth said. "She doesn't remember because he drugged her with a date rape drug and had his wicked way with her. He told Sinead and me what he had done, and I found a used condom in our bedroom."

Horrified, Jules glared at Seth. It was bad enough her dad knowing about the assault but giving him the fine details too was too much to bear. She looked at her dad and wished that the floor would swallow her up. "I'm sorry, Dad."

"Why are you sorry?" he replied. "You did nothing wrong. Men like him prey on the innocent. He has brainwashed that poor young girl up there. You have to stop him from hurting others and file charges against him. That's what we all think you should do. May has locked him in the servants' quarters until you decide what you want to do."

"Do you think I should, Seth?"

He sighed, "I do. He says he needs help, but that is probably a ploy. He is like a trapped rat up there. He will say anything to get away with it."

"You do know that you shouldn't have hit him," Mike said crossly. "He could claim he has been assaulted."

Jules gasped. "Oh, Seth! You idiot!"

"I don't care. I am not sorry. He deserved a lot worse. I don't think that anyone saw it happen," he said, looking towards Mike. He was shaking his head. "Please say you didn't see me."

"You are going to have to address that temper of yours. I don't want Julia running to me one day saying you have hit her!"

"He wouldn't, Dad!" Jules said defiantly.

"Please don't ever think that I would hurt her."

"Mm… I should think so. Look, I have no idea why Tom has a sore chin. I think we were all looking at that poor girl he had strapped to the bed."

Seth smiled and then looked down at Jules. She was clinging to him. "We need to call the police. I won't leave you, I promise."

"But I can't remember anything. How can they prosecute him if I can't remember what happened?"

"I kept the evidence, and Sinead and I can tell them about how he attempted to abduct you and what he told us."

"What do you mean, you kept the evidence?"

"I found a dart with some ketamine still in it and blood on the needle. I put that and the spent condom in a storage box and hid it in the bushes that run along the side of the summer field."

"That is so gross! Why did you do that?"

"I freaked out doing it, but I just knew that it was the right thing to do. It was wrong to throw them away."

"That was a clever thing to do. When did this all happen?" Mike asked.

"Over a year ago," Seth said.

"Oh dear, that's a long time ago. But there is a chance that they will be able to get a DNA sample. Both yours and that nutter upstairs."

"This is like a nightmare. Please don't show me that box, Seth. It will make everything feel real."

"Shall I call the police for you?" Seth asked.

Jules nodded and sighed. She looked across at Darragh, who was awake and staring at her. "Can we give Darragh his dinner first? I just need time to process everything. Oh, Seth. I can't believe that we are going to have to face dealing with the police again. Aren't they going to think that it is odd that this is the second time that I have been violently assaulted?"

"No, of course not. Sometimes we get more than our fair share of shit thrown at us."

"A second time?" her dad questioned.

"Dad, there are some things that happened at Farm End, that I couldn't really talk about with you because you were so ill. I'd rather not talk about it now. It is bad enough you knowing about May's brother raping me. Was it rape?"

"It was. You didn't give your consent," her dad said. He was looking tearful.

Jules sighed. "I'm feeling a little sick. Let's all go back home and sort out Darragh. Seth, will you drive?"

***

While Seth spoon-fed Darragh his cauliflower cheese, Jules showered and let the hot water flush away the day's events. The thought of Tom abusing her was making her tremble. *Why is he here? Why would you come back to the scene of the crime and know that you could be arrested? There must be something wrong with his head. He clearly doesn't think that he has done anything wrong. I don't want to do it, but I need to speak to him. Speak to him alone and find out why he is here. He said he was here to say sorry to me. Do I believe that? When Darragh is in bed, I will drive down to the Manor House and talk to May. She will understand why I need to do this. Right, I now have to tell Seth about my plan. He is not going to like it.*

Seth wiped the last of Darragh's dinner off of his face and picked him up off the sofa, and then realised that he had it on his tiny hands too. There was cheese sauce and apple pudding on the seat cushion. "You are a messy thing. We really are going to have to get you a high chair. Come and let me wash your hands under the tap." He carried him over to the kitchen sink, and holding him steady, he sat him on the edge of the sink and let the warm water run. Darragh laughed and reached out for the water. "Let me test it. I don't want to burn you. Just a little more cold water, and then we will be good." Seth tested the water after adding more cold. "You do realise that this is going to be your bath for a while, don't you? You are not big enough to go in the shower yet."

Seth looked up and saw Jules leave the bathroom. She smiled weakly at him. She looked around the living area to make sure that her dad was not around. *Good, he's in his room.* She could hear the radio playing. "I need to talk to you. It's about Tom."

"You don't want to call the police, do you?"

"No, it's not that. I know I should, but first, I need to talk to him."

"No! Why?"

"I just do. Why did he come back here? He says he needs help. I need to understand why he did what he did. I need closure, Seth."

"Christ, no! That man is a maniac."

86

"He might be. I have to speak to him. Otherwise, I will fear him for the rest of my life, and the not knowing will torment me."

"Then I will come with you."

"I don't think that is a good idea. He will make you angry again."

"I don't care. I can't bear the thought of you two being alone together."

"I won't be. May will be there with me. I am not stupid."

Seth sighed, "I really don't like this idea, but I understand. Fuck! Sorry! You didn't hear that, did you?" he asked Darragh.

"I'll be ok. Don't tell Dad. He will go nuts."

"Don't you think you should let the police handle this?"

"I am a Hearn now. Don't the Hearns handle their own affairs?"

Seth scowled. "In the past, but not anymore."

"When you hit him, you took the law into your own hands. All I am going to do is some light interrogation. That way, I will be able to face him in court one day."

Seth sighed again and then smiled. "You do realise that you are one amazing girl, don't you?"

"You are not so bad yourself, Mr Hearn. Seth? Are you planning to bathe Darragh with all his clothes on?"

Darragh was happily playing with the water and was completely soaked. "I think that we might have gotten a little carried away with the handwashing. Would you mind getting us a towel?"

***

Jules placed Darragh in his cot and covered him up. *You look so peaceful when you are asleep. Just like your dad.* She had left Seth watching TV, and she knew that he would be asleep too when she returned to the living room. Her dad had stayed in his room reading. It had been a relief as she knew he wanted to ask her questions about the rape. *Rape is such an ugly word. Is that really what happened to me? Why do I feel like it happened to someone else? What is wrong with me? Now is a good time. I will slip out and go and see him. Is this madness?*

***

Seth woke up with a start. For a moment, he had forgotten where he was. It was such a relief to find himself lying on his sofa in his own home. The TV was still on, but the program he had been watching had finished. He looked at his phone and saw that it was quarter past seven. *I'm starving. I should put some pizza and chips in the oven for us all. I wonder where Jules is. Probably in the bathroom.* Carefully, he got to his feet, limped over to the kitchen and turned the oven on. His knee was sore, and his knuckles were throbbing from hitting Tom. He looked at his hand and noticed that his first two fingers were starting to swell. *Christ, I am broken all over.* Seth opened the freezer and took out two pizzas. As he placed the boxes on the work surface, he saw Mike come out of the bathroom. He was looking sad, and his face was red. *Has he been crying?* "Are you alright, Mike?"

"I just had a really hot shower. I couldn't work out how to add cold water. I hope that was ok."

"Of course, it was. You don't have to ask. The cold-water tap works in reverse. I made a small error when I fitted it. I plan to catch up with all my DIY jobs over the next few months. Is pizza ok? Jules usually makes her own, but tonight we will have to have shop-bought ones."

"That will be fine. I'm not that hungry. It has been quite a day. You do know that Julia has gone down to the Manor House to see him. I heard you two talking. I heard her leave. We should have gone with her."

Alarmed by this news, Seth looked towards the front door and could see that the car had gone. He had a very bad feeling about her seeing Tom and knew that he had to go and stop her. "When did she go?"

"About ten minutes ago."

"Mike, I am going to get her. It is a crazy idea, her talking to him. Would you keep an eye on Darragh for me?"

***

Jules stood in the hall of the Manor House and shuddered. The house was eerily quiet, and she was almost certain that it did not welcome her. The walls and dark furnishing leaked out sadness and lament. *Be strong, Jules, you can do this. If May comes with me, then there will be a row. I know Seth will be mad with me, but I must do this alone.* Taking a deep breath, she headed for the kitchen to get the key for the door to the servants' quarters. *I must be mad.* With the key in one hand, she made her way up to the top of the house, her other hand sliding along the top of the polished wood banister. When she reached the tiny landing a few steps below the door to the servants' quarters, she paused and stared out of the window into the darkness. It suddenly dawned on her that the storm had ended, and the sky was now clear and the stars bright.

Her attention turned towards the door. She heard the door lock click and then watched as the door handle moved down. Jules exhaled with surprise, and she fully expected the door to open. Her heart was pounding in her chest, and she held her breath, waiting for the captive to appear. She heard Tom swear and smiled anxiously, her eyes still wide with fear. The door remained locked.

Jules found Tom's predicament amusing, and she laughed.

"Julia? Is that you?" she backed up a little, shocked that he had identified her by her laugh.

"Yes, it's me. I need to talk to you."

"It is you. Julia, please open the door. I shouldn't be locked in here like a common criminal."

Jules stared at the key in her hand and was not willing to use it to free him. "I can't. Why are you here?"

"I came back for you!"

"Were you going to drug, rape and throw me into your boot again?"

"No, I shouldn't have done that. I promise you that I didn't rape you. I am truly sorry if I hurt you. I love you. That's why I came back."

"You don't know what love is."

"If thinking about you every day and not being able to sleep properly because of you isn't love, then I don't know what else you would call it."

Jules sighed; her worst fears had been confirmed. A stair creaking below her made her jump, and she spun round. Seth was running up the stairs towards her. Sweat was running down his face. He looked angry but relieved to see her. Swiftly she brought her finger to her lips and shook her head at him, warning him to be quiet. She stopped his advance and watched him limp quietly up the last few steps to join her. Silently, he wrapped his arms around her and drew her to him. His body was hot, and his clothes damp from exertion. *He must have run all the way here. His poor knee.* His embrace was reassuring, and she was glad that he was there.

"Julia, are you still there? You love me too, don't you? There is chemistry between us, isn't there."

"Look, Tom. I am going to be blunt with you. You are old enough to be my father. You disgust me. You violated me. I have never and will never love you. I am a married woman. You need to go back to Australia and leave us all in peace. Do you hear me?"

"I can't."

"If you love me, then you will do this one thing for me."

"Or she will fucking call the police and get you arrested!" Seth said sternly.

"Fucking marvellous! Now your gypsy boyfriend has joined us!"

"He's my husband. Seth, you need to go downstairs."

"I'm not leaving you with this moron."

"There is a locked door between us. I am not in danger."

"You said you were going to ask May to come with you."

"I changed my mind. You need to be quiet."

"You've got to let me out of here. I said I was sorry for treating you like the other girls. I know now that when we made love, it was special."

Jules felt Seth's fist clench, and she stroked it to get him to relax. "You need help, Tom. You are not listening to me, and you are delusional. There is nothing between us. You mean nothing to me."

"Why does my cock say differently? You are making me so horny."

"If you ever say anything like that to her again or come near her, then I will kill you," Seth yelled. "We are going to call the police. We have evidence and witnesses that you raped Jules," he leapt forward and banged the door with his fist.

"You are pathetic. You don't scare me. Julia wouldn't do that."

"No, Tom, you are wrong," Jules said. "You need to pack your bags and go. You need to get help. If I ever hear or see you again, then I swear that I will call the police and I will tell them what you did to me. We are going now. You have ten minutes to get out of here." She looked at the key in her hand and then bent down and slid it under the door. It scuttled under the door and along the floorboards towards Tom.

Seth stared at her in horror. "What the fuck did you do that for?"

"This chapter in our lives is over, Seth. We need to move on. He won't bother us again."

Chapter Eleven

The sun shone down on Jules as she walked down the track to the Old Barn. She had helped Sinead take the cobs to the summer field. Connor had followed her sleepily, his large hoofs catching on the cobbles as he walked. They had been back nearly a month, and she hadn't ridden him yet. As she waited for Sinead to open the gate, she had put her arms around his neck and promised him that she would take him out for a hack when May was free to babysit. She needed Seth to go with her as she was sure she would lose herself in the estate's maze of fields and woodland.

Seth had been out with Moss and was working on improving his condition. Concerned that his horse had lost so much weight, he had called the vet. It turned out that he just needed some of his teeth filing, and he was assured that Moss would be able to eat more comfortably and regain his weight. After just a week since Moss had his teeth filed, Seth had picked her up, hugged her and had spun her around, declaring that his horse was as good as new.

Jules smiled and looked up at the sun. It was only the beginning of March, and yet it felt like today was the first day of spring. Despite Seth's initial reaction, he had taken her decision to let Tom go and to draw a line under what had happened as she had requested well. Only once had she caught him staring at her, questioning her decision. Her dad, however, had not forgiven her. A tear pricked her eye as she remembered saying goodbye to him and wanting a hug from him so much. He had climbed into the horsebox cab and had wound the window down. She knew that he was disappointed with her. His last words to her were that she should take care of his grandson and be sure to send him photos. A small voice in her head told her that he didn't love her anymore. Jules shook her head. There was no point dwelling on the matter. Soon she would call him for a chat and do her best to become his kitten again.

A large bird swooped down in front of her. It was a bird of prey with dark brown feathers. She stopped for a moment and realised that it was carrying a rabbit in its talons. By some miracle, the rabbit wriggled free, dropped into the field next to her and then scurried away. *Oh, thank goodness, that was close!* Unfazed, the bird continued on its way, scouring the land for its next victim.

As she approached the barn, she could hear Irish music playing. Her eyes narrowed in the bright sunlight as she realised that Gemma was standing by the window and was watching what was going on within. *She's spying on Seth! Crap! What is she wearing? Why would you tie your t-shirt up to show your waist off on a cold March day?*

Gemma spun around when she heard Jules behind her. "Oh, it's you. I thought it was someone else. My nerves are on edge," she said, looking flustered. "Seth is dancing with Darragh. He didn't hear me knock."

"What do you want, Gemma?"

"I was wondering if you both wanted to come running with me. It's a beautiful day."

"I didn't know that you ran."

"I used to, but I promised that I would take running up again. I know you and Seth are going running today."

"We have to run separately, so someone minds Darragh."

"I could go with Seth. He might be able to give me some running tips."

"We weren't planning to run today as we have to practice for The Elbow tonight. We've got a few new songs to go through."

"Oh, I don't like running on my own. I could listen to your new songs if you like and let you know what I think."

"That's ok, Gemma… I um… we are a little shy to play in front of you." *Why did I say that?* "You must be freezing," she said, looking at her skimpy t-shirt and erect nipples. "You should be wearing a sweatshirt to keep yourself warm." She looked down at her shoes and shook her head. "You weren't thinking of running in those shoes, were you? You need to get yourself some proper trainers." *She wasn't going to run at all, was she? She really is after Seth.* "How are you finding the mobile home? It must be nice to have your own place."

"It's ok. A bit lonely, though. I miss Tom. You shouldn't have asked him to leave."

"He was too old for you. You need to find someone else."

"I have, but he doesn't know I exist."

She means Seth, doesn't she? "Finding someone is tough. You will find the right person one day. Someone that is not weird or married! Someone your own age."

Jules took off her wellies and stepped into the warm barn, quietly closing the door behind her. Seth hadn't seen her come in. She was glad to be rid of Gemma. She had gone back home with a bitter look on her face.

Seth was teaching Darragh a reel dance, and their baby thought that it was hysterical when they whirled round together. Barney was winding his body around Seth's legs, and it was by some miracle that he didn't get kicked. Seeing Jules standing there, Barney ran to her for attention. Jules stroked him, glad that he had settled back into their home so well.

The music stopped, and Seth picked up his phone and cleared the YouTube channel he had been using. He saw Jules and laughed. "Did you see me making an arse of myself?"

"You weren't. Darragh was loving it. I don't think that he will remember the steps, though."

"He knows the steps. Just wait until he is walking, and then he will be joining us at The Elbow for a dance. Dancing is in his blood. Barney is coming along nicely too!"

"Talking of The Elbow, we should work out what songs we are going to sing tonight. If I go and get my guitar, shall we go through a few of your new songs? You haven't heard the melodies I've written for them. You might not like what I've done."

"I know that I will love what you've composed. Yes, let me put Darragh in his playpen and then he can watch us rehearse. I don't like putting him in it, but now that he's crawling like an Olympian. We have no choice."

Jules got her guitar and then sat on the sofa next to Seth. He still looked hot from dancing, and she could smell his sweet body, citrus and something else. *Roses, perhaps.* Seth's eyes were sparkling and his mood high. For a moment, she forgot why she was holding her guitar. All she wanted to do was feel his body next to hers. *Darragh will go down for a nap soon, and then perhaps...*

"Will you sing for me?" Seth asked. "I love listening to you sing. I don't think that I will ever forget when you first sang for me. It was like listening to an angel singing."

Returning to reality, Jules laughed. "Ok, but I am no angel. What would you like me to sing?"

"Will you sing Ed Sheeran's Photograph? You sing that really well."

"Do I? Ok then." Jules strummed her guitar and started to sing. Seth was mouthing the words with his eyes shut. She knew that it wouldn't be long before he was singing too. He let her sing half the song and then, smiling, joined in, sending shivers down her spine. *He can't help himself.*

He is so hot when he sings. It is no wonder Gemma has been throwing herself at him. She keeps visiting us. May shouldn't have let her continue living on the estate.

"So, what shall we sing next?" Seth asked. "Do you want to try 'Beautiful in Blue'? I wrote that song for you."

"I did wonder. Am I the girl in it with the hair like hay?"

"Yes, the one that makes me wanna say that I love you more each day," he said, laughing.

"Seth?"

"Yes, my sweet girl?"

"I want to have another baby!"

"Christ! What, here and now?"

"Yes! As soon as possible."

"Really? Don't you have enough on your hands with our wee boy?"

"I love being a mum. Is it so wrong to just want to be a Mum to lots of children? Oh, and a rock star, of course!"

"No, that's great. You are not going to turn me into a baby-making machine, are you? I've heard about women like you."

Jules giggled. "Of course not. I'll give you breaks and let you teach and work the land now and again."

"Thank God for that! I don't mind. I've always dreamed of having a big family."

"Good, I am pleased we are on the same page."

"So, Mrs Hearn. Shall we sing Beautiful in Blue then?"

Jules smiled mischievously and put her guitar down. "I need a hug." She moved along the sofa, and Seth put his arm around her. His body was warm, and feeling reassured, she lay her head on his strong chest.

"I love you, you know. When Darragh is asleep, I will show you how much," he said, squeezing her.

"I'd like that," she replied. Her heart was beating a little faster. Darragh called out, and she turned her head to see their baby standing. He was holding onto the bars of the playpen, and she could see his big brown eyes watching them through the bars.

"Are you jealous that I am holding your Mam and not you?" Seth asked him.

"Seth, he's standing. This is the first time. Is that normal for a baby of his age?"

"He's nearly a year old now. He is a strong little thing. Do you realise that we have been married for nearly a year now? It will be our wedding anniversary on 19 April and Darragh's first birthday. We should have a party and invite a local band to play."

"I'd like that. You miss dancing, don't you?"

"I do. I like it when friends and family come together. I guess I miss being with people."

"When we are famous, we will be singing to thousands."

"So, you think that we are going to make it big then?"

"I know we are. Then you will never be alone."

"Isn't that a song?"

"We could cover that song tonight. Here let me find it," she said, sitting up and reaching for her phone that was lying on the coffee table.

"Do you remember the words to that one? You probably do. How do you know the words to so many songs?"

"I had a lot of time on my hands when I was in prison. I made it my mission between writing songs to learn a new song every day. Once I read or listen to the lyrics of a song, then that's it. They are printed in my mind. When I sing, I see the words scrolling up like on a karaoke machine."

"That is amazing. I think that you have a photographic memory. I wish I did." Jules pressed play on her phone, and they listened to 'Never be Alone.' "I like that one. We've sung that song before. You are never going to be alone, Seth Hearn, not when you have ten children and me to look after."

"Just ten?"

"We'll see. I don't want to wear you out!"

***

Jules lay in long grass in a cornfield, wearing only a blue sundress. She could smell hay and see the cloudless sky. Bees were humming nearby as they collected nectar around her. Seth was there with her, his strong naked body above her, his skin soft and smooth.

Back in their bedroom, Jules opened her eyes and gripped the bedsheets tighter as Seth worked his magic, bringing her closer to orgasm. She could feel his tongue between her legs, caressing her, making her wet, making her pant like a crazed animal. "I need you now," she whispered. "Please, before it's too late... I can't hold on for much longer." She closed her eyes again, not wanting to leave the cornfield. Memories of them making out there filled her mind. From nowhere, she felt his hot breath in her ear and then she gasped as she felt him enter her. Skin against skin, urgently seeking her, desperately wanting her, loving her and making her want to explode. For a moment, she saw Tom over her, and she grimaced, pushing that thought away. *Stay in the field, Jules.* Seth stopped. She opened her eyes and saw Seth's face above hers, his big brown eyes concerned for a moment.

"Did I hurt you?" he whispered.

"No, don't stop, Seth, please." He smiled and kissed her passionately, his kisses becoming urgent as he took her back to the edge of ecstasy. A hot breeze shot across the cornfield, and she was lost in it. She was part of the earth, part of Seth. Lost in him.

Gently, Seth kissed her and then, exhausted, he lay next to her as he got his breath back. "I love you," he said, still out of breath. "There! Baby number two on its way," he whispered. "I think this one is going to be a girl and have hair the colour of hay. She will have eyes the colour of cornflowers and smell of vanilla."

Jules sighed as the bedroom came into focus again. "That was heaven. I love you too. Me getting pregnant the first time was a bit of a fluke. Somehow, I think that it is going to be a lot harder this time around. When we get pregnant again, then I am going to savour every moment. Being pregnant for one day and then having Darragh the next day was a bit disappointing."

"I don't think that you will have any problems. You bleed each month, and you eat a healthy diet. When you were pregnant with Darragh, at least, you didn't suffer too much with all the sickness and whatnot. If you do feel bad this time around, then I will be there for you. I will bring you tea in bed and a bucket too."

Jules laughed. "Oh goodness, I hope I am not going to get sick."

"Well, it is too late now. Juliet Hearn is on her way."

"We can't call her Juliet. Can we?"

Chapter Twelve

Despite the day being sunny, the evening had turned on Jules and Seth, and they shivered and zipped their jackets up a little higher under their chins, wishing that they had brought a winter coat. The streets of Cork were eerily dark and quiet for a Saturday night. As Jules and Seth made their way, hand in hand to The Elbow, both their hearts began to beat a little quicker as they thought about performing in front of a large audience.

Jules squeezed Seth's hand as she remembered him driving them to Cork. She liked watching him drive, and she could tell that he really liked being at the wheel. This was their second journey together in May's old car, and the car seemed to purr as they drove along, happy to be out on the road again. "Wasn't it good to drive to Cork instead of getting the bus? Did you like driving here? It must feel good to have your licence back."

"I have missed driving so much. It was grand. The old Jaguar is a bit of a beast and a bit of a fuel guzzler, but she is smooth to drive. Saying that, it felt good to step out of our house and into a car without freezing our nuts off waiting for buses."

Jules laughed, "I love that car. It gets hot inside so quickly and smells of polished wood and engine oil."

"It does; you are right. Are you looking forward to performing? You are looking especially beautiful tonight in that frock you are wearing. And makeup too!"

Jules laughed. "Seth, you crazy thing. You are sounding more Irish every day. Who says frock these days? Is that an Irish word?" she asked as they turned into Elbow Lane.

"I don't think so. My sisters used to say… Holy cow!" Seth exclaimed. "Look at the queue of people waiting to get into The Elbow."

"Goodness! I wonder who else is performing here tonight. They must be pretty famous to attract so many people."

"You don't suppose they are our fans, do you?" Seth asked and then noticed that they were nearly all looking their way. "Christ! Some are coming towards us with pens and paper. Should we run?"

"No, it will be ok. We need to please our fans if we are going to sell any records."

"Ok then, but if it all gets too much, then tell me, and I will rescue you."

"It might be the other way around. Most of the fans are girls, and I think that they are more interested in you than me."

After a good ten minutes of signing and shaking hands, Mick, the landlord, came out and, seeing that they were being swamped with an adoring crowd, helped them in and then through to the backroom, where Jules and Seth collapsed into chairs to recover. Signing autographs had been exhausting.

Mick was beaming at them. "I put a Facebook event notice out yesterday that you were playing tonight, and I think half of Ireland has turned out for you. How does it feel to be celebrities?"

"I wouldn't call us that? Are you sure they didn't mistake us for someone else? We haven't played for nearly a year."

"S&J are getting a name for themselves. I am proud to have you play at my pub," Mick said, beaming. "The Elbow is going to go down in history because of bands like yours. Let me get you both some of the bubbly stuff to celebrate."

Jules grinned. "I can't believe how happy people were to see us. Well, you mainly, Seth. Thank you, Mick. I appreciate your kind offer of bubbly, but just lemonade for us would be great. Seth is driving, and I shouldn't drink before a gig. I am so excited. I can't wait to go on stage."

Seth frowned. "They want to see us both sing, Jules. I would be lost without you on the stage. You signed your autograph too."

"I know, but you really are the star attraction. I like it, though. I know all your songs are mostly about me, and those girly fans can only dream of you being with them."

"I am having trouble getting my head around this. It is great that S&J has become so popular, but I didn't think that most of our fans would be hysterical teenage girls lusting after yours truly."

"It is inevitable; you are gorgeous and hot. Teenage girls are our target audience. They are the ones that will buy our records. It really doesn't bother me."

"I am not comfortable with that. We are going to have to cut the love ballads from our playlist."

"But that's stupid," she was getting cross. *What's going on in his head? I said I didn't mind him being more popular than me.*

Mick was looking concerned. "Now, here's the thing. You two are something special, and you are destined to do well. Success brings its rewards, but there is also a price to pay. Is it so bad to have a few girls looking starry-eyed at you when you are bringing them so much happiness? It would be wrong not to share your songs and music with the world. Who knows how long your success will last? Grasp this opportunity with both hands and enjoy the moment."

Jules looked over at Seth and hoped that Mick's words had sunk in.

"With this Coronavirus thing, it is looking like that the pubs will be closing for a bit soon until they get this flu under control. So, I say again, enjoy the moment while you can. Tonight might be your last opportunity to play for a while."

"Do you think so? Christ, you are right." *I am an eejit.*

Jules noticed that Seth was smiling. "Well, that's a relief."

"Ok, we will keep the love songs in, but if you spot any women wanting to hurl their knickers at me, then I want to be the first to know!"

She laughed. "You are going to be knee-deep in them!"

And Gemma's will be on the top.

Chapter Thirteen

Jules and Seth were standing by the edge of the stage, waiting to go on. A new band, Music Crime, having finished their hour, were clearing away their equipment. The crowd had cheered them when they had sung their final song.

"They were good, really good. Mick certainly can spot talent," Seth whispered. "They remind me of Coldplay, a little. I was going to say, I'm sorry about earlier. I guess I am in shock. It's not every day you get girls hurling themselves at you for your autograph. It's almost as if we have become famous overnight. I can handle it now."

"It's ok. I am loving the attention. I just wish we could actually sell our songs somehow. We need to get ourselves to a recording studio as soon as we can."

"I'll look into it later. Is it ok if we sing Snow Patrol's Chasing Cars first? I just want everyone to know that it's you that I want to lie with me and not them. We will save Beautiful in Blue for another day. I think we need to practice that song a bit more."

"Sure, only if I can sing Stuck With U," she said with a serious look on her face. Seth gave her a worried look, and she smiled. "I am stuck with you in a good way, silly. That song is really popular at the moment. My heart is pounding, is yours? There're so many people here tonight." She felt her phone buzz and looked at it.

"A little, but when you are beside me, I feel like I can take the world head-on. Did Sinead message you? Is Darragh all right?"

"No, it's not Sinead. I was waiting for a message from Jane. Oh good, they can. I wasn't sure if they could make it."

"I'm confused. You mean Shawn Smith's girlfriend, Jane? Shawn from Sonar Cell? Aren't they in America?"

"They were, but they came back. They fell out with their manager. Well, actually, he has been arrested for tax evasion. Their contract has been cancelled, and Roger owes them a ton of money."

"Now there's a surprise! So, they are here in Cork then?"

"Yes, and we are going to meet them in a pub on the edge of Cork after we are finished here. They didn't want to meet us in The Elbow in case they got mobbed." Jules quickly typed a message back. "It's ok if we go, isn't it?"

"Yes, that's good news. I am looking forward to seeing them. I am stoked. We are going to have to tell May and Sinead that we are going to be late back, though. I told her that we would be back at midnight."

Jules smiled. "It's ok. It's all arranged. She and Sinead know that we are going to be out late and they are going to stay over at ours. Little Darragh is sleeping through now, so he won't be any trouble."

"You've got this all worked out."

"I wanted to surprise you. That is part one of the surprise."

"Really? So, what is part two?"

"You will have to wait and see."

"No, Jules, you have to tell me. I can't sing for two hours not knowing. The suspense will kill me."

"No, my lips are sealed. I just hope you like our idea."

"You wicked thing. Our idea? Please tell me, I can't bear not knowing."

***

105

The crowd cheered and erupted with applause when Jules and Seth had walked onto the stage. They had sung their hearts out, enjoying every moment. Singing made them feel alive, and watching the crowd respond to each song sent thrills through them. As well as their own songs, including Waterfall Way, their signature tune, they had sung 'Just Say Yes' by Snow Patrol, and the audience had called out and whistled when they started singing that song. Being famous was turning out to be an adrenaline rush.

The back room was quiet, and the sound of the crowd screaming and cheering was still ringing in their ears. Seth pulled Jules to him and kissed her, and then held her face in his hands and smiled. "I love you, you know. I can't get over how well we are doing."

"I love you too. We are doing amazing, and not a pair of knickers in sight! I actually get shivers when a girl screams when you start a song. I feel their love for you. It is then that I realise how lucky I am to have you."

"Crikey! Some of them are a little odd. Did you see a crowd of them doing a funny dance when we were singing one of our tunes?"

"They were doing a TikTok dance."

"TikTok? What's that?"

"Surely you know what TikTok is?"

"No, not a clue."

"It's just a site where people record themselves doing these dances or put up short videos of themselves singing or making something. Teenagers use that site a lot, and that dance they were doing has gone viral. We really need to get going on the social media front. Perhaps we could record us dancing or singing together."

"I don't know. I am getting a bit old for that kind of thing."

"Old people dance as well. It's really funny."

"Thanks a lot! Are you trying to tell me something?"

"No, silly. I'll show you later. Come on, we better get going and meet up with Shawn and Jane. I don't think we should go through the pub to get out. Is there another way out? As much as I like being famous, I have a feeling that we are going to be ripped to shreds if we walk through the crowds."

"It's ok, we can go out the back door like proper rock stars."

Seth put the guitar on his back and held out his hand. Jules took his hand and smiled mischievously at him.

"Are you ready for your surprise then?"

"You're not going to rip my clothes off in the back alley, are you?"

"No, Seth! It's a bit cold for that! Come on, I don't want us to be late."

Shawn and Jane's chosen meeting place was a grotty pub tucked away behind the hospital. The pub was filled with alcoholics and the dishevelled who were staring miserably into the pints as they lamented.

"This is really not the kind of pub I would normally like to bring you to," Seth whispered.

"It's ok, at least they have some nice Irish tunes playing. Look, Shawn and Jane are sitting by the window." Jules waved to them, and they walked over to see them.

Seth smiled. "Now, here's a surprise. I didn't expect to see you two so soon. It's good to see you, though. Can I get you both a drink?"

"It's good to see you too. We are fine for a drink. You should try the black stuff here. It's meant to be the best in Ireland," Shawn said as he got up and shook Seth's hand and patted his arm.

"I'm not really a Guinness man, but I'll try a half. What would you like, Jules?"

"Just a Diet Coke, please."

Seth went off to the bar, and Jules grinned at Jane. "I haven't told him yet. I want you to ask him. It is so good to see you both. We have missed you."

"It's a shame that we had to come back so soon. But it's for the best. I didn't like staying in America. I missed my family too much. It is good to be back. Although I don't think they are pleased to see me."

Seth returned with their drinks, noticing that his beer mat was torn. After asking, he took one from another table. "You have chosen a peach of a pub here, Shawn, but I understand. We had to leave by the backdoor at The Elbow and escape our fans. I can't believe how many people turned out to see us tonight."

"Your break hasn't made a difference then? You seem to be doing really well."

"Not so bad. I am sorry that things didn't work out in America and Roger turned out to be a maggot."

"It was actually a blessing in disguise. He was causing us grief anyway, and we missed Ireland. I think they are going to stop flights in and out of the country soon until they get this virus under control. I have a feeling that we got back just in time," Shawn said, taking a sip of his Guinness.

"What are you going to do about your music career?" Seth asked.

"So, we all had a chat, and we have decided to start up our own record label. Guy, our guitarist, is taking care of all the legal stuff. From Monday, Sonar Cell is open for business under the name of Sonar Cell Music, and we will be free to record what we like. I think for our first record we cut, we should record Waterfall Way with you. A fifty-fifty profit share. What do you think?"

"That's grand! No, that's amazing! Is this what you were being so mysterious about, Jules?"

"No, this is news to me. Seriously. You want to make a record with us? I can't believe it."

"When can you come to the studio?" Shawn asked. "I say that though, we are just renting a studio a few days a week until we can get our own premises and equipment. Monday, Friday or Sunday is good for us."

Seth glanced at Jules, and it was wonderful to see her so happy. *We needed this. Perhaps I won't have to plough the fields. Perhaps this is going to be a proper career for us and pay the bills. I think that something is wrong, though. Jane is smiling, but she looks sad.* "There's something else that you are not telling me. I am looking at you both and can see in your eyes something is going on."

Jane sighed. "We are getting married next Saturday in a hotel. I was wondering if you would be available to be Shawn's best man. Jules is going to be my maid of honour, and my twin sister is going to walk me up the aisle. It will only be a small wedding and not in a church which has upset our families. We wanted to be wed before the baby came."

Seth grinned, "I'd be delighted. Christ, a baby too! Not on the day, I hope… Oh, but I am working on Saturday. I am sure that I can do a shift swap. What time is the wedding?"

Jules laughed, "The wedding is at two, Sinead is doing your Saturday, and you are doing all her lessons on Sunday!"

"You all had this planned. I am so happy for you. Are you having a shindig after?"

"We are. At yours, actually," Shawn added. "If it is ok with you. We haven't got that many guests coming now that we have turned our backs on a church wedding. I think that we are getting our wedding in just in time. Since a second person has died of the Coronavirus, there is talk that they are going to shut down the bars and lockdown Ireland. I hope the hotel doesn't cancel our wedding. By the way, nobody but you two know that

109

Jane is pregnant. If our Mam's found out that we are having a baby, then we will be disowned for sure."

"Don't you worry, I will keep my lips sealed. Our old barn is just the place for a party. Jules and I will play you a few songs if you like."

"We were hoping that you would say that," Jane was crying. "Sorry, I keep crying, but I really am happy. Jules, did you cry all the time when you were pregnant. Or perhaps it's us not talking to our families that is upsetting me. I don't know."

Jules took her hand. "It's ok. We are here for you. You are going to have an amazing time at your wedding. May has started organising the catering, and Seth and I will take care of the music and the bar. It is going to be the best wedding ever."

***

"So, are you looking forward to being Shawn's best man?" Jules asked as they walked back to the car.

"I am, but it's a shame they have fallen out with their parents. Weddings here are a big thing for families in Ireland. I am puzzled why Shawn chose me. He could have chosen one of the band members to be his best man."

"I guess he didn't want to show favouritism. You are a good friend to him. When you are together, you can see that you have something special. You are not used to having friends, are you?"

"No, you are right. I have always preferred socialising with my brothers and sisters. I should have stayed in contact with him when I was in prison. I feel bad now. He called my absence a break. I wonder if he knows that I was in prison."

"Well, if he does, I don't think that has hindered your bromance. He..." Jules stopped and looked ahead. "Crap, I think that some girls have spotted you. Look in the doorway of that pub up there. Two girls are pointing at you. They are coming towards us. I wish they wouldn't. I want to get home."

"It's ok. I will tell them to leave us alone. Politely, of course. I don't want to upset our fans."

***

From a dark alleyway, coughing and starving, Tom watched his beloved Julia and her stinking gypsy husband walk past him. Bile entered his throat, his stomach sickened by just seeing the fool. He spat phlegm and bile out of his mouth and on the floor. Gritting his teeth, he watched as pretty girls crowded around Seth, eager to be with him. *What has he got that I haven't? Look at the sick bastard, lapping up the attention. My poor Julia.*

Chapter Fourteen

"Hey, come here and let me see you, my gorgeous girl. You are looking stunning!"

Jules looked down at the long, pale blue bridesmaid dress and sighed. "I am not sure I look that good. The dress is really figure-hugging, and oh no, I have Darragh's lunch on it. Will you pass me a damp cloth, please?"

Seth picked up the kitchen cloth and rinsed it under the tap. "Here, let me do it for you." He kneeled down and wiped away the baby food from the hem. "There, perfect, it will soon dry. Are you ready to go?"

"Is it that time already? I still have to dress Darragh and get my hair to comply. Jane wants me to wear it in a messy bun on top, but I don't know. She will be shocked when she sees my version of a messy bun."

"You look beautiful as you are. You are glowing just like you did on our wedding day. You are not pregnant, are you?"

"No, I don't think so. I don't feel pregnant." *Oh God, I really am looking fat!* "Jane wants us to all look similar, so I will have to do battle with this crazy mop. Please, will you dress Darragh? All his clothes are laid out on the bed. I hope he behaves at the wedding. It's a shame nobody was free to look after him, but never mind. I'm sure he is going to love going to his first wedding."

"He will be fine as long as he can see us from his pram. A biscuit might help too. You go and finish getting ready, and I will see to our boy."

"You need to change too. You weren't thinking of wearing jeans and trainers, were you?"

"I was," he said, looking down at himself. "Shawn said dress smart casual. I didn't realise that you were all going to wear proper bridesmaid dresses. You are right. I'd better change."

"I think that you'd better. Why don't you wear your wedding clothes? They are hanging up in the wardrobe on a padded hanger, so they shouldn't need an iron. I think your dress shoes are under the bed. They might need a polish. Oh God, we are going to be really late. I hate being late for things," Jules said as she rushed to the bathroom. "Don't forget to bring the rings with you." *I wish I had time to straighten my hair. I should have attempted this bun thing earlier.*

They got to the hotel with just minutes to spare. Jules strapped Darragh into his pushchair and stood back to admire him. "You handsome boy, in your bow tie. Are you going to be a good boy for your Mam and Dad?"

Seth chuckled. "You are sounding more Irish every day. Come on then, let's find our places. I hope that they are not all waiting for us."

Jules couldn't help but stare at Seth. He was looking so handsome in his white shirt and dress trousers. Just like he did when they got married. He was making her feel hot and flustered. *He doesn't realise what he does to me.*

As they entered the hallway, a young woman with a freckled face and ginger hair swept up into a messy bun appeared. For a moment, Jules thought that it was Jane. *Jane? No, it must be her sister.* She was wearing a similar dress to Jules, and she was looking troubled.

"You must be Jules. I was worried that you had gone to the wrong hotel. The media think that the wedding is going to be held at one on the other side of town. I'm Jackie, by the way. Jane's sister. We are all upstairs waiting for Shawn to arrive. Shawn is always late for everything. It is going to be the bride waiting for the groom at this wedding," she added, laughing. Even her laugh sounded like Jane's.

"I am glad that it wasn't us that were holding you up. You've done your hair beautifully. I did my best with my hair."

"You look perfect. Jane, however, is not looking her best. She is a bit tearful today."

"Oh, nuts!" Seth exclaimed. "I've left the rings in the car. Give me ten minutes, and I will be back with them. I don't have any pockets in these trousers. I'm really sorry, Jackie, I won't be long."

"Ok, be quick, I..." Jules watched Seth run down the hallway, and she could see that his knee was still hurting him. "Oh dear, now we are really going to hold things up."

"It's ok. We told Shawn that the wedding was at two, not half-past, so we have plenty of time. Is this your wee boy? He looks just like Seth. Look at those big brown eyes. He is going to melt a few hearts."

"Darragh is a sweetheart. I hope Jane doesn't mind me bringing him. I couldn't find anyone to mind him. He is usually good and quiet. He will like listening to the music and watching everyone."

"No, of course, she won't mind. What is a wedding without children? Let's go in the lift. Jane is waiting upstairs for Shawn to arrive. I hope he gets here soon."

Jane was sitting by the window in her hotel room. An elderly woman was smoothing down her wedding dress, and she tutted as a stubborn fold of material refused to lay neatly. A photographer was walking around the room taking shots of Jane, her bouquet and detailed photos of the embroidery on her dress. Jules wondered who the old woman was. *It can't be her Mum.*

"The dress is fine, Mary. You've done a wonderful job on it. If only my Mam could see it."

"Don't you worry yourself about your Mam. She is a foolish woman. Young people don't have to get wed in a church if they don't want to. She will regret being so stubborn. Still, you will have some wonderful photos to show her when she sees the error of her ways. Jane, I'm going downstairs and will take my place. Don't mind me if I start arranging your dress as you walk up the aisle. I'm a perfectionist. I like the dresses I make to shine. I can't help myself."

Mary left, and Jane stood up and came towards them smiling. Jules barely recognised her as her make-up and her beautiful ginger hair piled high on the top of her head made her look like a film star. *Oh dear, her red lipstick clashes with her ginger hair. Should I say something? No, she does look beautiful.* "You look amazing!"

"Oh, Jules, you are here, thank goodness. Is Shawn here yet?"

"We didn't see him when we came in, but I am sure that he won't be long."

Jane's face crumpled, and she looked like she was about to cry. "You don't think that he has got cold feet, do you? Dad was really nasty to him about us not wanting a church wedding. Perhaps Shawn has had enough of my crazy family and me."

"Don't be daft," Jackie said. "He loves and adores you. You know that he does. You have been going out with each other since school. It is about time he made an honest woman of you. He knows that."

"When he brought the rings over to us yesterday, he said that he couldn't wait to get married," Jules added.

Jane sighed. "I guess that you are right." Her phone started to ring. She picked it up and, seeing that Shawn was ringing her, took the call. "Where are you?... Oh no, how many journalists are following you. So, you are going to be late? It's not just an excuse, is it? You do want to marry me, don't you?... Keep your hair on!... Ok, I'll see you in a minute... Love you too, babe!"

Jane put the phone back on the table and then smiled at them but looked a little embarrassed. "He's on his way. I'm sorry about that. This baby is making me far too emotional. Did you feel like you wanted to cry all the time, Jules?"

Jules shot a look at Jackie and was relieved to see that she didn't look shocked with the news about the baby. "Darragh was born on the day I found out I was pregnant, so I can't say about how I felt before. Since he was born, I haven't been the same emotionally. I cry over stupid things. I think it takes about a year for your body and mind to get back to normal. So, Jackie knows that you are pregnant, then?"

"I couldn't not tell my twin. She'd never forgive me."

"So, you really are twins. Are you identical?"

"Yes, we are, but personality-wise, we are like chalk and cheese."

Darragh called out Da and put his arms out to be taken out his pushchair.

"Oh dear, he's had enough of being in his chair." Jules unstrapped him and picked him up. He looked so happy to be free and in her arms.

"I'm going to like having a baby if he or she turns out to be as cute as yours."

"He is a sweet thing, but he will cry and have a tantrum if I put him back in the pushchair. I might have to carry him up the aisle in a minute. Will that be ok?"

"Of course, that is what weddings are about, families coming together," she looked like she was about to cry again.

"Things will turn out fine," Jules said, trying to sound confident and then felt a little guilty that she hadn't rung her dad. "When you and Shawn have your baby, then your families will welcome you back with open arms. You'll see..."

There was a knock on the door.

"Come in," Jane called.

Seth opened the door but stayed in the doorway. "I just wanted to tell you that Shawn is waiting for you downstairs. He has a message. Now, this is embarrassing, but I promised that I would say it word for word. He says he loves you with all his heart, and could you please get a move on and not be late for your wedding."

Jane smiled. "Thanks, Seth. How funny, he thinks that he is early for once. We will be down in a minute."

***

It was good to get back to the Old Barn. Seth unstrapped Darragh from his car seat and then lifted him up gently, trying not to wake him. His spiky hair brushed Seth's cheek as he laid his head on his shoulder.

Jules was gazing at their house and was looking concerned. "It's very quiet here. I thought that May and Sinead would be hard at work setting everything up for the reception party. There are no decorations outside. I hope everything is ok. Let's go in and see what is left to do."

As Seth got to the front door, he noticed Sinead's Mini racing towards them. "Hey Jules, I can see Sinead. She's driving like a loon. She looks like she's in a rush."

Sinead parked next to their car and jumped out. "I've had a bit of a day, and I've got behind. May has come down with the flu, and I've just had to drive her home so she can rest. She is cross with me, but she really didn't look well. Did you know she was an asthmatic? Flu and asthma do not go well together."

"No, I didn't. I feel bad that you had two weddings to deal with today."

"She loves being busy, but sometimes she does too much. We found a puffer thing at the back of the bathroom cabinet, and she promised to use it. It was a few days out of date. I hope that it still works."

"Oh dear, poor May," Jules said as she unlocked the door. "Is there much more to do?"

"So, we have half an hour before everyone arrives, and all that needs doing is to take the covers off the food and pour some champagne. Seth, you're in charge of the champagne and sorting out the music and the band when they arrive. I just have to fix the banner and balloons up outside. I asked Gemma to come up and help when she has finished at the yard. She was eager to help."

"Ok, that's fine," Seth said. *We could probably do without the bunny boiler's help.* "I'll just put Darragh in his cot and hope he doesn't wake up." He looked at their home, and he was impressed with all the decorations. The walls and windows were festooned with pale blue and white balloons and silver ribbon. There were small round tables covered with long white cloths at the far end of the barn. He guessed there were around fifty chairs with bows on and, as always, enough food laid out to feed an army. The sofa and coffee table had gone, leaving enough room for everyone to dance. *I am so looking forward to dancing with Jules.* "Wow, this is just perfect. It has to be said. You and May have done an amazing job and have transformed the place. Don't you think so, Jules?"

"Thank you so much. It really is perfect! Jane and Shawn are going to be so happy."

"I'm just going to put my boy down for a nap. I won't be a moment, and then I will be able to help," Seth said as he headed off towards Darragh's room. He nearly fell over the sofa. *So that's where the sofa went to.*

"How did the service go?" Sinead asked.

"Ok, I guess. It was a bit odd and rushed. I had to carry Darragh up the aisle. He was tired and didn't want to go back in his pushchair. Nobody seemed to mind. There is talk that there won't be any more weddings for a while until they have got this virus thing under control."

"I hope they don't stop the weddings. That is going to be a bit of a blow financially if we can't hold them here."

"I know. But it's a bit worrying that people are dying from the virus. I think everyone thought it would burn itself out by now. Things are getting serious, aren't they?"

"No, it's not looking good… Are Jane and Shawn having their photoshoot in the park now?"

"I doubt it. When we left the hotel, there were reporters outside. I don't think they will be able to go to the park. They will be followed for sure. It's a shame. It's very pretty there with all the daffodils," Jules said as she started to remove the cling film from the plates.

"Oh, dear. It's a bit cold to have photos taken outside, anyway. The orangery looks stunning. It's a bright day. They should have some photos taken there."

"That's a good idea."

A face appeared at the window, and Jules' heart sank. Gemma was waving at her. She was wearing a very tight white dress, exposing almost all of her breasts. Her blonde hair was tied back tightly, and she wore heavy eye makeup and red lipstick, the same colour that Jane had been wearing. *Should I be wearing lipstick that colour?*

"Christ! Gemma looks like she's going to a nightclub," Sinead declared. "I asked her to dress smartly but not like that." She opened the door and let her in.

Jules noticed that Gemma was wearing black riding boots, which made her outfit look bizarre. In her hand, she held a pair of white six-inch heels.

119

"You're early. Did everything go ok with the four o'clock lesson?" Sinead asked.

"No, it was a no show, so I unsaddled Beth, and I got changed and came up to help. By the way, I saw some cars pulling up at the Manor House. I think that your guests might think that the reception is being held at the orangery."

"Didn't you think to go down there and tell them to park in the stables car park and walk down to the barn?"

"No, I didn't think Anyway, it's a long walk down to the Manor House."

"Fuck! I'd better drive down and send everyone up here. Gemma, please will you help Jules take all the covers off of the food. We are running behind here."

"Ok," she said, taking off her boots. "I'm not sure if these shoes go with my dress. What do you think, Julia?"

"You should have worn something flatter. Your feet are going to kill you later. That's the least of your worries. Are you sure that you are going to stay in your dress?"

"What do you mean?"

Seth came out of the bedroom with Darragh in his arms. He was awake and smiling. "It's no good. This little man has had his nap and doesn't want to miss a thing."

Seth put him in his high chair, and Jules found him a few things for him to eat from the fridge. Seth picked up something from a platter and offered it to Darragh. He took the cheese twist eagerly.

"Seth, some of the guests are down in the Manor House car park. Sinead is going to get them. Gemma, please can you help me? We have loads to do here."

"Fine, but can you tell your husband to stop staring at my tits."

Seth felt shocked. *Was I staring? No!* "Sorry, I didn't mean to. What on earth are you wearing, Gemma? You are going to shock a few guests wearing that dress."

"Gemma, you need to change," Jules said firmly. "Have a look in my wardrobe and see if you can find something more suitable for a waitress to wear."

Chapter Fifteen

With merry Irish music playing in the background, Seth opened a bottle of champagne. The cork popped and fired off towards the ceiling, and the contents began to spill. He laughed and, not wanting to waste any of the valuable liquid, poured it out into the fluted glasses lined up in front of him. *This champagne should have been chilled.* Most of the guests had arrived and were waiting by the door to greet the happy couple. He looked out of the window and saw a white limousine pull up outside. *So, they made it back here without the press following. Thank goodness.* Gemma came over to him with a tray. She started to load it with some of the glasses and seemed to be in a mood and nearly knocked some of the flutes over.

"Careful, I would only take a few at a time. They are bound to go over if you take too many," he said, trying to not sound too bossy.

"Fine! I'm not stupid!"

"I didn't say you were." She had changed and was now wearing a white shirt and black skirt. *My girl's clothes are too tight for her, but she looks better than she did. What was she thinking of?* Her shirt, however, was buttoned too low and displayed her ample breasts. He tried not to look but couldn't help himself.

"Do you like what you see," she whispered as she walked off to serve the guests.

Crap, she caught me looking. This girl is going to be so much trouble. I just know she is. I'm just going to have to keep my distance and be cold. He picked up a glass and took a sip of the warm champagne to calm his jangled nerves. *Why am I feeling so guilty? It is flattering to be sought after, but Gemma is really doing my head in.* He looked around the busy room, searching for Jules. He spotted her sitting at one of the tables. She had Darragh on her lap, and she was talking to an old couple. The old lady was smiling broadly, and she was stroking their baby's cheek. *Good, Jules didn't see any of that. I guess I should do my best man speech. Now, where's my bit of paper? It's in the car. Damn! I'll just have to do my best to remember it.*

Seth turned off the music and picked up a spoon, and as Jane and Shawn came in, he tapped on a glass. "If I could just have everyone's attention for a moment... Welcome to you all, I am Seth Hearn, the best man, and it gives me great pleasure to give a warm welcome and congratulations to the beautiful bride Jane Smith and my best mate, the groom, Shawn Smith. This is just a little speech, as, like me, you must all be in need of a bite to eat and are looking forward to dancing into the night. Shawn and I met at The Elbow, and from the very first day I heard his band Sonar Cell play, I knew that this man would go far. He is the most talented musician I have ever met and has the biggest heart. I am proud to call you my friend.

"Jane, you are looking stunning today, and it has to be said that this beautiful bride has waited a long time to marry Shawn. I am sure that you will agree that they make the perfect couple. I have known Shawn for a while now and know, Jane, that he thinks the world of you and will always be there for you even if he is always half an hour late!" Everyone laughed. "Both Jules and I wish you the very best for the future. May you have many children and both live a long and happy life together. Please raise your glasses and wish them well... To the bride and groom!"

"TO THE BRIDE AND GROOM!" everyone repeated, holding their glasses high in the air.

"If you'd like to help yourself to food and wine," Jules called out, "then please do. As usual, May and Sinead have done a wonderful job, and they have provided enough food to feed an army!"

***

The afternoon slipped into evening, and the reception had gone better than expected. A large band played all the best traditional Irish tunes, and it was hard to sit still. Nearly everyone was dancing, and for a moment, Jules was transported back to Crow Farm, where she had first danced with Seth. She had surprised herself on how well she remembered the steps. It was good to be dancing again, and she had skipped, spun and twirled as Seth led her through each set. His dark eyes shone, and he was grinning broadly at her. *He just loves to dance.* She was having fun too but felt a little guilty that Sinead was holding Darragh for them. *Just one more dance, and then I will try and get him to bed. I doubt that he will settle. He is enjoying the music and the attention far too much.*

As the dance ended, she noticed that Gemma had changed back into her tight white dress and was staring at them with her arms folded, and she had a cross look on her face. *Why is she looking so angry? Christ, she's coming over. What does she want now?*

"I think that it is my turn to dance with Seth!"

"I am actually quite happy dancing with my wife," Seth said sternly.

"Fuck you!"

Seth was shocked. "That's not a nice way to be, Gemma. Why have you got a cob on?"

124

"What do you know? You act all happy when you know you want to be with me. I see the way you look at me. You've been separated for nearly a year. There is no way that you could still love her."

Jules was getting angry. "Gemma, you need to go home before you make a complete fool of yourself. I am not going to ask you again."

"Go home and stop all your nonsense. I love my wife, and I don't know why you are being like this."

"So, is that what you are going to say when our baby is born?"

Jules glared at Seth. "Did you sleep with her?"

"What, are you crazy? I can't believe that you would ask me that? Gemma, tell her the truth. For God's sake."

A sly smile spread across Gemma's face. "I am not going to lie. The baby is due on your birthday, Seth, September the thirtieth. We need to talk. YOU NEED TO STOP LYING TO YOURSELF AND FACE UP TO YOUR RESPONSIBILITIES. IF YOU FUCK A GIRL AND SHE GETS PREGNANT, THEN YOU NEED TO DO THE RIGHT THING," she yelled and then she walked off, leaving Seth and Jules staring at each other in shock.

"When were you going to tell me?" Jules asked with a tear rolling down her cheek.

"Right! I'm not having this! We are going to sort this out here and now." *I've got to stay in control.* "That woman is spinning a web of lies. I have never touched her, and I never will. Yes, she has the hots for me, and yes, she will say anything to split us up, but I am not having you think that I am the father of her baby. That is just sick. Christ, Jules!"

Jules looked hard into his blazing eyes but could see that he was telling the truth. She lay her head on his chest and put her arms around him. He didn't pull away. She was so relieved. "I'm so sorry, Seth. I didn't mean that" she sobbed.

"It's ok, please don't cry. She is just a stupid child. If she is having a baby, then it will be Tom's or any Tom, Dick or Harry's but certainly not mine."

"I know, she just sounded so convincing. And she reminds me so much of Ivy Brown."

"Christ! That hurt!"

"Don't listen to me. I know that you would never go with her. What are we going to do? She has a big mouth, and she is going to be telling everyone that you are the father."

"Nobody is going to believe her. Everyone saw Tom fucking her without protection." An image of Tom standing there naked and erect without a condom filled his mind. He shook his head to dispel the image. "We just tell her where to go if she comes near us. Let me get you a drink. I don't like to see you so upset."

"No, I'm ok now. I really feel bad for saying what I did. I do trust you. I really do."

Seth hugged and kissed her. "I believe you. We are going to have to work together to get that witch off my back. Let's see what Sinead thinks we should do."

"Ok, but first, we need to put Darragh to bed. Poor Sinead has been entertaining him for hours."

"I'll sort him out," Seth said. "He is going to play up. There is too much going on in here. Let me try and get him to sleep with my dulcet tones. I can see him rubbing his eyes. He is tired. You go and chat with Sinead and tell her what happened. She will put your mind at rest about the Gemma thing. When I come back, then we should do a few songs for everyone. The band could do with a break. Are you up to singing a few tunes with your wayward husband?"

"That's really not funny. Of course, I am. I just hope people don't see that I've been crying."

"Let me look at your wee face. Perfect and beautiful. Did I tell you today how much I love you?"

"Yes, when we woke up this morning and at the wedding service."

"I did too. I would tell you every hour if you would let me."

They walked over to Sinead, and Seth took Darragh from her. "You poor, tired wee lad. Are you coming with your Da for a little song? Have you been good for Sinead?"

"He is tired, I was on the verge of coming over to you, but then I saw Gemma yelling at you both. What's going on?"

"Jules will fill you in. Come on, Darragh, let's go to bed. Kiss your Mam goodnight."

Jules hugged and kissed Darragh and feared he would want to come to her. Before he could put his arms out, Seth took him off to his bedroom.

"Have you been crying, Jules? You haven't had a row with Seth, have you?"

"No, not a row. I feel really bad. Gemma just came over and told Seth that he was the father of her baby. She says that she is pregnant. Oh, Sinead, that really hurt, and for a moment, I thought he was…"

"Fuck! You do know that he is the most loyal person that you are ever likely to meet. He loves you to bits."

"I know, and that's why I feel so terrible. I shouldn't have said what I did. I guess I am just scared of losing him. Emotionally, I haven't been the same since having Darragh. He says that we are going to have to work together to sort this out. Oh, Sinead, she is going to be spreading vicious lies about him. I can't bear it."

"Look, nobody is going to believe her. She has a bit of a reputation, and everyone knows that Seth idolizes you. You have nothing to worry about. I will talk to her if you like. For some reason, she is scared of me. I guess May is her nice employer, and I am the bad cop. I am the one that tells her off if she does something wrong. She has just got a teenage crush. I'll sort her out. She won't bother you again."

"Thank you. There I was lecturing Seth about having to deal with obsessed fans, and it is me that can't handle it. She might need your support if she is pregnant. Don't be too mean to her. Oh, I was going to ask. How is May?"

"I'll be kind if she doesn't get on my nerves. May is worrying me. It is really weird. She says she is ok and she has gone to bed early with a hot water bottle. I am so used to her being up chatting until one or two at night, and it just seems so odd that she is in bed already."

"A good night's sleep is what she needs. You'll see, she will be up and about tomorrow as good as new."

"I hope so. Look, Seth is heading back over to us. That was quick."

"He has the magic touch with Darragh. He is such a good dad. How could I ever have doubted him?"

"Look, don't beat yourself up about it. He is smiling and has forgotten what you said. He has that look about him that says that you are going up on stage. You are, aren't you? I can't wait to hear you two sing again. S&J is fast becoming my most listened to music. You so need to live stream some records. I've practically worn out that CD that Jane made you."

"You are right. We just have to. We are going to record Waterfall Way with Sonar Cell next week, so that is a start."

"How is my gorgeous girl? I hope you've been saying good things about me."

"Of course, Sinead is going to warn Gemma off for us. You got Darragh off to sleep quickly."

"I didn't even have to sing to him. He was asleep before I even got him to the cot. We'll check on him after we've done our songs. Are you ready? I want to sing 'All Of Me' first. Shawn and Jane could do with a few slow numbers to give everyone a rest, and then I will sing My Heart is Your Heart, the one I sang to you when I proposed. What do you say?"

"You do know if you sing that song, then I will be sobbing. I love it when you sing that one to me."

"As long as it is tears of love, then I will take my chances."

"I love you, Seth, and I didn't mean to hurt you."

"I know. No harm done. Come on, my beautiful girl, I want to sing to you."

Chapter Sixteen

The roads through Waterfall were eerily quiet and the sky a stormy grey. Sweat dripped from Seth's face as he ran, and he was badly out of breath. This was his third run since his knee felt strong enough to run on, and although he knew he shouldn't be running so hard, he was determined to beat his personal best and complete his ten-kilometre run in less than forty-five minutes. He was doing his best to forget Gemma's outburst too. It did not sit well with him being accused of adultery.

Despite tears from the shock of the announcement, he was pleased with how well Jules had dealt with the situation. He had forgiven her for doubting him. *We should talk to Gemma today. Both of us. I can't ever be left alone with that girl. I think she is obsessed with me. Jules says she reminds her of Ivy. I suppose they do look similar and that type of girl I would have been attracted to in the past. But not anymore. Thank God I've got my Jules now. This Gemma thing is doing my head in. I don't want everyone thinking that I have been a bastard. I am not like my Dad. Christ, no!*

The timer on his phone went off, telling him that he hadn't achieved his goal. He reached the foot of Waterfall West's drive and sighed. *Just a few seconds out, so not too shabby. I should focus on running and not slow myself down thinking about yesterday's fiasco.* It was then that he noticed the ambulance in the car park of the Manor House, and alarmed, he felt his heart pound. *Please let it be one of the guests and not May. It's May, I know it is. Fuck!*

Seth ran up the path, and as he reached the door, May was being wheeled out in a chair. A yellow blanket was placed over her and was tucked up under her chin. She had a mask over her mouth, and she was being given oxygen. She was gasping for breath, and her eyes looked wide, and he could see the fear in them.

"Seth!" she called out desperately. "Don't let them take me."

He looked at the two ambulance workers for answers. They were both wearing blue surgical masks, which made them look cold and distant. *Why are they wearing masks? Is May contagious?*

Sinead followed her out, and she was crying. He had never seen her cry like that before.

"I had to call an ambulance. She couldn't breathe. Please tell her I did it for her own good," she sobbed.

"You were right to call us. May, you mustn't be afraid. You are very sick, and you are in good hands. You are having a severe asthma attack, and you need specialist treatment. Is this your mother?" the ambulance man asked Seth.

"No... As good as."

May freed a hand from her blanket, and Seth took it and noticed how cold it felt.

"I don't want to go to hospital," she said breathlessly.

"You have to. Did you not hear the man? You are not well. You need to go. We'll come with you so you won't be alone."

"I'm really sorry, but as I've explained to Sinead, because of the pandemic, the hospital is not allowing patients to be accompanied."

"Well, that can't be right. Not even family?"

"I'm really sorry, but we can't risk others getting infected with the virus. These are difficult times."

"I see. May, we will walk with you to the ambulance. You understand, don't you? I'm sure that you will be better in no time and back home again. Sinead and I will be on the end of our phones to chat, and I'll come and collect you when you have got your breathing sorted. You have your phone, don't you?" May nodded, but Seth was not sure if she did. He looked at Sinead to confirm this, but she was shaking her head.

"She doesn't know where it is. She is a bit confused. I don't think it has been charged for a while. I said that I would ring the hospital and see if they would take a phone through to her. May, I am going to call you this evening. I'm sorry I can't go with you."

Seth and Sinead stood side by side, and they watched the ambulance pull out of the car park and head down the drive to the main road. Sinead was sobbing. Seth hugged her. He could feel her body shaking, and he held her a little tighter.

"She's not coming back, is she?" she said, staring off into the distance.

"Don't say that. They just have to sort her breathing out, and then she will be good as new."

"I really wanted to go with her. She was so frightened."

"I know. There is nothing we can do. May is strong, and she will get over this. Come up to the barn and stay with Jules and Darragh. You shouldn't be on your own. Do you want me to take your lessons today? I really don't mind."

"No, it's ok. I only have a few to do. Luke is taking the hacks. If I teach, it will stop me from thinking about her. Oh, Seth, I love that woman and now…"

"Don't cry. It's ok. It's only an asthma attack."

"I hope that's all it is. Life here wouldn't be the same without her."

***

Jules stood in the shower and let the powerful hot jet of water wash over her cold body. She had gone out for her run with a heavy heart. Hearing that May had gone to hospital had upset her. Halfway through the run, the heavens had opened, and she had walked home crying. She was sorry for May and sorry for herself. She felt sad for May and hoped that she wasn't feeling alone and frightened. She knew what that felt like and then realised that old memories of being without Seth had resurfaced. *I shouldn't be thinking like this. It's May that I should be crying for, not myself. Get a grip, Jules!*

When she emerged from the bathroom, she was feeling much better. Seth and Darragh were watching television. The news was on, and she shivered as she heard that the death toll was increasing.

"This thing is getting out of control," Seth announced. "I don't know what they are waiting for. The government needs to lock down the country now before things get out of hand. Look how quickly the virus spread in Italy."

"I guess the scientists know what we need to do. You don't think May has it, do you? One of the symptoms is breathing difficulties."

"I doubt it. There's been no cases in Waterfall."

"But May has guests in the Manor House from all over the world. They could have given it to her."

"You might be right. I guess they will test her. She is over seventy. It won't be good news if she has. I didn't like the way she looked. Poor Sinead was so upset about calling an ambulance for her, but it had to be done."

"I know. I can't believe that we can't visit her. Sinead should stay with us tonight. There're only two guests staying at the Manor House, and Gemma can look after them. Seth, I was thinking we should go and see Gemma and sort out this baby business. If we go together and bring Darragh, then everyone will stay calm."

"I was thinking the same. I won't lose it, not with you and Darragh next to me. We should go now and get this out the way, and then we can go out for a drive after lunch. Do you see all these eejits on the TV bulk buying toilet roll? Have you ever seen anything like it? Why are they going crazy for it?"

"When people feel threatened, they panic, and if they see someone else bulk buying, then they copy. I guess it is their survival instincts kicking in."

"But why toilet roll? Do we have enough?"

"Well, I added some to our online order, so with a bit of luck, we should get it in our delivery this afternoon. I have to admit I did order extra. It would be awful to have to use old newspapers, wouldn't it? I might have ordered an extra bag of pasta and custard creams, too," she added, feeling a little guilty.

***

It seemed an age away that Seth and Jules had lived in the mobile home with Sinead. As their old home came into view, Seth was surprised by how small it was. The old orange curtains looked drab, and the white exterior was covered in a green mould. *It could do with a jet wash, but it might be too far gone for that.* He was carrying Darragh, and he hoped that Gemma was going to be civil. For a second, he saw a shadow in one of the windows, and he shivered as he thought about facing the bunny boiler again.

Darragh pointed to the summer field, and Seth realised that he wanted to go and see the horses. "Do you want to see Moss and Connor? You like horses, don't you? We have to go and see someone first, and then I will take you to see them. Is it ok if I take Moss out for a ride this afternoon? I wish that you could come too."

"You don't have to ask, of course. Let's get this over with. Sunday is her day off, isn't it?" she asked as she knocked on the door. "This place is looking really grotty. How did we all ever live in it?"

Seth nodded. "It's so small and sad looking."

Jules knocked again. "I don't think she is at home."

"I swear I saw someone in there. Perhaps she doesn't want to face the music. Gemma, we need to talk to you," he called. "I still have a key, so if you don't come out, then we'll just come in."

"We can't do that. Gemma, we'll come back later. We all need to talk about last night. We are not angry. We just want to help."

"Do we?"

"Yes, Seth! She is going to be a single mother soon, and she is probably scared."

"Oh right. I see."

"We are just going to see the horses, and then we will knock again on the way back. We do need to talk."

Seth breathed a sigh of relief. "So, my wee boy, shall we go and see Moss and Connor. This field is a bit muddy, so I'll get them to come and see us. Look, I have apples in my pocket. Your Mam's horse is crazy for a bit of apple. You should ride again. You used to love it. You haven't ridden since we got here. This afternoon, you could take Connor out, and I will look after Darragh."

"No, you go. I just need to go out with you and Moss one day and we can try and find us a good route that I can remember. I don't want to get lost. This estate is like a crazy maze. I don't like to ask May or Sinead to babysit too often. In a couple of weeks, I will ask May. Oh, May, I forgot. I hope that she is doing ok."

"We'll ring the hospital and get an update when we get back. Now, where is my Moss? He usually comes running to see us."

In the distance, at the edge of the field, they could see the coloured cobs and Moss standing around an old yellow bath which served as their water trough. Some of the mares' ears were pinned back, and their tails swished angrily.

"They don't look happy," Seth said as he moved closer to the fence to get a better look. "There must be something in their water trough again. They won't drink if there is a dead animal in there. I can't say I blame them. Last week I had to pull out a dead magpie. Here, hold Darragh, and I'll go and check." Seth passed Darragh to her and climbed through the rails. Moss, seeing him approach, ran down to him.

When Moss was a short way from Seth, he stopped and pawed the ground. Seth went up to his horse, and he patted him and knew that he was agitated too. "It's ok, don't fret. I'll sort out your trough. Are you thirsty then?"

It took a while to walk up the field, and Moss galloped on ahead and joined the others around the water trough. "What's going on? It's only a bird." Seth pushed his way through the horses to see what the trouble was. It was the smell that hit him first. There was an odour of roses and something else - a metallic smell. He stopped short and gasped. He could see something larger than a bird in the tub. Dazed, he stepped forward, fearing the worst. He focused on the red water within the tub and saw below the waterline an ashen face. Lifeless eyes stared up at the sky. "Fuck! It's Gemma!" He hoped what he was seeing was just a cruel trick of the light, and he looked up at the stormy sky for a moment and begged all that was good to release him from this nightmare. He looked back down at her, and the scene was just as ghastly as he remembered it to be. He hadn't noticed it before, but one of Gemma's arms was visible too, revealing not only a cut wrist but the sleeve of his jacket. "NO! PLEASE NO!" *She's only gone and killed herself. Is that my coat? Shit! This can't be happening. Oh God, no!*

Seth stood there frozen to the spot trying to make sense of what he was seeing. *What do I do now?* Horrified and feeling like he had a punch to his guts, Seth made his way back to Jules. *Is it my fault this has happened?*

Chapter Seventeen

Jules knew instantly that something was wrong. Seth had been gone too long, and Darragh was starting to wriggle, wanting to be put down so he could examine what was below them. By the time Seth got back to Jules, his face was as white as a sheet, and he was shaking. Darragh put out his arms wanting Seth to hold him, but he didn't notice. "What's wrong? You look bad. Are you ok?"

"Something really bad has happened." Gemma's lifeless eyes staring into nothing filled his head. "Gemma's taken her life."

"I don't understand. We heard her in the mobile. You must be mistaken."

"No, she's lying in the horses' water trough with her wrists cut." Jules inhaled sharply.

"We are going to have to call the police or an ambulance. Both, I guess."

For a moment, Jules stood by the silent pool at Farm End on that hot summer's day. *This is Ivy Brown all over again. Only this time, Seth is getting his phone out to call the police. What will they think? This isn't good. Seth is known to the police. Gemma was obsessed with him, and the fact that he has found her body is a disaster. They are going to take him away. Send him back to prison. I just know it. I can't have that.* "Seth, you can't ring the police. Please don't. I'll say I found her. I don't want you getting involved."

Seth shook his head. "I have to ring. I found her, and if she has ended her life because of me, then it is my duty. It is the least I can do."

"No, you mustn't, please. I can't have them take you away again."

"They won't do that. I haven't done anything wrong. I might have to go down to the police station and make a statement, but that is all. Why do you think they will take me away?"

Jules was trying to stay calm for Darragh's sake, but she was having trouble keeping herself together. "Seth, seriously! This is all wrong. Don't you think it's a bit odd that she has taken herself halfway up the summer field to end her life? Why didn't she just end her life in the mobile? Something isn't right. I just know there has been foul play."

"So, you think that it is murder?" Seth asked, feeling alarmed.

"I don't know. I just think that it is odd, and you need to keep out of it."

"Who would want to kill her? She got on a lot of people's nerves but not enough for anyone to commit murder."

"So, what do you think the police are going to say when they find out about her yelling at you at the wedding and accusing you of being the father of her baby? You have a record, and this isn't the first pregnant girl that you know that has been found dead in a watery grave. Not to mention that you were raised by a serial killer."

"Christ, Jules! What are you saying?"

"I think you told me once that mud sticks, and it will be an ex-convict that will get the book thrown at them, guilty or not."

Seth glared at Jules as her words started to sink in.

"I can't let you deal with this alone. No, I have to do this. I was never questioned about Ivy Brown's death. Anyway, my footprints will be near the water trough, so it is best that I ring the police. It is better, to be honest. Otherwise, things like this can turn on you. I was wrong to leave you to deal with Ivy Brown."

"Please, Seth, I don't want you to." She was crying now, and Darragh, seeing her sobbing, started to cry too.

"Oh, God. I have to. Now you're both crying. Look, go back home and give Darragh his lunch. I promise nothing is going to happen to me. If it was murder, then that person needs to be found and punished… No, stay with me. I don't want you walking alone when there might be some nutter on the loose. There was someone in the mobile, wasn't there? Perhaps they know a little more about this. Please don't cry both of you, everything will be ok. I can't believe this is happening."

"Seth, I'm scared for you. For us."

Seth sighed and climbed through the post and rail fence. "Let me hold you both. Seeing you so unhappy is tearing me apart. Let's go back to the barn and ring from there." He hugged them both, trying his best to calm them. *I am innocent. Perhaps I should take my jacket off her body. No, I'd better not. Fuck!*

As they waited for the police to arrive, Jules gave Darragh his lunch, and as she spoon-fed him, she watched Seth pacing up and down the living area, doing his best to remain calm. *Why is he looking so agitated? Everything is going to be ok? I mustn't cry again.* "We should tell Sinead. She is going to be worried when she sees a police car driving our way."

Seth looked at the time. "She will be teaching her last lesson. I will message her. She is going to be shocked and emotional. May will be too. I should ring the hospital and see how she is. It's been quite a day for us all. Do you think I should go to the mobile and see if anyone is in there?"

"No! Hell no! Let the police look. You might destroy crucial evidence if you go inside."

"You really do think she's been murdered, don't you?"

"She just doesn't look the type to take her own life. She was always so full of life and… confident." *A nuisance.*

"You can't always tell what people are feeling inside. I think that she was pretty miserable. I found her crying in the horses' barn once."

"Did you? You never said." *What else haven't you told me?*

"Jules, you do trust me, don't you?" he asked as he typed a text out for Sinead.

"Of course, I do. I am just feeling a bit emotional. It was not so long ago that Dad tried to take his own life."

"I'm sorry. I shouldn't have said that. I know you do. This is a really shitty day."

"There, I have messaged Sinead. I've just asked her to come up here so we can tell her some bad news about Gemma. Now I am going to ring the hospital to see how May is. No, hold on. The police are here. I'll go out and talk to them. You stay here and lock the door behind me. I need to know that you are safe while I take them to the summer field. They might want me to move the horses to another field so, I might be a while. In fact, I will move them. They need clean water. I'll move them to the lower field. Promise that you won't leave the barn until I come back."

"You are going a bit over the top. Whoever it was is probably long gone."

Seth frowned at her. "Ok, I promise. I'll tell Sinead about Gemma. Oh, Seth, I'm scared now. You don't think there is a nutter on the estate, do you?"

Seth hugged and kissed her. "Be strong. It's going to be ok. I won't let anyone hurt my beautiful wife."

Jules watched him leave, and he turned back and pointed to the door, reminding her to lock it. Sighing, she walked over to the door and fixed the security chain in place. *Why did this have to happen? Are we cursed or something? Please don't let them take him away.*

***

With her heart beating hard, Jules opened the door to Sinead, forgetting that she had left the chain on. The door jarred, and Jules cursed as she removed the chain. She opened the door and saw Sinead's puzzled face. "Sorry about that."

"Why have you got the chain on during the day? Why is there a police car out here?"

"Oh, Sinead, you are never going to guess what has happened. Come in and sit down."

Sinead came in and looked around. "Gemma's not been here threatening you, has she? I gave her a piece of my mind last night when I went home from yours. I found her outside here, lurking in the bushes like a deranged stalker. That one is not right in the head."

"So, what did you say to her?"

"You really don't want to hear. She foul-mouthed me, so I fired her and told her to pack her things and go."

"Christ! Did she seem upset?"

"No, not really. She was angry and told me where to stick the job. I felt a bit sorry and later…"

"So, she wasn't distraught then?"

"No, just angry. Why? What happened?"

"Seth and I found her in the summer field."

"What do you mean found her?"

"Oh, Sinead, she's cut her wrists. She's dead."

"Oh my God! Really? Dead? I shouldn't have been so mean to her. I should have checked to see if she was ok," she said, sitting down heavily on a kitchen chair. "Is that why the police are here? Do you think I should tell the police what I said to her?"

"You will probably have to make a statement. Look, it's not your fault or Seth's. Seth has just taken the police over to the summer field. I wish he hadn't gotten involved. There is something not quite right about all this. Why would Gemma walk all the way up the field and get in a water trough and then cut her wrists?"

"Is that where you found her?"

"The horses were having a strop by the trough, and Seth went up there to see if another bird had fallen in the water. He found her. I was waiting with Darragh while Seth got Moss and Connor down to pet. It's just all wrong. If I wanted to end it all, then I would probably get drunk at home and take some pills. That is why I think that someone killed her, cut her wrists open to make it look like suicide and then dumped her body in the bath. When we visited the mobile, we thought there was someone at home. We were going to try and reason with Gemma. I bet you anything that it was the murderer we caught sight of. Now Seth's got me locking myself in here because he thinks there is a nutter on the loose."

"What a nightmare. If only… I doubt there is a nutter on the loose. Seth is just being cautious. He is just a little bit overprotective after what happened with you and Tom. It is odd that Gemma chose to end her life that way. She can't stand the sight of blood. You should have heard the fuss she made when she cut her hand once. I think you are on to something. Perhaps she has been to all the stable hands and said that they are the father of her baby and one of them lost it and accidentally killed her."

"Who would do such a thing?"

"It could have been Luke. He's had her. He's got a temper, too, but I don't think it's him. He is a nice guy. No, it's not him. We will just have to wait and see what the police make of it. Why do you think the police are going to arrest Seth? Does he know that you think that?"

Jules sighed. "Yes, I hope I haven't upset him. I know he's innocent, but because he has a record and we both seem to find ourselves in murder cases, then I worry that they will think he did it. I can't bear the thought of him in prison again. I was willing to say I found Gemma to keep him out of this."

"Don't get yourself stressed out. They would have questioned him later anyway. They will question me too. He is doing the right thing reporting this. Nothing is going to happen to him."

"I hope so. Things were going so well for us. And now this. Oh, and May too. Seth was going to ring the hospital, and then the police arrived. Will you stay here tonight? I don't like to think of you all by yourself in that big, creepy house."

Sinead looked really sad for a moment, and she was about to cry. "I would like to stay. I rang the hospital when I walked up here. May is in intensive care, and she is on a respirator. They are pretty sure she has the virus. She wasn't well enough to speak to me. They have put her in a coma."

"Oh, Sinead, I am so sorry. There's me prattling on about my worries, not giving you a chance to tell me yours. Do you want a cup of tea?"

She nodded, and a tear rolled down her cheek. "I didn't realise how much I loved her. I wish I had told her that before she went to the hospital." Embarrassed, she wiped the tear away.

"You will be able to tell her that soon. They say that the virus is a bit like pneumonia, and I am sure they have something for that. Don't be sad, May is strong and is a fighter." *I hope she doesn't die.* "If it is the Coronavirus, then don't we all have to self-isolate for two weeks?"

"I guess so. Do you think I should get tested? Do they test relatives? If I have it, then I might have given it to everyone who came to the weddings."

"I think they only test you if you have symptoms. If May tests positive, then we all will have to stay in for two weeks. That's going to be a lot of fun! You and Seth will have to get Luke to cover all your lessons. Have you been in contact with Luke recently?"

"Of course, I see him nearly every day. He will have to self-isolate too. We will have to cancel all the lessons and close bed and breakfast down. Fortunately, there are not many bookings at the moment for either. I think people are feeling wary about going out since all the pubs closed. If May has the virus, then how do you think she got it? Do you think one of our guests had it? I haven't seen anyone coughing."

"Some people don't have any symptoms and just pass it to each other without realising it. It seems to be affecting older people more."

Darragh called out in delight as Barney jumped up onto the table and walked towards him. Sinead stopped him from getting too close and started to rub him underneath his chin. Barney purred loudly. "I wouldn't go near Darragh unless you want banana in your fur. Look at those hands."

"Oh my, he is a state. Let me clean you up, you messy pup. I know you are having fun mashing it into the table. I guess you've finished your lunch. Your Daddy should be back soon." *I hope he comes back. I just have a bad feeling about this.*

The door opened, and Seth smiled at them both. "My ears are burning. Were you talking about me?"

Chapter Eighteen

Seth sighed. He was ready to teach far too early. He was sitting in the warm riding school's booking office, looking through the planner for the day. Feeling frustrated, he leant back in the chair and stared out of the window for inspiration. *Monday is usually much busier than this!* He had one private lesson at ten and then a hack at midday with two new riders. *Well, that's not going to pay the bills. So, let's see, each horse needs their hooves trimmed every ten weeks, that is just over a hundred pounds a year, their vaccinations, beet and nut feed and their teeth looked at, which is another two hundred. Say two hundred and fifty pounds a year, and we have fifty horses here. So, I think that's twelve hundred and fifty pounds a year.* Seth got his phone out to work out what they needed to bring in each day to cover their costs. He tapped in the figures and then sighed. *Thirty-five pounds a day to find for the horses without any vets bills to pay or maintenance to the yard. I guess there is some money left over for my wage. I have just got used to being busy. The virus has a lot to do with this lack of business. But let's not get too down. Everything should be back to normal by the summer.*

Seth yawned and looked over at the kettle. *I need to wake up. To think, I could have stayed in bed with Jules an extra hour this morning. It was hard to leave her. I never tire of waking up with her in my arms. She was so stressed out yesterday. I don't like to see her like that. All I want to do is make her happy. She is so afraid of me going back to prison. I hope Gemma's death was just suicide. Does her wearing my jacket make me look guilty? Let's not think about it.*

The names scribbled on the planner for ten o'clock caught his eye. *Shawn and Jane Smith*. Jane Smith's name was crossed out. *He should be on honeymoon with Jane in Dublin. I hope everything is ok. I wonder why Jane's name is crossed out. This pandemic is causing people to cancel their holidays. 2020 is going to be a lean year for us all.* Seth saw Sinead walking by the office. *She looks awful. I bet she didn't get a wink of sleep last night. I wonder where she is going. Probably down to the Manor House. I'll go and see how she is.* He opened the office door and was surprised at how fresh the wind was. He rubbed his hands together to keep them warm. "Sinead, do you want a cup of tea before you go down to the house?"

She turned and smiled weakly. "No, I'd better not. Mrs Perkins will be waiting for her breakfast. I'm late already. There's not many lessons today, are there?"

"Not a lot. If you need anything done, then just let me know."

"You couldn't chop some wood, could you? The wood bunker at the house only has a couple of logs left in it."

"Yes, sure, no problem."

"I think your ten o'clock is here. Did you see that Shawn and Jane have booked that lesson? They are early. It's only nine-thirty. I can only see Shawn. Seth, he is running. He thinks he is late. I'll see you later," Sinead called as she continued on her way.

Seth waited in the doorway for Shawn. He arrived at the office out of breath and red-faced.

"I'm sorry, mate. I don't know where the time went. I am sure I gave myself plenty of time to get here, and then I got a call about the studio we wanted to hire. It doesn't look like we can rent it after all. So, if I am too late, then I will pay for the lesson."

Seth smiled. "You are half an hour early. It wasn't Jane that booked the lesson, was it?"

"Get away with yourself. I swore Jane said the lesson was at nine."

"No, it's written down in the book as ten. Sounds like she has set you up to get you here early. To be sure!"

"Anyone would think that I am late all the time," he said, laughing.

"So come and have a cup of tea first. There's been a lot going on since your wedding on Saturday."

Seth handed Shawn a cup of tea and sat down at the desk again. Shawn stood by the office window, looking out at the yard and the sand school beyond. "You know I've never had a riding lesson before. I used to ride my sister's pony when I was small, and I guess I just learnt to ride by myself. Jane thought it would be good for us to get some proper training."

"So, where is Jane? I thought you two were going to Dublin for your honeymoon."

"We will soon when they get on top of this virus. Today the government has asked the pubs to close until the end of the month. They are calling the virus Covid-19. Did you notice that? We were lucky to fit our wedding in. I will feel really bad if anyone at the party passed the virus around. Things are getting out of hand. They are going to lock everyone down any day now. Just like they have in Italy."

"The sooner they do it, the better. Business is suffering, and a couple of weeks of everyone staying in has to stop the virus spreading. It has to be done to get things back on track and to stop people dying."

"Jane has been asked to do extra shifts at the hospital. She is working in the Covid ward. It is tough going. That's why she cancelled her lesson."

"I wondered why her name was crossed out. I thought she was ill. I am glad she is ok."

"She's grand, and the pregnancy is going well. I am a lucky man. So, what has been happening here then?"

"Well, it has been a crazy weekend. You know May wasn't well and couldn't be at your reception. She's been taken into hospital, and they think she might have the Coronavirus... Covid. We are all hoping that she just had an asthma attack. She is in intensive care. Probably in Jane's ward."

"No, that's awful. I wanted to thank her for organising everything for the wedding. I'm sorry to hear that."

"Yesterday, something else happened. It is going to take me a while to get over it. One of the waitresses at your do took her own life. I found her in the horses' water trough with her wrists cut yesterday."

"Geez! That is so sad. Did you know her well?"

"She has worked at the stables and in the Manor House for a while. She, Gemma, was the one that was shouting at me at the reception."

"No! The one that accused you of being the father of her baby?"

"Oh, you heard. Yes, the very same. I think everyone heard her."

"There's no truth to the matter, is there?"

"Christ, no! I would never do that to Jules. Never in a million years!"

"Sorry, mate, keep your hair on. I didn't mean to offend."

"No offence taken. It's just so hard to hear people question my loyalty to Jules. She means the world to me."

"I know. I'm really sorry."

"Did the poor girl leave a note?"

"I don't know if she did. I told the police what she had been saying about me. I think she was obsessed with me. She has been wearing my instructor's jacket and has been making advances. She was wearing it in the water trough. I should have told the police that, but if it was suicide, then it is not going to matter what she was wearing when she died."

"What do you mean IF it was suicide?"

"Jules thinks she was murdered. I hope she is wrong; otherwise, there is going to be a full-blown enquiry. We really don't need another

149

police investigation in our lives. Not after what happened on our wedding day."

"Christ, I wouldn't worry about it until the autopsy is carried out. That's what they will do, right?"

"Oh yes, all suicides are treated as suspicious. I guess we will hear this week. If they cart me off, then you will get Jane to keep an eye on Jules, won't you?"

"Look, you are jumping the gun. It won't come to that. It is not as if you have been involved or anything. Perhaps you should have told them about the jacket."

"No, if it comes up, then I will say that I gave it to her. I don't know, perhaps I will call them. I will have a think about it."

"Christ! Waterfall West is becoming notorious! Soon you will be getting coach loads of people wanting a ghastly history tour."

"Thanks very much!" Seth said with a smile breaking across his face. "We might just have to do that to bring in some revenue and keep the horses fed."

"Are things that bad?"

"The coffers are empty, but we have just enough lessons to cover costs. I am sure things will be back to normal by June. Now then, don't worry. With Jules by my side, we will overcome any obstacle that comes our way. So, what horse do you want to ride? They are all rearing to go."

"Something kind and willing."

"I think Soldier might be the horse for you."

"So, do you want me to pay now or later?"

"We'll see how you do first. I don't want to rob you." Seth stood up and passed him a riding cap. "There you go, I will be gentle with you. I think your canter could do with working on but to be honest…"

Sinead burst into the office, her face was white, and her mascara was smudged down her cheeks. "Seth, she's gone. May has died. The hospital just rang me. I want to see her and say goodbye, but they won't let me. Oh, Seth, she's gone!"

"No? Seriously, no! That can't be."

Sinead was sobbing. "Come here." Seth held out his arms. She complied, and he put his arms around her, doing his best to comfort her. He could feel her shaking. He looked over at Shawn, who looked shocked. He hoped Shawn wasn't judging him for holding her. *He would do the same, surely?*

"I am sorry for your loss. Do you think it was the virus then?" Shawn asked.

Sinead nodded. She could barely speak for crying. "They said that she had it. She looked ill yesterday but to die the next day is shocking. What is this disease? How can it just take people like this? It is all wrong."

"No, no, it can't be," Seth declared, trying his best not to cry and to be strong for his friend.

"When Jane finishes her shift at the hospital, I'll see if she can get you into the hospital to see her in the chapel. Surely that is allowed. Leave it with me. I will see what I can do. Seth, don't worry about the lesson today. We should leave it for today. I will rebook."

"If you're sure. I feel bad."

"No, don't. I will ring you later after six. I am really sorry for your loss. Jane will be too. I'll call you later."

"Thanks, Shawn."

Shawn went back to his car, and Seth sat Sinead down. She was shaking. He took off his jacket and put it over her shoulders. *She's stopped crying, at least. I can't believe what's happened.* He put on the kettle and sifted through the cupboard for her Redbush tea bags. He added sugar for shock, hoping that she would like it sweet.

"So, what do we do now? Should I call her only living relative?" Sinead asked with her head in her hands.

"Fuck no! Tom doesn't care if she is alive or dead. But we need to tell Jules. She is going to be so upset."

Chapter Nineteen

It was lunchtime and a week into lockdown. Both the riding school and the Manor house bed and breakfast had been closed until further notice. The horses and ponies had been turned out into the fields and thought they were on holiday. Only Pringle, the laziest pony, waited patiently by the gate, ready for work. His work ethos surprised them all.

With no riding lessons to teach, Seth had put on his overalls and had been trying to fix the old tractor he had found in one of the outhouses. With the prospect of possible food shortages, the plan to till the land and grow arable crops had become all the more urgent. Fifteen sacks of seed had arrived and needed to be sown before the end of April. Tinkering on the old tractor was distracting him from thinking too much about May and Gemma. Sinead was also worrying him. He didn't know how he had done it, but he had upset her, and he was sure that she was avoiding him. *I guess she has been working all hours to avoid me and to stop herself from hurting. I can't believe that May is being buried soon, and we can't go. No wonder Sinead is upset with me. Shawn couldn't get us into the hospital to see her. Maybe that is why she is cross. Damn this virus. What time is it?* He looked at his phone. *Just after one. Lunchtime. I'm starving.*

He let himself into the Old Barn and saw Jules standing by the kitchen table. Her hands were on her hips, and her back was to him. A shaft of sunlight lit up her mass of hay-coloured curls. Darragh was sitting in his highchair and was concentrating on eating his lunch. She hadn't heard him enter, and the idea struck him to creep up and hug her. Not wanting to scare her senseless, he was about to call out when Darragh spotted him and called out Da. Jules whipped herself around and smiled.

"You weren't going to surprise me, were you? Our baby gave the game away. Did he call you Dad?"

"I think he did, and he did blow my cover. He's got your back. Come here and give your old man a hug and a kiss."

Jules looked him up and down and then deciding that his overalls were not too greasy, hugged and kissed him. He smelt of engine oil and of Seth. She could have easily stayed in his arms for the afternoon, but Darragh needed his yoghurt and perhaps something else as he was always hungry.

"I love you," he whispered in her ear.

"I love you too. I haven't made anything for lunch yet. Is cheese on toast ok?"

"That sounds grand. Do you want me to make it, and you feed our little man?" he asked, looking at various scraps of material, micro cloths and old clothes piled on the table. "What are you up to?"

"I am going to make Darragh nappy pants that we can wash. I saw a clip on YouTube, and it looks pretty easy to make. I thought that would save some money. We only have a little bit of our savings left, and nothing coming in. Nappies are so expensive, and I am frightened that there is going to be a shortage. I feel like we are all on rations at the moment. We hardly got any of our Tesco's order yesterday. Pasta, toilet roll and eggs are all in short supply."

"You don't have to do that. I am sure that this pandemic will be over in a couple of weeks, and we can all start working again."

"No, I want to make them. I know used nappies are just burnt and are causing pollution. This is going to help the environment. I am also going stir crazy in here and need something constructive to do. I know that we are isolating to protect others from getting the virus, but after one week, I feel like a bird trapped in a cage."

"The thing is, your life hasn't changed much. I think before all this, we have spent a few weeks now and again without leaving the estate."

"I know, I keep telling myself off for feeling sorry for myself, but I do have a yearning to go to Cork and look round the charity shops. This caged feeling is all in my head, and I will go for a walk later to feel the wind in my hair and the sun on my cheeks. I will be fine after that."

Seth laughed. "That's my girl."

"There's something else I want us to do later when Darragh is napping."

"Do you want to take me?"

"No, that can wait until tonight," she said, smiling. "Behave! What I want to do is sing together on TikTok and get ourselves known. I've set up an account for us. We will have to use my phone for now, but it should be ok. I've been having trouble finding a popular song that we can sing for a minute and showcase our voices. We need to think of a song that is popular and lively. Can you think of any?"

"Waterfall Way gets going pretty quickly if you miss out on the intro."

"I thought of that, but perhaps we should find a song that is likely to go viral and then bring our own songs in later on. Popular songs are ones like Savage Love. That one is going crazy at the moment. How about Galway Girl or Memories? They are lively. I was thinking of doing a minute song each week. I have big lockdown plans for us."

"I feel safe in your hands. Let's listen to some of these songs over lunch. How about the chorus of Counting Stars?"

"Maybe. Or Hey Brother or Blinding Lights. There are so many songs to choose from."

"I love it when you are on one of your creative missions. Your eyes go all sparkly and light up. So, what other plans do you have for us?"

"Mm… just one other plan. I'm not sure how much this is going to cost, but I think we should get some second-hand recording equipment and create our own S&J record label. Poor Shawn is not going ahead with his music label for a while, and we really need to get our music career off the ground."

"Goodness, I didn't expect that. If I know you, then you've already found us some equipment on eBay."

Jules smiled. "I might have, but I haven't found any equipment I want to buy yet. I've got a bit more research to do. I think that we will need to spend about two or three hundred pounds. I know that's a lot, but we can upload our music to iTunes and all the other stores and make money when people download them. We can set up social media accounts to advertise ourselves. You are looking a bit shocked. You think it is a bad idea, don't you?"

"I think that it is a great idea. The acoustics in the barn lend themselves to making recordings." Seth sighed. "It's just that I was going to ask you if it is ok if I order some parts for the tractor. The engine is sound. You can't go wrong with a fifty's diesel engine, but it has been sitting in that barn for over fifty years, and rats have eaten the electrics. If I do all the work myself, then I think we are looking at a couple of hundred pounds for materials. We will need a new battery too."

"You don't have to ask me. We need to get the tractor running. We can wait for a while to launch our label. Let's get ourselves known on TikTok first. Soon the stables and the B&B will be running, and there will be money coming in. I will just get us some microphones for now. They are not expensive."

"That sounds like a plan," Seth said as he started to wash his hands. "Do you want to go for a walk after lunch? I could put the carrier on my back for Darragh. I want to show you the fields that I am hoping to use for our farm. They are not far from here, and the land is flat and fertile."

"Yes, that will be lovely. It's such a beautiful day. Later I was thinking of spring cleaning the Manor House. It's not had a decent clean for months. Let's face it, cleaning is not Sinead's forte."

"Forte?"

"You know, she doesn't shine in that department. When we come back from our walk, shall we go down and see what needs mending or cleaning. Sinead hasn't been down there since May died. Nor have you, come to think of it. Do you like being Lord of the Manor then?"

"No, not at all. It feels strange to own or part-own an estate."

"Well, we don't own it yet. Probate has to go through first. The solicitor said six months at least, didn't he?"

"It could be longer. Ok, I'll come with you, but we should tell Sinead what we are doing. We don't want to upset her."

"Why do you say that? We are not moving in. We are only going to do a bit of maintenance before the guests come back."

"She is really touchy about the house. I didn't tell you, but when I asked her about contacting the solicitor and about the will, she told me to fuck off."

"Seth! Darragh!"

"Sorry! I know May hasn't been buried yet, but I only wanted to get all those that needed to know rung or written to. I don't care about owning the house. In fact, it could turn out to be a millstone around our necks. That place haemorrhages money. Have you seen the bills that have come into heat the place? I think that we should sell it and give the money to charity. I am happy half owning the land and the stables. That will do us."

"But May loved that house. She would be so sad if you sold it. No, that is a bad idea. I know it is a bit creepy, but the guests love it, and there are weddings booked well into next year."

"I guess you are right. The house makes money. I just wish I could make it up with Sinead. She really is not talking to me, and she is working herself into an early grave. Would you talk to her?"

"Are you sure she's not talking to you? She adores you. You must be wrong. I haven't seen her giving you the cold shoulder. I think that she has just gone into herself and is grieving. It is not very nice not being able to go to your lover's funeral. I will go and see her after lunch and take her something to eat. Like you say, she has thrown herself into work to keep her mind off things. I will take her some lunch and see how she is. I won't say you sent me. I'm sure she will be mortified if she knows you are upset. I will sort it out."

"Thanks."

"Don't worry. Seth, I'm starving. Can you make me two cheese on toast? Darragh can have a little of mine. He has a big thing about cheese at the moment."

"Ok, but have you seen our boy when he gets hold of a piece of cheese on toast? You will be lucky if you are left with a crust."

***

With a lunch bag in her hand, Jules searched for Sinead in the stable block, the office and the hay barn, but she couldn't find her. *Perhaps she's gone down to the Manor House, or she's poo picking in one of the fields. I don't miss doing that. Although I should. Connor does his fair share.*

She was thinking of walking down to the lower field to see if she was there but changed her mind as she was wearing her trainers and the track leading to the field was very muddy. She was just about to turn around and head back home when she realised that she could hear music. The tune was familiar and was coming from Sinead's Mini. *That's where she is. She's listening to Waterfall Way. How funny. We can't be in her bad books if she is listening to our music.*

Not wanting to frighten her, Jules walked over to the car and walked in front of it and waved. She saw Sinead look up and then scream. *Oh, dear! I've scared her. I didn't mean to.* Sinead smiled and beckoned her to come and sit in the car with her. As Jules got in, she turned off the music.

"I'm sorry I scared you. I notice you've got very good taste in music. That wouldn't have been Waterfall Way by any chance, would it?"

Sinead sighed. "I like listening to your voices. It helps me to relax. Why are you here? Is everything ok?"

"Well, I'm here because I was worried about you. I have hardly seen you since we went into isolation. You haven't eaten anything that I've left for you this week, so I have brought you some lunch. I don't want you to waste away. I'm not going to ask you if you are ok because I know that you're not."

Sinead went quiet for a moment. "I haven't been myself lately. Not since... I appreciate you making me lunch, but I am having trouble swallowing anything, and when I do eat something, it just tastes like cardboard. You mustn't be worried about me. I have got over worse."

"We can't get our heads around May passing like that either. I know it's hard for you, but I am sure that May would want you to soldier on without her. She wouldn't like to see you so sad. Seth is worried about you too."

"Is he? The last time we spoke, all he could talk about was wills and probate. I'm surprised he hasn't moved into the Manor House already!"

Jules was surprised at how cross she had become.

"Actually, he wants to get rid of the house, and he wants to give the proceeds to charity! I think that would be a shame after all the work that you and May put into the business."

"Did he say that then?"

She is sounding sad now. "He did. He thinks you are avoiding him, and he is upset that you have misunderstood what he was trying to say."

"Oh fuck! I have been a real bitch to him. I just needed some alone time, and... I'll make it up to him later."

"So, I guess, between us all, we will keep the wedding business and the B&B going until further notice. If it is ok with you?"

"Of course, it is."

"Seth and I want to go down to the house to see if anything needs doing. I was going to clean all the rooms ready for the guests. We have bookings for the beginning of April. If you don't want us to, then I will understand."

"Oh God, I'm so sorry. I feel really bad now." She started to cry.

"It's ok, we'll get through this together. We will make May proud, won't we?"

"I miss her so much."

Jules squeezed her hand. "Are you sure you don't want any lunch?"

"I had some cardboard soup earlier. Leave it in the fridge for me, and I promise that I will try and eat it later."

"Ok, but if you are still like this tomorrow, then maybe you should make a doctor's appointment."

"I will be fine. I don't think they can mend a broken heart."

"Sinead. I am, we are, here for you. You know that, don't you?"

"I know."

Jules wound her way down to the Old Barn, doing her best to avoid the potholes. *We are going to have to do something about this road. I wonder how much it would cost to have it repaired. Probably a small fortune. Seth is going to be so pleased when he finds out that Sinead isn't cross with him.* She walked a little faster, eager to get home. As she approached the barn, she saw Barney in the flowerbeds digging. *Well, that's nice. Now I know why it smells like cat's wee every time we open the front door.* Barney flicked his paws and then ran along the front of the house and into the shrubbery.

Jules got to the front door and looked through to see if she could see Seth and Darragh. *I wonder where they've gone to.* She felt in her pocket for her keys and then saw a filthy hand come out of the bushes and push Barney away. The hairs on the back of her neck stood up, and her heart began to pound. Finding the right key to open the door, she fumbled to get it in the lock.

"Julia, help me," whispered a man.

She knew the voice. "Tom? Is that you?" she whispered back. Her heart was still pounding in her chest, and her mind was racing.

"Please help me."

"You shouldn't be here... Why are you here?"

"Help me. I need food."

She got a little closer, and Barney started to rub himself against her leg. She picked him up and then pulled back the bush and gasped when she saw Tom. He was sitting on the floor, hugging his knees. His skin was dirty, and his blond hair had been hacked off. What was left was grey and grimy. With a pathetic look on his face, his eyes met hers. They were watery and sunk deep into his sockets. He was having trouble speaking.

"I need food and somewhere to stay," he mumbled.

"I can't help you. You shouldn't have come back here. I can give you food, but then you must go. If Seth finds out that you're here, then God knows what he will do to you."

"I don't care. I am dying."

"Do you have Cancer or Covid?"

"I might as well have. You have done this to me. I cannot live without you."

"I have nothing to do with the state you are in. Do you hear me?" He was making her cross.

"I need food. I haven't eaten for a week."

"Here then. I've got a bag of lunch. It's not much, but it will help." She held it out for him, not wanting to get too close. He grabbed the bag and ripped it open. She watched as he desperately stuffed a sandwich into his mouth. *Christ, he is like a crazed animal. How did he get himself into this state? Why didn't he go back to Australia? Why is he putting this on my shoulders? Where will he go? He is not strong enough to find somewhere else to go. Would it hurt if he spent one night at the Manor House?* She took the key to the Manor House off her fob.

"You can stay in the house tonight. Just tonight, though."

"I was going to ask my sister to take pity on me, but the house is all locked up. Where is she?"

"May is... May is away, and Sinead is staying with me." *I can't tell him that she's dead, can I?* "Here's the key." She dropped it at his feet. "Just one night, and then you must go. The house is closed because of Covid. Do you understand? Leave the key under the plant pot by the front door when you go. We are going out for a walk in a minute, so you will need to keep yourself hidden until we are gone."

He nodded. "Thank you. You have saved my life. I knew you would."

Disgusted, Jules let the bush flick back, and it was a relief not to see his scrawny body or his wretched face. Still holding Barney, she turned to go.

"I love you, Julia."

Feeling cross, Jules said nothing and walked away. She found Seth and Darragh sound asleep on their bed. Seth's arms were around Darragh, and she stood there mesmerised. Their faces were so peaceful and serene looking compared to Tom's. *How can he say he loves me after the way he has treated me? What does he know about love? I should have called the police. I shouldn't have helped him. What have I done?*

Chapter Twenty

Seth had been awake for an hour and was sitting up in bed, with his earphones on, watching with some amusement various TikTok videos. Jules and Darragh were fast to sleep, and he was doing his best not to disturb them as some of the posts were making him laugh out loud. He had found an Irish dad dancing in his dressing gown to Blinding Lights with his teenage children, and it was cracking him up.

Realising that he had been watching these videos for far too long, he dragged himself away and checked their TikTok profile to see how their video was doing. He was surprised to see how many people had liked them singing together and had left them messages. *I'll have to go through the inbox later and reply.* It had taken them a while to choose a song that would showcase both their voices. Jules had left him to choose a song as she couldn't decide, and she seemed to be having trouble concentrating. S*he wasn't herself yesterday. I hope she hasn't come down with the virus. She was so restless in bed last night.* Seth clicked on their first video to watch it. They had finally chosen Maroon 5's 'Memories', and he had been pleased with their efforts. It was strange seeing himself singing. He wasn't sure if he liked watching himself. *We will sound so much better when the microphones arrive.* Bringing his phone closer, he studied Jules' face and then shook his head. *She looks like she wants to cry. Something is going on.* He put down his phone and looked down at her, and stroked her hair gently. *Will you wake up and talk to me?* He knew better than to wake her up when she was sleeping deeply, but he really needed to find out what was eating her up. *So, it is six-thirty, and Darragh will be awake soon. I'll get her a cup of tea and a hot cross bun. The smell of a bun toasting is bound to bring her round.*

Jules knew she was dreaming. She was walking up the stairs in the Manor House. She could hear the grandfather clock in the hall ticking in words – *don't go, don't go, don't go*. She had forgotten why she was going up the stairs anyway. She knew she was afraid but not sure why. A huge cat was sitting at the top of the stairs. The cat was a large tabby cat, and it had a disturbing smile on its face. Jules tried not to look at the cat's eyes, but she knew that it wanted her to come to him. She had seen those eyes before. She told it to shoo and to leave her alone and that she wasn't looking for a cat.

Jules turned over, trying to wake herself up, but the dream persisted. She was looking for someone, but she was fearful that they would appear. *I must wake myself up. I don't want to carry on with this dream. Who am I looking for? I can smell toast. Is someone cooking toast? Is it Easter already? Wake up!* She opened her eyes and saw Seth standing by her bed. He put down a cup of tea and a plate on the bedside cabinet next to her. He sat on the edge of the bed and kissed her.

"Is my beautiful girl awake now?"

"Oh, Seth, you've made me breakfast. You sweet thing. What time is it?"

"Nearly seven. Are you ok? You tossed and turned last night, and I was starting to worry. Let me feel your head." He placed his hand on her forehead and ran the back of his finger down her cheek. "No, you just feel bed warm." He smiled at her and felt relieved that she didn't have a fever.

"I am fine. I was just dreaming a lot last night. Did I wake you?"

"Not really. You know what I'm like. Awake at the crack of dawn. So, I was looking on TikTok, and you'll be amazed to know that we have nearly fifty followers and over a thousand likes. I think 'Memories' was the right song to sing in the end. We'll sing some of our own songs when we have more followers."

Jules sat up and picked up her tea. "I told you we'd do well," she said smiling. "We will have to do another song in a few days' time. It's strange having you home in the mornings. I am quite liking being brought tea and breakfast in bed. Lockdown is suiting me. Just another week to go, and things will be back to normal."

"I aim to please. So, what shall we do today? I can't do much on the tractor until the parts arrive. We didn't go down to the Manor House yesterday. Sinead said that she will come down too, and we can all work out what needs doing. I don't know what you said, but she came and gave me a hug and said that she was sor..." He stopped talking. *What have I said? She looks like she has seen a ghost.* "So, what's going on? You're not still upset with me about me ringing the police about Gemma?"

Jules stared up into his big brown eyes, surprised by how perceptive he was. *He knows something is wrong. Keeping it from him is tearing me apart. I can't hide what happened yesterday any longer. He needs to know about Tom. But Tom will be on his way soon, and then no harm will have been done.*

"Jules?"

No, I have to tell him. We promised to always be honest with each other. "Please don't be mad with me, but something bad happened yesterday."

"With Sinead?"

"No, after I went to see her. I should have come and got you to sort it out, but I was afraid that things might get out of hand."

"Out of hand?"

"Oh, Seth! Just let me tell you, and you must promise you won't do or say anything until I've finished."

"I promise. Just tell me what happened?"

"So, when I got back home, there was someone waiting for me. At first, I didn't recognise him, and I thought it was a tramp. He was filthy, and he begged me for food. I gave him Sinead's lunch. He was so hungry he couldn't stand. He needed a place to stay, and I told him that I couldn't help but then..."

"So, you know this man?"

Jules nodded. "Take a deep breath, and don't be mad."

"I'm not mad, but I will be driven mad if you don't tell me."

"Oh, Seth, it was Tom!"

"Tom Stone?"

"Yes. I panicked and told him he could stay one night at the Manor House to recover, and then he must go in the morning. He was emaciated and weak." She looked at Seth, waiting for the red mist to descend, but he was managing to stay calm.

"You should have come and got me. How did he get into the house?"

"I gave him a key. I told him to leave it under a flowerpot when he went."

"Don't you realise that he was playing you? Too weak to walk! Did he crawl here? I have no idea why he is back or why he was in the state he was in, but there is something not quite right about this. He has probably got wind of May's death and thinks he owns Waterfall West. We have got ourselves a squatter!"

"He doesn't know that May has died. He said he knocked on the door, hoping that she would take pity on him."

"That man is devious. I don't believe he knocked on the door. No, he is not going to get away with it. I'm going down to the house, and I am going to make sure he leaves the premises. Fuck! Why did you give him a key?"

Jules was beginning to panic. Seth was starting to lose it. "You should have seen him. It was no act. I barely recognised him. I know I shouldn't have helped him, but I took pity on him. I'm sorry, but as much as I hate that man, I couldn't let him die outside our house." She started to cry. "Do you hate me?"

Seth's mind was whirling, and he was having trouble controlling the urge to go down and throttle Tom. He couldn't understand why she would want to help this man. *Does she care for him in some twisted way?*

"Seth, I'm sorry. I really am. Please hold me. I couldn't bear it if you hated me."

He felt her hand in his, and she was squeezing it, doing her best to make him listen to what she was saying. *Why is she asking me if I hate her? No, I never want her to think that.* He could see her tear-filled eyes and was distressed that she was in pain. The rage he had felt a moment ago was beginning to subside. "Of course, I don't hate you. Please don't cry." He hugged her and then kissed her. "You mean the world to me. I just can't bear the thought of that man near you. Not after what he did to you. I am going down to the house to make sure he is gone. If he is still there, then I think that he needs to know about May and who owns the estate now before I see him on his way."

"I'll come with you."

"No, I need to do this alone."

***

As Seth walked down to the Manor House, he saw Sinead standing in the middle of the sand school, free reining one of the horses. Sparkle, a tri-coloured cob, was cantering around her and bucked occasionally, enjoying being schooled. Seth stopped for a moment and considered whether or not he should tell her about Tom. *The thing is, if he is still in the house, then I am going to lose my temper. I know I am. If Sinead comes with me, then she will be able to diffuse any unpleasantness. Will Jules be annoyed if I ask Sinead to come with me when I turned her down? No, she'll understand. I want him to have nothing to do with her.* "Sinead? Can you spare me a moment?"

She looked over at him and waved.

She thinks I am waving at her. He walked towards her, and Sinead asked Sparkle to stop. The horse cantered up to the far end of the school and then came to an abrupt halt near to an inviting patch of grass. Eagerly, with her head under the fence, she cropped the grass.

Sinead opened the gate to meet Seth. "Where were you off to, then?"

"I was going down to the Manor House to evict an unwelcome guest. Will you come with me? It would help if you were there. I don't want to lose my temper."

Sinead looked puzzled. "But we don't have anyone staying there."

"We do now. So yesterday, unbeknown to me, Tom Stone turned up and gave Jules a sob story saying he was starving and needed somewhere to stay. She's only given him a key to the house and let him stay there last night. She says he doesn't know about May. I am not so sure."

"Shit! What is he doing back here? I thought he was in Australia."

"I don't know. I'd like to say it wasn't because of Jules, and he has hit hard times, but I think that it is unlikely."

"Yes, I'll come with you. We should tell him about May and about the will. Oh, and about Gemma too. Why do you think he is here because of Jules?"

"Just a gut feeling," he replied as they made their way out of the stable courtyard and towards the Manor House.

As they got closer, they noticed smoke coming out of the chimneys.

"Well, someone has made themselves at home. Does that look like the actions of a dying man?" Seth asked.

"No, not really."

After checking to see if the key had been left under the flowerpot and seeing that it hadn't been, Seth opened the front door and was relieved that it opened. "The door hasn't been nailed up. That's something, I suppose. I thought we were going to be dealing with a squatter."

"Where do you think he will be? Do you think he has gone up to his old room in the attic? Fuck, it's hot in here!"

"The smoke we saw coming from the chimney was coming from one of the reception rooms. He is probably sitting in a wingback chair by a blazing fire and smoking a victory pipe. Just wait until we tell him who May left the estate to. I can't wait to see his face."

They walked through the lounge. The fire was lit, but there was no sign of Tom. The parlour fire was lit too. Seth felt one of the radiators. "He's only got the heating on as well. What is he playing at?"

"It was freezing last night. This house is damp and cold when nobody is... Seth, I heard something!"

"I didn't. All I can hear is all that wood that I chopped going up in smoke."

"There! I heard it again. Someone is calling for help. I think it was coming from the hall."

They walked back into the hall and stood in silence, and listened.

"Help..."

"I heard it then. It was faint but not that far away. TOM?" Sinead called.

"Help..."

"I think it was coming from upstairs," Seth said, looking suspiciously at the staircase. "I don't trust him. It's probably a trick. You should wait here in case he jumps out on us. I don't want you getting hurt."

"No, don't leave me here alone. He sounds feeble, and if it is a trick, then two against one is better."

"Ok, but if there is any trouble, then keep back. He's a lightweight, and I can handle him. Let's see what the Toad has in store for us."

"Help... Julia, help me."

What the fuck does he want with her? He is going to get a shock when he sees me.

Cautiously, they climbed the grand staircase, looking upwards at the landings above for any sign of movement. They didn't have to go far before they came across him lying at the top of the first flight of stairs on the landing. Seth was shocked to see the state he was in. He was filthy and ragged, just as Jules had described him to be. Not believing his eyes, Seth nudged him with his foot to make sure he wasn't seeing things. Tom mumbled something, and they weren't sure what he was saying, but they both heard Julia's name being mentioned again. He was drifting in and out of consciousness, and his eyes were not focusing properly.

"He is asking for Jules, I think," Sinead said, frowning.

Seth looked down at him in disgust. "Christ, the man looks like he is dying."

"Should we call an ambulance for him?"

"I don't think he is ill. Jules said he is just starving. You can't call an ambulance for that. Anyway, they are busy enough with Covid cases."

"I guess he just needs feeding and water then. We could try that, and if he gets any worse, then we will ring for one," Sinead said, feeling the pulse in his wrist.

"Or we could carry him out of here and leave him on a grass verge for the crows to do their bit." Seth shook his head. "I didn't mean that, but I can't be nursing this bastard."

Sinead sighed. "I will get him some soup. We will have to get him into a bed and sit him up. If you take his shoulders, and I'll take his feet, then we will carry him through to the annexe. It will be easier to nurse him there, and then I won't have to walk through this creepy house."

"You are joking?"

"No, Seth. He will die if we don't look after him."

Seth huffed. "I can't believe I am going to help this man. This can't be happening!"

Seth's phone started to ring. "Hold on, let me take this quickly. I am waiting for seed and tractor parts to be delivered." He got his phone out and, seeing an unknown number took the call.

"Is that Sebastian Hearn?"

Seth shuddered as only the police used that name. "It is?"

"This is Detective Inspector Lucy O'Leary. My colleague and I would like to visit today at eleven and take a statement from you. We would like to have a friendly chat about the Gemma Day case."

"A friendly chat indeed! When have the police ever wanted to have a friendly chat?"

"We need to talk to you."

"The thing is, I won't be able to see you face to face as we are all having to self-isolate at Waterfall West. The owner of the estate, May, died of Covid a little over a week ago."

"I am well aware of the situation, but it is most urgent that we meet with you."

"Can't this be done over the phone?"

"We are willing to chat with you over the phone, but as we will be recording our conversation, we would prefer it if we were able to see you."

"You say record. Am I being questioned then? Is this about the jacket? I was going to tell you that she was wearing my jacket when I found her, but it slipped my mind. Apart from that, I have told you everything I know about Gemma's suicide."

"Mr Hearn, this is a homicide case. We need to eliminate you from our enquiries. When we arrive, please remain inside your house where we are able to see you. We will call you, and we would prefer it if there were no other members of the household present."

"I see. So, it wasn't suicide?"

"No, Mr Hearn, Gemma Day was murdered. We will see you at eleven."

Seth put his phone back in his pocket and could see that Sinead was alarmed. "Did you hear all that?"

She nodded. "So, she was murdered?"

"It seems so. I am not looking forward to telling Jules. Will you come up to the barn and be there when I tell her that they are going to interview me. I know she is going to freak out."

"Sure, she's not herself at the moment, and this arsehole being here is not helping. I know he is disgusting, but we need to get him sorted first. I would hold your breath when we pick him up. I think he's shit himself."

Chapter Twenty-one

Listening to Blinding Lights on the radio and gripping a hot cup of tea in both hands, Jules sipped the liquid and looked anxiously out of the window, willing Seth to return. It had been over an hour since he had gone down to the Manor House, and she was starting to worry. *I hope Tom has gone. What will happen if he is still there? Something must have happened. Seth has been gone too long. Shall I ring him? No, I'm sure he will be back in a minute. I am so relieved that I told him about yesterday. All things considered, I think Seth took my dark secret very well. Tom was in a terrible state. I hope Seth isn't too hard on him if he is still there. I must stop myself from thinking about what might happen. Where are you, Seth? Why am I waiting at the window? I need to do something to keep myself busy and stop myself from fretting.*

Three black crows landed on the front path and started to fight. One of the crows had another on its back, and the third crow was pecking at the defenceless crow's stomach. *God no, they are going to kill it. How horrible! Why are they doing that to their own kind?* She knocked on the window hard to stop them. Frightened by the noise, all three crows took to the air, and she watched the victim fly off, fleeing for its life. The other two crows followed in hot pursuit. *Life can be so brutal sometimes.*

Darragh called out 'Da' from his bedroom, and she smiled. *I am going to be really busy now that my little man is awake. I can't wait to see his sweet face light up when I walk into his room. I wonder if he will ever learn how to say Mum?*

As Jules walked back into the living area with Darragh on her hip, she found Seth and Sinead standing in the kitchen talking. She hadn't heard them come in. *I wonder if Seth has told Sinead about Tom. Yes, he is sure to have.* "So, how did it go?" Just the look on their faces told her all she needed to know.

Sinead was the first to speak. "He was still in the house."

"We found him on the first landing, too weak to walk or talk. He is going to have to stay in the house for a few days until he is strong enough to leave. We took him through to the annexe, and Sinead fed him some chicken soup."

"I told you he was in a bad way."

"Why do you think he has let himself go like that?" Sinead asked. "Why do you think he came back here?"

"He's here because of me. Yesterday he said that it was because of me he was wasting away." She hadn't meant to say that, but it had come out of her mouth without thinking. She looked across at Seth, and she could see that he was in pain. "I wish he hadn't come back here. Needless to say, I won't be visiting the patient." She carried Darragh over to his highchair and put him in it. "There you go, my sweet boy. Are you ready for breakfast?"

"He kept saying that he needed to see you. I think that man is obsessed with you," Sinead announced.

Jules saw Seth scowl. "Seth, don't look so worried. You know what it's like to have someone fixated on you. I used to fear Tom, but now I just see him for what he is. He is just a sad old man that preys on young girls. He can't help himself. He is sick. Does he know what happened to Gemma? Another of his victims."

"No, he wasn't with it enough to hold a conversation. About Gemma," Seth said, looking worried. "Now, I don't want you to panic, but the police are coming here at eleven for a friendly chat. Like you thought, it wasn't suicide. Gemma was murdered. They are going to take a statement over the phone. We are in quarantine, so we will be inside the house and the police outside."

"Seriously? Gemma was murdered? What happened?"

"I don't know. They did ask that they speak to me privately, but they can't expect me to turf you and Darragh out into the street. They are going to record the conversation."

Jules frowned. "That doesn't sound much like a friendly chat. Oh, Seth, this doesn't feel right. There must be something that is making them think that you are connected."

Feeling uneasy, Seth shifted his weight a little. *Should I tell her about the jacket?*

"Gemma was wearing Seth's jacket when they removed her from the bath. They are probably going to ask him why." Sinead declared. Seth shot her an irritated glance.

Jules gasped. "You're joking. Did you know about this?" she asked him.

"Look, I didn't want you to worry. Sinead says she has been wearing it for a while. I didn't give her it or anything, and I certainly didn't ask for it back."

She shook her head. Her mind was whirling. "There is more to this Gemma thing than meets the eye. So, you told the police about the jacket then?"

"I did."

"Good. Just because she was wearing your clothing doesn't mean that you murdered her. We need to think this through. So, you were with me that night she was murdered, right? Did you go out without me knowing?"

Seth was shocked and amazed as he watched her process all the information. He didn't know whether to laugh or cry. "No, I didn't slip out while you were sleeping and commit murder. You really should have been a detective, you know. Christ, I hope the police don't think that I killed her!"

"Seth, this is no joke. We have to make sure your story is water-tight. I am going to stay by your side. Sinead, will you take Darragh for a walk when they come?"

"Yes, of course. I'll take him to see Pringle. That pony is missing the kids."

"I would like you to stay with me, but the police might not let you."

"They can't do anything about it if it is just a friendly chat. If it is more than that, then you can refuse to speak unless there is a solicitor present."

"I am sure it won't come to that."

***

Detective Inspector Lucy O'Leary and her colleague appeared at the window and knocked on it, taking them both by surprise. Seth and Jules had been expecting to see a police car draw up and were sitting at the kitchen table waiting to be interviewed. Their glass-fronted house allowed them to see both police officers from head to toe. They were surprised to see that Lucy was wearing a black suit and high heels.

"I bet she struggled to walk down the track in those shoes," Seth said, picking up his phone, ready to take her call.

"We really need to do something with the road; it's a death trap. Should I offer them tea or coffee?"

"No, we don't want to infect them with Covid."

"Jules, don't you think she looks like one of my sisters? Charlene, perhaps? She has the same long dark hair and dark brown eyes as most of my sisters. They are so similar. How old do you think she is?"

"I guess she is in her thirties. Yes, she does look like a Hearn."

DI O'Leary smiled and pointed to her phone. Her colleague, a much older man, dressed in a thick tweed overcoat, was holding an old-fashioned tape recorder and held it up to show them that he was pressing play. Seth's phone started to ring.

"Well, here goes. I'll put it on loudspeaker so that we can both hear." He laid the phone on the table, feeling apprehensive and knew that this was going to be more than a friendly chat.

"Good morning. Can I confirm that I am speaking with Sebastian Hearn, born 30 Sept 1989, current address The Old Barn, The Waterfall West Estate, Waterfall?"

"You are. I have my wife and advisor here with me, Julia Hearn."

"We were hoping to talk to you on your own."

"I have nothing to hide. And I think I need a witness here to make sure my words are not manipulated later on. You haven't cautioned me."

"You are not being arrested, but I have to tell you that this interview is being recorded and may be used as evidence in court should you be prosecuted. Today all we need from you is a statement."

"So, this is an interview rather than a chat with a statement thrown in. I told you everything I knew on the day I found Gemma. I have nothing more to add."

"Not everything."

"No, but I told you about the jacket when I spoke to you earlier this morning."

"If you don't mind, I'd like to start at the beginning. We need a record of the events that led up to the death of Gemma Day."

"Ok then."

"How did you know Gemma Day?"

"She worked at the stables here and later in the Manor House as a cleaner."

178

"How long have you known Gemma Day?"

"For around four to five years."

"Were you ever in a relationship with her?"

"No. Definitely not!"

"You are sure about that?"

"I'm sure."

"I am going to show you a picture of Gemma's bedroom in the mobile home. If you could come closer and have a look, then I would appreciate it."

Seth stood up, picked up the phone and went to the window. The detective held the A4 photo against the window so he could see.

Gemma had been staying in the same bedroom as he and Jules had shared when they had lived in the mobile home when they first came to Waterfall West. The walls of the bedroom were festooned with pictures of him. Some had been taken at the stables, and some had been taken when he and Jules had been singing at The Elbow. He noticed that any photo showing Jules had black marker pen across her face. There were even a pair of his riding gloves pinned to the wall. "Christ, I didn't know that she had all that stuck on the wall."

"Can you confirm that you have seen multiple photos of yourself pinned to Gemma Day's bedroom wall?"

"It seems so."

"So, you have never visited Gemma in her home?"

"No, of course not." Seth walked away and sat back down next to Jules. She was looking shocked and had managed to see the photo from where she was sitting.

"Gemma obviously had a thing for me."

"Does that make you angry?"

"No, but it creeps me out to see how obsessed she was."

"Did you lead her on in any way?"

"No, I never even looked at her. She must have been star struck. Jules and I are making a name for ourselves in the music industry and have a following. Sometimes fans get a bit carried away. We got mobbed by girls the last time we played in Cork. So, if she didn't take her life, then what happened to her?"

"We were hoping that you might be able to tell us that."

Seth didn't like where the conversation was going.

"So, for the record, can you please tell us what happened on the evening of Saturday 14 March 2020, the night of the Smith's wedding? It has come to our attention that there was a row with yourself and Gemma Day that night."

"I wouldn't call it a row exactly. I was dancing with Jules, and Gemma came over to us and demanded that I dance with her. When I refused, she started shouting at me and accused me of being the father of her unborn baby."

"Are you the father of her baby?"

"Of course not! I've never been with her."

"Did her accusation make you angry?"

"Yes, she was making me look like a right bastard in front of everyone."

"You have recently served time at Ford prison. It seems that you have a bit of a temper. We have a report that you struck another inmate and broke his jaw."

Seth went quiet for a moment and looked anxiously at Jules. *Fuck, I've never told her about that. She's frowning.*

"That was years ago. Look, I shouldn't have hit him. He called me a dirty gypsy, and he was picking on a young lad. I do have a temper, but if you are insinuating that I killed Gemma in a rage, then you are wrong."

"Can you tell me where you were between the hours of 1am, and 4am on the morning of 15 March 2020?"

"I was in bed, asleep with Jules. That's correct, isn't it, Jules?"

"Yes, it is."

"So, you didn't leave the barn at any point and go over to the caravan and see Gemma Day?"

"I told you I was in bed with Jules all night."

"I don't think you should say anymore," Jules whispered.

"No, you are right. I want to terminate this interview now." Seth ended the call.

"Well, that wasn't pleasant, was it?" He watched DI O'Leary look at her phone, surprised to see that he had cut her off. His phone started to ring again. "I guess I should answer." He could see her pointing to the recording machine, and she was indicating that she had turned the machine off. Seth took the call. "I've said everything that needed to be said. You have your statement. If you want to ask me anything more, then I think I will need a solicitor present."

"That's fine, Seth, we have everything we need. You do understand that we have to leave no stone unturned. Gemma was murdered, and we need to find her killer."

"I understand. How do you know that it was murder?"

"I am afraid we can't disclose that with you. Do you know of anyone that might want to harm Gemma? An ex-boyfriend, perhaps? You said that you both saw someone in the caravan just before you found Gemma in the water trough. Do you have any idea who that might be?"

"It could have been anyone. I don't like to speak ill of the dead, but Gemma did have a bit of a bad reputation, and it could have been any of the lads that work at the stables here."

"You should talk to Tom Stone," Jules said.

Seth shot her a surprised look.

"Who is Tom Stone?" DI O'Leary asked.

"He is May's brother. May died of Covid recently. We haven't told him yet. He is staying at the Manor House. He used to be Gemma's boyfriend. He is probably the baby's father. The last time we saw them, they were having unprotected sex."

"Really! I am sorry to hear about May. Why haven't you told him about his sister's death?"

Jules sighed. "He is not well himself, and we were not sure how he would take the news."

"Do you have a contact number for him?"

"No. I don't think he has a phone at the moment. Yesterday, he came to Waterfall West in a very sorry state. He didn't appear to have any possessions with him," Jules said, holding Seth's hand.

"I see. Is he in isolation? Do you think he has Covid?"

"He has been in contact with us."

"Is he showing any virus symptoms?"

"No, I don't think so. He is just weak and malnourished. He looks like he has been sleeping rough," Seth said. "I think he has mental health issues."

"Would he be able to talk to us? What do you think, Rufus? It does seem odd that he has appeared out of nowhere in such a sorry state."

"Yes, he is an ex-boyfriend. I think that we should talk to him."

"Would you be able to let us into the Manor House?"

"I don't think that we should go into the house. How do we know that Tom Stone hasn't got Covid?" Rufus said, looking agitated.

"Damn this pandemic. It is making our job impossible," DI O'Leary was looking cross. "Seth, would you be able to go down to the house and allow Mr Stone to use your phone? Would you be able to help him to a window?"

"Christ, no! I am not going near that man again!"

"Why is that?"

"Let's just say we don't see eye to eye."

"I'll have to go then," Jules announced.

"I don't think so."

"Sinead then?"

"No, it's ok. I'll do it. He will probably have to lean on me to get to a window. I'll go. It will be interesting to see what he has got to say."

"We'd prefer it if you left the phone with him and collected it later."

"Oh, for God's sake! Fine! I will meet you in the carpark at the bottom. Take care walking back to your car. The road needs fixing."

"Thank you for your cooperation."

"No problem. Can I ask you a personal question?"

"Ok... What's that then?"

"Your family are from Dingle, aren't they?"

DI O'Leary looked shocked for a moment. "I have family in Dingle. I was born there."

"I thought as much."

"You haven't heard of Jethro Hearn, have you?"

"I have, but that was a long time ago. Why do you ask?"

"I would bet my shirt off my back that we have the same father. I can spot a Hearn a mile off."

"I don't think so. My Da and I are really close."

"I would ask your Mam a few questions tonight, and you might be surprised to find she has a dark secret."

"I don't think that I want to. I am happy with the Da I have."

"Fair enough."

***

Seth drove the Jaguar along the track towards the stable yard. He gritted his teeth like the bottom of the car caught on the road as he disappeared into a pothole. *I need some hard-core. Where am I going to get that from? Let me think... I know. I could demolish one of the old brick pigsties and borrow some gravel from the main drive. If only the tractor was working, then I could put the rubble in a trailer and pull it along. I guess the wheelbarrow will have to do. Let's get this ordeal over with, and then I can set to work on the road. I wonder if the Toad is able to walk yet.*

Seth reached the lower carpark by the Manor House and noticed that DI O'Leary was looking through her boot for something. She was wearing only one shoe. The other was lying on its side on the tarmac in two pieces. *Waterfall West is not really the place for high heels.* For a second, he remembered his mother wearing heels in the garden behind the house, and he shuddered as he closed that thought down.

He parked the car up and, keeping his distance from Lucy O'Leary, possibly his half-sister, approached and smiled as he watched her pulling on a pair of bright pink trainers. *Nearly all the Hearn girls love the colour pink.* "I should have warned you about the road leading up to the barn. I hope you didn't hurt yourself," he called. "The track will be patched up the next time you visit. Hopefully, you won't have to."

"I'll live. So which window shall we stand by to talk to Tom Stone?"

She's sounding a bit pissed off. I hope I didn't upset her by suggesting we might be related. "He is in the annexe at the back of the house. There is a conservatory attached to it, so I will bring him in there. I hope he has had a wash. He didn't smell too good the last time I saw him. I'll see you round there," he said, walking towards the front door. *I really don't want to do this, but it has to be done.*

Seth found Tom sitting in the annexe on the sofa watching television. He didn't hear him come in and visibly jumped when he saw Seth. He had some toast in his hand and dropped it on the floor. Seth was pleased to see that he had showered and changed. *Is he wearing some of May's clothes? Surely not!*

"What are you doing here? Where's Julia?"

"She's not coming. Look, you have to forget her. She is my wife now and wants nothing to do with you."

"You don't understand. My life is not worth living unless I can be with her."

"So why were you with Gemma then?"

"She meant nothing. I don't expect you to understand."

"This has to stop, here and now! I want you out of here by sundown. You don't look too bad today. Perhaps your pathetic state yesterday was all just an act. You were strong enough to light all the fires, and somehow you are up and dressed today and seem just fine."

"It was no act. I am not strong enough to go anywhere. Anyway, this is my home."

"Look, there are things you need to know. May died of Covid just over a week ago, and she has left the estate to Sinead and myself. So no, this is not your home. You are not welcome here."

"NO! YOU LIE! My dear sister?"

"Don't give me that shite. You didn't care for her."

"I don't believe you. She wouldn't leave everything to a scumbag."

"And Sinead. Not just me. I can show you a copy of the will if you like."

"She wouldn't cut me out of the will. Not my dear sister."

"Look, I haven't got time for this. It is what it is. The police are here to ask you some questions about Gemma."

Tom looked shocked. "They're here?"

"Yes, they are outside and want you to go through to the conservatory so they can talk to you via my phone. Because of the Covid thing, they can't see you face to face."

"Why, what's happened to Gemma?"

"I will let them tell you that. Are you strong enough to walk? Do you need a hand?"

"I can manage."

Seth's phone started to ring. He passed it to Tom. "Her name is DI Lucy O'Leary and Rufus. I didn't catch his last name. They are waiting outside to interview you."

"Who told them that I was here? Was it you?"

"No, it was Julia, actually."

"I don't believe you. She wouldn't betray me like that."

"Stop the theatrics. Take the call, get this over with and get your backside out of here after. You really don't want me to drag your scrawny body out of here. I am that close to doing you serious damage!"

Chapter Twenty-two

Seth wiped the sweat off his brow with the back of his hand and let the mallet rest for a moment. The March spring sunshine was beating down on him, and he was tempted to take off his t-shirt. *Whoever built these pigsties certainly knew what they were doing. Just a few more blows, and I should have enough rubble to fill all the holes.*

Seth shuddered and looked around himself nervously. This was the second time that he had been down to the piggery, and he didn't like being there. Something was spooking him out, and he couldn't work out what it was. The cobbled courtyard was covered in weeds and moss. On the far side of the yard was an ugly red brick outbuilding where fifteen pigs had once been housed. The outside walls were stained black where the guttering leaked rainwater. Opposite the sad-looking building were six individual brick-built pig pens with a small covered sleeping area. The tiled roofs had fallen in, and the walls between each sty were crumbling. The wooden doors had long since decayed, and piles of rotting wood were entwined into a mass of brambles and weeds in each sty's open enclosure.

He was pretty sure that the farm in Dingle where he had been born had a dilapidated pig farm nearby, and he was sure that he had visited it with one of his brothers, but they had been warned off by an angry farmer. He remembered the sound of angry pigs squealing and crying out as he and his brother ran home, frightened for their lives. *Was I with James, or was it Charlene?* He struggled to remember his childhood in Ireland. It seemed to be such a long time ago. All he could remember was being at Crow Farm in Sussex. *Maybe I'll remember everything when I am old and grey. Perhaps all your memories come flooding back when you have nothing better to do than pass the time of day.*

Seth didn't feel too bad about demolishing the end pigsty as two of the walls had fallen in on themselves. Recovered and ready to swing the mallet, he gazed down at the remains of the walls choosing where to hit next, when he noticed that pig's trotters and several jawbones with teeth attached were littered on the floor. *Surely pigs weren't slaughtered here! How strange that there are bones here. I wonder if Sinead still wants us to help her convert the piggery into her home. Would a vegetarian want to live in a place like this? I wouldn't fancy living here. It's way too spooky.*

Seth took a deep breath and lifted up the heavy mallet but stopped when he saw Sinead running down the track towards him. *Oh heck, her face is bright red, and she looks fuming. Perhaps I should have asked her first before demolishing this.* He waved at her and waited for her to yell at him.

"WHAT THE FUCK DO YOU THINK YOU ARE DOING?"

"I'm sorry, I should have asked. I need some hard-core to fill the potholes."

"I know, Jules just told me. I don't go around smashing down your home when I feel like it. You are such an arsehole sometimes!"

"I said I was sorry. You are not going to be living in these old pig pens, are you? They will need clearing before you move into the piggery. This one was practically rubble anyway." *Good, she is calming down.*

"I want to keep pigs in them, actually. Ok, I grant you, this one was not that great, but the other five can be fixed up."

"Why do you want to keep pigs? You are not going to become a meat-eater, are you?"

Sinead's eyes narrowed for a moment, and then she smiled. "Are you mad? I like pigs. I want to have a sanctuary for rescue pigs."

Seth laughed. "I've heard it all now. I promise I won't touch the rest. So, are you going to live here and be our distant neighbour, then?"

"That is the plan. But…"

"We should start working on the piggery and turn it into a home for you. It looks like lockdown is going to go on into May. We have plenty of time on our hands to get this project going. It shouldn't take much to fix the old place up. I guess there is a water supply somewhere."

"So, are you willing to help your grumpy old friend fix it up then?"

"Of course. I just need to plough the fields and sow my seeds, and then I am all yours. Have you made a plan yet?"

Sinead shook her head. "I was going to live in the annexe with May, so no, I haven't. This is plan B. I'm sorry I yelled at you just now. You are not an arsehole."

"You've called me worse before. I don't take much notice. You have a bit of a hothead. I know you like me, really."

"Oh Seth, I really am sorry, I haven't been a good person lately. My mind has been all over the place. I need something to take my mind off things, and perhaps converting the piggery will be just what I need. I will take some measurements later and see if I can download an app that will design a living space for me. I'm hopeless at that kind of thing. I want it to be open plan like your barn. I know the piggery is cottage-like, but I would like to have no walls inside if that is possible. Maybe just one wall around a bathroom, perhaps."

"Jules is good at designing layouts. She did the layout for our barn. Give her the measurements, and I'm sure she will come up with something."

"Thanks, I will. I was going to ask. How did the police interview go? Seth, there's…"

"Not the best. Did you know that Gemma was practically stalking me? She had photos of me all over her walls. The police wanted to know if

189

after she accused me of being the father of her child if I was angry enough to kill her."

"Oh, Seth, that's horrible."

"If they arrest me, then you could tell them how well I handled things at the wedding."

"Why would they arrest you? You were with Jules when she died, weren't you? Have you ever been alone with Gemma?"

"I don't know what you are getting at. Of course, I haven't. You are sounding like the police now." He tried not to think about him waking up and finding Gemma fiddling with the button on his trousers.

"I'm sorry. I didn't mean it to sound like that. May's death and Tom's arrival is fucking with my mind."

"It's ok, I understand. Jules sent the police down to see Tom. I had to lend him my phone, so they could talk to him through the window. You should have seen his face when I told him about May and that the police were there to see him."

"No! What did he say? I should go down there again and see if he needs anything."

"I wouldn't bother. I waited in the kitchen while he talked to them. I didn't want him to have my phone a moment longer than he needed to. He was only with them for ten minutes. I wasn't supposed to listen, but I couldn't help myself. He said that he had been staying in Cork for the past few weeks and had friends that could vouch for him on the night of the murder. He was overly polite to the police and said how shocked he was that Gemma had died. I swear I heard him sob a little. What a prick!

"I am pretty sure that he was faking being ill. Yesterday when we found him on the floor, I think he was hoping that Jules was going to find him and then feel sorry for him. That man is obsessed with her."

"I don't know, Seth. He didn't look well, and I am quite sure that if he was with it enough to know that we had found him, then he wouldn't have let us carry him through to the annexe. You should have seen the look of disgust on his face when I appeared with food for him."

"There is something off about all this. He is up and about now. I told him that he must leave the house today and that he must forget about Jules."

"Do you think that he will? Go, I mean?"

"Not a chance. There is something wrong with that man. He knows about May passing now, and somehow I don't think that he will be leaving Waterfall West in a hurry."

***

With Darragh down for an afternoon nap, Jules opened the front door wide and stood in the doorway with her eyes closed, letting the warm afternoon sunshine wash over her. She could hear the birds singing, and a gentle breeze whistled in the treetops. *I think spring is truly here. It's so nice just to stop for a moment and gather my thoughts. I swear that the birds are singing louder since lockdown.*

"It's a perfect day for a ride. I'm sure Sinead will keep an eye on Darragh for a couple of hours for us."

Jules opened her eyes and saw Seth emptying a wheelbarrow of gravel into a pothole. His shirt was off, and she couldn't take her eyes off his broad chest and muscular arms and shoulders. *Oh my, he is looking so hot today!*

"Let's take Moss and Connor out and explore the estate. I'm done here. What do you say?"

"Ok then, but come in for a shower first. You are covered in brick dust."

Seth put his head on one side and smiled. "You weren't thinking of taking advantage of me, were you?"

"No, not at all. I promise I will be good... Now that you mention it. Our baby is sleeping, and it wouldn't hurt to see if there is room for two in the shower."

Seth shook his head. "I knew it. You will have to be gentle with me. My body is broken from repairing the road. I think Sinead has forgiven me for demolishing one of her pigsties."

"Oh, I'm sorry. I was going to ring you to warn you, but then Darragh wanted a drink and..."

"You know she wants to keep pigs now as well as look after all the horses? She is worrying me. I just know there is something she is not telling me. I'm sure she will tell me what it is soon enough. When I've done my farm duties, I said I would help her convert the piggery. I said that you would design the layout for her. She wants it to look like our place." He wheeled the wheelbarrow over to her and left it leaning against the wall.

Jules looked down their road and could just see the roof of the piggery at the end of the track. She could also see that Seth had filled all the potholes. She hadn't realised how many there had been. The potholes towards the stables had been filled too. "Goodness, you have been busy. Good job! We will actually be able to drive the car out of here without wrecking it."

"I'm quite pleased with myself. So, are you ready for me? I'm all yours."

"You do realise that you have brought this on yourself?"

"Why is that?"

"You shouldn't be walking around with no shirt on looking so hot. It's too much for me."

"Well, we are going to have to even things up. You have far too much on. Let me help you with your t-shirt."

Jules felt his hands around her waist. She giggled and pushed him away. "No, not on the doorstep!"

"Ok, into the shower room with you then. No, it's no good. I'm going to have to take you there myself." Seth scooped her up and carried her through to the bathroom, and then set her down. "So let me get some of this dust off first, and then we will test your theory," he said, kicking his shoes off and undoing his jeans.

"I'm pretty handy with the soap, and I don't think a little brick dust ever hurt a girl." Jules took off her t-shirt, and he smiled when he saw her pert breasts.

"You don't like wearing a bra, do you?" he said, taking off his socks.

"No, not that much."

Jules pulled off her jeans and underwear and stepped into the shower, turned on the jet of water, forgetting that it would take a moment to warm up. She squealed and then gasped as she felt his strong arms around her. His lips were on her neck. His skin was still warm from the sun, and her body tingled at his touch. Not letting her go of her, he pulled off his jeans and boxers and stepped into the shower and pulled her to him. The water was warm enough. He was aroused and ready for her.

"We need soap," she said breathlessly, passing him the citrus shower gel.

He smiled at her mischievously, and his dark brown eyes smouldered as the desire to take her grew. *I want you so badly. I don't think we will be in here long.* "So, where do you need soaping first?"

***

Jules picked up her guitar and sat on the sofa next to Seth. She looked across at Darragh, who was standing in his playpen, and he was holding the top and calling out to her, wanting to come out.

"It's not going to work. I know it won't take long to record a song for TikTok, but it will not sound good with our boy complaining in the background. We should wait until later when he is in bed."

"Let's try," Seth said. "He usually goes quiet when we sing."

"So, we will do a minute of Hey Brother," Jules said, hitting the record button on her phone. It was propped up against a cup on the coffee table. She sat down quickly, smiled at the camera and started to play her guitar. Seth started to sing, and after a few bars, Jules joined in.

Darragh called out louder or joined in with them. She wasn't sure which. "No, this is not going to work," she said and stopped playing.

Seth laughed. "I thought he sounded grand. We are going to be like the Jacksons soon. I'll hold him, and if he starts to sing, then don't stop. I think that everyone will love to see him try and harmonise with us." Seth got up and went over to Darragh, and lifted him out of the playpen. "Is that better, my wee boy? Do you want to sing too?"

"I don't know. Anybody can see these videos. Paedophiles too. I'd rather not. Let's try again later. Do you mind?"

"No, that's fine. The thought never even entered my head."

Seth's phone started to ring. He took it out of his pocket, and immediately, Darragh reached out for it.

"I know my phone is better than your plastic one. Better not play with this. Here, let me pass you to your Mam? It's Shawn."

Jules put her guitar down and took him into her arms. He wriggled to get down, and holding her knee, he stood on the floor, happy to be standing.

"Are you alright there, Shawn, how are you doing? I am pleased to hear that. I am going to put you on loudspeaker. Jules is here. She wanted to ask you something."

"I did? Hi, Shawn, how are you and Jane?"

"Not bad, at all. Jane had her scan today, and it looks like we are going to have a boy too."

"I'm really pleased for you. Have you come up with any names yet?" Jules asked.

"My Mam wants to call him Patrick after my Da, but Jane is not keen."

"No, I don't think Patrick is right," she said, remembering Seth's grumpy brother. She was pleased that they were talking to their families again.

"So, what was it you wanted to ask me? It wouldn't be about us recording Waterfall Way together, would it?"

"That is the very reason I am ringing. We thought we could do a Zoom recording and go live on Facebook. Since we were all on lockdown, a lot of groups are getting together and are singing on Zoom. What do you say?"

"Yes, that's a good idea, but don't you need a computer for that?" Seth asked.

"You can use my laptop. It has a camera on it," Sinead said, walking into the kitchen area. "It would be better than using your phones."

"Thanks, Sinead. So, Shawn, what is this Zoom thing, then," Seth was puzzled.

"It's a bit like joining an online meeting. We will all be able to see each other on a split-screen. Although I say we will be live on Facebook, we thought it would be best to just sing fifty percent of the song and then Guy will work his magic on it and distribute our record to sell the whole version. We will send you the recording over, and then you can upload it to all your media channels."

"We have only been TikToking so far," Seth said. "We need to open a Facebook account. I've never bothered with Facebook."

"We have an S&J Facebook page. I created one a few weeks back," Jules added. "There's not many posts on it yet, but I am working on that. Posting Waterfall Way on there will really help get us followers and might get people to buy our records."

"I didn't know," Seth said, looking at her with surprise. "It's a good job you have got our social media side of things sorted. I haven't got a clue."

Shawn laughed. "It's a good job the girls have their heads screwed on the right way; otherwise, we would get nowhere. We were thinking of creating a donation link to fund the food banks in Cork so that they can buy essentials for those with no income. Not everyone is getting furlough funds, and they are having trouble feeding their families. That was Jane's idea."

"Brilliant! We would like to do our bit to help those in need." Seth said. "When were you thinking of holding the Zoom thing?"

"Tomorrow at ten, if that is ok with you. Jane is off tomorrow and is going to run the Zoom session. We will message you with all the details on how to join the meeting tonight. We will have a warm-up and make sure we are all connected properly, and then we will go live at 10:30am. That is the real-time, by the way. Guy was moaning that it was early but never mind. I promise I won't be late," he said, laughing.

"No, ten will be good for us. With a bit of luck, Darragh might be having his morning nap. I'm looking forward to it. Our microphones are going to be delivered today," Jules said. "So we should look like we know what we are doing. Thanks, Shawn, that's just what we needed. Things have been a bit crazy here the past few weeks."

"I know, I wasn't going to mention it, but I saw that Waterfall West was on the local news yesterday. I didn't realise that Gemma Day had been murdered."

"Really, I've only been looking at the main news now and again, just to keep up with what is going on with the pandemic. That's odd. I haven't spoken to the press," Seth said, looking at Sinead. *So that is what she has been hiding.* "Did you know about this, Sinead?"

"No, I didn't."

"They spoke to an odd fellow named Tom Stone. I've not seen him before. Is he a relative?" Shawn added.

"Oh, for Christ's sake!" Seth exclaimed.

"He said that he suspected that gypsies had killed her. Do you know who I am talking about?"

"Unfortunately, I do. Gypsies indeed! We've got May's brother staying with us in the Manor House. That's it, I'm going down there, and I am going to turf him out. It's high time he left."

"Well, good luck to you. I don't think he was quite the ticket... Look, you two, I will see you in the morning. I've got Seamus calling me. He's a Zoom virgin too," he said, laughing. "Bye for now."

"Yes, see you tomorrow," Jules said, looking anxiously up at Seth.

Seth cleared the call and sighed. "He can't stay here any longer. What is that man's problem? People are going to think Waterfall West is a home for unhinged vagrants."

"It could be," Sinead said, sitting down in the armchair. "This Covid thing is getting out of hand, and it doesn't look like hotels and guest houses will be opening anytime soon. When we come out of isolation, why don't we go round Cork and look for people that need a place to stay and help them get back on their feet again?"

"Mm… perhaps," Seth said, stroking his chin. "I don't see why not, but we would have to be careful who we pick. As much as I'd like to help all the homeless, there are those that need specialist help. Did you know that the majority of people that sleep rough have mental health, alcohol or drug dependency issues? We would have to feed them too. It's a shame we didn't start farming last year. There would have been plenty of spare food to go round then. If Waterfall Way sells, then we could use some of the profit to fund this project. Would that be ok, Jules?"

"I think this is a great idea. I would like to try and make a difference to other people's lives. This pandemic makes you appreciate what you have and makes you want to help others."

"So that's a yes then? Good." Seth laughed. "I am sure that his Lordship down there will be delighted when the hotel starts filling up with homeless people."

"Seth, you can't do this just to spite Tom." Jules said.

"No, I have actually thought about doing something like this before. It would be better if the Toad left of his own free will. Like Shawn said, he is not the ticket, and I think if I dragged him out of the Manor House, then it would be like putting a stick into a hornet's nest. Jules, please don't go near him, ever. I am afraid for you."

"I won't. Who knows, he might be packing as we speak. He didn't have anything with him. I wonder what happened to his belongings."

"He probably sold everything for drugs," Sinead said, holding Darragh's hand so he walked to her. "You are the cutest thing... I saw needle marks on his skinny arms when we carried Tom to bed."

"Oh, Goodness!" Jules exclaimed. "I think you are right. Now I am doubly afraid of him. I don't like the idea of a drug addict staying here. What if he starts to sell the furniture for drugs?

Seth, we need to talk to him. He is obviously in trouble. He owns a big pharmaceuticals company in Australia, and he has money and a home, but his addiction has broken him. I know I am right. Sinead, will you look after Darragh for half an hour while Seth and I go down and talk to him."

"Yes, sure, but I am not sure he will open up with Seth there. You need to speak to him alone."

"No way!"

"He might listen to me. If you are not there."

"Hell no!"

"You could hide yourself, and then if I need you, I will call out."

"I don't like this idea."

"You know this makes sense. If we want him to leave us alone, then this is the only way."

Chapter Twenty-three

With shaky hands, Tom Stone scoured the cupboards for food. Hunger and the constant agonising craving for drugs and sex were always with him, clawing at his insides, and were in his mind like vicious and hungry beasts, night and day. *It's all Hannah's fault. I shouldn't have let her inject me. I shouldn't be so hungry. What was in that smack? The first time was amazing, but now I wish I just kept to my old friend ketamine. What is wrong with me? I can't seem to focus on anything. Not even Julia. How long have I been here? A week? Two weeks? What the fuck is wrong with me? I can't stay. Not now the police know I am here. That pikey would just love me to walk out! Fuck him!*

Hannah? Did I lock her in the flat? I should go back to the flat. I don't remember. If only I could get money out of my bank accounts, but they are all frozen. There's May's gold necklaces! Of course! I could pawn them, but I might need ID. But no, I have just the perfect solution that will take that smirk right off his face. May's address book has made some interesting reading!

He found a box of frosted Shreddies and ripped open the box and bag, desperate to feed his cravings. The box fell over, spilling its contents on the countertop. "Shit!" Scooping up a handful, he rammed the cereal into his mouth and then nearly choked as he tried to swallow. "So fucking dry!" He ran the cold tap, drank directly from it and choked again. Taking a deep breath, he stood up and shook his head. *I need a lift back to Cork. Julia will take me. I just need one more shot and then no more. If I am going to be with Julia, then I need to be clean and pure like her... Only she's not, is she? She's been with that fucking bastard too. What do women see in him? That bitch, Gemma! She tried to tell me that the baby was mine. How could she lie like that? I saw the pictures on the wall of him. Fucking bastards!*

***

Hand in hand, Jules and Seth walked through woodland carpeted with wild daffodils. The spring flowers smelt new and fresh, and their yellow heads looked up at the sky, waiting eagerly for sunshine to filter through the budding trees. The copse backed onto the garden of the Manor House and allowed Jules and Seth to approach the building without being seen. Using the row of rhododendrons that edged the lawn as cover, they silently watched the back of the house and waited for Tom to appear.

After waiting for ten minutes and hoping that he might have actually gone, their hopes were dashed when they saw him open up the patio doors of the conservatory and come outside. Tom pulled one of the patio chairs out from beneath a table, grated it along the flagstones, sat down and lit a cigar.

"I didn't know he smoked cigars," Jules said. "Where did he get those from?"

"May used to keep a box of them in the study for her special guests. He's just helped himself, the bastard."

"This is a good time to talk to him. I'll walk up the lawn, and you will be able to make your way through the shrubbery and get closer so you can hear everything he says. Don't let him see you."

"I still don't really understand what we will gain from you talking to him."

Jules put her hands on each of his cheeks and looked up into his smouldering brown eyes. She could see that she was hurting him. "Listen to me. You don't have to worry, I will be perfectly safe, and if he really cares about me, then I should be able to get rid of him. I can try anyway. Promise me that you won't come charging out if you hear something you don't like. I am going to warn you now that he might say he loves me."

"Oh fuck!"

"Promise me?"

"Look, I can't… Ok… I will try." Jules looked at him sternly. "I promise. I promise that I will only come to your aid if you need me to."

"Good. Let's get this over with." With her heart beating hard in her chest, Jules started to make her way up the lawn towards Tom. *Please just listen to me and don't make this hard for me. Oh crap, he has seen me.* She could see him smiling at her, and this made her feel nauseous. *Is he wearing May's clothes?*

"Julia, my darling. I knew you would come and visit me," he called.

"Oh, for fuck's sake!" she said under her breath.

He stood up and put his arms out as if he wanted to embrace her. Stopping near the edge of the patio, she sighed and shook her head. "You don't get it, do you? I am not here because I want to be. You are making my life impossible. I am sorry if something bad has happened to you, but you really need to go back to Australia and leave us in peace."

Tom sat down heavily. "I can't go back to Australia. Not without you."

"Ok, this has got to stop. I think that we might have been through this a thousand times. I am a happily, and I emphasise 'happily' married woman, and I have a one-year-old that needs a stress-free mother. You are making my life hell."

Tom looked shocked, and his eyes narrowed. "I didn't know you had a child. Is it his?"

"You didn't know? I don't believe you. Gemma must have mentioned it. Of course it's Seth's."

"Oh Julia, how could you? I can't believe that you have a child with him."

"You are joking? There is something wrong with you."

"Does he look like you or him?"

"I am not going to answer that. You need to pack your things up and go home. Where are your things?"

"They were stolen or lost. I am not sure which."

"Sinead said she saw needle marks in your arms. Are you on drugs or something? How can you not be sure what happened to your belongings? Unless you were out of your head and high on drugs."

"That stupid dyke should learn to mind her own business."

"You are not a very nice man, are you?"

"I used to be, but then I met you, and things changed..."

"Don't you dare blame me for your downfall! Perhaps the police need to know about all your dirty habits."

Tom frowned. "I can change. If you would only give me the chance to prove..."

"Please, Tom, you must go home. All you need to do is to ring the Australian passport office and bank and get your passport replaced. The phone line in the house is still working. If you care about me, then you will do what is right."

"I can't go home. It's complicated. Oh, Julia, I have done some bad things, and yes, I do have a bit of a habit, but I know if I had you in my life, I would be a new man. I need a hug. I need you to tell me that everything is going to be alright."

He got up and walked towards her with his arms open again, his cigar dropping ash as he walked. Jules stepped back, stumbled and fell back into the grass. "SETH!"

Tom stopped and sighed. "So, he's here then? I should have guessed."

Seth pushed his way through the bushes and ran to Jules. He helped her up and glared at Tom. "Don't you dare touch her, or you will have me to deal with."

"Oh, how pathetic!"

Seth got out his phone and started to dial a number.

"You are not calling the police, are you? There's no need for that."

"No, it's your lucky day. I am paying for a taxi to take you to the Australian Embassy in Dublin."

"But I have a home here with Julia. And anyway, I am sure the courts will be interested to hear how a gypsy jailbird got May to change her will."

"Go ahead and take me to court, but you are still getting in that fucking taxi!"

"Seth, we are in lockdown. I don't think the embassy will be open, and I don't think planes are flying at the moment. He is going to have to stay here until the lockdown is over."

"Over my dead body!"

"I knew you'd help me," Tom said, looking pleased.

"I am not helping you. WE have no choice, and I promise you if things were normal, then I would let Seth ring you a taxi. Do you understand me? You can only stay here on the understanding that you go when lockdown is over. I don't want you to come anywhere near us. You mean nothing to me and never will. You revolt me, and there are things that I will never forgive you for!"

"You are so sweet when you are angry."

She could tell by his wry smile on his face and distant look in his eyes that he had not absorbed her words.

"We need to go home, Seth, and forget about this sad bastard."

"Run along, gypsy boy!"

Jules saw Seth's fists clench. She took his hand and started to walk away with him. She knew that if Tom made one more comment, then Seth was likely to punch him. "Just keep walking. He is not worth it."

"I hate him so much," he whispered.

"I know. I do too."

***

Connor snorted, and his soft velvet muzzle brushed her neck, making Jules giggle. "Have you missed our rides together? Do you like living in Ireland with all your new horsey friends?" She turned and patted his neck and hugged him. "I have missed going out with you too. Do you forgive me for not riding you as much as I used to?"

"Of course, he does," Seth said, putting his saddle on his back. "He understands and is devoted to you. A bit like me, really," he said with a grin. "Will you be ok getting on him, or do you want me to hold him for you?"

"No, that's ok, I will be fine. You get Moss sorted, and we will stand in the courtyard together and admire the view."

"There's not much to see from here. Wait until we get into the fields... You mean me, don't you?"

"Maybe. You get my heart racing when you are sitting on your black steed. I think it is something to do with you being my white knight. Or, in your case, a hot black knight."

Seth laughed, "You still have the hots for me then?"

"Of course," Jules said as she jumped up onto the mounting block and then slipped onto Connor's back. "Forgive me for loving you too much. And for having wicked thoughts."

"I should take you out riding more often, although I can't imagine why you see me as a knight."

"You were there for me when Tom was being such an arse. Let's forget about him. I am looking forward to exploring the estate, but I do feel a bit guilty."

Seth mounted Moss, who immediately started to walk off. "Why is that then?"

"Well, we seem to be asking Sinead to mind Darragh a lot, and I don't want her to think we are taking advantage of her."

"She doesn't mind, and I think it gives her something to do. She is a bit of a lost soul at the moment, and Darragh is the perfect distraction. He loves her and will be as good as gold. It's good for you too. You've been suffering from cabin fever, and getting out of the house and into the fresh air will make you feel so much better. We can forget about all the shit that is going on and live a little."

They followed the track down past their barn and continued until the path ended by the piggery, and Seth opened the gate, allowing Jules and Connor into the field. "Turn right Jules, I was thinking of ploughing the next two fields. They are flatter than this one. The only thing is that there is a stream at the bottom of the second field that floods occasionally. Tell me what you think. I can run a water pipe from the piggery down to each if I need to set a sprinkler up to water the crops in the summer."

The first field was huge, with a line of oak trees evenly spaced around the edges. Jules could barely see where the field finished. "You are really going into farming in a big way. Are you going to be able to manage all this on your own?"

"I was thinking of getting help in to harvest the crops, but with this pandemic going on, it looks like it's going to be you, me and Sinead harvesting. Are you up for a challenge?"

"Yes, I guess so." For a moment, Jules had an image of herself thrashing corn by hand wearing a long white dress.

"What are you going to grow?"

"I have changed my mind a few times. Initially, I wanted to grow superfoods like kale, but now I think we should grow crops that we can sell easily around here, so I have settled on cauliflowers, broccoli, carrots and potatoes. Oh, and swedes too."

"That sounds sensible."

The second field was even larger than the first, and the new spring grass was lush and verdant. As they entered the field, hundreds of rabbits scurried this way and that. Connor seemed unfazed by the rabbits' flight and continued down the side of the field without even flinching. Moss, however, had taken fright and charged off, taking Seth by surprise. It took all of his strength and skill to slow him down and turn him around. Embarrassed, he trotted Moss back to Jules. "Damn rabbits! They won't be so happy when the ferret man comes."

"Why, what do you mean?"

"We can't be having rabbits living here if we are going to grow crops."

"So, what does the ferret man do exactly?"

Seth looked at her concerned face and then realised that she would not be happy when he told her that he was thinking of having the rabbits exterminated. He remembered the ferret man coming to Crow Farm and how happy everyone had been when they were given rabbit stew. He, of course, being a vegetarian, had passed on that meal. "He just sends the ferrets into their burrows, and they chase the rabbits out into nets."

"We could rehome them on the other side of the stream," Jules said, pointing towards the horizon to where she thought the water might be. "Do rabbits swim?"

"I don't think so. We could use the first field instead, but I thought that Sinead might want that one for her pigs. This field is too wet and liable to flood over, anyway." *I can't tell her what else the ferret man does. My poor sweet dote, she has no idea. Let's change the subject.* "It's a big day tomorrow. My tractor parts and seeds are going to be delivered, and we are going to release our first single. Are you excited?"

"I am so looking forward to it. Seth, you know that our lives could be changed forever. Wouldn't it be amazing if S&J and Sonar Cell became household names? I just know everyone is going to love Waterfall Way. Have you seen how many TikTok followers we have already?"

"No, a few thousand?"

"More like one hundred thousand!"

"Wow! I didn't realise."

"When Darragh is in bed, we should do another popular song. How about 'All of Me?' That is going crazy in the pop charts at the moment."

"I like it. I will leave my future music career in your capable hands. Do you think we should answer all the messages in the TikTok inbox? Some of the questions were a bit off the wall."

Jules laughed. "I think we should avoid those. I don't want anyone knowing if you are good in bed."

"Oh, you saw Rude Boy's comment, then?"

"We should reply, but like I said, just to those that are our true fans and thank them for their kind words. After all, they will be the ones buying our records."

"We better get started when we get back. It's going to be a long night."

Chapter Twenty -four

Nearly lost our lives when the sun went down
To a crazy man and his plans and a withered clown
We fled golden fields for county Cork
Too poor to eat, so we found work
We declared our love with a Claddagh ring
now all we do is laugh and dance and sing
You laughed and stole a kiss, and I stole one back
looked up at the sky and the stars, and I made my wish

If we are going to Waterfall Way
oh, then can we stay?
I need you today
Say you'll take this ring and be my wife
Oh, how long, I've waited all my life
And if you're planning on leaving, then listen, dear
I'll do whatever it takes to convince you that you should be here

Don't dance with that badass guy. He'll make you cry
Oh, be with me instead, he's in another girl's bed
You cringe, you hang your head because you know it's true
When all I want is to save this dance for you.

If we are going to Waterfall Way
oh, then can we stay?

I need you today
Say you'll take this ring and be my wife
Oh, how long, I've waited all my life
And if you're planning on leaving, then listen, dear
I'll do whatever it takes to convince you that you should be here

Together we can climb our tree
Seal our love
Just you and me
We don't need to think
Just let our bodies sink
And I'm crazy; you're in my head
You're in my bed
In my head

(Listen to Seth singing Waterfall Way by clicking on this link https://youtu.be/cV4f8GtzBdA)

Grinning from ear to ear, Sinead applauded and whistled and then looked at Seth with wide eyes and a worried look to make sure she hadn't ruined the recording. Seth gave her a reassuring smile and then, moving his microphone out of the way, sat down in front of the laptop and waited to see if the recording had been a success. Jane appeared next to Shawn, and the other band members were all smiling, pleased with their performances too.

"That was perfect," Jane said, hugging and kissing Shawn. "Well done, everyone, you sounded great."

Shawn was smiling. "I think that went really well. Guy, do you think that was good enough?"

"That went way better than I expected. I don't think there was any feedback." Guy ran his fingers through his bed hair and looked at another screen. "Yes, I should be able to tweak the recording and turn it into something decent, although it would have been so much better in a studio."

"These are crazy times, Guy. We have to work with what we've got." Shawn was starting to look cross.

"I loved singing with you all," Jules said as she put her guitar down and sat down next to Seth. "Perhaps we could do another song together soon. Seth has written so many while he was away. Some of them are really good."

"Let's see how this one does first," Seth suggested. "Is it ok if we put a minute's worth on TikTok and add a link to buy the record?"

"You do that, Seth, and don't forget to add the 'Just Giving' link. I don't know anything about TikTok. We will send you over the recording when Guy has polished it. The hard part is promoting the track. I guess we will work out what to do as we go along. So, any marketing ideas you two might have will be really welcome." Shawn was smiling again.

"Are you guys ok?" Jane asked. "It's so weird us not being able to meet up in person. I'd like to say that we could all see each other soon in The Elbow, but things are really grim at the hospital at the moment. I wouldn't be surprised if we will be in lockdown for months."

"Oh, dear. We are really lucky. Our lives haven't changed that much. The estate isn't making any money, but at least the horses have grass to eat, and we can go out in the fields for walks," Jules replied.

"Oh, I was going to ask. Have they buried May yet?" Jane asked.

Seth shook his head. "No, not yet. She is going to be buried on Friday, but the local church is not allowing any mourners to attend. We were going to walk down and pay our respects during one of our exercise walks. We will all be out of isolation by then, and they can't stop us from walking past the church if we are going that way anyway."

"I guess not. That really is sad, though. You could have a little service when things get back to normal. I forgot that you had been in contact with Covid. I can tell by your voices that you are fine."

"No, I don't think we have contracted it," Seth replied.

"Did you know that some people have been admitted into hospital with no symptoms at all and all these people had low oxygen levels?" Jane said gravely.

"Did they? Christ, we could all be contaminated and not know it. We are all really well," Seth said, feeling Jules' forehead.

Jane laughed. "You look well. Don't listen to me. I just can't get my head around how bad this pandemic is turning out to be. Roll on Covid free days!"

"So, Seth, is May's mad brother going to accompany you down to the churchyard?" Shawn asked, half laughing.

"You are joking? Never in a million years! He is probably far too busy selling the furniture to worry about going to his sister's funeral."

"You don't think he is?" Sinead asked in a worried voice.

"No, he wouldn't dare," Seth replied. "Not if he knows what's good for him."

Jules looked at the time. "I've got to go. We've got to get Darragh up. He was as good as gold and fell asleep right on cue, but if I leave him sleeping any longer, then he won't want to go to sleep tonight."

"No, that's fine. We've got to go shopping, although I am not looking forward to queuing. Last week, we waited outside Tesco for an hour. It is so nice to go out and not have crazed teenagers following us. That's one good thing about the lockdown," Shawn said, looking for the Zoom meeting exit button.

"We will send over the track in the next couple of days. To make sure you are happy with it before it goes live," Jane added.

"I just know Waterfall Way is going to do really well. You were all awesome," Sinead declared.

***

Seth lay awake, his mind too busy to sleep. He had spent hours answering TikTok inbox messages and was overwhelmed by the support and encouraging words he and Jules were getting. There was, of course, the odd, weird message which he ignored. Someone had asked him if he liked chicken soup, and he wondered if that was code for something. He was looking forward to getting the tractor running, and this was the main reason that he was unable to sleep. All the parts had arrived, and he was looking forward to fitting everything. In his mind, he had run through a fitting schedule several times, and he just couldn't stop himself from thinking about it. *I need to sleep, or I will be good for nothing in the morning.*

Feeling thirsty, he slipped out of bed and made his way to the kitchen. With just the cooker clock for light, Seth ran the water. Barney jumped up next to the sink and started to purr. Seth stroked him and smiled. *Are you happy to see me? I haven't given you much attention recently, have I?* Barney rubbed his head against his hand. Seth's attention turned to a light travelling up the wall next to the windows. Are those headlights? He could hear a lorry making its way towards the barn. *Who can this be? Nobody should be driving this way. Not at this time of night. Perhaps they are lost.* A horsebox drove slowly past the barn, and he frowned. *This is not right. I'd better find out what is going on. They are heading towards the piggery, and that is a dead end.*

He tiptoed into the bedroom and quickly pulled on some trousers and a sweatshirt. He picked up his keys and phone and then quickly put on his trainers. The night was particularly cold, and he wished he had put on a coat. Seth could see the lorry making its way down towards the piggery and the thought of going there in the dead of night made him shudder. Feeling a little uneasy, he made his way down the track, and he shivered again. The horsebox drove into the piggery's courtyard and came to a stop. The lorry's lights went out, and Seth was plunged into darkness. *No, this is not good.* He stopped for a moment as he weighed up why a horsebox would be on their land at two in the morning. *Horse thieves? Holy crap! They've missed the turning to the lower fields where all the horses are. Should I call the police? No, let's go and see why they are here. They are probably lost and have decided to rest until morning.*

Seth was about to head over to the horsebox and then noticed someone approaching from the other direction. They were lighting their way with a torch. Curious to see who it was, Seth stepped off the track and hid in the shrubbery. The tall shadowy figure was getting closer and was muttering to himself. Seth silently cursed as Tom walked by. *What is he up to?*

He followed behind him, keeping far enough away so as not to be heard. He watched Tom walk up to the cab and saw him knock on the driver's door. The door opened and a large middle-aged woman, wearing a thick jumper and woolly hat with a pompom on top, jumped down to speak to him. She had a cigarette in her hand and held it like a man between her finger and thumb.

"Where have you been?" Tom snapped. "Why didn't you stop at the house first as we agreed?"

"Look, I'm sorry I'm late. I broke down, and now it is too late to pick up the horses." Her voice was deep and husky from too much smoking. "We are going to stay here until the morning and then round them up when it is light. It is too dangerous to do it now."

So, there's more than one. Seth got a little closer so he could hear them better. *What horses are they going to round up?*

214

"No, that's not good. We agreed that you would take them tonight. I'd prefer it if nobody knew about our deal. You did bring the five thousand, didn't you? You do realise that this is a chance of a lifetime. I would get three times as much if I took them to the sales."

Christ, he is selling the horses!

"I have the cash, but we need to rest, and then we will do the deal in the morning. First light, I promise. I will be discreet."

Seth was fuming and came out of hiding. He stormed up to them, doing his best to control his temper. "The horses are not for sale," he said to the woman. "You need to leave the estate, or I will ring the police."

Tom was shocked to see him. "Oh, for the love of God! Not you again!" Tom sneered and then turned his back on him. "Rosemary, don't listen to the farmhand. He has nothing to do with this. It was May's dying wish that the horses..."

"Dying wish, my arse! Until probate is granted, then nothing can be sold. This is not going to happen. I am sorry if you have had to come a long way, but I really must ask you to leave," he said to the woman. "And by the way, that goes for you too, Tom. Give me the key and get the fuck out of here."

"You'd like that, wouldn't you? I have a right to be here. I am going to call my lawyer and contest the will."

"Go ahead. You are all just hot air. It is obvious that you are in some kind of trouble. I can smell a toad a mile off."

"Well, I'm disappointed," Rosemary said. "I've had my eye on May's cobs for a while. They all do so well at the shows. Especially the black stallion."

"Mm..., that's my horse, and no, he is definitely not for sale and never will be."

"Look, I have a three-hour drive home, and as much as I would like to leave now, I don't think I have the energy. I have a heart condition. I have a bed in the cab and promise that we will be no trouble. We will leave first thing."

"We?" Seth asked.

"My dog, Toby. He goes everywhere with me."

"That's ok, please stay, but Tom, you and I are going on a little journey."

"In your dreams!"

"Oh, you are! Even if I have to drag your scrawny body into the car myself!"

"Where is Julia? She wouldn't allow this."

"This has got nothing to do with her."

"Are you coming?" Seth asked him, turning to go.

"You are having a laugh. Fuck off, gypsy shit!"

Furious, Seth spun around and punched Tom squarely on the chin, sending him flying. He hadn't thought about hitting him. It was just a knee jerk reaction. Tom lay in the semi demolished pigsty and moaned out in pain before passing out. His torch lay on the cobbles at Seth's feet.

Horrified, the woman gasped. "I think you have knocked him out cold. You are not going to do that to me, are you?"

"I should have done that a long time ago." Seth shook his head. "I don't hit women. I know I shouldn't have hit him, but he deserved it. He raped my wife. Will you watch him while I get the car?"

Chapter Twenty-five

Seth sat in the Jaguar and put the key in the ignition. The last time he had tried to start the car, it had taken him several attempts as the battery was nearing the end of its life. *Please start and not wake everyone up.* He turned the key again, and the car battery whined in protest and rapidly lost power. *Come on, this is not the time to start messing around.* Seth adjusted the choke and then tried again. The battery was flat, and he knew that the car was not going to start. In despair, he rested his head on the steering wheel.

A loud knock on the window made him jump, and he looked up and saw Sinead standing there. He opened the car door to speak to her. "I am sorry. Did I wake you?"

"No, I was just getting a drink. Where are you going?"

"Nowhere, it seems."

"What's going on? Do you need me to drive you somewhere?"

"That would be grand. I was going to take Tom into Cork."

"At this hour?"

"Look, Sinead, something bad has happened. Go and get some clothes on, and I will explain. I've got to get him out of here tonight."

Sinead's eyes narrowed. "I need to ask you something first."

"What's that then?"

"Promise you won't go mad?"

"No, I need to know what's been eating you up. I am not going to like the question, am I?"

"No, but I just need to hear this from your mouth, and I will know if you are lying."

"Go on then."

"On the night that Gemma died, I went over to the mobile home to speak to her. I had changed my mind about sacking her. When I got to the door, I could hear that she was with someone. I could hear them having sex. The whole building was shaking, and they were throwing themselves around the place violently. She was screaming out in ecstasy or pain. I am not sure which. Oh, Seth, she was screaming out your name as she came. Please tell me… It wasn't you, was it?"

"Fuck no! Seriously! You haven't been thinking all this time that I have been unfaithful, have you? You know I wouldn't go with her or anyone else for that matter. NOT EVER!"

"Don't get cross. I believe you. I know you wouldn't do anything to hurt Jules. But why would she call out your name when she was with someone else?"

"Fuck knows! Perhaps she was pretending it was me."

"It just reminded me of when… we did it."

Seth went quiet for a moment. "It wasn't me, all right! I'm not like that anymore. Back then, we were off our heads, and I'm surprised you remembered that night at all."

"Forget what I said. I know you are not lying. There's something else."

"Things are going fucking crazy tonight. Please don't tell me that you think I killed her as well!"

"NO! I don't think that. I know you are not lying. Please don't be mad with me. I have been going out of my mind with worry."

"It's ok, I'm not mad at you. You should have told me sooner. So, what else happened?"

"After they stopped having sex, it all went quiet, and I started to walk away. I heard Gemma yell out, 'you bastard.' Whoever it was hit her, and I heard her body crash against something, and then it went quiet again. I think whoever killed her did it there and then, with a single blow."

"Christ! Did you tell the police all this?"

"Not everything,"

"You didn't tell the police that you thought it was me, did you?"

"No, of course not! What I told them was that I went over to see her and heard her fucking. I told them that I heard someone hit her, and then it all went quiet and that I was worried."

"What else did you tell them?"

"I told them that I just thought she was upset and was sulking. All sorts of things were going through my head, and I didn't want to say that…"

"You thought it was me."

"Exactly! They asked me if I recognised who she was with. They asked me if I saw or heard you there. I swear to God I didn't say I thought it was you. Oh, Seth, I don't think they believed me."

"Great! Now they think I paid her a visit and probably killed her too. Now I understand why they kept asking if I had gone to see her that night."

"Seth, I just want this nightmare to be over with, and they find Gemma's killer. Who could it be? What the hell are the police doing to find him? There is nothing in the news about the murder, and we haven't heard anything more from the police."

"They are probably doing very little. Everyone is too preoccupied with Covid at the moment. They will find him sooner or later. I am just relieved that I haven't been taken down to the police station for further questioning."

"I will tell them again that it wasn't you with Gemma that night if you think it will help."

"No, it's ok. Best let sleeping dogs lie. Sinead, we really need to get down to the piggery and collect Tom. He might have woken up and run off."

"What! Now I am really confused."

"You are shivering. Get some clothes on and help me, please. I am starting to think I might have actually killed him."

"SETH!"

"I just punched him once, and now he is lying in one of those pig pens, out cold."

***

Sinead got dressed quickly and ran out to her car, clutching her keys and a first aid kit. Feeling worried, Seth waited for her in the Mini and was anxious to get going. As Sinead got in, she threw the first aid kit onto the back seat. "We might need this. We should take him to the hospital. He might have a concussion. Where in Cork were you going to take him at this time of night?"

"Seth sighed. "I don't know exactly. I was going to take him to the centre of town and drag him out of the car. If he is still unconscious, then perhaps the hospital is a better idea."

Sinead backed the car out of the driveway and headed down the track towards the piggery. "So why did you hit him?"

"He had arranged for one of May's friends to buy the cobs. It was only by luck that I was up and saw a horsebox drive past the house. The woman, Rosemary, was going to give him five thousand pounds in cash. If he needs cash that badly, then there is something seriously wrong."

"Oh my God! No wonder you punched him. The bastard!"

"I am not proud of what I did. He knows how to press my buttons, and he called me gypsy shit. I couldn't help myself. I thought that I had gotten on top of my temper. But obviously not. Fuck!"

"Don't..." Sinead screamed as Tom appeared in front of the car. She slammed on the brakes and hit him. He fell onto the bonnet. The side of his face hit the windscreen.

"Shit! I didn't see him," she exclaimed.

They got out of the car and watched as Tom pulled himself up from the bonnet and then, walking like a drunk man, continued on his way.

"That must have hurt. I don't think he's even seen us," Seth said, watching him weave his way up the track.

"He's definitely got a concussion. We should take him to the hospital. He might have a bleed to the brain. I'll turn the car around."

"Let me drive. If I go and get him, then he might resist getting in the car."

"Ok, but I might need a hand if he gets angry."

Seth got into the Mini and turned the car around. When he reached Tom, Sinead had caught him up. Seth drove past them both and then stopped the car. He jumped out and opened the rear passenger door, ready for Tom to get inside.

Sinead was talking to him, but he wasn't hearing her.

She ran up to Seth. "It's no good. He is in his own world. We are going to have to force him into the car."

Seth groaned. "Ok, I'll do it."

It was only seconds before Tom reached them, and Seth was ready for him. "Tom, you need to get into the car. We are going to take you home."

Tom looked confused and then nodded. "I need a lift home. I can't quite remember the address. Somewhere in Perth, or is it Sydney?"

"That's fine. I know where you live. In you get."

Tom looked at the open door and then fell onto the back seat and lay down. Pushing his legs in, Seth shut the door.

Sinead looked on in amazement. "That was easy. He's not right, though. He is not seeing us." They got back in the car, and Sinead looked back at Tom. "Will you put your seatbelt on?" Tom ignored her and then exhaled in pain and held his head. "Oh crap, he's not listening, and I think he is hurt."

"Let's not worry about seat belts," Seth said, pulling away. "This is going to be an interesting journey. Let's put the radio on to keep him entertained." He looked in the rear-view mirror and looked directly into Tom's eyes which startled him. *Well, at least he is sitting up now.* Tom was frowning, and he looked disturbed. "He is not right. I want you to watch his every move. People with head injuries can become agitated, and if he realises it is me, then he might lash out."

"Ok," Sinead said, twisting herself around to watch him. "What are we going to do when we get to the hospital? We can't take him in there as we are still in quarantine."

"I wasn't planning on taking him in. We will just take him to the entrance and leave him there."

"Mm… I don't know. Do you think he will tell the police that you hit him?"

"No, I have a feeling that he won't want the police involved. He won't be coming back here either. I will get his key off him before we leave him at the hospital."

"Seth, he is trying to get out of the car."

Quickly, Seth flicked a switch and locked all the car doors. "We are not there yet," he called.

Furiously, Tom pulled the lever and cursed. "I need to get out. I'm going to be sick." He then threw up into the footwell.

"For fuck's sake. That smells disgusting," Sinead said, holding her nose. "My poor car!"

"Just ten more minutes, and we will be free of this bastard forever. I'm sorry about your car. I'll sort it out for you in the morning," Seth said, opening the windows.

The roads leading into Cork were eerily quiet. A lazy fox sat in the middle of the road and scanned the gutters for vermin. When he saw the headlights of the Mini, reluctantly he got up and trotted off into the shadows.

"How is the patient doing," Seth asked.

"He seems relaxed enough now he's emptied his stomach, but I'm not sure if he knows where he is. Tom, are you alright?" Sinead asked. He said nothing.

Seth drove the car near to the entrance of the A&E department and then pulled up outside. "Tom, we're here. You just need to check-in."

"I don't think this is where I live," he replied.

"You need to ask the receptionist to direct you to your house. You need to tell her that you have hurt your head too."

"I'm so tired," Tom replied.

"I know you are. You will be able to lie down in a minute," Seth said, getting out of the car. He opened the passenger door and waited. "You need to get going before they lock you out."

Confused, Tom got out of the car and then held onto the door. "I don't feel well."

"Then, you are at the right place."

Seth could see that he was about to faint. He saw his eyes roll and his legs begin to fold. Reluctantly, he grabbed hold of his arm to stop him from falling. Holding him up, he managed to get Tom to the doors and then saw Sinead running up to him with a chair.

"I spotted this in the car park," she said.

"Perfect, I can't hold him for much longer."

Tom dropped into the wheelchair and then slumped forward and was sick again. Seth jumped back, doing his best not to get vomit on his shoes.

"So should we leave him here?" Sinead asked. "It doesn't seem right."

"We will push him into the reception area, and then someone is bound to find him. We can't risk infecting others."

"He could have Covid too. If we push him into the building, then he might infect people."

"I hadn't thought of that. You are right. Why don't we leave him here, go and park up and ring the emergency services and explain that we were out for a drive and saw this man fall over and hit his head? By bringing him to the hospital, then we might have contaminated him as we have been in contact with Covid. How does that sound?"

"Yes, let's do that."

"I'll just get the key out of his pocket first. I guess he has a key and didn't leave the Manor House unlocked."

Seth bent over his slumped body and, holding his breath so as not to smell his vomit, felt in his pocket for the key. He found it, and as he pulled it out, Tom grabbed hold of his wrist, digging his nails into his flesh. He looked hard into Seth's eyes and, for a moment, recognised who he was.

"Gypsy shit! She only has eyes for me," he growled and then passed out, releasing his wrist.

"Come on, Sinead, let's get out of here. I am not staying here a minute longer."

"Don't listen to him Seth, he is sick in the head. I'll ring for an ambulance. It is the right thing to do."

***

It was almost morning when Seth and Sinead returned home. As they walked into the barn, Jules was standing in the kitchen with her fists on her hips. Seth immediately felt guilty for not telling her that he had gone out. Her eyes were blazing.

"So, when were you going to tell me that you had to rush out in the middle of the night and punch Tom?"

Confused, Seth looked at Sinead and then back at her. "I didn't want to wake you. How did you know about Tom? Has someone rang you from the hospital?"

"The hospital? No. But a very nice but irate woman nearly bashed the door down to warn me that there was a lunatic on the loose."

"She must have meant Tom. He wasn't in his right mind. I shouldn't have asked her to watch him while I went to get the car."

"No, you knucklehead! She meant you! She told me that a man with black hair knocked Tom out and then left him for dead in a pigpen. She was beside herself, and I had to get her to sit down and convince her not to call the police."

Seth frowned. "She said she would be no trouble. Did she tell you why she was here?"

"She said there had been a misunderstanding, but she was too upset to say anything more. Why was she here?" Jules was starting to calm down. *He looks so tired.*

"Tom had arranged for her to collect all the cobs, including our Moss and Connor for a measly five grand. It was just a bit of luck that I managed to stop the deal going ahead. Please don't be cross with me."

"It's true," Sinead said wearily. "If it hadn't been for Seth, then we would have lost our beautiful cobs. Yes, Seth hit him, but Tom was asking for it. We thought he had a concussion, so we took him to the hospital. We took his key off him too and told him not to come back here."

"Oh my, she didn't tell me that. The sly bastard! But Seth, you shouldn't have hit him. What if he tells the police? They will just love to know that you have lost your temper again!"

"He won't talk to the police. I swear he is in some kind of trouble. I feel it in my bones."

"Do you think so?"

"I am sure of it. He won't come back here again if he knows what is good for him. I've made it quite clear that he is not welcome."

Jules sighed. "I'd like to believe you. At least we knew where he was when he was living in the Manor House. I just can't believe he is gone. We will have to check the house in the morning. It's been quite a night. You both look wrecked. We should sleep and talk about this all in the morning. Let's go to bed, Seth. But first, I need a hug. You really worried me."

"Come here and give your bad husband a hug then."

"Don't joke. You just seem to get yourself into so much trouble," she said as she felt his arms around her. She held onto him, eager to lose herself in his warm embrace, breathing him in. *Why does he smell of sick?* "Perhaps we can get on with our lives now without worrying."

"Everything is going to be ok, you'll see," he said, resting his chin on her head.

Chapter Twenty-six

After Seth had fitted all the new parts to the old tractor and started her up, the engine had sprung into life effortlessly. He had wasted no time and had set off to plough the fields. It was perfect weather for ploughing, and the ground was soft and not too moist. As he pulled the plough behind him, the grass turned over, revealing rich and fertile soil. Seth watched with immense satisfaction as the field slowly turned from a verdant green to a rich brown.

The wind had a slight chill to it and stopped the spring sunshine from drying out the earth too much. The plough carved its way through the turf like a hot knife through butter. After removing the rust and oiling the old plough, it was as good as new. There was nothing more satisfying than driving a tractor with a plough behind it and creating neat farrows.

A flock of seagulls suddenly appeared from nowhere and followed behind him, snapping up worms in the newly ploughed earth. *Where have they come from? It was the same at Crow Farm. As soon as the ground is being churned up, the gulls appear. I guess we are about the same distance from the sea as we were in Sussex.* He smiled. *I am actually my own boss. I couldn't be happier. Things are going really well for us now.*

A week had passed, and there had been no sign of Tom the Toad. He wondered if he knew that his sister was due to be buried that day. It was likely, as Sinead had said, much to her annoyance, that Tom had opened all the post that had arrived. Fortunately, there had been nothing from the solicitor regarding probate. *I must stop thinking about him. He keeps invading my thoughts, and I rather that he didn't.*

With the first field ploughed, he thought about moving on to the next but knew that he wouldn't be able to plough the whole field before lunch. He didn't like the thought of leaving it half done. After lunch, they were going to walk down to Goggin's Hill Catholic Church and hope to see May's coffin being lowered into the ground as they walked past. He hadn't realised that May had been a Catholic. *Poor May, I miss her.*

Feeling pleased with himself, Seth drove the tractor past the piggery and then headed towards the outbuilding near their converted barn. He saw Jules walking towards him with Darragh on her hip. She was wearing a short dark blue denim dress. Her curly blond hair shone in the morning sunshine, and he remembered why he had written Beautiful in Blue. *I am the luckiest man alive. I have such a beautiful sweet wife and the cutest baby. I wonder if our fans would like to hear Beautiful in Blue. Now we have more than a hundred thousand followers on TikTok, we can go live and sing a whole song for our fans. I guess we should see how Waterfall Way goes first.* "How's my beautiful girl and wee boy?" he asked as he drove up to them. Not wanting to scare Darragh, he turned off the engine.

"We are grand. We have come to see how you are doing. Have you ploughed both fields then?"

"No, just the one. I will do the other when we get back from the church." Darragh put his arms out for Seth.

"Do you want to drive the tractor? Come and sit up here with me, then."

Jules passed Darragh to him, and Seth sat Darragh on his lap and let him hold the steering wheel. "Do you want to go for a ride back to her shed? You can help your Dad drive if you like."

"Do you think he will be safe?"

"I won't let him go, I promise. He will love it. It won't be long before he will be driving the tractor himself."

"Oh, don't say that. I don't want him to stop being a baby."

Darragh smacked the centre of the steering wheel. "You are not looking for the horn, are you? He is so clever. He's obviously watched us driving and has learnt a thing or two. Come on, let's start the old girl up and go for a ride. Do you want to hop up too? You could stand on the step and hang on."

"No, it's ok, I'll follow. Oh, Seth, I was going to say. We had a delivery. I thought that someone had sent us a picnic hamper, but it's actually the ashes of my old pony. I nearly opened it up to look and then read the delivery note. I'm not sure where we should bury them. I don't think we should bury Barney in the summer field. It doesn't feel as special now. Not since Gemma was found there."

Seth laughed. "It would have been a bit of a shock to see all those teeth in the ashes."

"You are joking?"

"I doubt if they ground them down like they do with human ashes."

"Gross! I'm glad I didn't look."

"We'll think of somewhere new. There's a pet cemetery behind the orangery in the Manor House garden. How about there?"

"Maybe. Do you think his hooves are in the ashes too?"

Seth laughed again. "Probably. Come on, my wee boy, let's give you your first tractor ride."

***

May was due to be buried at two, so at half-past one, all dressed in black, Sinead, Jules and Seth pushing Darragh in his pram, headed down the lane towards the church. They hoped that they had got their timing right and would pass by the graveyard as the burial was taking place. Sinead was carrying a wreath from them all, and they planned to leave this at the gate and hope that someone looking after the graveyard would take pity and leave it on May's grave for them later.

Jules smiled as she watched Seth steer the pushchair down the lane. He was a little too tall for the stroller, and he didn't look comfortable pushing it. "Do you want me to push him, Seth? It's a shame we can't raise the handles any higher."

"No, it's ok. I am not suffering in any way. We are watching out for bears, aren't we, Darragh? There are bound to be some in the trees along the road here."

Jules laughed. "You do realise that he hasn't got a clue what a bear is?"

"Well, that's no good," Sinead sounded surprised. "The next time we are allowed into the shops in Cork, I will pop into Pinocchio's and get him one. It's good to be out, isn't it?" Sinead said, smiling. "It's good to be out of isolation and free to go for a walk."

"It is lovely, but it feels weird too. I am feeling guilty for leaving home. Are you doing ok?" Jules asked Sinead.

"Not too bad. In a way, I am glad that May hasn't had to see her business fail and witness what is happening in the world. She died when the world was normal, and all we had to worry about was making a living."

"Things will be back to normal in the summer, and I am sure the Manor House will have guests again."

"If things carry on as they are, then we will be bankrupt in a few weeks' time. The house just eats money. I'm hoping that we qualify for government assistance."

As they walked towards the church, they noticed that there were quite a few families out for a walk too.

"I think others have the same idea as us and are going to walk past the church and pay their dues," Seth announced as he waited for Jules and

Sinead to catch them up. "I hope they don't stop at the church. Otherwise, the police might fine them for gathering. They won't, will they?"

"They shouldn't. I think the whole of Waterfall is here to say goodbye. It feels strange, doesn't it? Seeing people again. It's a little scary," Sinead said, looking at a family walking close behind them.

"I think that you are both right. They are going to see May off," Jules said. "I just know it. May was really popular in Waterfall, and I bet she taught lots of these people how to ride or entertained them with one of her stories."

"It's a shame they can't come back to the house afterwards. May would have liked..." Seth stopped talking. He could hear loud music coming from an open-topped car ahead. "Do you hear that music? That's way too loud and disrespectful. I don't think we are allowed to go on joy rides at the moment." He could see two people sitting in a Mercedes, but he wasn't sure who they were. The sun was in Seth's eyes, making it hard for him to see clearly. As he got closer to the car, he recognised the man sitting in the driver's seat. "Oh, for fuck's sake!" he said out loud and then regretted saying that in front of Darragh.

"SETH!" Both Jules and Sinead said in unison.

"I know, I'm sorry. I will train myself not to swear in front of our baby. But for God's sake! Do you see that white car up there? You'll never guess who else has come to the funeral!"

Jules looked hard at the man and woman in the car. "Oh no. Why is Tom here? He's brought a child with him." She watched him nodding in time to the music. His arm was around a young girl with blonde curly hair, not unlike her own. He looked their way and then pulled the girl to him and started to snog her.

"Is he for real! Will you wait here while I tell him to fu... move on?" Seth was annoyed but in control of himself.

"No, we will just walk by him and take no notice," Sinead said. "He can see us coming, and he is just showing off. Where did he get that car from? And what has he done to his hair?"

Jules frowned and shook her head in disbelief. His grey stubble had been dyed yellow. *Does he think that he is making me jealous? That poor girl, I'd rather kiss shit than him.* "Sinead is right. We will just ignore him. He wants a reaction from us, and he is not going to get one."

"Do you hear that? I can hear a siren in the distance," Sinead said. "I bet someone has called the police. You just can't stop your car like that and not expect a visit from the police."

"He's not going to hang around. It would make my day if he got arrested," Seth said.

With the police car approaching, Tom pushed the girl away from him and started the car. He turned off the music and sped off down the road toward them. He was looking directly at Jules as he passed. He slowed a little and tried to make eye contact with her. Jules ignored him and kept on walking. Her heart was beating hard, and she was beginning to feel frightened. For a moment, she remembered him on top of her, panting like a dog. She gasped as this flashback taunted her. Tom wheel spun the car as he put his foot down on the accelerator and then shot down the lane away from them.

As they reached the church, a police car was parked outside the front.

"I don't think we have seen the last of him," Sinead said as she leant the wreath on the wall outside the graveyard. Others had laid flowers there too.

"I don't think he was here to say goodbye to May," Jules replied as she tried to read the cards as they walked.

"No, he wanted to make sure you saw him with that girl," Seth said bitterly. "You do know that he is obsessed with you."

"Don't say that."

"We need to get a restraining order sorted. That was harassment."

"He didn't say or do anything,"

"I know, but he will. Here, Jules, take the pram. I am going to have a word with the police officers and tell them which way the Toad went."

Chapter Twenty-seven

Jules was sitting on the chair in their shower room and was checking all their songs on TikTok to see which ones their followers liked best. It had been hard to concentrate on this task. She had set a timer on her phone and refused to look at the words in the window of the pregnancy kit until she heard the alarm go off. Sinead was playing with Darragh, and Seth was out in the fields surveying the newly ploughed fields to see if the soil and weather were right for sowing. Feeling anxious, she glanced over at the white wand sitting on the lid of the toilet seat and was thankful that she was a safe distance away from it. *This is probably the longest three minutes of my life. Why am I so worried about this? If I am, I am. If I am not, then it doesn't matter. We've got lots of time to have another baby.*

Her alarm went off, and it made her jump. She found herself rushing over to the testing wand, and she picked it up, put the light on in the bathroom so she could clearly see the blue writing properly, and she gasped. '*Pregnant.*' "Surely not! I can't be." There was no denying it. The blue writing below the little window was as clear as day. *Well, that was quick; there is certainly nothing wrong with my fertility. What is Seth going to say?* She was two weeks late and had ordered the testing kit online with the vague hope that she might be pregnant. She smiled and then grinned at the thought of going through a pregnancy from the beginning. Finding out she was pregnant with Darragh and then giving birth on the same day had not given her the chance to enjoy the experience. *I mustn't get too excited. I can only be a few weeks pregnant - six weeks perhaps. Should I tell Seth or wait until*

I am a bit further along. No, I can't wait. Darragh and I will go over to see him and tell him my news.

Jules walked out into the living area and found Sinead sitting at the kitchen table with Darragh on her lap. She was showing him a moth-eaten teddy bear and was pretending that the bear was talking to him. Sinead had given the bear a Cork accent, and it was making Darragh giggle.

Jules quickly hid the testing kit behind her back, not sure if she should tell Sinead that she was pregnant.

"I've given Darragh my old teddy bear. I know he is old, but he is still soft and needs someone to love him. Do you mind if I give him to Darragh?"

"Are you sure? Won't you miss him?"

Sinead laughed. "We were inseparable when I was a kid, but Mr Ted has spent thirty years in an old suitcase with other keepsakes. I think it is time that he found a new home."

Darragh started to fiddle with Mr Ted's plastic nose and then eyes.

"He loves him. You are a dear thing. Oh, Sinead, I have some news. I know I should tell Seth first, but somehow, I think he already knows." She held out the wand and came over to her so she could see the blue word clearly.

Sinead smiled. "Pregnant! That was quick work! I can see that you are happy about it. Aww, I can't wait."

Seth came through the door and stood on the mat. His boots were caked in mud. "I have a little job for you both if you are up for it. I'm going to attach the potato hopper onto the back of the tractor, and all you two have to do is sit on the seat on either side of it and drop the seed potatoes down the hole as I drive the tractor along. I was going to put Darragh on my back in the carrier rather than leave him in his pram on the edge of the field." He looked at Jules and Sinead; they were smiling at him. "So, what's going on then? Why are you both grinning like Cheshire cats? Have I brought too much mud in?"

"Seth, you know how we talked about having another baby? Well, I reckon that we are about six weeks pregnant," she said, taking the wand over to him so he could see.

"I knew it! I saw it in your eyes when you and Darragh came down to see me the other day. I must have a second sense for seeing when a woman is pregnant." He picked Jules up and spun her around, hugging her. He put her down and then drew him to her and kissed her.

"I take it then that you are pleased," Sinead said.

"I am the happiest man alive. Now I am feeling guilty that I am asking you to work in the fields."

"I'm not sick, Seth. Just pregnant, and I've never felt better. We have to be realistic, though. Six weeks is really early, and we really shouldn't tell anyone until we reach the twelve-week mark."

"Ok, but it's going to be hard not to say anything. Will you help me with the potatoes before the weather turns bad? Rain is predicted tomorrow, and I want to get everything sown by this evening." He then looked down at the mud on the wooden flooring. "Look at the mess I've made on the floor. There's mud everywhere. I promise that I will clear it up later."

"I'll let you off," Jules said, laughing. "It's not every day you are told that you really are going to be a father." *At least he knows that this baby is his.*

***

Seth helped Jules and Sinead onto their seats next to the hopper and stood back to check that he had lined the tractor correctly with the drill in the earth. He couldn't help but smile at his puzzled workforce. They were both dressed in blue overalls and had their hair tied up in headscarves and reminded him of Second World War land girls. "So, the idea is that you take turns to throw a spud down the shoot, so they drop a foot apart. We will give it a go and see how far apart they are. In the past, they would have dropped them by hand and would have spent hours bent over, doing it. We are lucky that they used to farm potatoes here, and we have some apparatuses left for us."

"Apparatuses?" Sinead questioned. "This machine looks like it should be in a museum."

Seth laughed. "Sometimes these old machines are worth their weight in gold and are more efficient than a modern machine. Mind you, it will all be down to you two to throw the potato down at the right time."

Jules looked at the sacks of sprouting potatoes in the trailer next to her and stretched to get one. "I think you need to move these sacks closer to us and mustn't drive too fast. What do you think, Sinead?"

"I can't believe I've agreed to do this. I'm bound to get distracted and forget what I'm doing."

"I would let you drive the tractor, but it's hard to keep it straight. It does tend to pull to the left," Seth said as he moved the sacks closer to them. "Just shout when you run out. I've got fifty more sacks in the shed."

"No, it's ok. We'll give it a go but don't go mad if the spuds end up clumped together," Sinead said, picking up several potatoes ready for action.

"I won't; we will have a trial run first. I'll just put my boy on my back, and then off we go."

Seth started the tractor and then looked over his shoulder as he drove slowly forward. Jules and Sinead took turns to throw the seed potatoes down the shoot. Slowly he worked his way up the field and then felt Darragh's tiny hands on his head. "Are you doing ok, my wee boy? You like being out in the fields, don't you? You are going to have a brother or a sister soon, and then you will never be alone." *I wonder how my brothers and sisters are doing back at Crow Farm. I'll give Charlene a call later when we...* He heard a scream and saw that Sinead was lying on the earth. He stopped the tractor and jumped down. When he got to her, she was lying on her back in the mud, laughing.

"What happened?" he asked as he helped her up.

"We just went over a rock," Jules said. "It's like being on a fairground ride."

"I didn't expect it to be so bumpy," Sinead said, climbing back onto the wooden seat.

"Is it too much?" he asked Jules, suddenly concerned that he was causing them pain.

"No, I think we need to get some cushions and then we will be fine. These benches are really hard."

"I'll go and get some from the house. I can't have my workforce black and blue. Shall I get the cushions off the sofa?"

"Don't worry," Jules said. "I am sure we will get used to it. I think that we have done a grand job. Have a look, Seth. The potatoes look evenly spaced."

Seth looked down the row and placed his foot between the potatoes. "That's not bad, but they could be a little bit closer. Are you able to speed up a fraction?"

"We'll try," Sinead said. "We need to get a rhythm going."

"We could sing," Jules suggested.

"You don't want to hear me sing."

"I could sing a sea shanty or Ed Sheeran's 'The Shape of You.' That's got a great rhythm."

Sinead laughed. "This is going to be so crazy. Who knew that I would end up planting potatoes, in the middle of Ireland, in time to The Shape of You!"

***

With her lower back and bottom aching and her hands sore, Jules gently lowered herself into bed, eager for the soft mattress to suck her in and soothe her pains away. Dressed only in his boxer shorts, Seth was standing at the end of the bed with his arms folded, and he shook his head. "You should have let me get you cushions. I've nearly killed you and Sinead. I am a cruel husband. You should have told me to stop if you were in pain."

Jules gave him a weak smile. "I was fine until we got home. I actually really enjoyed planting those potatoes. It was strangely satisfying, and it was good to see Sinead laugh. We actually haven't laughed so much in a while."

"I still feel bad. I think I had the easy job driving the tractor. Do you want me to rub some deep heat into your backside?"

"Just my back, please. That would be lovely, but I doubt if you can use that stuff if you are pregnant."

"No, I suppose not. Baby oil then?"

"Mm... that sounds good, " she said, flipping over and then moaning in pain. "I just need a massage, and I will be right as rain."

Seth smiled. "I think I can manage that."

"There's some oil in the bathroom. I bought some for Darragh after he's had a bath. I haven't used it yet." *Do people use baby oil on babies, I wonder?*

Seth went off to the bathroom, and when he returned, he saw that Jules had gone off to sleep. *Better not wake her up.* He sat on the side of the

239

bed, and as he covered her up, he noticed her oak tree Dara knot tattoo on her back. *The inks still look vibrant and new.* He traced his fingers over the S&J and smiled. *I love you so much.* He kissed her back and then covered her up.

As he climbed into bed, both Jules and his phone pinged simultaneously. He picked his phone up and noticed that they had both received an email from Jane. She had attached their new single Waterfall Way to the email, and Seth looked across at Jules sleeping soundly and wondered if he should wake her so they could listen to their song together. *I can't wait until the morning.* He connected his earphones to the phone and, feeling a little anxious, clicked on the attachment. Waterfall Way started to play. He shut his eyes as he listened. Jules mumbled something and turned over, groaning a little. He unplugged one of his earphones and gently placed it in her ear so she could hear their song too. Seth was shocked as he listened, and he couldn't believe how good Sonar Cell and S&J sounded together. It was like listening to a famous band. *This is all a bit surreal. This has to be a hit. How could it not be*? He snuggled down and, facing Jules, watched her face as the music seeped into her dreams. He saw her smile, and he knew that she could hear them singing. Sleepily, she opened her eyes and smiled. "That's not half bad, is it? I think we all nailed it. You do know you really turn me on when you sing?"

"You're pretty hot yourself," he said, kissing her on the lips. "Sleep now," he said, pulling her into his arms so he could feel her body next to hers. He couldn't hold his eyes open any longer and drifted into a deep sleep, the music filling his dreams too. "Everything is going to be ok," he heard himself whisper.

Chapter Twenty-eight

The rain beat down hard on the windscreen, drowning out the radio, as Seth drove Jules and Darragh down to the Manor House. "Are you sure you want to start cleaning the house today?" he asked. "There's really no need until we have guests again. Who knows when that will be?"

"Exactly. Lockdown might be lifted next week, and then we will end up running around like headless chickens as we try to get ready. Anyway, there is not much we can do in the fields if it is tipping down, and I really need to get out of the house and do something constructive."

"It's a shame about the rain. I wanted to get the cauliflower seeds in. Perhaps it's a good thing I didn't. They might have all got washed away. Darragh, do you want to have a look around your house with me?" Darragh was mesmerised by the windscreen wipers and took no notice of his dad.

"I guess he will inherit the house one day. Along with Sinead's children. If she has any."

"Maybe. If Tom doesn't win his claim to the property, that is."

"I don't see any solicitor's letters. He is definitely in some sort of trouble; otherwise, I am sure we would have had a letter through by now. Let me sort out the annexe. I'd rather you didn't go in there and clean up after the Toad."

"If you want to, but honestly, I don't mind. In a way, it will be therapeutic for me if I scour and cleanse the annexe until it shines like a new pin. It will feel like I am getting rid of him once and for all."

"I hadn't thought of it like that. I can't say I had the same experience when I cleaned up his puke from Sinead's footwell. I am almost gagging

241

just thinking about it. I still want to keep you out of the Toad's lair. Darragh and I will make a great team. Can you hear him talking to the rain?"

"No, he is singing, actually. Do you not recognise that he is singing along to Blinding Lights? He knows that one well," she said, turning the radio down a little so they could hear his voice.

Seth laughed. "It won't be long until he is singing with us. We will have to call ourselves SJD- no, not SJD. That sounds too much like STD. How about 'The Hearns Three?'"

Jules laughed. "I am sure we can come up with something catchy."

As they entered the house, the smell of mould and soot filled their lungs, making them all cough.

"Christ," Seth said, looking around for evidence of damp climbing the walls. "This is no place to bring a baby," he said, putting Darragh into his pushchair. "I swear this house is deteriorating before our very eyes, and before we know it, the walls will start to crumble, and we will be dealing with a pile of damp bricks."

"Oh, don't say that. Waterfall West is not feeling loved at the moment. It's almost as if it is wringing its hands and crying. I think it misses May."

Seth smiled. "I wouldn't go that far. We need to keep it heated, but keeping the boiler on would cost a fortune."

"We should keep the fires burning then. We have plenty of wood on the estate. Would it take a lot of work to keep the fires going until the house is dry? When summer comes, it will be ok."

"That's a good idea. We will have to do that, or the guests won't want to stay here. There should be some dry wood at the back door. Darragh and I will go and get some logs. The pushchair will come in very handy."

"I'll start upstairs then and strip all the beds. Let's see if I can remember what needs to be done in each room. Do you realise that it's been nearly a year since I worked here? Oh, Seth, do you realise that it is Darragh's birthday and our first wedding anniversary on Wednesday?"

"Is it?" he said, smiling. "It's not a day any man or woman is likely to forget."

"You haven't got anything planned, have you?"

"I might have."

"Oh no! With everything that's been going on, I haven't even thought about it until now. Is that bad of me?"

"I am wounded."

"Really? I am so sorry."

Seth looked at her horrified face and couldn't let the teasing go on. "I'm only joking. To be honest, I haven't thought of anything to do yet. That's actually not true. There were lots of things I would have liked to have done. Had it not been for lockdown, I was going to take you to Blarney Castle so you could kiss the Blarney stone and then I was going to take you for a nice meal somewhere. We've never been out for a romantic meal together, have we?"

Jules smiled. "You remembered that I wanted to kiss that stone. Or see it, at least. I think they hang you upside down to kiss it, which is a bit worrying. You are sweet for remembering that I want to do that. I don't think I would like to be hung upside down, though."

"Another idea I had, which would be my ideal date, would be to take Moss and Connor down to the beach, and we could ride along the sand together. Moss loves going in the sea, and I am sure that Connor would too. Did you know we are only forty minutes from some amazing beaches?"

"I am really feeling bad now. All I can think of is baking Darragh a birthday cake and getting us in a take-away. That is if we can afford it."

"Don't feel bad. I like take-away. I don't see why we can't. Who knows, we might make our first million when Waterfall Way goes live, and we will be able to treat ourselves more often. It does sound so good, doesn't it?"

"I uploaded a minute's worth to TikTok this morning," she said, feeling her back pocket. "Oh damn! I've left my phone at home. I wanted to see how many hearts we've got. Jane said the full version will be on the radio tomorrow. Can you believe that we are going to be listening to ourselves along with famous singers? It's crazy. Of course, it's all down to Sonar Cell. If we tried going it alone, it would have taken us years to get this far," Jules said, picking up the post from the doormat.

"I don't know; we're pretty good. I get little butterflies in my stomach when we sing together. If I do, then I am sure others will too. Ok, I am going to pass out if we stand here much longer. It smells like someone has died in here. Let's get going and bring this house back to life before this little one starts yelling for his lunch."

***

It took Jules and Seth longer than they expected to clean the Manor House, and Darragh was getting irritable. Gemma had not been a good cleaner, and she had let mould accumulate in the shower rooms. There were stains on the carpets that took a lot of work to remove. Jules, who was now feeling exhausted but exhilarated, found Seth in the reception room, sat on the sofa talking to Darragh. The fire was burning brightly, and the room looked like it was coming alive again. Seth was telling him about the history of the house, but Darragh wasn't paying attention and wanted to get down onto the floor and explore.

"He's hungry," Jules said. "We need to go home and give him his lunch. I'm starving too. How did you get on with the annexe?"

244

"All clean. There was a surprising amount of Shreddies on the kitchen floor. The lazy git could have cleaned up after himself. There is a pile of laundry in the laundry room to be done. I picked up his old clothes with tongs and burnt them.

Darragh was wriggling and impatient to go. It's ok, my wee boy. We are done here. Are you hungry then? You get him in the car. I just want to get the fireguards out and cover the fires. I don't want a log to fall out while we are not here. The last thing we need to do is to burn the house down."

Seth got up and passed Darragh to Jules. "I'll bring the pram out in a minute. I won't be a moment."

"Ok, see you in a second. Don't forget to double-lock the door. We don't want the Toad to get back in." Jules carried Darragh back to the car and tried to get him into his car seat, but he arched his back, resisting. "It'll only be for five minutes, and then I can get you a piece of cheese until I've made your lunch. What do you want today? Macaroni cheese? I thought so. That won't take me long to make." Darragh started to cry as Jules did up his straps. "Just five minutes." She shut the door, and then she got into the passenger seat and waited for Seth to appear. *Come on, Seth, we have a wild, hungry baby on our hands.* She looked back at Darragh, who was moaning that they were not going anywhere. She held his foot to try and comfort him. The driver's door opened, and Jules was relieved that Seth had made it back before Darragh started crying again. She sighed with relief. "We are going to have to go like the wind…"

Jules could see long, thin fingers holding the steering wheel. *Seth? "Nooo!"* she gasped. Her eyes followed the hand to the wrist and then up the arm until her eyes settled on an emaciated face. She could barely breathe; her fear was so great. "TOM!"

"Surprise. You didn't think this would be the last you would see of me, did you? Pass me the key. I need your help."

"I can't help you. I've got to feed Darragh."

"Oh, so that's its name."

"I haven't got the keys," Jules said desperately. "Seth has them. He will be out in a moment." She stared at the door, willing Seth to appear.

Tom sneered. "I'm not stupid. I saw you open the car up with a key. I just need half an hour of your time. And if you don't mind, I would like to leave before your bodyguard appears. Do you know he nearly killed me? Shit like him needs to be locked up."

"I don't want to help you. You need to go, or I swear I will call the police."

"I don't think that would be wise. Not when I happen to know that there is a knife with Gemma's blood on it in a plastic bag at the bottom of a certain someone's toolbox."

"You bastard! You've planted it there, haven't you?" Jules was feeling alarmed. "It was you. You killed Gemma. Oh my God!" Jules put her hand on the door handle, ready to bolt and then looked back at Darragh. She was frightened that Tom might hurt him.

"If you get out, then it would only take a second or two to smother that brat. Keys, please."

"A knife in a toolbox doesn't make Seth guilty. The police aren't stupid. They will know that it was planted if you tip them off."

Tom sneered. "I don't think the police will see it that way. The man you have married is dangerous; he has a record and is a jailbird. Now keys, please, or I will go straight to the police with this crucial bit of evidence. Look, Julia, all I need is half an hour of your time, and I will let you and the brat go."

Angrily, she threw the keys at Tom, and they hit the window, and they dropped down between his legs. He swore, and she could see that he was starting to panic. *He's seen Seth.* She could see him locking the door.

She wound down the window and yelled. "SETH!... SETH, HELP!" He spun around, hearing her calls for help and then started running up the path towards her. Tom started the car, but it wasn't keen to start. He pulled out the choke and then, cursing, turned the key. The car coughed and started. Silently Jules swore. I can't believe it started. He has the luck of the Devil. Tom reversed the car at speed and slammed into a tree stump, knocking the rear number plate off.

Seth ran into the car park and touched the boot but could do nothing to stop Tom from stealing Jules and Darragh away. "NO!" he yelled and threw his arms in the air and held his head as he saw Tom drive off. "FOR THE LOVE OF GOD, NO! PLEASE NO! NOT AGAIN!"

Chapter Twenty-nine

"PLEASE, TAKE ME BACK. I don't want to go with you. Poor Seth, he will go crazy."

Tom shot her an angry glance. "You really don't see it, do you? That scumbag doesn't deserve you. You will thank me one day."

Alarm bells were ringing in her head. *This is kidnapping. Where is he taking me? I mustn't show him that I am afraid, or he will know that I am on to him.* Darragh started to complain, and she could see that he was getting on Tom's nerves.

"Can't you make him be quiet?"

"We need to take Darragh back, and then Seth can give him his lunch. He's hungry. I'll come and help you with whatever it is."

"Nice try, but unfortunately, the brat is going to have to come with us too."

Jules huffed. "Look, I don't know what is going through your head, but there is no way I am going to help you when we get to where we are going."

"Oh, you will. All it takes is one phone call, and the police will arrest the bastard."

"What makes you so sure that Seth touched that knife?"

"Because it wasn't me who cut her wrists. She was fine when I left her. I found the knife outside your house in a carrier bag."

Jules ignored his last comment. "So, you were at Waterfall West on the night Gemma died."

"No, I was talking about before."

"I'm not stupid. This is what I think. On the night Gemma died, you came up to see her and possibly me too. After all, you were in a relationship with her or just enjoyed the sex at any rate. You went to the mobile home looking for a bit, and then she told you that she was having your baby, and you freaked out, and you accidentally killed her. Then you took her up to the water trough and cut her wrists to make it look like suicide. Am I close?"

"See, that is what I like about you. You have a vivid imagination."

"Why are you looking flustered? I'm on to you, aren't I?"

"I didn't kill her. Sometimes when we were intimate, things did get a bit out of hand. She tripped and hit her head, and passed out. I wasn't feeling well, so I left and spent the night in the hay barn with those stinking horses. I didn't have enough money for a taxi home."

"So, you left her to die. Didn't you think to stay with her and make sure she was all right?"

"Now you are being dramatic. She didn't hit her head hard; it was nothing. As for staying with her, I certainly didn't want to spend the night at hers with all those pictures on the wall of that gypsy bastard."

"So, you just left her to die. In my book, that is murder or manslaughter at the very least."

"I am not a monster. I went back the next day to see if she was willing for a second round, but she had gone."

"So, was it you we saw in the mobile just before we found her body?"

"If it had just been you, then I would have shown myself. But that fucker was there as usual, and I am quite sure he would have had me by the throat."

Jules had a quick look back at Darragh to make sure he hadn't heard Tom's foul language. Fortunately, the motion of the car was sending him off to sleep.

249

"So, what happened to you after that? How did you end up in such a terrible state? When I found you outside the barn, you looked like you were about to die."

He sighed. "You'd look rough if you were withdrawing from heroin and had Covid. That was Hannah's fault, by the way. I told her not to go near anyone that was coughing. Stupid bitch!"

"So, are you Hannah's pimp then?"

"NO! Of course not. She is a freelance entertainer. She does live performances for businessmen. I am not quite sure what she does, but it makes her rich. The girl is obsessed with me, obsessed with sex and obsessed with the idea of us having a child. She is barking up the wrong tree if she is hoping to have a baby with me. Children are only good for one thing. I always use protection, and I plan to remain a virgin until you and I are wed."

"A virgin! Seriously!" *Did he just say until we are wed? I am in so much trouble here. He is delusional.* "What about Gemma? I don't remember you using anything with her."

"Yes, I am a virgin. I have been saving myself for someone special. With Gemma, it was a bit different. I don't want to go into that."

What a weirdo…

"Before I found you half dead in the bushes outside our barn, how long had you been hiding at Waterfall West?"

"A few weeks, I'm not sure. My mind has been playing tricks on me. I did go into Cork a couple of times to see Hannah."

"Mm… Where have you been staying? Please don't tell me that you were staying in the Manor House when you had Covid."

"I am not sure where I stayed. I think it was mostly in the hay barn. I was ill, I told you. I don't remember much. I needed money and food. May

250

keeps a cash box in the annexe. While she was out, I got in through a window and had a look round. All I found was a bag of crisps."

"Did you touch anything while you searched the annexe?"

"Of course, I did. Why?"

"You do realise that it was you that gave her Covid? Your germy fingers contaminated her belongings. You make me sick!"

"I am well aware that it was me that accidentally gave her this horrid virus, but I didn't do it on purpose. Thankfully, May being dead has solved all our money worries."

"You are cold and callous, and I don't want to be with you."

"You stupid girl! I have rescued you. You just need time to get over him. Your so-called husband was fucking Gemma and then killed her. God knows why. A jealous rage, perhaps. His sort are animals at heart. Anyway, Gemma told me that the baby was his, just as I was about to ejaculate. What a time to tell me that! It was a kick in the balls, and I shoved her away. Look, I know this is a lot to take in, and it will take time to get over him, but I do believe we can be happy together."

"You are a liar. You just said Gemma said the baby was yours. Listen to me, I am happily married and know that Seth wouldn't cheat on me or kill anyone for that matter." For a second, she saw a flashback of Seth and his Dad fighting to the death in the silent pool at Farm End. Angry for firing up that memory, she chastised herself. "In fact, we have another baby on the way."

"Oh Julia, I'm so sorry. We can get rid of it and that thing too," he said, looking over his shoulder at Darragh.

"You bastard, you have gone too far!" she yelled. She was beginning to lose it. "So, you found the knife that was used to cut Gemma's wrists. So what! When we stop at traffic lights, then I am going to get out of this car and scream for help. You are out of your mind."

251

"You wouldn't do that, Julia. I know deep down you want to be with me." Darragh had woken up, and he was yelling out to her, angry that he wasn't getting his lunch.

"I swear that the child is a gypsy demon. How long do you think it would take me to silence him while you are calling out for help? Thirty seconds, perhaps?"

"You touch my baby, and I swear I will rip your eyes out with my bare hands!"

"You are not being very kind to me, and it hurts. You know that I love you, don't you? All the hundreds of girls I've been with mean nothing to me. When we make love, it is so very different. So pure."

Jules went silent. Not sure how to respond. *He's a total nutcase. Be strong, Jules, don't rile him. For Darragh's sake, you have to play this nightmare of a game.* "I'm sorry. So, you said you needed my help. Was that just a ploy?"

"I knew that you would come round. Yes, I do need your help. I need your help with Hannah."

"Who is this, Hannah? Is she the child I saw you with your tongue down her throat?"

"You're not jealous, are you? I thought that you might be."

"No, I wouldn't say that exactly." *Don't rile him.* "I was just surprised, that's all."

"Hannah is my live-in girlfriend, my honeypot, and although she would like it to be more than friends, I cannot give my heart to her because it belongs to you."

Jules closed her ears to the last bit he had said. "Ok, so what is wrong with your honeypot?"

"She wants to leave me. I need you to talk to her and convince her to stay."

"So why do you want her to stay if you don't love her?"

"We need her. Mr Steel has needs. She is our worker bee, and she will bring in the money until we get your half of the estate when you divorce that gypsy fraudster. Then she can leave."

Jules frowned as she tried to take in everything he was saying. She was horrified and didn't like to ask who Mr Steel was, but she had an idea. "I thought you had money and owned a huge pharmaceutical company."

"All lost! I'm bankrupt and penniless," he lied.

"So, Hannah isn't going to want to stay, now I'm here. Wouldn't it be better if we both got jobs and let her go?" *I'd better play along and see what the Toad has planned.*

Tom grinned a crooked smile at her, and it freaked her out. "We sound like a married couple already. No, she needs to work. I can't have you soiling your pretty hands. We're nearly home," he said as he turned into the Dough Cloyne Industrial Estate.

Jules' heart sank as they passed rows and rows of rust-coloured units with blue doors closed up because of Covid. *No sign of life here. Not a soul!* Any hope of getting her and Darragh help was slowly slipping away. Tom stopped the car by a black gate and looked at her.

"You need to open the gate and let us through. I know you won't run because I have your brat."

Saying nothing, Jules got out of the car and looked around to see if there was any sign of life. *No one!* She shut the gate and then followed the car to the back of a large white building. She could hear Darragh crying, and she couldn't help but cry too. The building was on the edge of the estate and backed onto wasteland. If she grabbed Darragh, she could start running through the estate. She knew that she wouldn't get far before the Toad caught up with them. When she got Darragh out of the car, he was sobbing.

"What's wrong with him? Can't you shut him up?" Tom asked as he lifted a shutter up to let them into the building. It wasn't locked. *That's a good escape route, but what a noise the shutter makes. I need to find a quieter way out.*

"I told you, he is hungry and probably thirsty. All I have with me is his water bottle and a nappy."

"Hannah bought some food yesterday. There's probably something in the fridge he could eat. Come and meet my honeypot."

He led her through an empty building and then up some stairs with the word office printed on the wall.

"This used to be one of my company's distribution units. The building is up for sale, but there is no interest at the moment, so this is home. Hannah and I have made it into quite a luxurious pad, and we want for nothing."

Jules said nothing and just rocked Darragh to calm him. He had stopped crying and was looking at his new surroundings with interest. At the end of the corridor was a door with the words Staff Room painted on it. Tom unlocked the door and opened it to allow her through. She stopped and looked at him.

"Why was the door locked, and where is Hannah? I can't hear anyone in there."

"She's a lazy bitch. She's probably sleeping."

"You go in first. I don't trust you."

"Oh, for Heaven's sake!" he said as he walked into the room. "Look, there is nothing to worry about. Hannah, get up. We've got a guest."

Cautiously, Jules ventured into the staff room, fully expecting him to be lying. She looked around and was surprised to see how nicely the room had been furnished. They were standing in a small kitchenette, and a large silver fridge with an ice dispenser caught her eye. At the end of the room was a brass bed with a princess net hanging down from the ceiling. Hannah, with blond curls like her own, lay in the bed. She was awake and smiled to herself, lost in her own world.

"Is she ok? She doesn't know that we are here."

"Oh dear, I told her not to do drugs when I'm not here. She nearly overdosed last week. She will come round in a couple of hours. Help yourself to anything you want."

He opened the fridge door to reveal an interesting array of snacks. *Christ, they are living on rubbish. Please let there be something in there I can give my baby.* She got closer and peered into the fridge and noticed a pack of yoghurts at the back, some cheese and a large bottle of milk. "Is it ok if I give Darragh a yoghurt?" Jules looked around, but Tom did not answer. She heard the door lock and realised that she had been imprisoned. "No, please don't leave me here." *I shouldn't have come in. He would have hurt Darragh if I didn't do as he wanted. Shit!*

Hannah lifted her head and grinned at her. "Welcome to paradise!"

Chapter Thirty

Seth raced up the gravel drive to the stable yard, the loose stones slowed him down, and his leg muscles and sore knee screamed out in pain. He had no time to lose. He had to find Sinead and ask her if he could borrow her Mini. *They can't have gone far. They were heading towards Cork, and there aren't that many cars on the road. I am sure I can catch up with them. Where would Sinead be? Please be in the office.*

She wasn't there or in the stable block. Each minute that passed by was lengthening the distance between him and the Toad. He would have to go and get Sinead's spare key and hope she didn't mind him borrowing her car. It was a few minutes run down the track home. Seth stood in the middle of the stable yard, debating if it would be quicker to hot wire her car. Better *not, she will go mad. These new cars have a casing around the wires like Fort Knox, so it would take me a while to start it.* He glanced at her Mini, feeling a little downhearted and then saw her. *Sinead!* She was sitting in her Mini reading, and he had never felt so relieved. He ran over to the car and flung the driver's door open. "I need your car. That fuckwit has kidnapped Jules and Darragh!"

"My God! You nearly gave me a heart attack."

"Quick, budge over; they are getting away. We haven't got a moment to lose."

Sinead jumped out of the car and ran around to the passenger side, and got in. Seth shot into the driver's seat and started the car, and reversed as Sinead shut the door. They sped out of the stable yard and down the gravel drive in hot pursuit.

"What happened, then? Seth, be careful. You are driving like a lunatic."

He slowed a little, not wanting to freak her out. "I'm not sure. We had just finished cleaning the Manor House, and Jules went ahead to put Darragh in the car. When I came out, I caught Tom driving them both away. She cried for help out of the window, but I couldn't get to her in time. I've let her down again! I could kick myself for not being more careful. I should have known that he would come back for her."

"That's crazy talk. There is nothing you could have done."

They flew by the Manor House. "If I put my foot down, then I am sure I can catch them up. This is going to be one hell of a ride. Do you want me to drop you off?"

"No way. It will only slow you down if we stop. SETH! There's another car."

Seth hit the brakes, and the Mini spun round on the gravel drive, narrowly missing a police car. The police car screeched to a halt.

"NO! What does that eejit want now?" They watched as a red-faced man climbed out of the car. Rufus and two other police officers jumped out of the car and ran towards him.

"Something bad has happened," Seth said. "Please don't let it be a traffic accident. That old car is hard to handle. Please let them be alright."

Fearing the worst, Seth got out of the car. "What's happened? Are they ok?"

Rufus looked confused. "I don't know what you are talking about."

"Tom Stone has kidnapped Jules and my wee boy. Have they crashed?"

"No, I'm not here about that."

"So, what are you here for then?"

257

"I've got a warrant to search the premises for a murder weapon. Please can you show us where you keep your toolbox?"

"You are having a laugh? Don't tell me. You got a tip-off from a man with a very English accent. Perhaps a hint of Australian in it. The very same man that raped my wife and has now kidnapped her."

"I don't know who gave us this information."

Seth got a bit closer to Rufus and looked at his name badge. "Look, Rufus Parvel, I really haven't got time for this. I need to go and save my wife. If you want to go and search for whatever, then help yourself. You will find my toolbox in the tractor shed next to our house. I need to get going. Can you not send a car to look for my family too? They are in danger. I know they are. Tom Stone needs locking up."

Rufus scowled and shook his head. "If we find the knife, then we will have to bring you in for questioning."

Seth was starting to get cross. "So, you are saying that you would rather question me than stop a psycho hurting and possibly killing another girl. Tom Stone is not stable; he is the one that killed Gemma Stone. I just know it. Please help me find Jules and Darragh before it is too late."

"I can't. I have to follow procedure."

"Sure, you can. Fuck procedure!"

Sinead appeared by his side. "Look, I know Seth didn't kill Gemma. It has to be Tom Stone. I heard him hit her and heard her hit the floor. When I checked on her in the morning, she was stone cold dead. I panicked, and I don't know why I did it, but I carried her up to the water trough in the summer field and tried to make it look like she had killed herself. The fingerprints on the knife are mine, not Seth's. I hid the knife in a bag in the bushes outside the old barn. Jules found Tom hiding in those bushes. He must have found the knife and planted it in Seth's toolbox."

Seth stared at Sinead in amazement. *Why would she try to make it look like a suicide? Unless... she was trying to protect someone. She was trying to protect me!* "Oh Sinead, you poor girl," he exclaimed, hugging her. "You crazy thing!" *I am not sure she is telling the truth, though. That is one crazy story.*

"Are you going to arrest me?" she asked Rufus.

"Not at this stage, but you are both definitely going to have to come in for questioning. Although you will have to drive there yourself. If you think your wife is in danger, then we can search for the car. Do you have the registration number?"

"That would be a great help, but we are wasting time. I might be able to find them if I put my foot down."

"I can't let you go driving around Cork like a ne'er-do-well vigilante. And anyway, I would have to arrest you for driving unnecessarily during lockdown."

"But…"

"Seth, we are going to have to do as he asks, or we will get arrested, and we will be no good to anyone."

Seth sighed and shook his head in defeat. *What a jobsworth!* "When the Toad reversed, he knocked the registration plate clean off, so the number plate is in the car park here. The car is a dark green classic Mark 1 Jag, so it will be an easy car to spot. Especially with a number plate missing."

"This isn't a domestic, is it? Wives go off with other men all the time."

Seth was losing patience. "Christ, no, Jules was screaming for help. You just have to make a call."

"Fair enough, I'll make a call, and then we can proceed to your house."

"Thank you, but please do your best. I've got a bad feeling about this. I guess once you've got the knife, then we will follow you down to the police station. Do you all wear masks at the station? I don't want to get Covid."

"No, nor do I. We have few masks available. I'd rather talk to you here, but the powers that be insist that we have a formal chat at the station."

"A formal chat? I don't like the sound of that. So will DI Lucy O'Leary be at the interview?"

"No, she's been taken off this case."

"Oh no. Why's that then?"

"It is not appropriate for her to be involved in a case when a suspect is a half-brother."

"Oh wow! Christ! That's a shame. She's really good at her job." *I knew it. Why am I a suspect?* "Rufus, we are running out of time. Please just make that call. I need you to find my wife and child."

"First things first, let's get this knife," Rufus said, pointing up the drive. Five minutes is not going to make much of a difference."

Oh, for fuck's sake!

***

The interview room in Cork police station smelt of disinfectant, and the mask Seth was wearing was doing nothing to hide the smell of bleach and pine. The small room was making him feel uneasy. It was too cell-like. He had been sitting there for half an hour, and he was getting annoyed. He wanted to be out looking for Jules and Darragh and didn't know what else he could do to help bring them back. He didn't think Rufus Parvel had taken him seriously.

I wonder if they have checked to see if the Toad has a criminal record. Will they even tell me if they have? If only Sinead had knocked on the mobile door and seen him with Gemma. We have no proof that he was there at all. What was Sinead thinking of, saying she moved Gemma? I can't believe that she would be able to carry Gemma that far. She was quite a lump. I wonder what she is going to say about that. Christ, this is such a mess!

Rufus came into the room, wearing full PPE clothing, and suddenly the mask Seth was wearing felt like it was pathetically inadequate.

"Oh, Christ! You look like a Martian."

"Mm… I can't take any chances. I have a weak immune system."

"Oh, I see. I'm sorry to hear that."

"We could have done another of those through the window interviews."

"We could have, but our interview policy has been revised. Sebastian Hearn, this meeting is going to be recorded. I am going to ask you your name, address, and age, so don't get cocky. This recording could be used in court…"

"I don't actually have to say anything. I've told you everything I know already."

"True, but it would be in your interest to repeat your sorry tale."

"I don't like the sound of this." *He is bluffing.* "I only have to say who I am and then say no comment to any questions you might ask me. Or I need a solicitor present. I think this is the way it is going to go. I really have nothing more to say. I have told you everything you need to know."

"Mm… There are questions I need to ask you about the Ivy Brown case."

"That had nothing to do with this."

"You say that, but you have to admit that it is strange that a young girl, similar looking to Ivy Brown, ends up dead in a watery grave."

Did Jules say something like that? "Like I said, no comment. That had nothing to do with me."

"Your Mam said that it had a lot to do with you."

"You can't take the word of a mad woman too seriously. So, no comment. You should ask my Dad questions about that." He wished he hadn't added that on, but the words just spilt out of his mouth. *Thank God we are not recording this. Just say No comment, Seth, you eejit.*

"So where is Jethro Hearn? Your Mam said that he went back to Ireland. There is a warrant for his arrest, but nobody has been able to find him. Any idea where he might be? Lucy O'Leary would like to find him, it seems."

Seth went quiet for a moment and wasn't sure how he should respond. *Say nothing!* "Look, I really can't help you. If you are going to arrest me, then arrest me, and I will get a lawyer. If you have no solid evidence, then you have to let me go. I am innocent."

"That's not what Sinead is saying."

He is bluffing. Sinead is not going to say anything to get me in trouble. Is she? No, he is bluffing.

"I have nothing more to say."

"Ok, but it is not looking very good for your friend. It seems that her fingerprints were on more than the knife."

"What are you trying to say?"

"Someone is lying to us, and that won't look good in court."

"Well, it's not me!" *He is trying to trick me. Just say nothing more. Of course, her fingerprints are all over the mobile. We all lived there once.*

"Look, Rufus, you don't have to play bad cop with me. I have seen it all before. I really am going to say nothing more about this." He folded his arms and looked defiantly at him. "What about Jules? Any news about my wife and wee boy?"

"Oh, that. No, we haven't been able to trace the car yet. We need to wait 24 hours before we declare them as missing. Repentant wives usually come home the next day."

"24 hours! My foot! She is with a dangerous man. Have you checked to see if he has a record? I bet he does."

He doesn't seem that bothered. I am going to have to find them myself.

***

Seth was sitting in the Mini, waiting outside the police station for Sinead to appear. He wondered why she was taking so long to come out. He was not impressed with Rufus Parvel, and he would have been quite happy to give him the kick up the arse that he so badly deserved. He was really cross with him. He was the most irritating man he had ever come across. Needing to listen to music to calm himself down and possibly distract his brain from overthinking things, he pulled out his phone and noticed that he had several messages in the TikTok inbox. With a heavy heart, he opened up the TikTok app and looked at the videos he and Jules had recorded. He played Walk Me Home and smiled as he saw Jules sing. It was good to see her sweet little face and listen to her sing. A tear ran down his cheek, and he wiped it away, not wanting to appear weak in front of her. "I will find you and walk you home. Be strong and never give up hope. Someone must know where you are. There must be a fan that can see that car outside their window. See where he has taken you and Darragh," he exclaimed. An idea was forming in his head. *I wonder if I can ask our fans to look for me. They will find her. I know they will. If I go live on TikTok for an hour each day, then people can send me comments. Now there's an idea. There is just the smallest chance that we can find you both.* He was crying and laughing at the same time. *Come on, Sinead, please come out. I need to get home and start a live broadcast.*

Seth sat in the car for another hour and was tempted to do a live TikTok broadcast from the car. It then occurred to him that he would probably have to shave first as the stubble on his chin might make him look like he was desperate. He didn't want to shock their fans. He breathed a sigh of relief as a pasty-faced Sinead got into the car. "So, you made it out of there alive. At least you didn't have Parvel interviewing you. How are you doing?"

"I am just amazed that they let me go. I did have the pleasure for the last half hour. Parvel is a fucking nightmare! He wanted me to say I killed Gemma. He kept going over the same old ground, and in the end, my mind was playing tricks on me. He fucked with my mind so much that I almost believe that I did commit murder. He kept calling it manslaughter. He said that you thought I killed her. I didn't believe him, of course. I know that he was just trying to trick me into a confession. Oh, Seth, please take me home. I need a hot bath and a bottle of vodka. Have you been waiting long?"

"An hour or so? I can't believe that you went to so much trouble for me. You really did think I killed her, didn't you?"

"We've been over this. You know that I'm really sorry."

"So, you carried her over your shoulder, all that way up to the water trough. That must have been hard going. She's a big girl," he said, smiling.

Sinead sighed. "You don't miss a trick, do you? No, it wasn't me that took her to the horse trough. They won't find my fingerprints on the knife either. I just said that so you could go off and look for Jules and Darragh. I did find a knife in a bag outside your house but I hid it in the hay barn. Do you think that could have been the murder weapon? Do you think the toad found it and planted it in your tool box? I am so confused."

"You crazy girl. You are going to get into so much trouble. Hell, you could go to prison for wasting police time and holding up a police investigation. I know you were only trying to help me, but what were you thinking of?"

"I don't know, I just wanted to make it up to you. I should have told the police about hiding the knife in the hay barn. I really can't face them now. When we get back home I will see if I can find it. Whoever killed Gemma was trying to make it look like you killed her by leaving the knife in the bag outside your door. I was trying to protect you."

"I do appreciate what you tried to do, but I am worried for you. They didn't charge you with anything, thank God!"

"They took my fingerprints, and I said that they won't find any of mine on the knife because it wasn't me. Because my story was so confusing, they ended up thinking that I was a crazy person. Seth, that was horrible. Did they grill you like they grilled me?"

"No, I didn't give them the chance. In fact, that weirdo Rufus Parvel didn't even turn on the recorder. I told him that I had nothing more to add and that I would do the no comment thing. You should have said that too."

"Fuck! I didn't think. When we find that bastard Tom Stone, we will beat a confession out of him. You're looking sad. There's no news, is there?"

"No, nothing. I have a plan, though. As soon as we get home, I am going to go live on TikTok and appeal to our fans to search for her. I want them to look out of their windows and look for the Jag."

"That's a great idea. It's a bit late, though. I would wait until the morning. It's too dark for people to be looking out of their windows at this hour."

"Damn! You are right. The morning it is then."

Chapter Thirty-one

It was beginning to get light, and Jules could see the sun just starting to appear on the horizon. Streaks of reds and oranges filled the sky, promising all those that believed in shepherd's warnings that it would be a glorious day. The barren wasteland beyond the perimeter of her prison mocked her and dared her to attempt to take a chance and run for it. *I am not a fool!*

Jules was tired and hugged herself miserably, missing Seth's warm and loving arms around her. *Oh, my poor Seth, you must be going out of your mind with worry. At least you know what's happened to me. You must have called the police. I hope you have called them.*

She hadn't slept, and she had been sitting by the window for hours, wondering what to do to free herself from captivity. The Jaguar was parked just below her in the car park, and it was tantalisingly close. She had thought of tying sheets together and climbing out of the window with Darragh strapped to her back but knew that could end in disaster if she slipped. *I will have to find a way to prise the door open.* She walked over to the kitchen to look for an implement to use. The knives and forks would be useless and too flimsy to use as a crowbar. She pulled out the largest kitchen knife from a block on the work surface and looked at it thoughtfully. If she did get out, then she would have to walk out of the estate with Darragh. She was sure that Tom hadn't locked the Jag's doors. *If only I knew how to hotwire a car. If I manage to prise the door open, then there is a chance we could escape.* Trying not to wake Hannah, she slid the knife in the crack in the door until she reached the lock and then, with all her strength, chopped down on it, trying to force back the bolt into its casing. Nothing happened, and tears of desperation filled her eyes as she tried again. "Please work. OH, FOR THE LOVE OF GOD!" she yelled. She withdrew the knife and leant her head against the door, hoping that it would open. The door refused to oblige.

Concerned that she had frightened Darragh, she put the knife back and went back to him. He was sleeping peacefully on the sofa, blissfully unaware of their desperate situation.

The night before had been an odd one, and she was thankful that Tom had gone out. She had tried her best to make her baby comfortable on the sofa and had surrounded him with cushions, so he didn't roll off in the night. He went to sleep at his usual time, and while he slept, she had rinsed out his wet nappy pants and had hung them on the radiator to dry overnight.

It was breakfast time, and she was hungry, but she dared not eat anything, worried that she would run out of food to give Darragh. Tom had not come back yet, and although she was thankful, she found it strange. *Where was he last night? Where did he expect us to sleep? With Hannah?* She looked across at her and checked that she was breathing. During the night, Hannah had yelled out in her sleep as if she was in pain. She suspected that the heroin must have been working its way out of her system and was causing these terrors. Jules sighed. *If only I had my phone with me. I always have my phone with me. The one time I really needed it, I left it at home. I can't believe how stupid I am! I wonder if Hannah has a phone. She must have.* Jules pulled open the drawer of the bedside cabinet, and to her horror, she realised that it was full of used needles. She couldn't see a phone, and she exhaled miserably.

"Tom, what time is it?" Hannah asked in a croaky voice. She patted the other half of the bed as if she was feeling for him.

"I have no idea. It's just gone eight," Jules answered crossly.

"What? Tom? Oh shit! So, you're here," Hannah wailed. She raised her head and squinted at Jules.

"So, you were expecting me, then?"

"Yes. No! Oh shit, he said he would give me another chance." She threw her head back on the pillow and winced. "You couldn't get me a black coffee and some painkillers from the kitchen drawer, could you? He should have left me some."

Jules frowned. "I am not your slave. Get them yourself. Or are you still too wasted to walk?"

"There's nothing wrong with me," she said, swinging her legs over the side of the bed. She then tried to stand up, but her legs didn't hold her up, and she face planted on the floor.

Jules felt a little bit sorry and would have laughed had she not been feeling so stressed. She couldn't help but notice how spindly her legs were. *She is almost a skeleton. She's a drug addict, there is no doubt.* "Look, I'll get you a coffee, but I need to know a few things. I know you are feeling rough, but I really need answers. We were kidnapped. I am not staying here. We are leaving as soon as I can, so you don't have to worry. You can have Tom all to yourself."

"We?"

"Darragh and I. He's asleep on the couch."

Looking incredibly weak, Hannah pulled herself up onto the bed and looked over at Darragh and smiled. "He said he would give me a baby."

"Did he? Well, it's not that one. He's mine. Anyway, Tom hates him. He won't let you keep him. He reminds him too much of Seth."

"Oh! Ok. Can I hold him when he wakes up? My baby was put into care. They won't let me see him."

"That's sad. I am sure they would let you see him if you can get yourself off drugs. Tom said that you have been using heroin."

"I can handle it. I really don't want to take it, but it helps."

"How can drugs help you? I thought you were going to die last night." Jules put the kettle on and looked in the cupboard for coffee.

"Tom says I should stick with ketamine like he does, but it doesn't help me at all," she said, leaning back on the brass bedhead. "I've heard Seth's name before, and I recognise you from somewhere, too."

"Have you heard of the band Sonar Cell and S&J? We just released Waterfall Way."

"Yes. I know where I've seen you before. You are on TikTok. Is Seth your boyfriend then? He's hot!"

"Seth is my husband, and he will be missing us. Look, Hannah, we've got to get back to him. Today! Please, please help me get out of here. I don't want to be here. My heart is breaking. If you have seen us on TikTok, then you must have a phone," she said with a glimmer of hope.

Hannah had a faraway look on her face and hadn't really heard her pleas. "I did have a phone. He took it off me a few days ago. He said he was going to get me a new one."

Jules' spirits sank to a new low. "Oh dear, this is not good. Why do you stay with that man? You do know he is using you?"

She looked at Hannah and saw a switch flip in her head. A haunted look entered her eyes, and Jules knew she had said the wrong thing.

"Look, I'm sorry..."

"You have no idea what it's been like for me, living alone in this miserable city. That man took me off the streets and gave me a life. He made me believe in myself, and he looks after me. I will love him until the day I die."

"So why has he brought me here, then?" Jules asked. She didn't want to upset her, but she needed to know what was going on.

Hannah looked towards the window silently as she prepared an answer. "He wants me to be more like you. He loves me, but all he does is talk about how perfect you are. I really don't understand what he sees in you. You are just like all the rest."

I am going to have to be sickly nice to her to get her to help me. "Nor do I. I am not a nice person. You are way nicer than me."

Hannah smiled, and then she frowned. "You want me to help you, don't you? I am not sure I can. He will punish me."

"He doesn't have to know that you helped me. I need the key to this door and my car keys. If you drug him, then I can get the keys out of his pocket and then leave. Then I will be out of your lives forever." Jules handed her a coffee and smiled. "Do you realise that we nearly look like twins, only I'm not as pretty as you? How old are you, Hannah? I think we're about the same age." *I think that I am getting through to her. I bet she says she's older than she is.*

"Fifteen," she said, her eyes widened with fear. "But Tom doesn't know that. He thinks I'm eighteen. You won't tell him, will you? Please don't."

"Why would I? I really don't want to get involved. So where is Tom? He didn't stay here last night."

"Oh, he goes off and does his own thing, sometimes. I wish he wouldn't. I miss him when he's gone."

"Why does he lock you in the flat?"

"He says that he does it to protect me from evil, but I think he is afraid that I will leave him. I tell him that I won't. I wish he would trust me."

"So how do you get food when he is away if you can't go out?"

"I order it online and get it delivered. When the van arrives, I lower down a bucket on a rope and haul it up through the window. I tell the delivery man that I am sick, so he can't come into the building."

"Are you having a delivery anytime soon?" Jules asked, a plan forming in her mind. "You haven't got much food left. I really need some baby milk and more food for Darragh. He's nearly eaten all your yoghurts."

"I'm sorry. I order everything on my phone, and I don't have it, do I?"

"Damn! Tom says that you are an escort. You must have to leave the building to see your clients."

"Did he say that? He likes to pretend I am. It turns him on. That's how we met. I am not a prostitute anymore. I dress up as a school girl and have tea with Chinese businessmen on the TV. I just have to look sexy and flutter my eyelids at them. They pay me heaps of money. If I touch myself, then they pay me extra. It's money for old rope."

"Oh goodness, I didn't realise that kind of thing went on."

"You should dress up too. They will pay double for twins."

"No, I don't think so..."

The sound of the door being unlocked stopped her talking, and she prayed that she would see Seth. *Please let it be you.*

Tom walked in. His eyes were bloodshot, and he had love bites on his neck.

Hannah stood up and glared at him. "YOU PROMISED THAT YOU WOULDN'T SLEEP WITH HER AGAIN," she cried out. Jules was surprised at her sudden change in mood. For someone so small, she had one hell of a loud voice.

"Honeypot, darling. You know she means nothing to me. I can't help it if Mr Steel needs to let off steam now and again. God blessed me with this gift, and I just have to share the love. It was the best fuck I've had in a long time."

Hannah hurled her coffee at him, and the cup hit him square on the chest. The contents spilt down him burning his body as it soaked into his clothes.

271

"YOU BITCH!"

Jules looked on in horror and was thankful that Darragh was on the other side of the room.

Tom ripped open the buttons on his shirt to get the wet material off of his body. "You know I will have to punish you. Think of Julia. You are embarrassing me. We have a new flatmate now, and she's not going to want to stay if you carry on like this."

Hannah started to cry. "I'm sorry, I will make it up to you and Mr Steel. I will cook you your favourite dinner tonight."

"Empty words, Gemma. EMPTY WORDS! You will be off your head again tonight, and you will be no good to anyone."

Hannah scowled at him but said nothing. Tom shook his head and then went off to the washroom to clean up.

"Did he just call me GEMMA?" Hannah asked.

"Yes, he did. Do you know who Gemma is?" Jules asked gently.

"No. He has lots of girlfriends. What is she like?" she asked.

"She was a bit like us, blonde, petite, but she had a big chest. Have you noticed that we all have similar-sounding names? Do you know what happened to Gemma?"

"No. He probably screwed her to death."

"Actually, he murdered her. He said he just pushed her, but it sounds like he pushed her over, and she hit her head, and he left her to die. To me, that is murder."

"I don't believe you."

"He told me what happened on the way over. You can ask him if you like."

"No, I'd rather not. I'm in enough trouble as it is."

"You can do better than him. What sort of relationship is it if he is talking about punishing you? Does he hurt you, Hannah?"

She glared at her. "I don't want to talk about it. I get what I deserve. Your Darren is getting off the sofa, by the way."

"He's called Darragh. When he's had his breakfast, you can play with him if you like." *I've got to keep her on side.*

Jules ran over to the sofa and just caught Darragh as he slid off, bringing the cushions with him. He giggled and then smiled at Jules. She picked him up and hugged and kissed him. "Morning, my wee boy. Did you sleep well?"

"Oh, he is so cute. He looks so much like Seth."

Tom returned from the washroom, and he was naked. Jules was surprised, and she did her best to ignore him. He didn't seem bothered that he was nude.

"Don't mention that bastard's name here. For fuck's sake, Hannah. Don't tell me that you know that bastard gypsy too!" Tom spat.

"I don't know him personally," she said quietly. "He's a pop star, so everyone knows him. So is Julia."

"What are you talking about?"

"S&J are famous. Haven't you heard of them then? I don't think it was a good idea bringing Julia here. You are going to get in so much trouble, Tom Stone."

"The police are probably scouring the country as we speak. Kidnapping is a criminal offence, you know," Jules said sternly. "It is only a matter of time before they track you down. Stealing a baby too! You will probably go to prison for a long time. If you give me the keys to my car, then I will go home, and we will say no more about this."

Tom's eyes narrowed. "We will have to get rid of the child and move to Dublin. Why did you have to bring it with you? You have fucked things up!"

Jules silently gasped as she realised what she had done. *What does he mean by 'get rid of the child?' Is he going to kill Darragh? Oh Jesus!*

273

What have I said! I might as well have thrown him under a bus. She held Darragh a little tighter and did her best not to cry. "Please don't hurt him. What do you want from me? We can work this out."

"That's more like it. All I want is for us to be one happy family. Hannah, you need to clean the flat, and if I see the tiniest speck of coffee on the carpet, then you won't get any treats this week. Julia, darling, I want you to give me a blow job. Mr Steel has been fed and needs satisfying and then later if you please him, I will go and get us all a takeaway. Do you like Chinese?"

Jules was speechless. His words kept replaying in her head, and she couldn't help noticing that he was becoming erect. She turned Darragh away, so he couldn't see and then looked at Hannah, puzzled. She could see her smirking. *What would happen if I don't satisfy him? Will he hurt Darragh? What am I going to...?*

"Julia, do you like Chinese? JULIA?"

"Yes," she replied in a small voice.

Chapter Thirty-two

Feeling low and hurting deep down inside, Seth stared down at his bowl of cereal, lost in his thoughts. At first light, he and Sinead had searched the hay barn for the knife but they had been unable to find it. *If only Sinead had given it to the police when she found it, then they would have arrested the toad and my Jules and Darragh would be safe....* He stirred the cornflakes without realising that they were breaking apart and turning into a soup. The morning had not come quick enough, and sleep had eluded him. The silence in the house was unbearable, and he longed to hear the familiar sounds of his family around him as they got ready for the day.

Sighing, he thought back to his conversation with Rufus Parvel at the police station, and he realised that he was not taking the search for Jules and Darragh seriously. *What do I have to do to make the police listen to me? If I get arrested driving around Cork looking for them, will they listen then? No, probably not. I wonder if DI Lucy O'Leary will help. We've got her card somewhere. Where would Jules have put it?* He put down his spoon and stood up.

Barney started to meow at him, wanting food. "Give me a moment, will you. I've got to find something." Barney followed Seth to the kitchen area and then jumped up on the work surface, purring. The purring and meowing went up a notch as Seth got near to the cupboard that stored the cat food. Unable to concentrate on the task in hand, Seth found himself pulling out a pouch and then fed Barney. Barney was starving and gobbled down the food with urgency. "There, are you happy now? Good. Let's look in the bits and bobs drawer." He pulled it open, and then after staring at

Lucy's card without seeing it, his eyes finally focused on her name, and he plucked it up, feeling a little more positive.

He took the card over to the sofa and picked up his phone. Jules' phone was next to his, and he stroked it gently, tears forming. *How is she going to ring for help, my poor wee dote? I mustn't cry.* Her phone battery was low, so he plugged in the charger, ready for her to use when she returned. He then realised that he would need her phone to record his live hour on TikTok as she had created the account.

Lucy had a mobile number printed on the card, and he was glad about this as he didn't fancy ringing the police station. *I bet they would put me through to that git, Parvel.* Squinting, he read the number out loud and tapped out the numbers on his phone. He was surprised at how quickly she answered his call.

"DI O'Leary speaking. Hello, Sebastian. Sebastian? It's Seth, isn't it?" she asked briskly.

"Yes. I prefer to be called Seth. Lucy, I needed to speak to you about Tom Stone."

"I'm sorry, Seth. I can't speak to you about the Gemma Day case. I've been taken off…"

"I know. Your not so pleasant, colleague Parvel, told me. Did you know that Tom Stone has abducted my wife and child?"

"No, I didn't. Rufus said that you were involved in a domestic issue, but he didn't mention abduction."

"I thought not. Yesterday the bastard carjacked the Jag and drove Jules and Darragh off. I ran after the car to save them, but he got away from me. He's got her and my wee boy, and I don't know what to do. I am going out of my mind with worry. She screamed out for help, for Christ's sake!"

Lucy went quiet for a moment. "Did you report this to Rufus? As you have told me?"

"I did, but I don't think he has done anything about it. He said he would try and track down the car, but when I asked him how it was going, he said that he hadn't heard. I don't think he likes me very much. As you say, he thinks that it is some kind of domestic dispute."

"And is it? Has your wife run off with Tom Stone?"

"No, of course not. She hates him, and as I told you, she called for help. I was too late. I feel like the longer she is away from here, the harder it will be to find her. Surely it can't be that hard for the police to spot a 1950's Jaguar with a missing number plate?"

"Have you reported her as being missing?"

"Well, no, I kind of hoped Rufus would open a file for her and my baby when I spoke to him last night. He mumbled something about procedure and 24 hours. There is something wrong with that man. I swear he has an issue with me. Perhaps it was because I was in prison, or perhaps it is because the Hearns were once travellers."

Lucy went silent for a few seconds and then whispered to Seth as if she was not wanting to be overheard. "Look, I am going to be brutally honest with you. I don't like to speak badly of anyone, but Rufus, how shall I put this; he is useless, and he is a bigot. I am not happy with the way he is handling the Day case, and he has or had a problem working with me. He is a chauvinistic pig and will, when I've finished with him, be given an early retirement. Mark my words. He isn't going to know what's hit him."

"I'm really sorry that you have had problems. I will be a character witness or testify that he is a complete eejit if you like?"

"That's kind of you, Seth and I would take you up on your offer if it weren't for the fact that we are related."

"So, you are my half-sister, then? I was right, wasn't I? I hope I didn't cause you any trouble with your family."

"It's ok; I think my Mam was relieved to tell me. We are not going to tell my dad. It would be better if he didn't know. Do you have any brothers and sisters? I haven't had time to check."

"Quite a lot. Fifteen that I know of, but judging by what I've heard, our Dad had children with many women, including his own daughters!"

"No! That's crazy. Don't tell me anymore. Some things are best left buried in the past. Like I said, I don't want to meet him. I am happy with my own dad."

Seth had a vision of their Dad at the bottom of the silent pool in Findon and then shook this thought away. He had more urgent things to think about. "So, will you open a case and find my wife and baby? I don't know if you did a background check on Tom Stone, but I wouldn't be surprised if he has a record. I am really worried about them, he is not a nice man. Last year he drugged and raped Jules. She can't remember this, but I know that he has hurt her, and I feel it in my bones that he means to hurt her again. Please help me," he asked with tears rolling down his cheeks. "Are you there, Lucy?"

"I'm here... It will be ok. I am furious that Rufus hasn't taken any action because Tom Stone is a wanted man. Rufus is an imbecile!"

"I knew it. What is he wanted for?"

"Interpol is looking for him. He is due to appear in court for carrying out sexual assaults on children and for downloading and storing images of children. You are right. He is not a nice man. Because of Covid, it took ages for the check to come back to us. Shit! All this could have been avoided if we had known sooner."

"We suspected he went with underage teenagers, but children? That is just sick! I am really worried now."

"I shouldn't be telling you this, but some of the children were very young. Still in nappies, in fact. The sooner we catch him, the better."

Seth felt sick. "My boy is only a year old. You don't think..."

"I'm sorry I told you now, but you need to know what we are dealing with. All I know is that I am going to take this case very seriously. Give me anything you can about Tom Stone. I will get the media involved. Are you able to do a live interview with the press? Do you have recent photos of Jules and your son? Darragh, you said?"

"Yes," he replied, looking at a family photo they had on the wall over the sideboard. "I have a really good photo of them both. Shall I email it to you? I've got your email address on your business card."

"Send it over now. We have a photo of Tom Stone, but we will have to Photoshop out all of that hair and replace it with grey stubble. He looks a lot different now."

"He has dyed his grey hair blond again. So, he has short, cropped yellow hair. A sickly yellow."

"Ok, I will get the photo fit artist to work on that. I will also get the traffic division to check the traffic movement yesterday. As you say, there can't be that many green Jaguars out on the roads yesterday."

"What else can I do? I can't just sit here and do nothing. I want to drive around and look for them. Parvel said he would arrest me if I did that."

"I know you want to go out and look, but you really have to leave this to the police. Do you use Facebook? You could create missing posts for them, but I would ask people to message you privately if they have any news. Or ring the police."

"Why's that, then?"

"If Tom Stone sees on Facebook that they have been spotted, he might panic, and who knows what he might do. Desperate men do desperate things."

"I don't like the sound of that. I don't have a Facebook account. I do use TikTok, however. S&J have over a million fans. Someone must have seen something. I was going to go live and do an appeal with a few songs thrown in to keep our fans interested. I will ask our fans to message me if they know anything. If I hear anything of use, then I will let you know. I was planning to go on at lunchtime. I guess people still stop for lunch when they are working from home. I want to catch as many people as possible."

"Well, there's a surprise. Who knew I was related to popstars? Yes, by all means, go on TikTok... Did you sing that new song with Sonar Cell? Waterfall something. I heard it on the radio earlier. Wow!"

"That's the one; Waterfall Way. I'm going to play it, or some of that song, this afternoon and then explain what's happened. I hope TikTok doesn't cancel our account. I'm not doing anything wrong by doing that, am I?"

"I don't know much about TikTok. No, I haven't heard of anyone else doing that, but you never know; it might work. I'll open an account and listen in at lunch time but if you see my name scroll up, for goodness' sake, don't say who I am."

"I won't," he said, his mood lifting. "I just know someone will have some news. I am going on every lunchtime until she is found." In his mind, he could see her in her blue denim dress with Darragh in her arms. She was standing by a window looking out onto fields as she waited for him to find her. *Be strong, my beautiful girl. I will find you and bring you both home.*

***

With the photo of the three of them together behind him, Seth's finger hovered over the record button, ready to begin his live TikTok session. He was feeling a little nervous and rubbed his chin anxiously, eager to get started but fearing that he might make a complete fool of himself. He had seen plenty of other TikTokers, sitting in front of the camera and answering questions from their followers. *I can do this. I just mustn't sound*

280

too desperate. Otherwise, I will be sitting here alone with nobody to talk or sing to. He stood up and checked himself in the mirror. With a heavy heart, he had worked out, showered and shaved with the hope that he might look half decent when he made his appeal. He was looking clean-shaven, and he knew that Jules would approve.

He took a deep breath, sat back down and quickly pressed start. For a moment, he froze as he thought of what to say. "Afternoon, everyone," he began. "I'm Seth Hearn from S&J. Have you heard our new song Waterfall Way yet? Our single came out yesterday. When I say our single, it wasn't just ours; it was Sonar Cell's single too. You might have heard our song on the radio. Tell me if you have heard it yet. I will play it for you." Seth had his phone ready and started to play the recording of Waterfall Way so everyone could hear it. "Tell me what you think of this song." He listened to Waterfall Way with a mixture of pride and sorrow. The song was about wanting to marry Jules, and he found it difficult to listen to. He was desperate to share his sad and harrowing news with everyone. When the song finished, he noticed that people were joining him live, names were starting to scroll up the screen, and some were giving him the thumbs up or sending emoji with hearts in their eyes.

Waterfall Way finished, and he smiled, doing his best to appear cheerful. "Thank you for joining me today. There is something I need to tell you, and I am going to feel so much better when I get this horrid news off my chest. So, here's the thing. You may have noticed that I am missing my wife Jules, the J in S&J. Yesterday, she was abducted. I need your help." Comments were starting to appear as well as little hands waving as their fans joined him.

leamoliner joined

darkwings2

Was Jules abducted by aliens?

Sab_riddle joined

Bindyvst71 joined

Chelsea_bun

"No, not aliens. Yesterday at lunchtime, Tom Stone, wanted by Interpol, took Jules and my son in our car. He has kidnapped them! This is where I need your help. Have you seen my wife and baby? Perhaps you saw them driving around Cork yesterday. If you haven't seen Jules or my son before, then if you look at the picture behind me, then you can see what they look like. Here let me show you a close-up." Seth picked up his phone again and scrolled through his photos until he found a picture of Jules holding Darragh. He held the phone near to her phone, so everyone could see them up close. "There, do you see? I am worried sick. Please help me find them."

stickylittlefingers
I'm sorry to hear that. Have you called the cops?

Grandmajones joined

"I have called the police. And you will probably see me on the news later, asking for people to come forward with information. While we wait for news, I was thinking of doing a few song requests. Let me know what song you would like me to sing. Jules and I have been covering most of the best 2020 songs. Be kind, nothing too sad."

lambchops
Where is Cork? I live in Zimbabwe

Majortom567 joined

Ericagere
I love you xxxxxxxxxxx

"Thank you, Erica; I love you too. Oh, I should have said. Cork is in southern Ireland. Is there anyone from Ireland out there? I believe that the Toad, Tom Stone, is holding my wife and baby in Cork. But who knows, they might be anywhere in Ireland."

44roadhome joined

angeldelight
What's your baby's name? He is like a mini version of you. By the way, you are awesome!

"Thank you, angel delight. We called him Darragh, which means strong like an oak tree. He is going to be one in a few days' time. I miss him so much. He likes Jules and me to sing to him. His favourite is Rockabye. Would you all do me a favour and look outside your windows to see if you can see that green Jaguar parked opposite? That's the car Tom Stone used to kidnap them. It's a really old classic car, and the back number plate will be missing."

carebear_26
That's terrible. Will you sing Rockabye? I will go and look ☺

283

"I can sing Rockabye, as I said, my baby loves that one. He just laughs, and he doesn't go to sleep, of course. Have you seen Jules and Darragh? This is really important. If you have seen them, will you message me in my inbox? We don't want the Toad, Tom Stone, to know that we are on to him. Would you do that for me?"

Seth started to sing Rockabye. He played the backing music on his phone and really missed Jules playing her guitar. He had to stay strong and not break down in front of everyone. It was hard going, but he managed to get through to the end of the song without crying.

Hairbear001 joined

brokenheart.5 joined

woodchuckberry
What's happened to Jules?

lucky_lucyOL joined

Seth smiled. *That has to be Lucy O'Leary.* "Welcome, if you've just joined me. Jules and my wee son Darragh have been kidnapped, abducted. Tom Stone is a wanted man, and I fear he may harm my wife and son. Please, if you have seen a 1950's green Jaguar reg ED1 05X or my wife and son, please message me privately as the police don't want him to know we are onto him. I really need your help to find them."

chantrysongs joined

"I'm just checking our inbox. Oh my! There are lots of messages, but all are well-wishing messages. Thank you so much. You all are really such lovely people. Please keep looking for Jules and Darragh Hearn and the green Jaguar. I just know that there is someone in Cork that saw them yesterday or knows where they are being held.

sandydune joined

shinypinner1111
I am sad that you are sad. You have us now, so you will never be alone. Will you sing that song for me?

birdbrain23 joined

"Never be Alone? Yes, I know that one. I know most of the current songs, all of Coldplay's songs and Ed Sheeran's songs. My Jules loves Ed Sheeran. Now, if I start crying, just ignore me. I have all you guys helping me? While I sing this tune for shinypinner, can you please send a message to my inbox and let me know if you have seen Jules or Darragh or the green Jaguar in or around Cork. We don't want to let Tom Stone know that we are on to him, so no live comments, please."

pearlgates_666 joined

lucky_lucyOL
You are doing a grand job. Call me when you are done here.

"Thanks, Lucy; I will give you a call in forty minutes.

So Never be Alone; that's Justin Bieber's one, isn't it. Let's see if I can remember the words. Dance with me under the diamonds... I am going to have to put backing music on. My brain is too fried to sing without."

Seth found it a lot harder to sing than he had expected. He knew that he was going to get emotional, and he did his best not to cry in front of everyone. When he finished singing, he hurriedly wiped away the tears that had escaped and forced a smile. "My heart is breaking. I can't be without my singing partner. I am lost without her. If you live in Ireland, please look out of your windows and see if you can see Jules and Darragh or the green Jaguar, Reg no ED1 05X. I know that together, we will find her. Message my inbox and so that the evil paedophile Tom Stone doesn't get wind of us and harm my family." *I shouldn't have said paedophile. Hell, I don't care. Everyone needs to know the truth.*

crowfarmjake joined

Seth gasped silently as the username registered. "Hello, brother?"

crowfarmjake
What are you doing on TikTok?

"It's a long story. How are you doing?"

bucketlizzy.tip joined

livingthedream
I am going to travel soon. Like you did. Come and visit.

Seth didn't know what to make of that comment. It was obviously someone that knew him.

rudeboy
Do you want me to bring you a hotpot round? Will you sing Wake Me Up?

"Thank you, but it's probably not a good idea to leave your home and get arrested... Is hotpot code for something? Yes, I'll sing that one for you. Let's just get the backing music going. Ok then." Seth started to sing Wake Me Up and could feel knots building in his stomach. For some reason, every word he was singing seemed relevant and poignant.

stringofpearls
Will you sing Perfect for me xxxxxxxxxxxxxxxxxx?

"Hello, stringofpearls. Yes, that sounds perfect. That is one of Jules' favourite songs. I will sing that in a bit for you when I have got over the last one."

crowfarmjake
How is Jules?

giant_peach joined

litterpicker101
Where's Jules?

taniabooklover
I downloaded Waterfall Way off iTunes today. Love it so much!

"Thank you, taniabooklover. Jules and I are really proud of our first song. So, a lot of you are asking where Jules is. If you didn't know, Jules and my wee boy Darragh have been kidnapped. If you have any information, then please message my inbox so we can keep things private. Any small detail, then please let me know. Any ideas where a woman and child could be held captive in Cork, then please let me know. I need to bring them home today before the nasty Tom Stone harms them."

crowfarmjake
Christ! I'm sorry, mate. Have you contacted the police, or are you doing it the Hearn way?

"I couldn't do this alone. The police are involved. Jake, would you tell Charlene for me."

bigheartgirl joined

jamesjoy joined

bubblegum67
I love you so much. My heart bleeds for you.

Burntbad
Check your inbox. I think I have some news.

Chapter Thirty-three

Doing her best to keep her composure and not wanting to put Darragh in any more danger, Jules picked him up along with a clean tea towel she was going to use as a flannel. "I am just going to clean and change Darragh," she said, heading off to the toilets. *I have no clothes for him, just one spare nappy. I can't bear the thought of him wearing yesterday's clothes. It will be ok; we will be out of here soon.* She entered the staff toilet, locked the door behind her and then started to sob as she realised how awful things had become for them. The thought of her giving Tom a blow job was beyond imagining. *What is wrong with that man?* "I am not going to let him hurt you," she whispered, cuddling Darragh. Darragh pushed himself away and looked up into her face, puzzled by her tears. "It's ok, your Mam will be fine. I need to stop my blubbering and find us a way out of here. You have to be a good boy and not cry. If you get on his nerves, then he will get rid of you." The thought of this made her cry harder.

A knock on the washroom door made her jump.

"Why are you crying? Are you not feeling well?" Tom asked gently.

She didn't reply. She had hoped that by locking herself away, it might give her time to think of an escape plan. She wanted to tell him to go to hell but knew that would not help matters. "I'm not feeling great. I'm sorry."

"It's going to take you a while to get used to your new home. If this is about Mr Steel, then Hannah can look after him. I understand. We need time to get to know each other properly."

289

"You need help. Who in their right mind names their privates Mr Steel?"

He laughed. "Look, I promise that I won't make you do anything you don't want to. We have the rest of our lives to get to know one another's funny little ways. Come out and have breakfast. I don't think you've eaten anything since you've been here. I'll get Hannah to cook you something."

Jules sighed, resigning herself to the fact that she would have to play happy families until she had worked out an exit plan. *It's only a matter of time before they both need to inject again. Be patient, Jules.*

"I can cook. I'd rather. I am just going to get us ready for the day, and then I will be out."

"Julia?"

"What?"

"I'm glad that you have decided to stay."

When she walked back into the living area, Hannah was on her knees, giving Tom a blow job. He was crying out as if he were in pain. He raised his eyebrows at Jules and looked amorously at her as she ran past them.

Keeping Darragh's back to them and praying that it would all be over soon, Jules entered the kitchen area, ready to cook. She knew that Darragh was hungry, but the thought of eating anything herself was making her feel sick. She knew she would have to eat to keep her strength up, or she wouldn't have the energy to run. *I have to eat. I'm eating for two now; I have to think about our baby growing inside me too.* With Darragh on her hip, she opened the fridge and saw some bread, eggs and cheese. It was going to be a job to cook and hold Darragh at the same time. She really didn't want to put him down.

Jules got everything out and then gave him a little cheese to eat while she broke some eggs into a hot frying pan. They splattered a little, so she turned the heat down, not wanting them to spit hot fat on them. She mixed the eggs up in the pan, not sure what she was making and then put some toast on. She looked for butter, but there was none. "Never mind, at least I have something to give you," she said, trying to ignore the yelling going on as Hannah did her best to satisfy Mr Steel.

"Please get it over with, for God's sake," Hannah exclaimed with her mouth full.

In desperation, Jules turned a radio on, hoping that music might distract Darragh from turning his head to see what was happening. News about the increasing Covid death toll began to compete with the lover's tiff going on at the end of the room.

"For Christ's sake, Hannah! You're not doing it right. How many more times do I have to tell you? Harder, bitch! I am feeling nothing!"

"Fuck yourself!" Hannah jumped up and, with her arms folded, stomped off towards the toilet.

"Well, that's fucking marvellous! You know what this means, don't you?" he yelled after her.

Jules' heart was beating hard in her chest, worried that he would ask her to carry on and finish the job. She put the eggs on the dry toast, and then with Darragh on her lap, she walked over to the table, put the plate and fork on the table and sat with her back to Tom. She just managed to move the hot food out of the way before Darragh grabbed some of the egg. "We've got to wait until it has cooled down." Darragh complained. Nervously she looked over her shoulder to see if Tom had heard him cry out. She sighed with relief. Tom had followed Hannah into the toilet. *Thank God. I wonder what is going to happen next. How does he punish her? Poor Hannah, she can't like being with him. What is wrong with her?*

Keeping the plate out of reach, she managed to cut a piece of toast and egg and blew on it before feeding it to her little bird. Darragh was hungry, and as he ate, she felt less tense. She ate a little herself and found it difficult to swallow. *I must eat.* A loud thud in the washroom made her jump. *What's happening now? Did he just hit her? Please no!* She heard another crash and prayed that Tom wasn't going to kill Hannah like he had killed Gemma. *How can I stop him?* She gave Darragh another mouthful of food and then carried him over to the washroom door. Feeling frightened, she knocked on the door. "Is everything ok in there?" The banging and crashing stopped for a moment.

Horrified, Jules went back to the table to continue with breakfast. The sound of two bodies wrestling in the washroom resumed, quashing any ideas about murder. Her attention turned to the radio, and she inhaled with surprise as she heard Seth's voice on the radio. A big smile went across her face as she heard his desperate appeal to find them both.

"Da?" Darragh said, his chubby little hand pointed at the radio.

"Yes, you are right. That is Dad. He sounds so sad and desperate. So, the police are looking for us too. We better keep this to ourselves," she said, getting up to turn off the radio. A small glimmer of hope filled her, and she smiled. "He's going to find us; I just know he is." She imagined Seth charging up the stairs, and she stared at the door, longing for him to burst through.

Tom's jacket, hanging up by the door, caught her attention. *Has he left the keys in his coat? I wonder.* She carried Darragh over to the jacket, and trying not to make a sound and hardly breathing, she felt in one of the pockets for the keys. By-passing packets of condoms, she felt the metal keyring and then triumphant, she pulled out her keys. With urgency now, she looked in all the other pockets for the door key.

"Are you looking for this? Tom asked. Jules spun around and saw his naked body and flaccid penis. He grinned a crooked grin and held up a key on a gold chain around his neck.

Fighting back the tears, Jules nodded. "I want to go home," she whispered.

"I know, but that is not going to happen, is it? Now be a good girl. Where's that breakfast you promised us?" Hannah joined him, her clothes were torn, and there was blood dribbling down the side of her face. She looked so sad and lost.

"We have worked up quite an appetite, haven't we?" he said, putting his arm around her.

"You've hurt Hannah!"

"Oh, it's nothing, just a scratch. There's no gain without pain. You like being punished, don't you, honeypot? Mr Steel is happy now."

Hannah said nothing.

***

Seth opened his eyes and saw Sinead standing by the bed. She was clutching a large roll of paper. "What's the matter? Have the police found them?"

"Sorry to burst in like this. No, they haven't found them yet. I couldn't wait any longer. I've had an idea. When I saw you on the news last night, they put up a missing photo of Jules and Darragh and a wanted photo of Tom on the screen. That made it all so real."

"Do you think people took notice then? It didn't feel like I was talking to anyone in that Zoom room. I kept thinking that I needed to look more desperate and less like a villain."

"You did just great. Seth, you are no villain. Don't beat yourself up. You couldn't have stopped him taking them."

"I know, but I can't help feeling guilty. If only I had come out of the Manor House with her and not gone back in to cover the fires."

"Seriously, you've got to think positive. No more 'if onlys.'"

"I'll try. So, what is your idea then?"

"I was going to make lots of posters showing all three of them and the car, and then we can stick them up around Cork." She held up the poster with an enthusiastic look on her face. Seth sat up and took one of the posters, and then sighed. "You've done a grand job, but who is going to see them when we are all confined to our houses?"

"We can still go out for food and exercise. I think we should stick them up at the entrances to supermarkets and petrol stations. We have to do something."

"That's not a bad idea, but I should go and put them up. We could both get arrested for going out on a non-essential journey."

"It would have to be a pretty mean copper to arrest us for trying to find a woman and child."

"Rufus Parvel would. I was hoping that Lucy would ring me with some news. They are sure to have found the car on video by now. If only that git, Rufus, had taken me seriously in the first place."

"Seth! No more 'if onlys!' Did anyone message you on TikTok? Have your fans seen anything?"

"There's been loads of caring messages but no actual sightings. Burntends said they had messaged me in my inbox with news, but they lied. There was no message. I haven't really slept. I've been checking the inbox every ten minutes. I will do a few more live sessions today, and I could stick one of your posters up next to me, so I don't have to keep explaining that I am looking for my wife and son. He fell back on the pillow, and he was nearly in tears. Sinead, will I ever find them?"

"You won't if you don't look after yourself. When did you last eat? Come on, Seth, you have to keep it together and not give up hope. Get washed and dressed, and I will make you some breakfast. When you've eaten, there's something you need to do which you won't like."

"What's that then?"

"You need to tell Jules' Dad and her brother. The news report only went out on local news, so they have no idea that she is missing. Unless the police have told them."

"Well, that's me done for! Mike is really going to hate me now. Can't you ring him?"

"No, it has to come from you. It is not your fault this has happened. He knows what Tom has done to her in the past. He won't blame you."

"Do you want a bet? It has to be done, I suppose. I just need a strong cup of tea first and cheese on toast if you are willing," he said, smiling cheekily at Sinead.

"Of course. It won't be as good as Jules makes it, but I promise I won't kill you. Come on, Seth, get up. We need to get printing and get these posters up pronto."

"What time is it? Jesus, it's early!" he said, looking at his phone.

"Come on, Seth, get up. The early bird catches the worm and all that. Or the Toad in this case. Seriously, we are going to get that bastard caught if it is the last thing we do!"

Chapter Thirty-four

Sinead held up one of her posters on a signpost at the entrance to Tesco, and Seth secured it with zip ties and then stepped back to see if it would catch the eye.

"You have done a good job, Sinead. I am glad we changed the headings from 'Missing' to 'Kidnapped. Have You Seen?' over Jules and Darragh's photo. I love that photo. The eyes look so bright and loving." He sighed. "I still think we should have added to the Toad's wanted banner that he is wanted for paedophilia. It has more of an impact."

"You didn't tell me that. Shit!"

Seth looked at the people queuing to shop in Tesco. "Do you think we should go down the line with one of these posters and see if anyone has seen them?"

"It wouldn't hurt, but don't get too close to them. We have to keep a meter away. It can't hurt to try."

As they walked towards the shoppers, Seth's phone started to ring. Hoping that it was Lucy with an update, Seth pulled out his phone from his coat pocket and looked to see who was calling. "Oh, it's Shawn! I won't be a minute, Sinead."

"Ok. I'll start quizzing the locals."

"Hi mate, it's not a good time. Is it ok if I call you back later?"

"No problem. Jane and I just wanted to check to see how you were doing and if you had any news. I'll call you later..."

Another incoming call notification sounded, and Seth realised that Lucy was calling. "I'm a bit broken, to be honest, Shawn, and the police are ringing me now. I'll give you a ring after lunch. Is that ok?"

"Sure..."

"Hi Lucy, any news? You must have seen where the car was going on video by now."

"Yes, we have seen the car travelling eastwards along Sarsfield Road."

"Well, that's great; they haven't gone far then."

"We are just checking vehicles moving on the motorway up to Dublin, but my gut feeling is that they are still in Cork."

"So, what happens now? Are you going to do door to door searches?"

"At the moment, I have patrol cars driving along the streets in the southwest quarter of Cork, looking for your car. The taxi driver that picked Tom Stone up from Cork and dropped him off at Waterfall West has contacted us straight after the news report last night. So, we are starting to build up a picture. This is confirmation that Tom Stone was at Waterfall West, as you said and that Jules and Darragh were more than likely kidnapped."

"Crikey! Was it ever in question? You haven't been listening to Rufus, have you?"

"No, I haven't been listening to him. You do understand that sometimes when a person is reported as missing, it is not always straightforward. It has been the case that the husband uses this story to cover up what actually happened."

Seth sighed. *She thinks I've killed my wife and baby.* "You do trust me when I say that I would never harm my family? I am lost without Jules and Darragh, and my life is not worth living without them."

"I do believe you, Seth. I just have to build up an accurate picture of what happened and build a timeline. I can hear it in your voice that you are hurting. We will find them, I promise. The moment we have any leads, then I will give you a call. Are you going to go back on TikTok again? Did you get any feedback from your fans?"

"No, nothing concrete. A crazy person in Dublin said that he was keeping them locked in his shed. You don't think he is, do you?"

"Mm... No, I don't, but I'd better check him out. Send me a screenshot of his message. Again, I can't rule anything out, but I am pretty sure they are still in Cork."

"I am too. Sinead and I are putting up a few 'Kidnapped,' 'Have You Seen?' and 'Wanted' posters around Cork. I have put the number you gave out on the news on the poster."

"Oh dear, I'll pretend I didn't hear that. Make sure you don't put them on council land, or you could get fined."

"They wouldn't, would they?"

"Believe me, they would. There's just one more thing. I notified Jules' family about her being missing. They didn't take the news well."

"Who did you speak to?"

"Um, I spoke to Michael Bridgewater, her father. He was very upset and had to pass the phone to his son."

"Oh no! I was going to ring him today. I just kept hoping that Jules would come home and I wouldn't have to call him. It is just sinking in that they really are missing. I am beside myself and don't know what more I can do to find them. My heart is breaking."

"Look, Seth. I know these are tough times for you, but you have to believe that things will turn out well and not allow yourself to let hope slip away. Sing some more, and the world will listen and help you find them."

***

Sinead had gone to do some laundry at the Manor House, and Seth, not wanting to sit brooding, decided to take Moss out for a gentle ride. Just being outside was making him feel so much better. The wind had dropped, and he could see clear sky in the distance. He tried not to think too hard and just absorb what was going on around him with the hope that the spring flowers and the trees with fresh new leaves would lift his spirits. Moss walked on steadily, understanding that any messing about would not go down well. They passed the potato field and then entered the huge oak tree-lined field that would soon bear broccoli, cauliflower, carrots and kale. This field, he decided, was his happy place. A good place to think and ponder on all that was good. The tallest oak tree in the middle of the field was calling to him, and he turned Moss to the left and carefully chose a path through the mud, avoiding the rows of seedlings. It had only been days since he had scattered the seeds, and already he could see tender green shoots sprouting. "Careful boy, keep a steady line. Let's go and rest under the oak tree. I promise when we get into the rabbit field, we can go for a canter. I need to ring Mike first. I don't want to, but it has to be done. What sort of son-in-law am I if I don't ring him? He is probably going crazy like me, waiting for news."

Seth dismounted and let Moss graze on the grass around the tree. "Don't you scoff the lot, though," he said, patting him. Seth sat with his back against the tree, hoping that it would give him the strength to make the call. The great oak spiralled above him, and he could feel its energy and almost hear words of encouragement whispering to him through the bark. He needed all the help he could get. He found Mike's number and half hoped that he wouldn't take the call. Mike answered immediately, taking him by surprise.

"Have they found them?" he asked with urgency.

"No, I'm sorry. The police are doing everything they can. I went on the six o'clock news last night, and Sinead and I have put up posters all around Cork. They think the bastard is holding them in Cork. They have police cars out looking for them too, and I have been asking all our fans to help."

"You must be going out of your mind with worry. If only Julia had reported that animal to the police, then this wouldn't have happened."

Well, there's a surprise, Mike is actually being pretty decent to me. "We both wanted her to, but she didn't feel that she could. I am sure that she will tell the police when they find them. I only wish I could do more. I am going crazy just sitting at home. I have been trying to contact our S&J fans to see if they have seen Jules and Darragh. We have quite a following. There must be something else I can do."

"I saw you performing with Sonar on Facebook. Peter showed me. I know I didn't say it before, but I am really proud of you both. That Waterfall Way song is going viral. That's what Peter says. I can see you are doing your best to find them. That song really says it all. There's something about it. Haunting almost. The world will hear it, and they will help you bring Julia and Darragh home."

"Viral, you say. I had no idea. I haven't had the heart to see how it is doing. Mike, I am broken; I am lost without them."

"We have to be strong. Jules is strong, and she won't let that man get away with it. She is a fighter, just like her mother."

"I hope that you are right. No, I know you are right. I just have to be strong, like you say."

***

Feeling more positive after talking to Mike, Seth started a TikTok live session. He had placed one of Sinead's posters leaning against a plant on the coffee table in front of him, and he was feeling hopeful that he would hear from one of their fans telling him that they had seen Jules and Darragh somewhere. He imagined that they had spotted her behind an upstairs window crying out for help. The thought of this made him shudder. He remembered her face as Tom had driven away, and that look haunted him when he tried to sleep. He didn't like to think of her being distressed. *Come on, Seth, pull yourself together and press record.* He started the session and decided to sing first before he explained to everyone why he had a missing and wanted poster in front of him. He couldn't explain why, but a song he had written months ago popped into his head. *Beautiful in Blue.*

"Hi, I'm Seth Hearn, from S&J. S&J and Sonar Cell, have just released a single - Waterfall Way, which I believe has gone viral. Thank you so much for buying and sharing. I will play that song to you later when a few more of you have joined me."

Names started to appear on the screen, and congratulatory messages moved up the screen too.

bucketlizzy.tip joined

karen_jones5
Love your new song. Love you both

"Thank you, we are thrilled about our new song, Waterfall Way, too. Only… if you look at the poster here," he said, pointing to it. "Jules has been kidnapped and is being held in Cork somewhere." *Should I have said that?* "Jules and my son are still missing. If you live in Cork, then please look out for a green Jaguar and for my wife and son. I have pictures of them all here, including the bastard that is holding them. Sorry for swearing and for not shaving."

sonarSmith joined

Bananabread55 joined

"Hello, SonarSmith" Seth smiled, recognising that it was Shawn. "Shawn, I will call you in an hour, mate; thanks for joining me."

sonarSmith
The band are out looking and are asking our Facebook fans to look too.

"Thanks, Shawn. Now I am feeling a little shy about singing 'Beautiful in Blue', but it seems apt. Please tell me what you think and private message me if you have seen my family. We don't want the Toad to know we are on to him."

Trying not to break down, Seth checked the continual stream of names coming in as he sang.

Did I tell you? You look so good in blue
I see you laugh and take my hand
And you know my heart is true
I am always going to love you.
Love you when you're wearing blue

You are my baby in blue
Can't live without you
You make my heart sing

WATERFALL WAY

Now you wear my ring
I will always love you
Cos you're my baby in blue
Beautiful in blue

Your hair the colour of hay
Makes me wanna say
I love you more each day
Love your sweet face
Makes my heart race

You are my baby in blue
Can't live without you
You make my heart sing
Now you wear my ring
I will always love you
Cos you're my baby in blue
Beautiful in blue

You've heard this all before
Can't help myself
I just want more
You let my heart be free
Your blue eyes cast a spell on me
Lost without you
You look so good in blue
I will always love you
Cos you're my baby in blue
Baby in blue
Beautiful in blue

Breadofheavan
<3 <3 <3 <3 <3 <3

"Did you like that song? Thank you for sending me hearts. Everyone is so kind here. I am broken and lost without them both. I don't like to keep going on about my wife and son being missing, but if you know anything, then if you could ring the number on the poster or message me in my inbox, then that would be great. I am going out of my mind with worry."

apple.storytime
If you don't find her. I'm yours

"I know we will find Jules!"

rudeboy
Look after yourself, stay strong.

"I am doing my best."

starfleet77 joined

jumpingjack joined

granny@pinkmoon
Bridie, Nathan and I send our love.

"Granny? My granny. On TikTok? No! It can't be!"

granny@pinkmoon
It's your cousin Nathan. I am setting Granny up on TikTok

"Why?"

granny@pinkmoon
She wants to do live readings and pass spirit messages. She's got a message for you.

"Really?"

granny@pinkmoon
The spirits have given her a picture

"A picture?"

granny@pinkmoon
She says, look for a large white building by a field of blood.

"Nooo... Are they hurt?"

granny@pinkmoon
They are both alive, but life hangs on a thread for a third

"Granny, you are talking in riddles."

granny@pinkmoon
She says that you need to be quick. Time is running out.

"Now you are scaring me."

granny@pinkmoon
She says that the pink moon will always shine on you. You have to go and find that white building and a field of blood.

"I need to speak to her. I will ring in a minute." Seth stared silently at the messages on the screen and wondered what he should do. He needed to look at a map of Cork and hunt for large buildings next to fields. "Well, you've all heard what my Granny has to say. I think I, or we, should start hunting for this white building in Cork, don't you? Message me if you have any idea where granny@pinkmoon might be talking about. I know she sounds crazy, but she is usually right about most things."

Not wanting to end the TikTok session prematurely, in case he got any messages with information, Seth played Waterfall Way to his fans and rang Granny to find out more about her crazy message. He wasn't sure if he should act on her vision or spirit message. The field of blood was also troubling him. He didn't want to find his family with their throats cut in a bath of blood. Memories of finding Gemma like that made him shudder.

"Granny?" He was thankful that his mother, Bridie, hadn't picked up. He hadn't spoken to her since finding out that she was his real mother and not the woman that had brought him up and who was rotting in prison for murder.

"You should be out there looking for them, not playing around on this Ticking Tok thing. The spirits are bombarding me with urgent messages. I can't rest for hearing them," she exclaimed.

"They haven't given me much to go on. What do you think a field of blood is? An abattoir?"

"No, not an abattoir. I see red fields through the eyes of a child. Darragh's eyes, perhaps. Also, I remember being in this field as a child. When we travelled, we stayed in Cork many times. I swear they are near that field that we used to stay in."

"Where exactly? Do you have an address?"

"Cork is not how I remember it. They are telling me South. Keep south of the river, Seth."

"Ok, thanks for trying to help. How did you find out about me being on TikTok?"

"Nathan, grandson number twelve, dances on there doing a shuffle sometimes - whatever that is. He thinks I should go on there and do live readings. I've seen some of those doing readings, and they should hang their heads in shame. Charlatans they are! I have a gift, and I'd like to give people some comfort in these hard times. It gives me something to do now I have been imprisoned in my home to avoid getting a cold. Bridie has locked me in!"

"I think it is a bit more serious than a cold. People of your age don't do well when they get Covid. Please stay in; I don't want anything to happen to you."

"Don't you worry about me; I am as strong as an ox, and I am looking forward to bouncing Darragh on my knee. So, you get yourself out and look for a red field next to a huge white building. You have until midday tomorrow."

"Why midday?

"Feck knows! That's what the spirits are telling me."

"Thanks, Granny, I have to go now... Waterfall Way is nearly over."

"Hold on, Seth... yes, I can see it now. The spirits are telling me that you need to look for a large wild cat. Now you be a good grandson and come and visit me when you find them. Won't you?"

"Yes, Granny, of course."

Seth sat down in front of the camera, lost in thought as the enormity of the task ahead was realised. *If I pick a route on the edge of Cork southwest of the river, then I am bound to find something. Sod lockdown. Should I tell Lucy? Or will she arrest me for breaking lockdown rules? Mm... That's a hard one. I don't have to tell her that I am going to be driving around Cork. If I tell her that I have had a tip-off that they are being held in a big white building on the edge of Cork, then she will be able to direct her search efforts in that direction. I need to tell her.*

Waterfall Way had stopped playing, and he smiled as he watched all the hearts, flowers, and kisses stream up the screen. "I know it is a little early, but I need to go now and let the police know what we have discovered today. Please message me if you know of any big white buildings in Cork and help me find Jules and my little boy. I am grateful for your love and support."

Chapter Thirty-five

With Darragh in her arms, Jules opened the window and looked down to see how far it was to drop to the carpark below. It was far too risky to climb down with a baby in her arms. Tom was out collecting the Chinese that Hannah had ordered on her phone. She had hoped that he would forget that he had given the phone back to her but, he gave Jules a sly look and shook his head and said, "I'm sorry, Hannah, but you won't be able to have your phone back until Julia has settled in." Hannah didn't object and started to clean the kitchen. Jules swore at him silently and did her best not to cry.

It was a beautiful day; there was not a cloud in the sky. Jules looked out at the wasteland with a heavy heart and sighed, willing the landscape to reach out for her and whisk her away. It was then that she noticed that the wasteland had been transformed into a sea of poppies. Their bright red petals gently bobbed and glowed in the evening sunshine. "Have you ever seen anything so beautiful as that?" she asked Hannah, who had finished in the kitchen and was now sitting at the table colouring in a peacock in a colouring book as she waited for Tom to return. She was engrossed and strangely quiet. "Have you seen the poppies outside?" she asked again. "They weren't there this morning."

"Are they those red flowers?" she finally replied.

"Yes, they are beautiful, aren't they?" Hannah didn't reply and was furiously scribbling away. "Do you like drawing?"

"No, not really, but colouring keeps me calm. Tom says I need to find a way to come off the heroin. I don't seem to be able to go a day without using. That can't be good, can it?"

"No, I suppose not." Jules came closer to her and sat down, and put Darragh on her lap. She noticed that Hannah's artwork was far from tidy, and some sections were scribbled in an erratic manner. There were beads of sweat on her forehead, and she looked pale.

"You don't look good. Is there anything I can do to help? Can I make you some sweet tea?"

Hannah shook her head. "I've made my own bed, and now I have to lie in it. That's what Tom says. I don't know why you are being so nice to me. I know you both want me out of here so you can be together."

"You know that's not true. You know I don't want to be here. Tom is delusional, and Darragh and I need to go home. Please help us get out of here," she said, a sob escaping as she spoke. Darragh looked at her and was worried.

"I can't; he will kill me. Like he killed Gemma."

"So, you know what he is capable of? Did you know that he drugged and raped me a while back, and I fear we may end up dead too if things do not go his way? I know you are hurting right now, but please help me if you can."

Hannah lifted her head and looked out at the sky, lost in thought. "There might be a way. We could make paper airplanes with a message inside and fly them out of the window. Someone might find the note if it goes far enough into the fields. Every morning dog walkers walk by. They might find your note."

"Do you mean like a message in a bottle? It is something I suppose, and that way you won't get into trouble, and you can pretend you know nothing about it. Hannah, you shouldn't let him hurt or punish you. You are worth more than that."

She looked angry. "You have no idea what you are talking about. I am a bad person, and I deserve everything I get." She pushed her colouring book with a pen towards her. "Quick, write your notes before he comes back. I need a fix, and then I will be all right again. Don't let him catch you. I know nothing, right?"

"Thanks. I won't say anything."

Tom returned in high spirits and laid various cartons of Chinese food on the table and then looked across at Hannah, who was lying on the bed laughing to herself as if she was witnessing something hilarious. It was dark outside, and Jules prayed that Tom wouldn't notice the paper planes lying in the car park. Only one had made it over the low fence and into the poppies. She hoped with all her heart that a dog would find it and bring it to its master. She had kept the message simple. URGENT CALL 999 Julia Hearn is being held in the white office block against her will. HELP was written in red on the wings.

"Hannah, honeypot, you need to eat. I told you not to take anything when I was away." She just laughed at him.

Tom shook his head. "You don't know what it's like living with a drug addict. I am at my wits end!"

"She needs help."

"I have managed to quit. Why can't she?"

Jules felt disappointed when she heard that. Another chance to escape had gone up in a puff of smoke. "You could stop her buying the stuff in the first place."

"I don't know how she buys it, but every now and then, this guy turns up on a motorbike, and she drops down a can on a string to collect it."

"You could take it off her."

"I have, but she goes seriously crazy if I don't give it to her. You've seen her attack me."

Jules knew that he was telling her tales just to make her feel sorry for him. She emptied some fried rice and a few vegetables from a black bean sauce carton and scraped off as much as she could, and fed it to Darragh. He made a strange face, but hunger made him eager for more.

"Hannah, you need to come to the table now, or you know what you must do."

Hannah sighed and slipped off the bed, lowering herself onto the floor. Jules watched her curiously, wondering what she was going to do. When she was on the floor, she pulled herself under the bed until she was hidden from view. She laughed again.

"Shut the fuck up!" he yelled.

The room went quiet, and then Darragh started to cry.

"Don't you start, or you can join her," he said to Darragh fiercely.

"You didn't have to yell. You frightened him," Jules said, brushing his tears away with her fingers. She offered him another spoonful of food, and he stopped crying. She was scared that Tom might hurt him.

"I'm sorry," he said. "She will behave now, and we can enjoy our evening alone. What do you want to do tonight? Shall we watch a film in bed together?"

She was shocked. "You are not going to carry on as if Hannah isn't there, are you?"

"We can watch a film sitting on the sofa together. Like normal people do." His face darkened for a moment, and then he smiled. "Of course, darling, you could always hold Mr Steel while we watch."

Jules nearly choked on her food. She couldn't bear being called darling. It sounded so contrived, and the thought of her touching him was too awful to even contemplate. *I have to make out I am happy. Just ignore what he said.*

"You choose the film. I'm easily pleased." Playing happy families was beginning to grate. *Please let this nightmare be over soon. Poor Hannah.*

Tom stood up and went to the kitchenette. He came back with a bottle of wine and some glasses. "We should celebrate," he said, opening the bottle. "This is the eve of a fresh start for both of us." He pulled out of his pocket a packet of pills. "I want you to take four of these pills, and by morning your womb will be cleansed, and you will be pure again."

Not believing what she was hearing, Jules could feel her ears ringing. His words were coming out in slow motion. He had gone too far. He was asking her to abort her baby. She glared at him. "NEVER!" she spat.

"We'll see. Let's get cosy on the sofa and watch Dirty Dancing. That's one of my favourite films. It gives me goosebumps. I don't need to take anything. Mr Steel gets very excited all by himself!"

He poured two glasses of wine and picked up a bowl of food, and sauntered over to the sofa. Jules continued to feed Darragh, her mind a whirlwind of crazy thoughts. She imagined herself smashing the end of the bottle on the table and ramming it into his groin, cutting Mr Steel off completely and then spearing his heart, so he died a terrible death. She shook her head as she thought of Darragh seeing his mother commit murder. Seth's mother's face filled her mind. *I am not like her.*

"Are you coming over? The film is about to start."

****

It was getting late, and Seth and Sinead sat at the kitchen table with an ordnance survey map spread out in front of them. After Seth had spoken to his Granny, he and Sinead had driven around Cork in a haphazard fashion looking for white buildings, red fields and wild cats. They had returned home tired and hungry and were feeling disappointed. Sinead had her laptop open, and she was virtually driving around the outskirts of Cork looking for large white buildings next to fields, and Seth could see that she was exhausted.

"I am not going to be rude, Seth, but your Granny is, how shall I put this… Bonkers!"

Seth gave her a weak smile. "I know, she is a little bit off the wall, but I do believe that she has what she calls it; 'the second sight'. She once helped a neighbour find their cat. It had been locked in a garden shed." He could see that Sinead wasn't impressed. "The spirits described where they would find the cat. They said that it was in a metal case and that it had multiplied. The neighbour found it in the lawnmower box with six kittens."

"Oh, I guess that was pretty accurate. So do you think we will find Tom in a field covered in blood with a wild cat clawing his eyes out?"

"I wish." Seth sighed. "It's all very well driving along virtually, but until you are actually out there, you are not really going to see a red field, a cat or a large white building. You are looking tired. You need to go to bed. Looking at the map, I can see which roads we missed today. By morning, I will have a route properly planned. I don't think that I can wait until morning, though. I just want to get out there and explore the roads and streets we have missed."

"Seth, it's dark, and we are exhausted. At least the police are helping us. Your DI Lucy said it would take until tomorrow to organise a proper search. Not even they are searching in the dark. You are going to be no good to anyone if you don't get a couple of hours of sleep."

"No, I suppose not. The sun rises before five. Do you mind if we head out then? If you are tired and need to lie in, then I don't mind going on my own. If we get stopped by the police, we might both get arrested for breaking lockdown rules."

"I am coming with you, no question about it. Seth, you're looking lost again. We will find them tomorrow; you do know that? Do you want me to keep you company tonight?"

Seth smiled. "You do know that I am a married man?"

"You do know that I prefer girls, and all I would do is hold you?"

"That's kind of you, but if my memory serves me correctly, you are a terrible fidget. I won't get any sleep."

"That was when we shared a tent in Singapore, and the temperature was forty-five degrees. I couldn't get comfortable. You are probably right; it doesn't matter what the temperature is; I do tend to toss and turn when I sleep."

Seth smiled and stood up, ready to go to bed and then saw Sinead's eyes widen.

"Oh, Seth! It has just come to me. I know what you're Granny meant by a wild cat." She grinned.

"Go on then."

"She meant your car. It's a Jaguar, isn't it? That's some kind of big cat, isn't it?"

"You clever girl. Yes, you are right. I think she is trying to tell us that the car is out in the open by that red field and white building. I am not going to be able to sleep now, knowing that. I am too hyper to sleep. Do you want some tea and toast?"

***

"Can't you shut the brat up? He is making the most annoying sound."

"He should be asleep in his cot. He is not used to watching late-night films. He is just a baby, and he is tired and is having a moan."

"He needs to be taught a lesson. Take his nappy off!"

"NO! Don't you dare touch him!"

"Well, tell him to shut up then."

Jules picked up Darragh and carried him round the corner to the kitchen. Darragh was rubbing his eyes and desperately wanted to be put down for the night. He was getting ratty. Jules had not seen him so grumpy before. She went to the fridge and took the milk out, and poured some in a cup to warm it up in the microwave. He was still on infant powdered milk, and she hoped that the cow's milk would be ok and not upset his stomach. She needed to find a quiet corner to sit in and rock him to sleep while he drank his milk. She hoped that the film would be over soon and she could lie on the sofa next to Darragh. She dragged a chair into the kitchenette, and with Darragh on her lap again, she let him sip the beaker of milk, hoping that it would soothe him and make him sleepy. Darragh looked up at her curiously and then at his surroundings. He was overtired and grizzled, pushing the milk away. "You are not a happy boy; we miss our home so much, don't we," she whispered gently to him. Determined to get him off to sleep, Jules put the milk on the side and lay him back and tried to rock him. Darragh sat up and pointed to his milk, complaining that he hadn't got it. "But you just pushed it aw…"

"What's going on? That brat has ruined my film. That's it, I've had enough!" Tom turned off the TV and then marched over to them both. "That brat needs some discipline."

"What are you going to do?" Jules jumped up and held Darragh close to her. She backed away from Tom. "You are not going to hit him, are you? He needs somewhere quiet to sleep." The bed suddenly looked so inviting, but then she remembered that Hannah was lying underneath it. *She is so quiet; I hope she hasn't overdosed.*

Tom smiled. "No, not that, although he deserves a slap. I have just the place." His eyes narrowed. "He can sleep in the car. Come to think of it, that would kill two birds with one stone. It will be nice and quiet in the car. Now where is a blanket? Where has Hannah put them? Oh yes, in this drawer". He pulled open a deep drawer in a sideboard and took out the blanket, and handed it to Jules.

"So, are we going to go for a drive to get him off to sleep?"

"Something like that. Follow me; we will all have a peaceful night this way."

The outdoor lights came on as they walked around the building to her car. It was so, so good to be out. Jules breathed in the night air, and for a moment, she was back home with Seth. Darragh seemed calmer, too and had stopped moaning. Tom opened up the car, and Jules put Darragh in his car seat at the back and covered him up with the blanket and tucked him in. His big brown eyes were looking sleepy, and she knew it would only be minutes before he was asleep. Tom was already sitting in the driver's seat, waiting for her to get in. She got into the passenger's seat, and it was then that she knew that something was not right. Tom gave her a sideways glance and looked uneasy.

You do know I have your best interests at heart, don't you?"

"I don't like the sound of this."

"I've arranged for Darragh to go to boarding school."

"You are joking? He isn't even one yet."

"In the morning, they're coming to collect the gypsy child. I will tell them where to find him. He will be quite safe in the car tonight, and then there won't be any painful goodbyes."

"NO, NO WAY! I won't let them take him. You can't leave a baby in a car all night. What if he chokes or needs his nappy changed... TOM, PLEASE! That is a crazy idea. We both just need time to get used to living here. Perhaps you could open up another room for a bedroom for him. He is usually the happiest of children."

"I despise him. He is only good for one thing, and not even I could use him for that. Julia, this will be for the better. You'll see. We will go upstairs, have a glass of wine, and if you take those pills, then I promise I will help you get over losing your children. You need to do this for me. For us."

"FUCK YOU!"

"I don't like your tone. I will have my way. I didn't want to come to this." He grabbed her thigh and stuck a sharp needle into her leg, and squirted a syringe of fluid into her. She tried to push him away, but he was too quick for her.

"What have you done?"

"It's just a sedative, your old friend ketamine. It will help you sleep. You are upset, and I understand. Nobody likes goodbyes."

"I can't stay here. I have to get away with my babies. I can't move my legs! I can't see properly. FUCK, WHY…? I don't want to sleep… PLEASE help me… Please…?"

Chapter Thirty-six

As it was starting to get light, Seth and Sinead checked on the horses to make sure they were all present and correct. The pasture was improving, and the herd cropped the new green blades of grass quietly, their tails swishing as the occasional fly landed on their hindquarters. Lockdown and the lack of work didn't seem to bother them at all. Moss, eager to greet Seth, trotted over to him and nuzzled his arm, asking him to reveal what he had hidden in his pockets. Seth patted him and put his arms around his strong black neck. Moss rested his head on Seth's shoulder and snorted. "You're wanting an apple, aren't you? Tonight, Darragh will give you one, I promise. Wish me luck, my boy. I have a good feeling about today."

"Let's get going. The sun is rising, and we have a lot of ground to cover," Sinead said as she climbed through the fence. "I think I should drive. Just tell me where to go. Do you have the map with you?"

"I do, but I doubt if we will need it. I couldn't sleep, so I virtually drove the route in my head many times, and now it is imprinted in my mind."

"Seth, you should have slept! It's going to be a busy morning. I bet you didn't have breakfast."

"Stop fussing, woman!" Seth said playfully, and then he went quiet for a moment. "I can't eat yet. Later, when we bring them home. Then I can start living again."

Painfully aware of his granny's warning to find his family by midday, Seth got his phone out to see if there were any messages from DI Lucy. They needed all the help they could get. She had promised to ring him first thing with an update. *She won't be up yet.* As they approached the edge of Cork City and the start of their route, Seth noticed that the sky was a dark red, streaked with a little orange. To farmers, this was a warning that the day might bring bad weather. He tried not to dwell on that and turned on the radio to see if there was any news. To his amazement, they could hear Shawn talking to the presenter about their new song, and he was asking everyone to look and then look some more for Jules and Darragh. The radio presenter put out an urgent appeal to find them, and then he played Waterfall Way on the radio, declaring that this new song had got to number one in the charts.

"Can you believe it, Seth? You and Jules have made it in the pop world. I am so proud of you both. I just love this song. I'd buy it. I might have to; I've nearly worn out the CD; I've been playing it so much."

"Thanks. Well, I never! A number one hit. I am happy, but the song is about Jules, and it is going to make me cry. I need to stay strong for her. I'll have to turn it off," he said, pressing the off button on the radio. "There is nothing worse than seeing a grown man cry. Shawn is a good mate. When I spoke to him the other day, he said he would do everything he could to put the word out. I…" He couldn't say any more; he was starting to tear up.

"We will find them," Sinead said, patting his hand. "Is this the turning you wanted to go down? I won't drive too fast."

Seth wiped his eyes on his sleeve, and he nodded, unable to speak. Sinead drove the car at a snail's pace, and they both kept a keen eye out for a white building, a red field and a Jaguar.

***

Jules woke up with a start and thought she was going to suffocate. She had thick tape over her mouth, and she gasped for air but couldn't draw

320

a breath. She was panicking. *Just breathe through your nose, don't panic; you are in bed. Just breathe.* There was a bitter taste in her mouth, and her stomach was cramping. She felt a little sick. Slowly she took the air in and out and did her best to stay calm. She wanted to rip the tape off her mouth, but both arms were above her head, her wrists tied together and tethered to the bedhead. "SHIT!" she yelled, pulling hard at the bedhead, her words muffled by the tape.

"Morning, darling. I had to tie you up for your own safety," Tom said, turning over in bed to face her. She could see a bare shoulder sticking out of the covers and knew he was in bed with her, naked. She also noticed the gold chain around his neck with the front door key clipped onto it. The key was annoyingly close and was just asking to be removed. "I can take off the tape now. You should have swallowed those tablets. I cut them in half, so you didn't choke." His long fingers came out of the covers, and he ripped off the tape.

"FUCK!" she screamed in pain.

"Now, that's no way for a lady to speak."

Her blood was boiling with rage, and her mind was being bombarded with last night's events and the enormity of the situation. "YOU BASTARD! YOU'VE GIVEN ME THE ABORTION PILL AND LEFT MY BABY IN THE CAR ALL NIGHT TO ROT. FUCK YOU!"

Tom sat up in bed, shocked by her words. "I am doing this for us. You must understand that. I have never met such an ungrateful person. Hannah would never speak to me this way."

"You have brainwashed that girl. She is so messed up that she will do anything you ask. I can't believe that you... we spent the whole night sleeping over her, not knowing if she was alive or dead. Have you checked to see if she's dead? She could be."

"You are being overly dramatic. Hannah is fine. She's learnt her lesson. I've sent her down with a banana and some water for the brat. We want him to be nice and calm when they come to get him."

Jules was starting to panic. "Please don't send him away. I promise that I will behave if you bring him back up."

"No, the deal has been done. They are going to collect him at nine."

Jules twisted her head and body around to see the kitchen clock. It was just after seven. "What do you mean, deal? It sounds like you've sold him. He's not going to a boarding school. What fucking school takes in babies? You've fucking sold him!"

"JULIA! I am going to have to put the tape back over your mouth if you carry on like this."

Jules had nothing more to say and yanked her wrist restraints angrily, twisted her body away from him so her back was to him and then cried out in pain as her stomach cramped again. *Please let it just be anxiety and not those tablets starting to work.* She ran her tongue around her teeth, looking for any trace of a tablet to expel and save her baby's life. Her mouth was dry, and she found nearly a whole tablet stuck inside her cheek. Feeling relieved and using her tongue, she managed to bring the piece of tablet to her lips. Gently, she spat it out. It dropped down onto the pillow. She moved her head slightly to hide it. Her body was feeling warm and damp, and an image of herself lying in a pool of blood filled her mind. *Have I wet myself? No, I desperately need a wee. Oh, please don't be blood.* "I need the toilet. You will have to untie my hands so I can go."

"I can unhook them from the bedhead, but we will keep them tied together for a little longer."

"Well, how am I going to manage like that?"

"I could help you."

"No way! I'll be fine."

"Hannah will be back in a minute. She will help you. I know how you girls like to go to the toilet together. I am so glad that you two are getting on so well. Perhaps I can video you together. It would really turn me on seeing you pleasuring each other."

Not listening to him, Jules looked up at the clock again and wished that time would freeze. The red second hand appeared to be racing along, eager to clock up another minute. Jules shut her eyes and thought about Darragh. *At least he is not alone, but he will need his nappy changing. I can't bear to think of him wet and sore. If only I could get to him. There must be something I can do. I wonder if Hannah knows who is coming to get him. Think, Jules. I need to get my hands free. Oh, that hurt. Am I having contractions? Please no. I can't lose our baby. Where are you, Seth? If you are looking for me, then this is the time to find me.* Tears began to roll down her cheeks, and she started to sob. She felt a spindly hand caress her shoulder to comfort her. She opened her eyes wide, and she was ready to yell at him. *If I say anything, then he will stick my lips together again.*

"Are you hurting? I will get you some paracetamol to help the pain. The cleansing will soon be over." He got out of bed, and she caught a glimpse of his scrawny naked body. Revolted, she shut her eyes tight and tried to imagine herself in the middle of the poppy field with Darragh in her arms. If she willed this to happen, then there was hope for her and her baby. Her heart was breaking, and she could hold back the tears no longer and cried like she had never cried before.

***

Seth and Sinead had been on the road for nearly three hours. They had been up every turning and every side road that led to fields. They had stopped many times and had gotten out of the car when they had seen a white house. They knew they were looking a bit suspicious, wandering up to people's drive and then circling their houses if they were able to, but they didn't care. Seth was glad that Sinead was driving; it had given him the chance to study the streets in detail. He was tired but determined to cover every street on the map. They got into the Mini and then continued up Sarsfield Road. A dark blue car followed slowly behind them. Seth had seen the car before, and he looked in the side mirror to see if he could see the driver. "Do you see that car following us, Sinead? I think I know who is driving. I can spot an unmarked police car a mile off. It's Rufus Parvel."

"Why is he following us?"

"He probably thinks we are up to no good."

"This might be a good time to ring Lucy and find out what is going on."

"It might just be a coincidence."

"No, I don't think so. He is definitely following us."

"Let's make a quick getaway then," Sinead said, starting to speed up. Rufus increased his speed too. "I don't like this. Let's give him a run for his money." Sinead put her foot down, and they sped off.

"Fuck no! Sinead, please don't. He will book us for speeding, and you might hit the curb. The last time I was a passenger in a racing car, it ended badly. Seriously, Sinead, slow down. I'll ring Lucy. We might have missed a white house driving this fast."

"You are no fun," Sinead said as she stopped the car. Rufus pulled up behind them and then got out of his car and walked towards them. Sinead wound down the window.

"I thought it was you two. You know you shouldn't be out going for a joyride. Can you explain why you are out this way and are driving erratically?"

"I have Covid," Sinead said, coughing, "and I needed some fresh air."

Horrified, Rufus jumped back, disgusted. Seth got out of the car. "I've got Lucy on the phone. We've got special permission to help look for my wife and child. Do you want to speak to her?" he asked, coughing too.

"No, that's ok. I shouldn't touch your phone if you are crawling in germs." Rufus backed away. "I hope you find them," he said, getting into his car and slamming the door. They then saw him spraying his hands and car with disinfectant.

"Did you see the fear in his eyes?" Seth said. "I will laugh if he gets it. No, I wouldn't wish Covid on anyone. I didn't actually have Lucy on the phone, but I knew he wouldn't want to touch the phone if I was coughing."

"So, what's next? We have done half of the southwest sector," Sinead asked.

"The Doughcloyne Industrial Estate is next," he replied, looking up Sarsfield Road, his spirits low.

Chapter Thirty-seven

Hannah let herself into the studio and then frowned when she saw the state Jules was in. She was holding a banana skin in her hand and lobbed it into the bin in a rage.

"What have you done to her? Why is she crying?" she yelled. "You haven't given her one up the arse, have you?"

"You stupid girl, she's in pain. I guess the second little demon bastard inside her is hanging on with claws. A few more hours, and it will all be over." Hannah's eyes narrowed. "What have you done?"

"Nothing to worry your pretty little head about."

"He's given me an abortion pill," Jules sobbed. "I don't want to lose my baby. Please, Hannah. I don't want to lose Darragh either. Please help me."

Tom scrabbled to get the reel of tape, not expecting her to tell Hannah everything. "She is as stupid as you are."

"Why is Darragh in the car?"

"He's sold..." Tom stuck tape over Jules' mouth before she could finish.

"I've sold the car for her. It will help pay for her keep, and you won't have to work so hard, darling. Darragh doesn't need to see her in such a state. I don't know why she is crying so much. It is only a car."

Jules yelled at Hannah the truth but only muffled sounds came out. She tried to tell Hannah with her eyes, but she wasn't looking at her. Hannah was staring at Tom suspiciously. *Please help me. I need you, Hannah; you are my one and only chance.*

"We need to bring Darragh in; he's not happy. His nappy needs changing," she looked at Jules.

"I don't want him to see Julia in this state. It might affect him later on. It's nearly nine, they will be here to collect the car soon, and then you can bring him in," he lied. "You are being so annoying, Hannah. For fuck's sake, stop asking me questions."

Jules roared beneath the tape and pulled at her bindings furiously, desperate to be heard.

"You've never been this mean to me."

"I'm not being mean. This is all for the greater good, and then we can be together."

"All three of us?"

"Yes, all three of us, my darling."

"And Darragh too."

Tom didn't reply.

***

Seth took DI Lucy's call as they drove into the industrial estate. He was feeling nauseous and wound down the window. *Perhaps I should have eaten something before I came out.* "Hi, Lucy, any news? Are you any closer to finding them?"

"We have been trawling the streets since first light. I have managed to get another voluntary search team involved. It seems they all know you well as pop stars and are raving about your new single. Seth, are you driving somewhere?"

"I am not going to lie to you. Sinead and I have been out in the car looking too. We haven't been near anyone. We just can't sit at home doing nothing. We did bump into the gobshite Parvel earlier. No doubt he will mention it to you. We haven't got Covid, by the way."

"It's ok; these are exceptional circumstances. I won't say anything. Where are you now?"

"We've just pulled into the Doughcloyne Industrial Estate. I don't hold out much hope, though. All the buildings here are very small and dull." A flash of red at the end of a road caught his eye. "Sinead, can you stop, please? I think I might have found something. Will you back up and go down the last road? Did you see what I saw?"

"What have you seen?"

"I am not sure, but I might have found the red field."

Sinead backed up and then drove at speed to the end of the road. As they got closer, they could see that the waste ground edging the estate was awash with bright red poppies.

"This has to be the right field!" she exclaimed. "This is the reddest field I've ever seen. Just like blood. Like your granny said." Sinead stopped the car, and they both leapt out of it and ran to the post and rail fence.

Seth's heart was beating hard in his chest. "Lucy!" Seth said a little breathlessly. "I know there must be a thousand fields of poppies in Cork, but this is the right one. I can feel it in my bones. I'm going to walk into the field and look at the estate from there. Maybe I'll see what we are looking for."

"Stay on the line. I am just going to see if we have any cars nearby. If you see any white buildings, then you will need to let us deal with this. Do you understand?"

"I do."

Seth worked his way through the red flowers, their petals shining brightly, willing him to continue so they could share their secrets with him. For a moment, he was in his and Jules' favourite field, walking hand in hand together. It was so quiet and peaceful here that he could hear his own heart beating. His anxiety was building. *Please let this be the right field.*

Sinead waited by the edge of the field, ready to jump in the car and drive if he found what he hoped to see. As he walked, he kept turning and looking back. As more and more of the estate came into view, he was starting to feel discouraged as all the buildings were very similar; brown brick rows of lockups with shabby blue doors. He was just on the verge of giving up when he noticed the corner of a large building at the very edge of the estate, partially hidden by lockups. The white paint shone in the morning light, calling out to him, begging for forgiveness. "Lucy, I've found it. I've found a white building at the edge of the estate. They've got to be in there. I just know they are."

"Stay where you are. I will be with you in twenty minutes. If Stone sees you, then he could panic and, well… let's not go there."

"Ok, but don't be any longer; I've got a feeling that we've only got minutes to find them. The spirits were wrong."

"The spirits?"

"I know this sounds foolish, but the tip-off was from our granny. You are not going to call the whole thing off now I've mentioned our mad granny, are you?"

"No," she replied. "Oh my! No, it's ok… You see, I am, well… I'll tell you about it some other time. Keep out of sight, and I will be with you in a moment."

Seth put his phone in his back pocket and ran back to Sinead.

"You've seen the white building, haven't you?"

"I did, but Lucy says we must stay where we are, and she will be over in a minute to look."

"So, are we going to just sit here like two muppets, or shall we get a bit closer and see if we can see the car?"

Seth weighed up her words. "It wouldn't hurt to look, now, would it? We just mustn't get seen."

"No, it wouldn't hurt, but I think we should walk through the field rather than drive. The estate is so quiet that you could hear a pin drop. Tom might hear our car, and we don't want the Toad to know that we have found him, do we? I hope you are right, Seth. You are going to be so disappointed if the building is empty."

"I have never been so sure. I could feel the earth and the flowers under my feet whispering to me."

Sinead laughed and then looked serious. "Let's hope Jules and Darragh are ok. I shouldn't have said that, should I?"

"He wouldn't hurt her, but I worry for Darragh. He likes to hurt children."

They walked along the edge of the field and noticed a man walking a dog towards them. The dog trotted past them with a paper plane in his mouth. The man tipped his hat to them and wished them a good morning.

"That's a curious thing to be carrying," Seth announced when the man had gone by. "You'd think the dog would be carrying a ball or a stick."

"I didn't see. What was he carrying?"

"A folded-up piece of paper."

The white building was getting closer, and they slowed their pace, not wanting to get spotted. Standing with his back against the wall of the last lock up on the estate, Seth stole a look into the parking area at the back of the white office building and sighed with relief. "I can see the Jaguar. Granny got that right. It's sitting bold as brass in the carpark, next to this red field."

"We should ring Lucy to let her know," Sinead said, picking up a paper plane that was lying on the floor at her feet. "Is this what the dog was carrying? That's odd; it's got HELP written on the wings." She gave the plane to Seth.

"It's probably kids. We used to make ..." He stared at the writing. "That's Jules' writing." He opened up the plane and saw her desperate message. "For the love of God! She's in there for sure. I can't wait any longer. It is doing my head in, all this waiting. When the police turn up, he will see their cars, and he might panic. I am going to sneak in somehow. I want you to wait here for me. I don't want you getting hurt, or in trouble with the police, for that matter. Will you ring Lucy for me? He asked, handing her his phone. I know she'll be mad at me, but I promise I won't kill anyone."

"Seth, you shouldn't. If you are going, then I am coming too."

"Please, Sinead, I love you like a sister. I'd never forgive myself if anything happened to you."

Sinead huffed. "Ok, but be careful. Seth, really, be sensible. You know what you are like."

"I will."

Seth, in stealth mode and looking up at the windows as he went, made his way across the car park without being seen. He skirted the building, looking for a way in. There was a back door, but it was locked. If need be, he could shoulder the door down, but he was hoping to find a lower window that he could smash and get through. Either option would make some noise. Keeping his back to the wall, he made his way to the front of the building. The parking area around him was empty, and he felt exposed. He took a quick look around the corner at the front of the building and was relieved that nobody was there. He could see lower office windows and a door leading to a reception room. Feeling a little unsure about what he should do, he looked at the black gate in the distance and wondered if it was locked. *If it is, then the police are going to have to cut the chain, and the Toad will definitely see them coming.* He could see a sign at the entrance that read TS Pharmaceutical Distribution. *How the fuck did the police miss that? If they are looking for him, then they must be searching all of his trading premises, surely.*

Seth scanned the front of the building again to see if there was a way in. Within touching distance, he could see a large shuttered door, but he feared that it would be locked too. His best bet was to go to the back door and try and break it down. *Maybe I should wait for the police. They will have a crowbar.* Not sure if he should break in, he started to walk back to Sinead. A loud zithering sound stopped him in his tracks. He jumped back to the side of the building and held his breath. The shutter was being lifted, and taking this opportunity to jump the Toad, he rushed around the corner to confront Tom. A young girl walked straight into him. She was holding one of Darragh's homemade nappies. She screamed, but he grabbed her and stifled the scream with his hand. "I am not going to hurt you. I just want to get my wife and baby back." She nodded, and she didn't look frightened anymore, so he took his hand away, hoping that she wouldn't scream out and give the game away.

"You're Seth, aren't you? God, you're fit!"

"Are they here?" he asked desperately.

"Yes, you need to be quick. Tom's gone to the toilet for a shite, and he has tied Jules to the bed."

"Where's Darragh?"

"He's in the car."

"Why? Are you going somewhere?"

"No, I am just going to change him. Look, you haven't got long, and if he finds out that I helped you, then I am going to be in big trouble."

"I won't tell him. What is going on here?"

"I'm not sure. I'll look after Darragh for a moment. Seriously. You need to be quick."

"Sinead is waiting in the field next to the car. Please will you give Darragh to her? I beg that of you."

"Ok."

"Where will I find Jules?"

"She's in the staff room. Go to the top of the stairs and turn right. The staff room is at the end of the corridor. The door is open."

"Thank you, whoever you are," he said, hugging her hard.

"It's Hannah," she replied, looking a little shell shocked. "Hannah Honeypot," she called as she went off to free Darragh.

Does that girl look a bit like Jules or even Gemma? Seth ran through the opening at the front of the building and nearly fell onto the white Mercedes. He would have kicked it to death if he hadn't been in such a hurry. He flew up the stairs and ran along the corridor towards the staff room. He was going to burst in but stopped himself, afraid of what he might see. *Please don't be lying naked on the bed with your wrists and ankles tied to each corner, like Gemma was.* Carefully he opened the door, and with his heart beating hard, he stepped into the tiny studio, fearing the worst.

Jules saw him immediately, and her swollen, watery eyes lit up. He looked around the room for the Toad, but he was nowhere to be seen. He ran over to her and sank onto his knees, crying. Tears rolled down her cheeks too. Her big blue eyes were brimming with happiness, and yet he could feel such sorrow seeping out of her. Carefully, he pulled away the tape from her mouth. He was truly crying now; he wasn't sure why. "My poor wee dote," he sobbed, gently stroking her face.

"Seth! My lovely Seth." she was crying happy tears. Her voice was croaky. "You came for me. I knew you would."

"Has he hurt you? Like he did the last time?"

"No... not like before. That man is insane. He gave me pills to abort our baby. Seth, I managed to spit out one of the tablets, but I must have swallowed the rest. He drugged me and put them in my mouth while I was

333

unconscious. I think I've hung on to her. I am so wet, though. Will you pull the covers back and tell me if I am bleeding? Please don't be angry if I am."

"No, never. It is not your fault." Seth frowned. "The police will be here in a moment. That man needs stringing up. How could he do such a thing? He unhooked her arms from the corner of the bed head, and then feeling apprehensive, he pulled back the covers. Her blue dress was soaked with sweat, but the bottom sheet was still white. "No, you're all right. You are wringing wet, though." He sighed and looked at her clammy face. "I can see that you are in pain. You're as white as a ghost."

He looked around the room for a knife to cut the zip ties that were around her wrists. In the kitchenette, there was a knife block with four knives sticking out of the five slots. He recognised the handles immediately. They had glitter in the black plastic, just like the knife Parvel had found planted in his toolbox. "The sneaky bastard!" Not wanting to touch any of the knives, he opened the kitchen drawer, pulled out a pair of kitchen scissors and then came over to Jules and cut each binding, shaking his head. "I hope they throw the book at him. Trussing you up like a chicken and trying to murder our child!"

Jules sat on the side of the bed and rubbed her wrists. She looked up at the clock anxiously. It was nine o'clock. "Seth?"

"Just wait until the Toad comes out of the bathroom. He's not going to know what's hit him."

Jules bent over for a moment and then held her stomach. "It hurts so much, but we need to get Darragh. He's arranged for someone to take him away. He's in the car. Did you see the car? Oh, Seth, it's nine o'clock. It might be too late!"

"No, it's ok, that girl... Honeypot came out with a nappy for him. She's going to give him to Sinead. She told me where to find you."

"Oh thank God! I need to see him with my own eyes. These people that are coming to get him are not good news. I can't bear it. I've got to see him and know he's all right.

The toad killed Gemma, you know. He told me," she said, standing up and testing her legs. They felt wobbly, but she could still walk. "I need a wee so bad, but that can wait. That's a good sign, isn't it? I always need to go when I'm pregnant."

"It's a good sign," he said, looking at her doubtfully. "I'll leave Tom to the police. Poor Gemma, that is one bastard, I tell you. You don't want to hear what else he has been up to. Do you want me to carry...?"

Tom came out of the bathroom, whistling. Seth glared at him, disgusted by what he saw. All he was wearing was a condom, and he was erect.

"I've fed Mr Steel. He needs some loving, Hannah. Hannah?" He froze to the spot when he saw Seth standing by Jules. His eyes widened with fear, and seeing the rage in Seth's face and the scissors in his hand, he bolted to the door and fled out into the corridor. Seth started to follow and then stopped and looked back at Jules. "I can't leave you. He won't get far, not like that; the police will be here at any moment."

"Seth, I don't feel good. I don't want to lose our baby. I'm scared."

He came back to her and put his arms around her, and pulled her to him. He held her face in his hands. "We have our wee boy, and you have no idea how much I love you both. Whatever happens, I will be there for you. I would go to the end of the earth for you." He kissed her on the lips and then drew her to him and hugged her. The tears were rolling down his cheeks. "Let's go downstairs and get Darragh. Lucy is going to be mad with me, but I had to find you myself."

"Lucy?"

"DI Lucy O'Leary. She's been helping me find you. It turns out she is my half-sister after all."

Jules stepped outside and felt a refreshing breeze on her face. Just being outside in the fresh air made her feel a whole lot better. Not wasting any time, they walked towards the car, and Jules looked up at the sky. It was almost as red as the field of poppies ahead. *So strange to be this colour so late in the morning.* Police cars drew up behind them, and as they approached the rear of the building, they both knew that something was terribly wrong. All the doors of the Jaguar were wide open. Jules spotted Sinead first and cried out. Sinead was lying on the floor in the middle of the car park in a pool of blood, her body lay lifeless, and her leg was twisted and bleeding. Hannah was leaning over her, trying to help her.

"Oh my God, Hannah, what's happened?" Jules asked, kneeling on the floor next to her.

"They've taken Darragh. I tried to stop them, but they pulled him out of my arms and then took him away. I didn't want to let him go. Tom lied to me. Those people didn't want the car; they wanted your baby. There's a bag of cash on the floor over there," she said, nodding in the direction of a black van. "This girl threw herself in front of the van, but it was no good. The bastards ran her over. I'm so sorry, Jules, I really tried. I think she is dead," she sobbed.

Jules held Sinead's hand. "No, she is still alive. I can see her breathing, and I can feel a pulse. Seth, that van," she said urgently, pointing to the corner of the car park. "I didn't see it before! Do you think Darragh's in there," she asked and then sprang up and ran towards it.

The black van revved its engine and started to reverse at speed. It looped back and then spun round to make a getaway. Seth was confused. "Hannah, is that the black van that ran over Sinead?"

Hannah was too upset to reply and looked blankly at him. Taking no chances, Seth ran over to Lucy, who was conducting a search at the front of the building. "Lucy, that van is taking my wee boy away. You've got to stop it."

The black van was coming straight for them. A police officer ran up to the car and banged on the sides of the van, and yelled at the driver to stop. The windows were blacked out, so it was impossible to see inside them. The van screeched to a stop, and this puzzled Seth even more. The way was clear ahead, and if he had been a kidnapper, then he would have sped away. The police officer spoke to the driver, and then after what seemed an age, he came over to them and shook his head. "No, child, I'm afraid."

"But you haven't checked in the back!"

"There's no need. They are CID. They got here just before us."

"I don't understand. Where is he then?" Seth cried out. Did they see the van that took Darragh?"

Jules came running over. "Hannah says it was a white van, not that black one. Please, you have to find it. Find our Darragh. We need an ambulance. Sinead is in a bad way."

Lucy made an urgent call to the search units to look out for the white van. "There is a good chance they will find the van straight away. My team is on it. I've called an ambulance too. Seth, you shouldn't have gone in to get Jules. I did ask you not to. Did you see Tom Stone up there? We've just done a search and found another girl in the downstairs office. She was tied to a bed but no sign of Stone."

"Fuck no! That man needs his cock chopped off. Seriously, he is sick! Is the girl ok?"

"Her name is Sandra James. She's a minor and has been missing for a month. She's is alive but is in a bad way. I don't think she has had much to eat or drink these past few weeks. I dare say she's been violated too."

Jules listened in horror to the news but was too distressed to say anything. Her mind was going at a hundred miles an hour, and all she could think about was getting Darragh back. She stared at Lucy's radio on her jacket, praying that she would hear it crackle and she would hear a voice telling them that a white van had been found.

"The Toad was here, but he made a run for it. I should have stopped him, but I didn't want to leave Jules. The bastard will know who the men in the white van are. You'll find him easily enough though, he is naked, hard and the shite has a blue rubber on. He was the one that called the bastards in the white van to come and get Darragh." He held his head with both hands. "This is a living nightmare." He looked at Jules; she was crying and sheet white. "Jules? Do you want to sit in the car? Are you going to faint?"

She shook her head. "No, I want to be with Sinead. She is conscious but only just. Oh, Seth, we will get him back, won't we?"

"Of course, we will. We just need to find the Toad first."

They walked over to Sinead, and she smiled weakly at them. "I saw both their faces. The woman had long ginger hair. I can draw them for the police. I really tried..." She started to cry and then winced in pain.

Jules kneeled down beside her and held her hand. "Don't cry," she was crying too. "We will find him. He is only a heartbeat away. It's going to be ok."

Seth stared at the poppy field, lost in thought. He needed guidance more than ever now. The poppies nodded and agreed with him.

Hannah stood up and looked at Seth. "I am going to leave him one day. I thought he was a good man, but I was wrong. I know that now."

"You don't want to be with a man like that. You do know he will go to prison for what he has done. I know you did your best for our little Darragh..." He saw something move on the far side of the car park. A scrawny white body ran from one large green bin to another. *Am I seeing things?* He shook his head. He looked down at Sinead and then noticed Tom running along the edge of the car park towards the field. Seth looked round at the police officers, but nobody had noticed him escaping.

"Jules, don't move. Stay where I can see you. I am going to catch the bastard and get him to tell me who's taken our wee boy." He charged after him and leapt over the fence, determined to catch his prey. It didn't take Seth long to catch up with Tom, and he rugby tackled him to the floor. The toad's skin felt slimy and wet with sweat, and his emaciated white body revolted him. Seth wrestled with him and could feel his erection in his stomach. It sickened him to think of him inserting himself into Jules. Ignoring it and finding Tom too weak to fight, he held him down by his thin neck. "Who's taken my boy? You bastard. Why did you have to go and do a thing like that? Are you some kind of sycophant?" You'd better tell me, or you won't see the sunrise again," he said, raising his fist, ready to strike.

"Get off me, you maniac," he gasped, his hands gripping Seth's hand around his neck. "I have no idea what you're talking about."

"You know very well what I am talking about. I wasn't born yesterday."

"I am doing you a favour. You know that child was mine, don't you?"

"You lying bastard," Seth said and brought his elbow down hard into his chest.

Tom yelled out in pain.

"You tell me where he is, or I swear I will hurt you badly next time."

"Don't hurt me. I don't know where he has gone to or who with. I just rang a number and put him on a click and collect service."

"You are talking shite." Seth raised his fist to punch him hard in the face and knew that he could kill him with one blow as he hated him that much. He looked up at the blood-red sky and saw Tom Stone dead, his face broken and distorted. Furious, he punched the ground by his ear and heard

his knuckles crack. Both Tom and he yelled out in fear and he in agony. He
didn't know how he had stopped himself from killing him, but he had. Seth
gritted his teeth and stood up, his eyes dark and dangerous, willing himself
to re-join humanity.

"Seth, leave him be!" Lucy called, her face red from running. We
will deal with this. We are going to arrest him anyway. Those two men in
the black van have a warrant for his arrest. They got the registration of the
white van. The owners of the van are known to us. We'll find Darragh. It's
going to be ok." Lucy sighed and got out her cuffs. "Will you stand him up
for me, please? I am going to arrest him."

"Nothing would give me more pleasure," he said, dragging Tom to
his feet. Tom resisted and looked unstable as if he might collapse at any
moment. Lucy read him his rights. Not only was he being arrested for
kidnapping, a series of paedophilia charges, but he was also being charged
for the murder of Gemma Day. Lucy cuffed him and then passed him to a
colleague that had joined them, and he led Tom away.

"Fucking gypsy," Tom shouted back at Seth and then spat on the
ground.

"He is going to go to prison for a very long time," Lucy said,
shaking her head.

Seth was almost crying. "I just want my wee boy back. I want to
hold my baby in my arms again."

"I know, Seth. Let us do our jobs. We will find him. I promise. If
we are right, then the traveller community has taken him. I shouldn't have
told you that, but I don't want you thinking that he has been taken by
paedophiles. He will be in safe hands for now, but that doesn't make it right.
You need to comfort Jules. She is going to pieces over there."

Seth nodded and sighed. "Murder? You arrested him for murdering
Gemma Day. You might want to check the knife block in the bastard's room

up there. One of the knives is missing, just like the one he planted in my toolbox. Jules said that he confessed that he killed her too."

"We worked that out. The knife did have Gemma's blood on it, but that wasn't the knife he used to cut her wrists with. We found the murder weapon, a kitchen knife from the caravan, hidden in your hay barn. We also found his footprints and his pubic hair on the side of the horse trough. It seems he is quite comfortable walking around naked. Did you know, and this goes no further, that Gemma wasn't dead when he cut her wrists."

"Christ, no, that's terrible. So, Sinead and I are in the clear then?"

"Not entirely," she said with a smile.

Seth looked shocked, and his eyes met her brown eyes as he asked her for answers.

"You are going to have to let me meet your - or our - Granny. I need to find out why she likes to encourage my half-brother to go all vigilante on me. You could have got yourself into a whole heap of trouble."

Seth sighed. "You had me worried there. You'll see. It's the Hearn way. Us new generation Hearns are known for our daring deeds. We are strong like oak trees but like to sing and dance too. You'll have to come over for a party and see how to dance the Waterfall Way." He looked down at the sea of poppies around them and sighed again. "We just need to find Darragh, and then Jules and I can laugh and dance and sing again. We won't be much company until we do."

"Where does our Granny live?"

"In Dingle."

"I remember now. I think we should pay her a visit. I think she knows a little more about this saga than she is letting on. It's no coincidence that travellers took him."

"Why do you think that?"

"Call it second sight."

341

Jules stood back as the paramedics worked on Sinead. She heard her scream out as they put her on the stretcher, ready to go into the ambulance. *Her leg is so twisted and broken looking. No wonder she screamed.* A sharp pain reverberated through her own body. It was the pain of loss, regret and guilt flooding her very being. *My little Darragh, there must have been something I could have done to save you. What can you think of me? Are you hurting inside like I am? Oh my God! I've been a terrible mother to him. Will he ever forgive me?*

"JULIA, TELL THEM THAT THIS IS ALL JUST A DREADFUL MISTAKE," Tom yelled as he was led across the car park to a waiting police car. Jules heard his voice and just stared at him, not hearing his words. *How ridiculous he looks, his erect penis leading the way. What is wrong with that man? He is a monster, and I don't have to see him ever again.*

"JULIA! Tell them the truth. Tell them that you want to be with me."

She laughed out loud sarcastically. "I HOPE YOU ROT IN HELL!" she screamed, turning her back on him, not wanting to ever see his face or his scrawny body again. She could hear him yelling at her to help him as he was forced into the police car. She let his words wash over her, oblivious to his pleas. *I just have to find my baby again, hold him and tell him how much I love him.* Her stomach contracted and contorted again, but it didn't hurt as much. *At least I haven't lost this one. I hope I haven't lost her. I won't let him take her from me.*

She felt warm arms around her and Seth's sweet smell as he hugged her. She turned around and hugged him back, losing herself in his hot body, not wanting to leave his warm embrace – ever again. The outside world was cruel and unforgiving. *My lovely Seth, I love you so much.*

"How are you doing, my poor wee dote? You know we are going to find him. Like I found you. The spirits are on our side."

"I don't know if I believe in anything anymore. At least I have you back. Oh, Seth, I tried everything, and I swear if I had the opportunity, then I would have stopped all this. I don't think that I will ever forgive that monster for selling our baby. I would have killed him if I had the chance. I swear I would have," she sobbed.

"Don't fret. The Toad will get what he deserves. Nobody likes paedophiles in prison. He is going to rot and burn there. Don't cry. It won't be long before we have our boy back."

"He's been sold to monsters who want to do terrible things to him," she sobbed.

"The police know who the van belongs to. They believe travellers have taken him. So, he will be well looked after for a few hours, and then he will come home to us."

Jules wiped her tears away and looked up at Seth's big brown eyes curiously. "You seem so calm. They ran over Sinead's legs. That doesn't sound like something rational people would do."

"We just have to be patient and do everything we can to get him back. We are strong like oaks, and our children are too. Everything will be alright. We'll have our boy back soon enough. You just wait and see."

She smiled weakly at him. "Do you think so?"

"I know so," he said, hugging her again.

Waterfall Way Play List

Rockabye - Clean Bandit (feat. Sean Paul & Anne-Marie
https://www.youtube.com/watch?v=papuvlVeZg8

Waterfall Way - Seth and Julia Hearn S&J (feat. Sonar Cell)
https://youtu.be/cV4f8GtzBdA

These Days - (feat. Jess Glynne, Macklemore & Dan Caplen)
https://www.youtube.com/watch?v=pjTj-_55WZ8

Giants - Dermot Kennedy
https://www.youtube.com/watch?v=Fi33qkv4Bjw

Photograph - Ed Sheeran
https://www.youtube.com/watch?v=nSDgHBxUbVQ

Never be Alone —-Shawn Mendes
https://www.youtube.com/watch?v=N7VCLNBNJQs

Chasing Cars - Snow Patrol
https://www.youtube.com/watch?v=GemKqzILV4w

Stuck with U - Ariana Grand & Justin Bieber
https://www.youtube.com/watch?v=pE49WK-oNjU

Just Say Yes – Snow Patrol
https://www.youtube.com/watch?v=vW1hv37imjw

Blinding Lights – The Weekend
https://www.youtube.com/watch?v–4NRXx6U8ABQ

Hey Brother – Avicii
https://www.youtube.com/watch?v=6Cp6mKbRTQY

The Shape of You - Ed Sheeran
https://www.youtube.com/watch?v=JGwWNGJdvx8

Walk Me Home - Pink
https://www.youtube.com/watch?v=J1OsKJW51HY

Wake Me Up - Avicii https://www.youtube.com/watch?v=IcrbM1l_BoI

Beautiful in Blue – Seth and Julia Hearn S&J

I hope that you enjoyed Waterfall Way. If you could leave me a small review then I would be most grateful.
Authors are lost without reviews. ☺x

You might be interested in reading the fourth book in the Waterfall way series 'Darragh.' I am writing this book at the moment and if you would like to subscribe to my mailing list then I will let you know when the next book is going to be released and other bookish news. Just head over to my website at https://cutt.ly/5fR483w and wait for the subscription form to pop up. You can get a free book if you sign up!

WATERFALL WAY

Natasha Murray is an award winning West Sussex author. She is a diverse writer and produces books for all ages. During lockdown, Natasha has written a romantic crime thriller Waterfall Way series 58 Farm End, Julia's Baby and Waterfall Way (The Waterfall Way Series). These books are set in Findon, West Sussex and Cork, Ireland. She says, "I enjoy writing and it is both a pleasure and a compulsion. There is nothing better in life than creating parallel universes."

Please follow me on social media

Author's website
https://cutt.ly/5fR483w
Facebook https://www.facebook.com/NatashaMurray3004 or
Twitter https://twitter.com/NatashaM_Author
Instagram @natashamurray1426
TikTok @natashamurray16